And then she understood.

This man, who had amassed a fortune telling other people how to get through the worst moments of their lives, wished he was someplace else right now.

Because he knew something she didn't know.

Something bad. Something seriously awful, life-changing bad.

Christina felt the prick of a thousand tiny toothpicks on the move, fanning out across her shoulders, down her back, and along her arms.

A tiny marching Army of Doom.

Outside, the fescue lawn crisped under a blazing sun.

Inside, the room turned airless and cold, like the inside of a refrigerator.

Christina shivered.

D1373937

By Margaret Carroll

RIPTIDE
A DARK LOVE

ATTENTION: ORGANIZATIONS AND CORPORATIONS
Most Avon Books paperbacks are available at special quantity
discounts for bulk purchases for sales promotions, premiums,
or fund raising. For information, please call or write:

**Special Markets Department, HarperCollins Publishers,
10 East 53rd Street, New York, New York 10022-5299.
Telephone: (212) 207-7528.   Fax: (212) 207-7222.**

RIPTIDE

MARGARET CARROLL

AVON

An Imprint of HarperCollinsPublishers

This is a work of fiction. Names, characters, places, and incidents are products of the author's imagination or are used fictitiously and are not to be construed as real. Any resemblance to actual events, locales, organizations, or persons, living or dead, is entirely coincidental.

AVON BOOKS
An Imprint of HarperCollins*Publishers*
10 East 53rd Street
New York, New York 10022-5299

Copyright © 2009 by Margaret Carroll
ISBN 978-0-06-165277-6
www.avonromance.com

All rights reserved. No part of this book may be used or reproduced in any manner whatsoever without written permission, except in the case of brief quotations embodied in critical articles and reviews. For information address Avon Books, an Imprint of HarperCollins Publishers.

First Avon Books paperback printing: October 2009

Avon Trademark Reg. U.S. Pat. Off. and in Other Countries, Marca Registrada, Hecho en U.S.A.
HarperCollins® is a registered trademark of HarperCollins Publishers.

Printed in the U.S.A.

10 9 8 7 6 5 4 3 2 1

If you purchased this book without a cover, you should be aware that this book is stolen property. It was reported as "unsold and destroyed" to the publisher, and neither the author nor the publisher has received any payment for this "stripped book."

For Katie Mae and Mom,
with all my love.
And Rand, who lives in my heart
and made all my dreams come true.
And Tim O. and Jodi S.,
with all my thanks.

ACKNOWLEDGMENTS

To Carrie Feron at HarperCollins, who I'm privileged to work with; her assistant, Tessa Woodward (ditto!); Sara Schwager, who has an awesome eye for detail; Christine Maddalena, for her natural enthusiasm, and the entire team. My agent, the fearless and wonderful Stephanie Cabot, who made it look easy to land me the opportunity of a lifetime. Kerri Carroll, who puts bad people in Suffolk County, New York, where they belong and takes time from her busy schedule to share her expertise with me. Chip Berschback, who does the same in Wayne County, Michigan, and Bob Stevens, who works homicide in Detroit. You all fight the good fight every day, and I hope my made-up detectives are guys you wouldn't mind working with if they were real. My sister Kate and brother-in-law Denis, for bringing back menus and wine lists (tough job, but somebody had to do it) and all my family and friends (yeah, Emmetts, I mean you), who drop everything every year no matter what and join us as far out on Montauk Highway as you can go, all the way to The End. Rock on. And finally, Buddy, who inspired the role of Shep and is really much nicer than Shep. Really. And finally, this book is dedicated to Gossman's Dock in Montauk, a special place of happy memories for many people, including me.

rip•tide (rip/tīd/), *n.* a tide that opposes another or other tides, causing a violent disturbance in the sea.

Random House,
Webster's Unabridged Dictionary

CHAPTER

1

I came to on a moonlit beach. I was running, or trying to. My bare feet made furrows in the cold night sand. My right hand was wrapped around the slim neck of a near-empty bottle of Jamesport Vineyards' Chardonnay. An onshore breeze played havoc with the sheer voile of my wrap dress. The bow at my waist had come undone, so most of the dress billowed at my side like a sail. It felt like I had an imaginary invisible twin.

This struck me as hilarious. I stopped so I could laugh as hard as I wanted. I felt that I should tell all this to Dan, explain to him about my imaginary twin, and how we could finally have that threesome he kept bugging me about.

But the wind tore away my words before I could say them. I hiccuped.

I heard Dan's deep, booming laugh behind me. He came up close and I felt his breath on my shoulder, which was bare except for the silk strap of my bra. I got a whiff of the hot cloud that was Daniel Cunningham, a thick stew of Old Spice and cigarettes, and the fruity scent of the wine we'd been drinking since lunch at Lenny's on the dock in Montauk.

His bare arms came up sharply around my waist, warm and muscled, marbled through with thick veins on smooth skin, pulling me back against him. I lost my balance and fell against his chest, melting into that cloud of his, slipping down and down and down . . .

"Christina?"

Christina felt their eyes on her. The circle was quiet, waiting.

Dan, his face, his scent, the knowing way of his hands on her bare skin, filled her mind. He was always there for her, the lover who lived in her head. Like a drug she could always come back to and use again.

But not here. Not now.

The counselor's name was Peter, and he leaned forward until he was in danger of slipping off the edge of his molded plastic chair. "Christina?" He said her name again, coming down heavy on the next-to-last syllable so it sounded like a question.

But it was not a question, not really, and Christina knew it. It was a command to spill her guts.

The group watched, like so many hyenas in the veldt waiting to pounce on a fresh kill.

Peter let a moment or two pass. He began to speak when Christina did not. "There came a day, finally, when I knew my number was up. I don't know why that day was different, but it was. I had hit my bottom, and I knew it." Peter picked up the folded napkin from underneath his styrofoam cup and used it to mop up the sheen along his upper lip.

Heat from outside seeped in around the edges of the heavy automatic doors and sealed windows of the rehab center despite the A.C., which was kept in arctic-blast mode to protect the patients from the merciless furnace that was Minnesota in August.

Beads of sweat poked through Peter's Polo shirt, dotting his midsection like chicken pox. "The way I was drinking, I should have been dead ten times over." He used the flip side of the napkin to blot at his forehead.

Nods and murmurs of assent moved around the circle like a wave through the stands inside a football stadium.

"But the day I finally got it, I was done. My number had come up. I had taken my last drink. And I knew it." The counselor leaned back until the plastic chair creaked, his gaze never wavering from Christina's face. "That's what we call hitting bottom, Christina. Have you hit your bottom yet?"

She looked at him, taking stock of the pale blue eyes and thinning blond hair, the face that was arranged into a permanent frown of understanding. He was a third-generation Norwegian-American whose drinking had taken him on a wild ride across the Midwest through two marriages, seven locked psych wards, and even a brief stint in prison. Until he had seen the light and found his way here, where he could dedicate all his time and energy to shining the beacon of recovery into the dark hearts of drunks like Christina.

"You don't need to hide anymore, Christina. You're in a safe place." Peter's blue eyes swam with compassion for her, so deep and so full, apparently, that he needed to press the napkin into service yet again to dab at them. He took a swig of coffee that went down with an audible gulp.

Signaling to Christina that it was okay, he had all the time in the world when it came to saving her soul.

God, she hated him.

She stared down at the carpet, a sculpted pattern in a drab mix of colors that was designed to handle high-volume traffic. She risked a glance at some of the faces she had gotten to know over the last six days, since she had stopped shaking and come off the IV, leaving the medical unit behind to join Peter and his motley crew. There was the bass player, HIV-positive, from the boy band Christina's son had once idolized. The wattle-faced CEO of the largest chain of dry-cleaning stores in the Midwest, who was facing indictment for tax evasion. A saw-voiced woman from Montecito who debated hourly whether she should sell her share in the family vineyard in order to stay sober. And Sylphan, Christina's roommate, whose flowing goth attire could not hide her tortuous thinness. The name was a put-on, like the black lipstick and spiky pink hair. The girl wept through the night even in her sleep. Yesterday in group she had hinted that her addiction had its roots in the bedtime routine at her stepfather's place in Bucks County.

No doubt about it, Christina thought, the carpet in this place was designed to take a beating. She cleared her throat, calculating whether she could get away with saying she preferred to listen instead of talk, just for today.

"Just for today" was Peter's mantra.

"It's okay, Christina," he said in a soft voice. "We're here for you, and we're not going anywhere."

That much was obvious. Most of her fellow recovering addicts had no choice but to stick it out, here by court order or the result of a workplace intervention. But Christina did not have a workplace, nor did she have any sheet from a judge. She doubted anyone from her life would even notice she was gone. Except Dan. He knew where she was. But he didn't count. He was not, strictly speaking, part of her world.

Christina's son Tyler was vacationing in Aix-en-Provence with her in-laws until the middle of August, when Christina and Jason would drive him down to The Hill School for opening weekend. And Jason? Her husband could be in the city, or in East Hampton, or who knows where. He hadn't offered to fly out here with her. She'd come on her own. The rehab would have provided an escort if she had wanted to pay for one, but that wasn't the point.

"Jesus Christ," Jason had said, wrinkling his nose at the sight of Christina lying on rumpled sheets in the guest bedroom.

She told him then what she was planning to do, her voice weak, her skull so heavy she was not able to lift it more than a few inches, just enough to sip water from the glass she'd thought to leave out next to the bed the night before. A drunk's trick.

"Jesus Christ," he said again, shaking his head. He sneered. And then, of all things, he laughed.

Even with the blinds drawn tight against the glare from the beach and her eyes swollen almost shut, Christina saw a white flash of teeth against Jason's tanned skin. It had been a long, long time since she had heard him laugh. She noticed this despite her skull, which was throbbing like it was two sizes too tight. She couldn't sit up. She fell back against the pillows.

She would remember him this way, standing in the guest room doorway of their beach house on a summer afternoon (or possibly morning or early evening, Christina didn't know which), throwing his head back to laugh at her plan.

Truth be told, and the truth was not something either Christina or Jason was in the habit of telling, it was an outrageous plan. But she had run out of options.

Jason laughed hard with a sound that rolled up from deep inside. He took his time until he was good and finished. He looked at her, for probably the first time in ages.

Christina did not like the look in his eyes.

He shook his head, planting one hand high on the doorframe. "Whatever." He turned to go.

Christina would always remember the squeaking sound his fingers made as he dragged them down the wood.

As though he were being tugged away by an unseen hand.

"Take a car service to JFK," he said over his shoulder. "Leave the Mercedes here."

Christina couldn't imagine how she was going to transport herself to Minnesota, a state she couldn't pinpoint on a map, when she wasn't able to sit up in bed without vomiting. But she had to. She had run out of ideas and couldn't think of anything else to do. Maybe commit suicide. But as the sun shone brightly down on the Cardiffs' oceanfront estate on Jonah's Path that day, Christina was too worn-out even to kill herself.

So she had landed here just over a week ago, in a place more foreign to her than any of the capitals in Western Europe, to do the unthinkable.

Quit drinking.

The problem was, once the shaking stopped, and she was transferred into the residential treatment program that had cured legendary sports figures, politicians, rock bands, a First Lady and, it was rumored, a certain individual who was less than tenth in line to the British throne, Christina Cardiff was caught off guard by something she never saw coming.

A wave of terror so big and so deep she nearly drowned in it.

When she stopped drinking, then what?

Christina's life stretched out before her like a vast uncharted wilderness, for which she had no map.

The fear was followed by a second wave of emotion, no less powerful than the first. Self-pity. It rose up and swamped her, flooding her, washing away her resolve.

Hot tears pulsed at the back of her eyes. When had her life turned into this, drinking shitty coffee from a vat while perfect strangers took turns spilling their guts?

She tried to swallow around the lump that formed in her throat. To her horror, a small sound escaped, one that was shapeless and feral. Like the sound made by the raccoon they'd caught in the attic last fall. The trap was supposed to be humane because the animal was simply cornered, not killed.

So much for Hav-A-Heart traps, Christina thought, clamping her teeth down tight to avoid making that sound again. She was pretty sure she knew just how that raccoon had felt.

"It's okay, Christina." Peter leaned forward, pressing his napkin into her hand.

Soggy as it was, she wiped her eyes, wet now with tears.

"This is a safe place," Peter said.

It was a weird place, Christina wanted to tell him, straight out of an old skit from *Saturday Night Live*.

Instead, she hunched forward in her chair, pressing the limp napkin tightly to her face. In that moment, she got a sense of herself floating high in an imaginary perch up near the acoustical ceiling tiles, looking down at the Christina below. And she glimpsed herself not as the person she had become, pouring her life out in the liquid measures of goblets and pints and liters required to get her through each day, but as she really was.

In the parlance of Alcoholics Anonymous, Christina Cardiff was a garden-variety drunk.

In that moment of mental clarity came an opening. Maybe, just maybe, she could do it.

Get sober.

Christina considered for the first time since she'd arrived here that she might succeed.

Which, in turn, meant she would have to begin the process of mental undressing that seemed to be at the core of what went on here. She would have to humble herself, ask for help. Take a chance that help would come from the random assortment of junkies and drunks seated around her in a semicircle, any one of whom the Cardiff fortune could have bought and sold ten times over.

"Stay with us, Christina." Peter was using his best *Dr. Phil* therapy voice. But he sensed the tug on the line, she could tell. His molded-plastic chair creaked, giving him away.

Murmurs rippled around the circle. The group wanted, more than anything, for her to seize this moment.

Carpe diem. Another AA slogan.

But it was so hard. She had never imagined it would be this hard, just to open her mouth and start. A surge of nausea, like the morning sickness she'd had with

Tyler, sprang up inside her, and she hunched over with her head between her knees. The nausea was followed by something far worse.

A wave of panic rolled in and crashed on top of her. Christina had not gone more than two days without a drink or a joint or a pill or *something* since high school.

Someone began to massage the back of her neck.

Christina practically hit the ceiling.

It was Sylphan, her roommate. "You can do this, Christina," Sylphan whispered. "I'll help you. We all will."

The simple act of kindness from frail little Sylphan proved Christina's undoing. Sobs rose up from deep within her, and Christina began to cry.

Christina seldom cried.

"It's okay," Sylphan murmured, patting Christina's shoulder. "We've all been there. We all know what it's like."

Christina took a deep breath, shifted around on her molded-plastic seat, and snuck a look at Peter.

God, she hoped he knew what he was doing.

The boy-band bass player from Studio City stopped tapping his foot.

"Okay?" Peter's pale eyebrows rose on his forehead.

Christina nodded. She cleared her throat while about a million snapshots of her drinking career whirled through her mind. She tried to sort through them and pick one to start with.

And then, just like in the movies, she was saved by a knock on the door. Two sharp raps.

They sounded really loud.

The door opened before anyone said it was okay.

In walked the head honcho.

"Peter. I need a few minutes with you."

Christina blinked. She recognized the man in the doorway from the dust-jacket photo of his book, which had been on the *New York Times* best-seller list for two years. Every nightstand in the place had a copy parked right next to a Gideon Bible and the blue book of Alcoholics Anonymous.

The room grew even quieter as everyone did the kind of double take they'd do if, say, Donald Trump popped his head in.

As rehab directors went, Christina thought, this guy was Elvis.

But he didn't look happy. He just stood there, gripping the doorknob with one hand.

Even Peter just stared.

Nobody interrupted Peter's group while it was in session. Nobody. The room always had gallons of coffee brewing, plus enough boxes of Kleenex to bail the *Titanic*. But how these things got here and when, Christina had no idea.

"Peter. Now, please." The director cocked his head in the direction of the hallway.

"I'm sorry." Peter's frown deepened, and he set his styrofoam cup down so hard it landed with a splash. "We're in session." His warm soft therapy tone was gone. His voice held a This-Is-My-Turf-Get-Out kind of edge, and for the first time Christina could see how Drinking Peter had a mouth that landed him in jail in his bad old days.

"Sorry." The director gave a quick nod of apology but pressed on. "I have something urgent to discuss with you. Now."

Peter looked really pissed off, like he was considering telling his big boss to get lost, but he must have thought better of it because he literally chewed his lip instead. "Take five, guys," he said to the room in general, then, to Christina, "hold that thought, Christina, okay? We'll pick it up in a minute."

Christina nodded, pretty certain they would not. Her moment had passed, or was passing before her eyes. She shrugged, became aware of the director's eyes on her, and glanced up.

Their gaze locked for a couple of seconds, no more. Long enough for her to read something there. Curiosity, and something else she couldn't put her finger on. Something that didn't match up with the I'm-Okay-You're-Okay therapy face that was a job requirement around here.

The moment passed. Peter was already on his feet, out the door.

The room let out its collective breath when they had gone. People stretched, made small talk, got up for another cup of coffee. Like a union shift on break.

Except it didn't last as long.

Peter was back in less than five minutes. "Christina? Will you come with me, please? Next door."

Everyone looked at Christina and got quiet again, even the loud-mouthed bartender from Manhattan who dreamed of doing stand-up.

Christina was being called to the principal's office, and it didn't feel any better than she remembered from school.

Sylphan gave a thumbs-up.

Peter stood back to let Christina pass.

"This way, Christina." He motioned that she should

go to where the director waited at the entrance to another, smaller conference room down the hall.

It had the feel of a Cold War prisoner exchange. Christina wondered what they'd do if she bolted for the exit sign at the end of the long hallway. Somehow, she couldn't imagine Elvis, the Rehab King, sprinting very far. But Peter the Ex-Con was coiled and ready to pounce. Christina did as she was told.

"I'll catch up with you in a minute," Peter said. He did not smile.

She wondered if they were kicking her out, if there was a problem with her health insurance. In which case Jason could wire the money, cover it till they worked it out. He'd be pissed, Christina thought. But too bad. He had paid cash at the Storm dealership in Southampton when he had his mind set on a brand-new BMW roadster last fall, so he could wire money here to cover her treatment.

Christina wanted to stay for the full sixty days. This realization startled her. She hadn't admitted it even to herself till now. She couldn't go back to that life. She wanted a chance at a new start.

Elvis the Rehab King moved away, giving Christina plenty of space to pass through the doorway into a small conference room set up with a table and Aeron chairs.

Someone had thought to set the table with several tiny paper cups full of water and a box of Kleenex tissues.

"Have a seat." He did not meet her gaze.

Christina was getting a bad vibe.

She sat.

He pulled out one of the chairs near her but not directly next to her. "Christina Cardiff."

She nodded. This fact was well within his reach. They had all been photographed and fingerprinted at check-in. Not to mention he had obviously just sent Peter in to collect her.

"Your primary residence is in Manhattan, on Fifth Avenue, is that correct?"

She nodded.

"And you have a second home on Long Island?"

"Yes."

"And that would be?" He let his voice trail off so she could supply the information.

"East Hampton. Only during the summer." They had a place in Aspen, but that was in her in-laws' name.

"Right." He gave another quick nod but did not check her answers against the paperwork in his folder, nor did he jot anything down using his Mont Blanc pen.

The temperature in the room dropped a few degrees. Christina folded her arms across the thin silk mesh of her T-shirt. "Is there a problem with my health insurance?"

"No," he answered quickly. "No, your insurance has processed the claim, and there is no problem with it. Everything is fine there."

He was stalling. He cleared his throat and reached for one of the tiny paper cups. He emptied it in a single gulp.

The Rehab King was nervous. The clarity of this realization caught Christina off guard. The fact that she noticed anything about him at all was out of character for her. Christina was not one to read other people's moods. Correction, she thought: Drunk Christina didn't notice other people's moods. Sober, Nervous,

Jittery, Jumping-Out-of-Her-Skin Christina noticed lots of things about other people.

Such as the way Rehab King was unfurling the top of his Dixie cup and shredding it into tiny pieces.

And then she understood.

This man, who had amassed a fortune telling other people how to get through the worst moments of their lives, wished he were someplace else at that moment.

Because he knew something she didn't know.

Something bad. Something seriously awful, life-changing bad.

Christina felt the prick of a thousand tiny toothpicks on the move, fanning out across her shoulders, down her back and along her arms.

A tiny marching Army of Doom.

Outside, the fescue lawn crisped under a blazing sun.

Inside, the room turned airless and cold, like the inside of a refrigerator.

Christina shivered.

The Rehab King saw it and leapt to his feet. "Let me lower the fan. Sometimes it's difficult to regulate the temperature in these smaller rooms."

She gripped the edge of the polished mahogany table so hard her hands hurt. "What's wrong?"

Careful not to look her way, he hunched low over the air-conditioning controls. "Some of these smaller rooms get way too cold in summer, and they overheat in winter."

"What is it?" Christina's voice rose.

Peter entered the room. He glanced from Christina to his boss, then back again, carefully closing the door behind him. "I'm sorry," he said, the expression on his face even more mournful than usual.

Rehab King shook his head, embarrassed. "She doesn't . . . I mean, I didn't . . ." his voice trailed off.

Men are cowards, Christina thought. She was on her feet without knowing how she got there. "What is it?" She directed her question at Peter.

He blinked. "Christina, I'm sorry. I have bad news. Please sit down."

"No." Edging back, Christina raised one hand in protest, as if she could stop whatever this was from happening if she could just keep the words from leaving Peter's mouth.

"Christina, I need you to stay calm now and be strong."

Something like the claw of a Tonka truck but bigger, went to work on her insides, scraping out everything between her shoulders and knees.

Peter's words floated past her with no weight, as Christina's gut rearranged itself around the hole left behind by the claw.

"No, no." She stood, not moving as a series of images, each more terrible than the last, flashed through her mind like static. "No." She was shrieking now.

The Rehab King flinched. He pressed himself as far back as he could against the console near the windows.

Peter, to his credit, held his ground. The look in his eyes, normally gooey with compassion, had solidified. "Sit down," he ordered.

Christina sat.

Lowering himself quickly into the chair next to hers, he cut right to the chase. "I'm sorry, we have received very bad news about your husband, Jason."

It isn't Tyler. My son. Tyler's okay. It isn't Tyler, or he would have said Tyler's name. He was talking about

Jason, not Tyler. They didn't call me in here with news about Tyler.

"Tyler?" The act of speaking her son's name out loud took away whatever was holding her head up, and Christina fell forward on the chair.

The room went dim, buzzing with a crazy hum.

Peter's voice had an urgent tone that was too loud.

He was scared, too.

"Your son is fine." Peter grabbed Christina's hand. "Tyler is okay. He's fine, safe and sound."

"You're sure?" Her voice was reedy and tinny and far away, like an old phonograph recording. She was going into shock at this moment but, like everything else surrounding this event in her life, it was a label that would not come to her until much later.

"Tyler is fine," Peter repeated. "Safe with your in-laws in France."

Relief splashed through her veins like a neap tide in spring, flooding her heart and filling her ears with sound. She barely heard what he said next.

"This is about your husband, Christina. Jason went for a swim in the pool of your East Hampton home sometime during the night. He experienced some difficulty swimming, and he drowned."

Jason never went in the pool at night. Christina frowned.

"Apparently your husband had been entertaining some guests in the home earlier in the night." Peter shifted in his seat, looked away.

That bitch. Christina nearly blurted the words out loud. Jason had a girlfriend. Lisa, from the Upper West Side. Christina had caught a glimpse of her once. She stared at the thin film of dust motes on the polished surface of the table. This room didn't get much use.

Peter met her gaze once more. "After the guests left, your husband went for a swim. The cleaning crew came in this morning . . ." His voice faded.

No doubt trying to spare Christina the images that were tumbling through her mind.

The counselor tightened his grip on Christina's hand. "The housekeepers noticed something was amiss shortly after they began work, and they immediately alerted the authorities."

The head housekeeper, Señora Rosa, was in her sixties. Tight-lipped, with a ruby-encrusted crucifix on a thick chain of gold that she wore around her neck. Her niece, Marisol, was sullen and beautiful and wore her hair in a black braid. She sent money back to Costa Rica to provide for a son with special needs. The pair worked in silence, mainly, and could be moved to tears on an average day.

The pool on Jonah's Path had just been redone, lined with tiles that had been hand-fired in Milan and shipped airfreight. They had installed an underwater stereo system and state-of-the-art lighting system that was radio-controlled.

The lighting system used some kind of high-tech diodes that operated on a sensor. As soon as anyone jumped in the pool at night, lights would pop on in red, green, blue, or yellow.

Christina blinked.

Peter massaged her hand.

A warning flare fired down in the deepest dark core of Christina's being, emitting a flash of white heat.

Dan on a ladder, paintbrush in hand, stopping long

enough to do something obscene with his tongue that only Christina could see. Jason, oblivious at her side, discussing options for a stucco finish with the contractor.

"Your husband doesn't have a clue," Dan whispered later, his breath tickling the place he had just licked inside Christina's ear. "He doesn't appreciate what he has."

The warning flare burned itself out, leaving only a trace of doubt behind in Christina's panicked mind, lingering no longer than a wisp of sulfur.

Sulfur.

Satan's calling card.

Christina sniffed. Her shoulders hunched, and her neck muscles constricted in a small movement that was, in certain people, an involuntary reaction to guilt.

Peter patted her knee.

Across the table, the Rehab King finally pulled out an Aeron chair and sat.

Nobody said anything.

Christina's mind, greedy now for reassurance, raced to Dan. She pictured his face with its stubble of five o'clock shadow, his musky scent, and the bruising weight of his lips on hers. But the staff here would not have interrupted the residents' morning group therapy session to bring her news of Daniel Cunningham. Nobody knew of her connection to him. She was not Dan's next of kin. He was a paint-and-plaster guy who worked for a contractor who had been hired to renovate the pool area of the Cardiffs' summer home.

Nobody knew Daniel Cunningham was Christina's lover.

If something bad had happened to Dan somehow, she would hear of it only as an afterthought. It would be a footnote to the shitty news Peter was telling her, brought up only after Peter was certain she had absorbed the news about Jason.

Christina couldn't wait that long. "Was anyone else . . ." Christina allowed her voice to trail off, hoping it sounded like a random expression of concern.

"No. Your husband was alone in the house." Peter kept his gaze steady, but his crow's-feet deepened.

She nodded, hugging her arms across her chest to try to stop shaking.

The Rehab King broke his silence at last. "We're all very sorry for your loss, Mrs. Cardiff."

Loss. *Her* loss. Except her husband hadn't belonged to her. The marriage had been a fake front for a long time, but the Rehab King's words placed a terrible burden of ownership on her.

Christina blinked.

Jason, her husband of nearly sixteen years, who had cheated on her beginning with their first married Valentine's Day, when she was pregnant with Tyler, was dead.

Which made her a widow.

A widow who stood to inherit approximately one million dollars for each and every year she had been married.

Her in-laws had stood guard over that trust fund like the Marines posted at Fort Knox.

And now it belonged to her.

This fact danced along Christina's nerve endings, already stretched taut like tuning wire. The result was a sensation that tingled its way out to the surface, releasing energy in the form of a sound that was halfway between strangulation and a giggle.

The vibration made it difficult to focus on the words that were flowing, warm and smooth like hot coffee, from Peter's mouth.

"It's okay." Peter reached for both Christina's hands, working them over inside his with his thumbs. "Whatever you're feeling now is okay. Just feel the feelings and move through them."

But the look in his eyes was not as open and supportive as it had been just a few minutes ago. Christina frowned, struggling mightily to wrap her mind around the fact that she had just became a widow, albeit one of respectable wealth.

Another sound zoomed up, unbidden like the first, through her mouth.

Both men looked away, grabbing at the same time for the last remaining Dixie cup. They fumbled and nearly spilled its contents.

This struck Christina as funny, and she tried to hold back a giggle but could not.

The Rehab King frowned.

"It's okay, Christina." Peter pressed the Dixie cup into her hands. "Everybody grieves in their own way."

2

The Terminal 3 arrivals hall at JFK International Airport thrummed at full capacity. Crowds of people, most with cell phones glued to their ears, gave status reports on their single, common goal: collecting their luggage and getting the hell out of there.

You could tell the natives from the tourists. The New Yorkers wore black despite the fact that the temperature outside hovered a few degrees above blazing. They were the ones jockeying for position at the bottom of the luggage chute, waiting to pounce. To hell with the uniformed staff checking bar codes at the door. Which left the straightaway sections of the luggage carousel wide open for the out-of-towners, who stood a polite distance apart.

This particular crowd of tourists appeared even more polite than usual.

Delta's nonstop had just touched down from the Midwest.

A scuffle broke out among the New Yorkers. Two women and a man were having a tug-of-war over a suitcase, the man on one side and the women on the other. He was pulling hard, but the women were giving him a run for his money.

Voices were raised, and more than a few people in the crowd lowered their cell phones long enough to glare at Suffolk County Homicide Detective Frank McManus.

McManus shot a look across the terminal at his partner, Detective Ben Jackson. Both were dressed in plain clothes, Jackson holding up a sign like a chauffeur. Doing his best to look nonchalant, which was easy since nonchalance was Jackson's MO, he caught the look in Frank's eye and grinned.

Even minus the uniform, people always pegged them for cops. Detectives wore shoes of their own choosing, but the county-mandated suit or sport coat and tie was a giveaway. Nobody wore suits at work these days, except homicide detectives and the President of the United States.

Frank McManus gave a quick lift of his eyebrows to say, *Yeah, they know who we are.* No words required. He turned his attention back to the crowd in black, where the dustup was ending. Some genius had thought to check the luggage tags.

McManus continued scanning the down escalators, spilling over with new arrivals who looked like they all shopped from the same Lands End catalog.

With one exception. A woman stepped aboard up top. Thirtysomething, with an expensive-looking face, which was to say a perfect nose and those big Aunt-Jemima-looking lips rich chicks all seemed to have now. That was as much as McManus could make out, what with the pink velour hoodie pulled down low and a giant pair of dark sunglasses.

Like Paris Hilton trying to duck out on a bad day.

Christina Cardiff would be deep into a bad day of her

own, based on what Frank McManus knew. And there was still a lot of day to come.

McManus shot another glance at his partner.

Ben Jackson gave a quick nod to indicate he'd spotted her, too. He stayed put, holding up the sign that spelled out CARDIFF in block letters, just in case she declined Frank's offer and went off in search of her own car service.

In which case, she'd have a bit of a wait. Detectives McManus and Jackson had taken the liberty of dismissing Mrs. Cardiff's driver, who took one look at the badge and headed back to the limo lot.

All that remained was for Christina Cardiff to accept their offer of a free ride out to Hauppauge, a landlocked town in central Suffolk that was famous not for any sandy white coastline but for an unpronounceable name thanks to the Wyandanch tribe of Indians, who were long gone. What Hauppauge had going for it, however, was the fact that it served as home base for much of the Suffolk County government apparatus and the tax revenues and jobs to go along with it. The acres of office buildings that lined Veterans Memorial Highway included the Suffolk County Medical Examiner's office, where at this very moment the remains of Christina Cardiff's late and not so very great husband were chilling.

She didn't have to go with them, of course. She had not been named a Person of Interest. Not yet, anyway. Nobody had. There was not one bit of evidence at the scene to suggest that Jason Cardiff's death had been anything more than a tragic accident. But when a guy with that kind of money drowns in his own swimming pool, at the height of tourist season in the Hamptons, it's bad for business. Which meant you could bet your E-ZPass the Suffolk County DA was going to keep an eye on it. And when the drowned guy turns out to be a Cardiff (as in *The* Cardiffs of Southampton) the DA was going to be on it like white on rice.

Enter Detectives McManus and Jackson.

Old man Cardiff played golf at Good Ground with the former governor of New York State. McManus had seen Cardiff around plenty, had even been on the receiving end of a free round at the bar when he was assigned to work crowd control at the '95 US Open. Nice enough guy.

The fact that his son Jason was probably the biggest prick on all of Long Island only served to make Frank McManus's job more interesting.

McManus strode quickly to the base of the down escalator, people scattering in front of him like the parting of the Red Sea.

Definitely the suit jacket and tie, he decided. People just seemed to know.

Christina Cardiff did.

She had singled McManus out by the time she was halfway down. She fixed those bug-eyed shades on him long enough to take it all in, right down to the heavy black shoes, all the while maintaining a tight grip on the rail with one hand.

Which was good, McManus thought, because Mrs. Christina Cardiff did not appear to be in shape to handle any sort of road trip.

She held a cell phone in her free hand, about to make a call. At the sight of McManus, she changed her mind and flipped it shut, dropping it into a shoulder bag the size of Delaware.

It would be nice to know whom she had been about to call.

She stepped off the escalator, one pointy mule at a time, and stood.

Waiting.

She knew, all right.

"Mrs. Christina Cardiff?" McManus extended his right hand, flashing his on-the-job smile. Courtesy first.

After the merest hesitation, she placed one hand inside his.

It was cold like ice and had about as much life to it.

She allowed herself to be led a short distance away, out of the stream of humanity that continued to pour off the escalators around them.

"How're you doing, ma'am?"

Her only reply was to tip her head down so the long blond bangs fell forward, shielding the small bit of face that was visible, what with the sunglasses and the hoodie. She dug around some more inside that giant bag.

A crowd of gawkers was already forming.

McManus glared, which was enough to get the Lands End set moving. The New Yorkers didn't budge. They sniffed a story, and they were right. Everything about Christina Cardiff screamed big money and quite possibly fame, from the interlocking gold letters on the sides of her sunglasses, to the dark blue jeans that hung too perfectly to be Levi's, to the teetering pointy-heeled mules pieced together from something that should have been slithering across a desert floor.

The tremors in her shoulders didn't look too good.

Neither did the odor coming off her. Frank McManus

knew the smell, adrenaline mixed with BO. Raw nerves from someone who had fallen out of the habit of regular bathing. Both were hallmarks of a junkie, or else someone likely to be involved in the commission of a crime. Very often, these individuals were one and the same. And if said individuals were having a bad run of luck, their paths would cross with that of Detective Frank McManus.

He breathed in and picked up the overlay of perfume, something heavy like figs, that probably cost a ton.

It was not working for her.

McManus's nose twitched.

Head bent, she continued rifling through her bag.

"I'm Frank McManus," he said in a low voice. "I'm here with my partner, Ben Jackson, from Suffolk County PD." He did not add the word "Homicide." "We are both sorry for your loss, ma'am."

She found what she was looking for at last and raised her head. "Oh. Thank you."

She had a voice like honey that oozed out from those oversized lips, coating the air between them so it felt soft and sticky and sweet. Sexy, if you wanted to know the truth.

Those designer sunglasses were opaque, even at close range.

Aiming them up into his face, she pressed something into his palm and for that brief moment, while their skin came into contact, McManus felt his breath catch in his throat.

He could only make out the barest outline of her eyes behind the shades.

"Are we parked near the terminal?"

Without waiting for an answer, she clattered past

him in her little shoes, and Frank got the impression she lived in a world where men could always be counted on to bring the car around.

"My partner's near the door. He's holding up a sign with your name on it," he began.

The hoodie bobbed once, and the back of her hand came up, signaling she got it. She made pretty good time in those heels.

McManus looked down. In his hand were the claim tickets for her bags.

The medical examiner had told her Jason's body was in good shape, like someone who had stayed too long in the tub.

About a hundred years too long.

Good shape, my ass, Christina thought. The ME must be so used to looking at dead people, he no longer realized how bad they looked. "Oh, my God, he looks like shit," she burst out, squeezing her eyes shut. She regretted it almost as soon as the words left her mouth. Any kind of emotional outburst, she knew, would brand her as unbalanced.

Like someone who had been sprung too soon from a nuthouse.

Nobody said anything. Not the ME, who appeared slightly wounded by her assessment, and not Detectives McManus and Jackson, who stood behind her and a respectful distance away.

Blocking the exit, but near enough to catch her if she fainted.

Christina Cardiff was not the fainting type.

God, I hate this. She hated everything about it.

Mundo Bizarro.

She closed her eyes in an attempt to block out the entire shitty scene, hoping maybe she'd wake up from the nightmare and find herself in the sunny guest room of the house on Jonah's Path, with the surf pounding at the southern edge of their property line, or maybe on the foldout couch in the den of their Olympic Tower condo that overlooked St. Patrick's Cathedral. That condo, smack in the center of the hustle and bustle of midtown Manhattan, had never felt as much like home to Christina, who was a country girl at heart, but she loved the power and privilege of living at one of the most exclusive addresses in the world. Step outside and Rockefeller Center was right there, with Saks Fifth Avenue just a few steps away. Tyler loved those windows at Christmastime, and, oh, Jesus Christ . . .

This was no nightmare.

Reality was a million times worse than any coke hangover she'd ever had.

There was only one way out of this, and that was through it. Christina allowed her eyes to flutter open. "That's him," she said to the medical examiner, who sat facing the monitor in the seat next to hers. "That's Jason Cardiff. My husband."

The ME gave a quick nod.

"That's it? That's what you need for an official identification?" She turned around to check with Frank McManus. Of the two, she had developed some small rapport during the ride out here, based on nothing more than the fact that his partner did the driving, which left McManus to make small talk. And thank God he had not done much of that.

McManus and his partner were here purely as a matter of protocol, he had explained.

He nodded now.

"Okay, then," Christina said. She had been relieved to learn the identification process would take place via closed-circuit video monitor rather than actually having to stand in the same room as Jason's body like on the TV show *Law & Order*. As if watching a video of her dead husband would make everything so much easier instead of having to ID him in person.

As if.

The reality of it, the fact that Jason was dead, slammed into her with the force of a hurricane that threatened to suck her brains out, blowing away her soul right along with it.

Christina tried to look away but couldn't resist one last glimpse of the grainy image of Jason on the screen, his skin waxy white and his lips a grotesque purplish stain. Frozen in place. Not moving.

The screen went black, and the image disappeared, ghostlike, into the ether.

Through the cinder-block wall, she heard measured movements that were, she somehow knew, the sound of hydraulics equipment.

Because heavy equipment was now required to move what was left of her husband from one place to another.

She pictured him hale, healthy, and suntanned, all six feet of him, laughing at a joke she'd made. Not Jason the husband who had grown tired of living with her, but Jason the boyfriend from so long ago who had brought her to parties to show her off to his friends from college and then slow-danced with her, whispering in her ear that he wanted to live with her.

Jason's metamorphosis, from living, breathing, upright person to the hideous horizontal thing she'd just seen on the monitor, was proof that the world had gone mad. Life was no longer safe. Jason was being stowed at this very moment in a refrigerated compartment so his body would not rot before they finished with it. This idea tumbled like a dry weed on the wind that was blowing through the hollow place that remained of her insides. Bile pulsed up high into her throat, and Christina swallowed hard, forcing it down. She winced with effort.

She did not want be sick in front of these men.

"Thank you, Mrs. Cardiff."

The ME pushed his chair back, signaling this was over. That was a relief.

"Do you need anything before you go?"

The list of things she needed was so long that, in the end, she could not settle on any kind of reply.

Christina stood.

The ME followed suit.

"I'll let you know once I figure out where to . . ." She couldn't bear to finish the sentence.

The ME was probably used to it, because he raised a hand to spare her the effort. "Fine. Let us know. Should be ready by day's end tomorrow."

Jason's corpse. Jason's corpse should be ready.

"Good luck to you, ma'am."

His hand, when she shook it, was surprisingly soft.

Christina followed the detectives through the subterranean hallway that smelled of antiseptic.

They rode the elevator in silence. It was oversized, lined with heavy steel bumpers and had two sets of extrawide doors that opened at either end, a fact Christina had not fully appreciated on the way down.

She checked her watch, a diamond-bezel Rolex tank that had been a gift from Jason on their wedding day.

Quarter past six. Dan Cunningham would be finishing up work if he were on a new job, which he very likely was. By placing the call now, she could reach him on his way home to shower and change before he headed out for the night. It was summertime in the Hamptons. Christina wanted to hear his voice more than anything. She wished she had the nerve to tell the two cops she needed to make a call in private, but she did not.

She had already spoken with her son Tyler today, and they knew that, just as they knew it was the middle of the night now in France. Tyler would be in bed early in preparation for his dawn departure from Marseille up to Paris, where he and his grandparents would board their transatlantic flight to JFK.

"I'm okay, Mom." Tyler had said those words to her this morning on the phone in a voice that was masculine, foreign.

He was managing her, she realized with a pang. Like Jason does.

Like Jason used to do.

The way her in-laws did, who were there with Tyler right now. While she, his mother, was six thousand miles away in the residence unit of a rehabilitation center for alcoholics.

The modern-day version of a loony bin.

She had failed her son. Again. And now, on the worst day of Tyler's young life, she was not there for him. Fate dictated that his childhood would come lurching to a halt in the space of a single summer's day, and he would either get through it or not, with no more help from his mother than she'd had from hers. Christina's shoulders folded inward like a bird with broken wings. She had gripped the phone till her hand hurt.

"We'll be back tomorrow night," Tyler had said.

Not "I'll be home," but "We'll be back." He was one of the Cardiffs, and she, Christina, felt like the in-law.

She sensed her son slipping away from her through the long-distance lines.

"Tyler," she said, unable to control the need in her voice. "Tyler," she said again, choking on a sob. She was the one who needed comforting, not him.

Her father-in-law had come on the line then. Calm, soft-spoken, as always. In control. Informing her of their travel plans, their estimated time of arrival tomorrow afternoon at JFK. There was, he said, no need for her to worry. They would handle everything. All Christina needed to do was get herself back to the East Coast. Just get her self through this, take it just a little bit at a time. They would handle the rest.

Christina wondered later whether it was coincidence that her father-in-law had used one of AA's big slogans, perhaps to taunt her.

One day at a time.

They rode east from the morgue in silence. Ben Jackson drove, with Christina next to him in front.

And all the while Christina needed a drink so bad she could practically taste a vodka burn at the back of her throat.

CHAPTER

3

Someone had stubbed out a cigarette in one of the potted geraniums.

The sight of it was irritating to Christina. Señora Rosa should have cleaned that up before she left. The patio furniture was askew, left at odd angles. The straw mat outside the back door had been pushed to one side into a bed of impatiens.

Christina frowned.

A tiger lily lay crumpled in the grass, its spine broken. The turf all around a side gate, rarely used, was bent and flat.

Two fresh tracks had been carved down the center, which was now a sea of mud.

Wheel ruts.

Of course, she thought, they would have taken Jason away through the side gate. He had no need of doors or houses anymore.

This realization had the effect of lowering the sky, dark and gloomy today, until it touched the top of her skull, making it impossible to breathe. Christina hunched low on the edge of the striped cushion of her patio chair and gripped the teak trim.

Detective Frank McManus got up from his chair with

its coordinated floral cushions. "Can I get you some water, Mrs. Cardiff?"

The patio set was supposed to evoke the feel of the Tuscan countryside. An oversized amber shade umbrella, not necessary today, had been carelessly left open to gather droplets of mist.

Christina shook her head without looking up.

"Water will help. Even without the sun, it's still pretty hot out here." McManus was already heading inside.

She could have directed him to the refrigerated bar, fully stocked, inside the pool house, but that would have required too much effort.

"Just take it easy, ma'am." Detective Ben Jackson walked around the side of the pool and stood in front of her, big enough to block the sun if there had been sun.

Squeezing her eyes shut, Christina sucked as much of the humid air into her lungs as she could, taking in deep breaths she remembered from her birthing class until the wave of panic had passed. She straightened up. "I'm fine."

McManus returned with a water bottle. "Drink this, Christina."

The thought of anything, even water, made her stomach heave. She raised one finger to the bridge of her nose and pushed her sunglasses back into place. She had kept them all day through the plane ride and even now, despite the gloom. "Can we please, you know, just finish with this?"

"No problem, Mrs. Cardiff." Detective Jackson was sticking to formalities, Christina noticed, unlike his partner, who had begun using her first name. Creepy. Somewhere in the back of her brain she remembered something about Good Cop, Bad Cop.

Detective Jackson walked back to the edge of the pool.

McManus sat once more, watching his partner, but Christina was aware he maintained a good peripheral view of her face.

"When we arrived, the decedent was lying here." Detective Jackson pointed to the steps in the shallow end of the pool.

Decedent. If that was a real word, Christina hated it already.

"After placing a call to 911 dispatch, your housekeepers managed to move the decedent from the deep end." He pointed to the area beneath the diving board, where today the water was a malevolent shade of blue.

Christina shivered.

The ocean waves were landing closer than usual today, just out of sight beyond the top of the dunes at the southern edge of the Cardiff property.

The patio was silent as a tomb.

Someone had turned off the pool filter.

"They managed to get it as far as the shallow end," Jackson continued, "but they were not able to remove the decedent from the water."

That word again. Meaning Jason. Christina pictured Señora Rosa and Marisol, their gray nylon skirts billowing around them in the water that was always kept at eighty degrees, as they struggled with Jason's lifeless body.

"At some point during this process, the landscapers became aware of the housekeepers' efforts."

"¡Ay, ay, ay, Dios mío!"

Señora Rosa's screams would have echoed off the walls of Cotswold stone they'd had built by a certified English mason. Whenever something upset her,

Señora Rosa would grab the crucifix hanging around her neck.

"The landscapers ceased work and entered the pool area to assist," Jackson continued.

The landscapers arrived each morning this time of year in an aging Ford pickup driven by Roberto, the foreman. They worked till sundown, pulling weeds and removing debris from the beds with miniature hand rakes. Jason absolutely forbade the use of leaf blowers except on mowing day. *What's the point of living on the goddamned ocean if all you ever hear is leaf blowers?*"

The landscapers, to the best of Christina's knowledge, spoke no English. They stopped work whenever she passed by, just long enough to flash smiles of white teeth mixed with crowns of gold. None of them were as tall as she, except Roberto.

Detective Jackson stood at the shallow end. "Even with the landscapers' help, they were unable to remove the decedent from the water. They began attempts at resuscitation here on the pool steps until East Hampton Police Department officers arrived on the scene."

The detective's dark jacket and thick-soled black shoes looked out of place against the backdrop of tumbled Cotswold stones.

Christina had argued with Jason over the cost of importing those stones, and she had won.

Detective Ben Jackson stared down at them now.

He was the larger of the two officers and younger by fifteen years, maybe more. It was hard to tell. He was supermodel handsome, his skin a shade of eggplant with the reddish tones that were common in certain parts of the East End. He'd be killer handsome when he smiled, Christina thought, but she didn't suppose he had much cause to do that in his line of work.

As if to prove her point, Jackson looked up and resumed speaking in a tone that was dry and matter-of-fact. "Two police officers arrived within approximately fifteen minutes of receiving the initial call. They continued resuscitation efforts and began external heart massage. They continued these ministrations throughout the transfer by ambulance to Southampton General Hospital, and for approximately twenty-five minutes inside the emergency room, at which time the attending physician performed an EKG, and the victim was pronounced to have expired."

Decedent. Resuscitation efforts. Expired. Death had a language all its own, Christina thought. She tried hard to concentrate on the chain of events that had just been described, but her mind was sluggish. "He must have been dead before they ever found him in the pool," she said at last.

Detective Jackson looked at her, his expression giving away nothing.

McManus was the one who spoke. "It would appear that way. We won't know for certain until the ME files his report. That'll probably be in the next day or so. We'll let you know as soon as we hear anything." His words were helpful, his tone a few degrees warmer than that of his partner.

Christina thought again about Good Cop, Bad Cop.

A dove cooed from its perch on the low branch of a scrub pine.

It was a mournful sound.

Christina wanted this episode to be done with, wanted these men to be gone. She didn't like cops. It occurred

to her they wouldn't leave until she took some action.
"Okay." She pushed her chair back.

Neither of them made any move to leave. "Okay," she
said again and stood.

After a moment McManus rose from his chair.

Ben Jackson walked around the pool.

Christina made no move to extend her hand. "Thank
you."

"If we can do anything at all, please don't hesitate to
give us a call," McManus said.

"We're compiling a list of the people who were
present in the house early last night," Ben Jackson
said. "Once we have that list, we'll talk to the people
on it."

Christina gave a quick nod, studying a stand of Queen
Anne's lace that was blooming in a bed just inside the
privet hedge. She had a pretty good idea who had been
here last night with Jason. Lisa. *Tramp*. Low-life *bitch*.

Now it was Christina's turn to keep her face impassive.
"Fine." She hugged herself, shivering against a sudden
chill.

McManus watched her. "Is there anything else you
think we need to know?"

Her mind flashed on the tabloid headlines after Jason's uncle divorced several years back. Details of the
breakup had made it into *People* magazine, and someone had even written a book about it.

No, Christina thought, if the police wanted to sniff
through her and Jason's dirty laundry, they'd have to
dig though it themselves. "No," she said, avoiding
McManus's gaze.

Storm clouds piled up overhead, and she watched,
wondering if there would be thunder.

There was silence. They were watching her, she knew. "Not really," she said for good measure. "No."

Neither man said anything.

Christina kept watching the clouds, waiting for them to thank her and leave.

But they did not.

McManus then sat, watching her, his eyes a grayer shade of blue than they had been earlier. It seemed to Christina they had changed colors somehow, to a shade resembling the dark centers of the storm clouds overhead.

Nobody said anything for a while.

"Well," Christina said, when she couldn't stand it any longer. "One of the housekeepers, Marisol, was having an affair with the head gardener, Roberto." She waited, relieved to have come up with some tidbit that might satisfy them.

McManus, the older one who had done most of the talking, merely continued to watch her. He did not so much as nod.

Ben Jackson gave a small nod but did not, she noticed, bother to write this information down in his pad.

McManus finally blinked. "And you are basing this statement on, what observation?"

Marisol and her beady eyes that lingered on things just long enough to let Christina know she'd seen things she hadn't been meant to see. Once, after she wiped vomit that had splashed up against the edge of the toilet seat, she said something in rapid-fire Spanish to her aunt with a cackling sort of laugh when she didn't know Christina was there.

Christina drew in a deep breath now, letting it out through her mouth. "Just a lot of little things. Roberto drives her to work sometimes. They sit together at lunch and talk. She has a kid, you know, somewhere in Costa Rica, so she must be married."

Neither man reacted.

Christina shrugged again. "I just thought you should know."

"Thank you." McManus gave a tiny nod.

Christina never felt good when Marisol was in the house; she'd tried on several occasions to convince Jason to get rid of her.

"You can't get rid of her unless you fire the aunt as well," he'd said. "And there's nothing wrong with their work."

And that was it. End of discussion.

"I just thought it was worth mentioning," Christina said.

Ben Jackson tapped his pen once on his writing pad. "This guy, Roberto, you know his last name?"

Christina shook her head. She didn't know much about anyone who worked for them. Jason handled all that.

"Thanks for the information," Ben Jackson said. "You remember anything else, you give us a call." He removed a business card from the back of his notepad and handed it to her. "You take it easy, Mrs. Cardiff."

Frank McManus fished one of his cards out of his breast pocket and did the same.

A wave of pure relief washed over Christina. At last, they were going to leave.

"Try to get some rest," McManus said. "Is there someone you can call? You want us to wait?"

There was, and she didn't. Shaking her head, Christina looked at the gate. Hint, hint.

Ben Jackson cleared his throat. "I guess we'll head out."

Christina nodded. She hated cops.

"You just take it easy now," Frank McManus said, and at last they were gone.

"So?" McManus hunched out of his jacket as Jackson eased the cruiser down the winding drive of pea gravel.

Jackson let out a low whistle. "Some spread."

A starling swooped from the boughs of an ornamental pear tree.

The wrought-iron gate swung open at their approach.

As they nosed through, a man straightened from his slouch against the side of a black Escalade and trained his camera lens on them.

"Smile and say cheese," Jackson muttered, pulling onto the road.

Seeing the county plates, the paparazzo snapped away but maintained a respectful distance.

"You low-life, scum-sucking moron," McManus murmured in a low voice as they passed.

Jackson nodded, giving the car some gas but staying well inside the speed limit.

Twilight was prime time for the weekend warriors to jog or roller-blade or take a spin on their titanium-framed bikes to get in an aerobic workout in the rarefied air that blew across their oceanfront estates.

McManus reached for a Marlboro Light. If the county meant business about banning smoking on the job, they would have to prove it by removing dashboard lighters from their fleet of Crown Victoria cruisers. Pressing the tip of his cigarette to the bright orange glow, McManus took a deep drag and felt better than he had in hours. "What do you think?"

"Couple of things," Jackson replied.

McManus took another long drag, enjoying the way the plume of bluish smoke mingled into the mist of the humid night. Ben Jackson was in the habit, common among Gen Xers or Gen Y or whatever the hell they were called these days, of thinking out loud. It was a quality Frank McManus disliked in the general population, but he had grown to appreciate in his partner.

Jackson's massive shoulders hiked up a bit before settling back down. "First, there's probably nothing in this. Guy got wasted and went for a swim. Too bad, man, what a way to go."

"Yeah." McManus shook his head. As the son and grandson of avid fishermen, McManus possessed a genuine love of the Atlantic that was matched with equal parts respect and fear.

"A man who ventures out onto the ocean in a boat had better know what he's about," his grandfather had taught him.

McManus's father, as always, had been more direct. "You go out alone in a boat, you better have your shit together, or your own mother won't recognize what washes up onshore."

McManus shuddered. It was hard to believe a guy could be wasted enough or just plain stupid enough to drown in his own pool, but McManus had been on the force for over twenty years. Plenty long enough to believe anything.

"The thing is," Jackson observed, "she's not too shook up."

McManus nodded. Christina Cardiff was clamped shut tight as a clam. Working homicide, they'd seen their share of widows. Therapists and defense lawyers would tell you some folks hold back and do their weeping in private. Everyone grieves in his or her own unique way.

Bullshit.

"True," McManus said. "Her counselor at rehab said she took the news on the chin."

"That's cool for her, I guess." Jackson arched an eyebrow. "Still, there's nothing at the scene."

McManus nodded. "Clean as a whistle."

"And she was nowhere near the place."

"True again. She was in Minnesota taking the pledge."

Jackson chuckled. "The politically correct term is 'getting sober,' my friend. And she just inherited one big"—he paused for effect—"big honkin' pile of cash."

To the tune of approximately seventeen million dollars, if Jason Cardiff's *Forbes* ranking was correct. McManus was a big fan of Google. "That she did."

"Lotta dough." Jackson whistled. "If it weren't for Cirie and the kids, I might just have to ask her out."

McManus, whose ex lived in Florida with his two kids, played along. It was an old routine. "Well, I'm gonna take a number and hang back at the end of the line, my friend. Things didn't work out so good for bachelor number one."

Jackson grinned. "That's probably wise."

"And there may be a couple of guys in line ahead of me."

"You never know, dawg. You could be right about that."

McManus raised an eyebrow. "We'll see." It was their job, after all, to figure that out. Old man Cardiff had not come out and accused his daughter-in-law of anything, at least not according to the part of the conversation that had trickled down to McManus and Jackson by way of the Suffolk County assistant district attorney.

In any event, the higher-ups had made it clear they

wanted all the t's crossed and i's dotted before any ruling
was made as to the cause of Jason Cardiff's death.

McManus watched for deer in the shadowed forest
of pin oak and scrub pine that pressed up against both
sides of the road.

This area had never been developed. No signs with
gold letters advertising some overrated vineyard, no
freshly paved streets named after flowering vines, not
even a U-PICK sign for strawberries. Nope. This stretch
of Montauk was as desolate as it had been when Frank
was a kid, passing through in his father's Ford Fairlane
on their way out to trawl for blues each June. The trees
grew gnarled and scruffy here, clinging with shallow
roots to the sandy topsoil left behind by the Wiscon-
sinan glacier that had scraped through about twenty
thousand years ago.

As forests went, the pine barrens of eastern Long
Island were not much to look at, but Frank had grown
up with them and liked them well enough. Frank
McManus was not one to be taken in by a pretty face.

Christina didn't get a good look at the cops' business
cards until she went through her pocketbook the next
day. At which point she gave thanks she hadn't called
Dan Cunningham till after they'd gone.

Printed in tidy block letters next to the same Suffolk
County logo she recognized from the medical examiner's card were two words Christina was certain neither
of them had uttered out loud.

Homicide Division.

*D*arkness came early, deepening the corners of the yard.

Anxiety swirled through Christina's mind like the mist blowing in across the dunes, riming the landscape with eerie droplets of silver. She had been dreading this moment since she left rehab this morning. No, her whole life if she thought about it.

Being alone.

Summer sundown was a busy time in the Hamptons, a time for heating up backyard grills, dressing to meet friends for dinner in one of the private clubs or Michelin-starred restaurants that dotted Long Island's East End.

Happy hour.

Christina thought of the bottles of Grey Goose that took up half the freezer, chilled and waiting.

There should be two cases in the basement, room temperature but ready to be pressed into service if needed.

She tried not to think about it, forced herself to stay put.

A great mournful emptiness, with a bottom and sides as deep and unknown as the ocean, opened around her. Gathering force to suck her away on a black tide.

The dove continued its steady cooing, the sound of a lover calling out and receiving no reply.

Christina felt her mind begin to unravel.

A drink would help.

On the beach, one wave landed harder than the others so the dunes shook, and she imagined the sea rising up to suck her away to an endless black eternity.

The dove fell silent.

Another wave hit.

Christina cried out.

There was no one to hear. She was alone.

Jason had been alone at the end.

How long did it take to drown? Did he know he was going to die? Did her husband, known on Wall Street for his nerves of steel, panic at the end? She pictured him flailing through the water, grabbing for air, coming up empty. How many moments passed? Long enough to realize that Tyler would grow up without him?

She had read once that drowning victims experienced a moment of euphoria at the end, after their lungs had filled with water. But the brief glimpse of Jason's face in the morgue told her this was a lie.

Jason did not like water. He had confided this to her long ago, when he was in love and shared his secrets, and this, she thought, was what marriage would be. He had almost drowned in Candlewood Lake at a barbecue when he was five, water filling his nose and eyes, losing all sense of which way was up, until he used the last of his strength to push off against the sandy bottom and rise, sputtering and coughing, to the surface. Saving himself.

Christina pictured the pool last night, roiling and heaving as Jason the adult struggled to find his true north. And failed.

She forced herself to look away from the pool. Therein lay madness. "No," she aloud.

Dan. She needed to see him or at least hear his voice.

She reached for her pocketbook. Sweeping the cops' business cards inside, she dug past the butterscotch candies Peter had provided for the plane (sweets helped calm the craving for alcohol, he'd said), the folded bits of paper with phone numbers and words of encouragement from her fellow patients at rehab, until her fingers closed around the slim cool surface of her cell phone.

She checked for messages and gave up before they were halfway through. Condolence calls from people wanting to know what the arrangements would be. Two from her sister-in-law in Southampton, including one placed a little while ago with an offer to come by and help.

Her sister-in-law had been to this house just once since they'd bought it. Five Christmases ago, when they were still all pretending to be on good terms. Snooping around in a dreary St. John cashmere suit that showed off her St. Barth's tan, gripping her highball glass till her skinny knuckles turned white.

Christina hit DELETE.

No calls from Dan.

She called him, using the speed-dial key that was easiest to find even in the dark—*0. The call went straight to voice mail.

"You got Dan's cell. Leave a message."

That voice, strong and virile. And alive. On a good day, Dan's voice heated up her core. On this day it made her fall apart.

"It's me," she began. "Dan, I'm in trouble and . . . I need to see you. Right away." A sob rose in her throat.

She forced the words out quickly before her voice broke down completely. "I'm home now, on Jonah's Path. Please call, or please just come. I need . . ."

There was another beep as his answering service cut her off. Her cell phone became a useless piece of plastic in her hand. She was tempted to hurl it into the pool. She toyed with the idea of throwing herself in along with it, filling her lungs with water and drifting down to the bottom, where she would wait for death.

Like Jason had.

The dove resumed its grieving call.

She needed to move, do something. Anything but sit here and wait to lose her mind.

She looked at the house, dark inside.

The Grey Goose was there in the freezer, a few short steps inside the door.

She couldn't go in there. Not by herself. Not yet.

The cedar shingles of the house next door rose above the privet hedge. The Brookses. They'd met on friendly terms just once, almost a decade ago. She had a vague memory of them, WASP-y and austere, a *New Republic* writer and his Birkenstock-wearing wife who came to their housewarming party but left before they started the buffet. The cops always showed up at the Cardiffs' parties after that when the band got too loud, saying only that a concerned neighbor had called.

"Straight out of *American Gothic*," Jason said once. "All they need is a fucking pitchfork."

If their cars happened to pass on the short stretch of lane they shared, Christina busied herself with something on the dashboard or at most dipped her head in a tight nod.

A studio executive owned the house directly across

the way. They lived in Bel Air, coming out just once a year to escape the "June gloom" of LA. But it was August, and the house was empty.

Christina didn't know anyone else. She had friends, of course, one from college who lived in Morristown and would be at her own summer place right now down at the Jersey shore with her three kids and her dog. Hours, if not days, away from rearranging her life to get here for Christina.

There was Clarke, her hairdresser from the city, who had a weekend half share at a group house in Quogue. But today was only Wednesday, and Christina had no idea if this was one of Clarke's weekends.

She was almost desperate enough to call Jason's sister. But not quite.

Peter had told them in rehab he hadn't realized how small his world had become until he landed in jail on Christmas Eve and couldn't think of anyone to call besides his dealer. "My world," he said, "had shrunk to the size of a barstool."

In the end, Christina decided to take a drive.

She could lose herself in the traffic that clogged Montauk Highway this time of year, pretending there was someplace she needed to be.

She grabbed her keys and cell phone, placing one more call to Dan to tell him where she'd be. The call went straight to voice mail again, which meant he had switched his phone off.

She remembered an afternoon in early summer. They had sipped margaritas and had sex in the pool house. Dan insisted she go on top, urging her on and on, until droplets of sweat flew off her. He wiped a finger across her nipples and licked it clean.

Christina had never felt so sexy.

Dan had ignored his cell phone until they were good and finished. When it rang for the third time, he checked caller ID, holding the phone in one hand and keeping a firm hold on Christina's ass with the other.

He snorted. "My boss." He switched the phone off and let it drop to the floor, grabbing Christina's buttocks now in both hands and tightening his grip. "I never pick up when I'm in the middle of a good fuck."

Christina dialed again now, groaning out loud when it went straight to voice mail again. *What was he doing?* Jealousy seeped into her gut like an injection of hot lava. They had never said they were exclusive. How could they? But they had played a game after they made love each time. He started it, a fact that thrilled her, growling into her hair when they finished. "If we were together, we'd do this every day." The game changed over time. "If we were together," became "If we lived together," became "If we had a place in Florida," and how they would live, how they would work.

Where was he?

Christina hit speed dial once, twice, and finally left a message. "Dan, please. I, ah, it's me again. I need to see you. Tonight, if possible. It doesn't matter how late. Please come by the house. Something's wrong, every-thing's wrong . . ." She lost her words as a sob rose up into the back of her throat. "It's, ah, Wednesday night, and I'm in the Hamptons and—"

The machine beeped, cutting her off again.

"Oh, my God," she cried aloud, angry now. Her mes-sage sounded desperate and pathetic, like she was losing her mind.

She called again, vowing to keep her voice strong this

time. "Dan, I need to see you. Everything's a mess. I don't know what I'm going to do." Her voice climbed into the high, desperate pitch. Into the zone of crazy homeless women who screamed at people walking past in Central Park. Christina didn't care. "I might do something really bad. I need to see you. Tonight."

The answering service beeped again, cutting her off.

If Dan cared about her at all, even if he had started seeing someone else while she was gone, he would call.

Satisfied for the moment, Christina flipped her phone shut, double-checking to make sure it was still on in case Dan called.

She headed for the garage.

An opaque plastic bag, rumpled and sealed tight with an official-looking paper pasted across the top, was lying on the ground just inside the brick wall of the backyard.

She knew what it contained.

Jason's swim trunks.

The only things he was wearing when he died. The ME had given it to the cops that afternoon, after sliding a manila envelope across the desk at her containing Jason's wedding band and Rolex watch.

Detective McManus had brought the bag back here and, after receiving no reply from Christina, set it down just inside the gate on his way out.

She picked it up now. Gingerly, as though it contained a poisonous snake. She tossed it into the shadows at the back of the three-car garage.

Her Mercedes sedan was still parked exactly where she'd left it nine days ago, next to Jason's coupe and the old Suburban, which they used just once each summer for the big move out from the city.

She climbed in, and the Mercedes started right up.

The simple act of heading out the drive with the windows down took away some of her claustrophobia.

The gate swung open on its sensor.

She caught a flash of movement and jammed on the brakes, thinking it was a deer.

But the man leaping at her car was no deer.

He came so close to the window she could smell his stale breath.

Christina screamed.

White strobes blinded her.

Christina was certain she was about to be carjacked.

But the man made no attempt to open her door. He was working the camera around his neck, snapping away with a powerful flash.

Her fear turned to anger as she realized he was paparazzo, like the guys who turned up for opening night of the Bridgehampton Classic. Christina always checked the next issue of *Dan's Papers,* loving the attention, hoping she'd look good in her dress.

But this was different. He was here to dig up dirt on Jason, on her, on their family.

"Fuck you," she snarled.

"Christina!" Her vision cleared enough to see that he was tall with lanky blond hair, worn jeans, and a vest. "Do you really believe your husband drowned by accident?" He had an English accent. Straight out of central casting.

"Fuck you," she yelled again, fumbling for the shift.

"Was it an overdose? Did he have a problem with substance abuse?"

"Asshole!"

He continued snapping away.

"How's your son handling this?"

Christina slammed the car into reverse, lifted her foot from the brake, and gunned it, glancing in the rearview mirror in time to see the metal gates swinging closed behind her.

She hit the brakes again, a moment too late.

The Mercedes collided with the gates in a screech of metal on metal.

"Yeow!" The photographer yelled at the top of his lungs.

Christina yelped, covering her mouth with her hands.

The photographer continued to snap away. "Easy there, tiger!"

He was making a game of this.

She fumbled for the remote to the gate while the paparazzo kept up a stream of questions.

"Talk to me, sweet. How are you getting on, my love?"

She gave him the finger and backed through the gate when it opened again at last, gunning the Mercedes through in a spray of gravel.

The photographer howled and jumped back, clutching his foot.

Christina screamed in horror.

But he was laughing.

She backed away up the drive as fast as she dared.

The gate swung shut, its iron scrollwork battered and tilting at a crazy angle.

The Brit with stringy hair dropped his camera at last so it came to rest on the strap around his neck.

She wished it would strangle him.

"I'm here if you change your mind," he called.

"Fuck you," Christina said once more, revving her car up the gravel drive. She was too shaky to attempt to pull back inside the garage, so she turned off the engine and sat.

What she wanted more than anything was to rest her forehead on the steering wheel and have a good cry, but she didn't dare. If she started now, she would never stop.

Instead, she collected her pocketbook and cell phone and headed inside. At the moment there was no alternative.

She climbed the steps and crossed the concrete porch. The house was massive, constructed of white concrete and glass, and had replaced the tiny Cape that had been here before. She unlocked the front door, custom-designed of leaded glass.

Inside, the house smelled of the lavender aromatherapy products she insisted the housekeepers use mixed with the briny smell of the Atlantic and something else. Stale cigarette smoke and beer.

The police said Jason had thrown a party last night.

Christina wrinkled her nose. "Party" was too nice a word to describe what Jason had been doing.

Through the glass that comprised the southern wall of the house, the tops of the dunes were visible as heavy shadows in the gathering darkness.

Inside, the house was silent as a tomb except for the tick-tick-tick of the sculpted-iron floor clock on the landing, purchased in SoHo years ago when they first got married and Jason still accompanied her on shopping trips.

There were signs everywhere of activity from the night before. Furniture out of place, couch cushions that still held the impression of someone's body weight. Dining-room chairs askew, clustered at one end of the long glass table. She could well imagine what Jason and his guests had been doing on its surface.

The floor needed vacuuming, and she could see into the kitchen counters cluttered with open bottles and dirty dishes. Several long-stemmed champagne glasses, liquid still pooled in their bottom, caught her eye.

The back of Christina's throat tingled with a desire so strong she grabbed the couch to hold herself back. She sank onto the rumpled cushions, clutching her purse to her chest like a shield.

She should fire Señora Rosa's fat ass, and her simpering niece Marisol, for leaving the place in such a state.

Later, she would find the upstairs bathrooms clean and the beds freshly made, tasks that would have been completed by the housekeepers, perhaps, before they discovered Jason's body.

The screen door leading to the yard was open, the way she had left it earlier, and she decided to leave it open to air the place out despite the scumbag paparazzo at the front gate. The Cardiffs', like the studio exec's house across the way, sported signs that promised ARMED RE-SPONSE.

They had installed a new alarm system when they redid the house last spring. They only set it when they were away. She could see the green READY button shining steady in its panel mounted on the wall near the side door, and made a mental note to set it before she went up to bed tonight.

Upstairs.

She wasn't ready to face those empty rooms. Not yet. Not the guest room she had taken over at the end of last summer, a move that had never been discussed. Not Tyler's room, which always felt empty and wrong when he was away. And most certainly not the master bedroom.

Jason's room.

Tonight the whole place felt haunted.

The steel clock chimed eight, and she nearly jumped out of her skin.

She cleared her throat just to make some noise. The sound was hollow and lonely in the empty house.

Those half-empty champagne flutes beckoned from the kitchen counter. Christina wondered whether her stock of Grey Goose was intact inside the freezer.

Her rehab counselor's face floated to mind. "Think before you drink," Peter had implored them with his priestly blue eyes.

It had been a day straight from hell, the worst of Christina's life.

Her throat itched at the back. Nobody would blame her if she took a drink. Nobody would even know.

Except her son, Tyler, would know. She pictured his face pinched down the middle when he was angry, the way his thin shoulders would stiffen, and he would pull back when she hugged him hello.

Tyler had learned at a young age to catch the scent of booze.

Christina vowed to ride this one out, fresh on that memory.

This decision behind her for the moment at least, she fell back on the cushions, exhausted. She had learned in rehab that all newly recovering alcoholics grew tired easily, unused to moving through life without alcohol to round out the sharp edges.

Peter had lectured them to monitor their moods in the first ninety days of sobriety. "Progress, not perfection."

Lessons for life that would fit on a bumper sticker, Christina thought sourly. Was there a catchy slogan for how to cope when your husband was found facedown in your swimming pool?

Christina thought of the interviews she'd watched on TV with 9/11 widows. Their eyes, their faces, their voices ravaged by a depth of pain she simply did not feel right now.

The truth was, if she looked back and reviewed the fabric of her marriage, she would not have seen a smooth bolt of strong cloth. Nor would she have seen a smooth fabric in the center, drawing the eye away from fraying and wrinkles at the edges.

What she would have seen was something shredded right down the center, hanging on by a few strands of thread. Fabric that, however tattered, would hold together way beyond its useful life.

For the threads that bound the Cardiff marriage were bonds forged of mutual need.

Jason Cardiff brought money and prestige to the marriage.

Christina Banaczjek brought beauty, a yearning to escape the crushing poverty of her childhood, and a desperate desire for financial security.

The problem was that, as time passed, both began to envision a life without the other. Their patience for each other frayed and grew thin. Looking back, Christina could mark certain turning points in their relationship.

One such turning point was the annual benefit for the Southampton Foundlings Home. The event had grown over the years from a sleepy potluck dinner to a high-powered corporate event that was the social highlight of the Hamptons' season.

Invitation lists were prepared months in advance, labored over by PR staff scurrying across fields and through humid tents on the day of the event, barking orders into cell phones with all the concentration and precision of launching the D-day invasion itself.

Only A-listers were invited, and there was no more coveted seat at the gala than to be at one of the Cardiff family tables.

Christina made a point of buying all the papers in the days that followed, scouring social pages for photos of herself in the outfit she always purchased especially for the occasion.

She had not been rewarded with a beauty shot this year in *Dan's Paper*.

She and Jason had made a grand entrance in his new BMW coupe. They had drunk way more than they'd eaten, with Jason spending most of his time at the bar chatting up the waitresses.

Leaving Christina to fend for herself in a sea of Cardiffs.

She made up for it by drinking more than she could handle, and table-hopping as soon as the main course was finished. She spotted a man at a nearby table whom she knew her husband disliked. So she made a beeline for him.

His wife, who had always been bitchy to Christina, had gone off to powder her nose.

Christina made herself at home in his wife's chair, ignoring the dirty looks being sent her way from her in-laws, and waved off the man's offer of a fresh drink. She drained his wife's glass instead.

Just two days earlier, she had read a series of sent e-mail messages in Jason's BlackBerry trumpeting the fact that he was getting the best head of his life from a girl named Lisa.

Christina threw back her head now and roared at something Jason's former business associate was saying.

His wife reappeared, freshly powdered, and stood glaring.

The man rose and reintroduced them.

Christina, none too steady, pumped the wife's hand. She managed to spill a glass of wine onto the woman's silk dress while she was at it. "I'm so sorry," Christina slurred, grabbing a linen napkin and taking aim at the wife's dress.

The woman backed away, directly into the path of a banquet waiter bearing a tray loaded with dirty dishes.

The tray landed with a loud crash.

Christina's chair tumbled over after it, adding to the mayhem.

The man's wife hissed and grabbed her husband for support.

Christina shrieked in surprise.

A hush fell over the tent, followed by a ripple of whispers and murmurs.

And more glares from Camp Cardiff.

"My God," Christina exclaimed, giggling. In her addled state, the incident was hilarious. She hiccuped loudly. "My God," she said again, breathless with laughter.

The man she had been flirting with was on his knees now, sweeping bits of broken china from the floor at his wife's feet.

Several waiters rushed over to help.

"Christina." Jason appeared, solicitous now. He grabbed Christina by her elbow. "Come back to our table. Coffee is being served."

Christina resisted. "Jason," she said in a voice loud enough to be heard all around the tent, "you've decided to join me. Won't your friends at the bar miss you?" She was just drunk enough to push the envelope, despite the warning light in Jason's eyes. "Um, your new girl-friends?" She caught a glimpse over Jason's shoulder of her in-laws picking over their dessert plates, desperate to pretend this wasn't happening.

"Come back and sit down," Jason ordered in a tight voice. "Let's let the staff do their job and clean up." He tried to steer her by the elbow back to their table.

Christina wrenched free of his grasp. "No."

"Christina." Jason's voice dropped low into the danger zone.

He could shove it. She was about to tell him so when she felt pressure on her other elbow.

It was Pamela's husband, Richard Lofting. "Let me give you a hand, Jason." Richard was all smiles and smooth talk, but the grip he had on Christina's elbow was a perfect match for the one Jason had on her other arm.

Tight, with not so much as an inch of wiggle room.

"I don't need a hand," Christina protested.

But it was no use.

They propelled her across the tent, directly to the exit.

"Sorry you're not feeling well," Richard said, loud enough to be heard by the hushed diners.

Christina was indignant. "I'm fine," she slurred.

They were outside by then, at the valet line.

Two men sprang into action at Jason's signal.

"Thanks, Rich," he muttered at his brother-in-law through clenched teeth. "I can take it from here."

Richard Lofting kept his death grip on Christina's arm. "You sure?"

"Yeah." Jason squeezed her arm so tight it hurt. She would wake up with bruises the next day, four purple blobs marching up her arm that would take more than a week to fade.

Richard Lofting nodded, careful to avoid eye contact with Christina, before heading back inside. "Good night."

Leaving Christina alone with her husband. "That was embarrassing." She spat the words out, furious, and tried to wrench her arm free from Jason's grasp.

He tightened his grip and lowered his face close to hers. "That," he said in a voice ragged with anger, "was pure bullshit."

The valet pretended not to hear, fiddling with the keys hanging from pegs on a wooden board.

"You can't tell me what to do," Christina shouted, belligerent now. She tried to wrench free once more, but all she managed to do was yank herself around so she nearly lost her balance. A few strands of hair tore loose from the up-do she'd gotten that afternoon at the salon. "Especially now."

"Shut up." Jason scanned the drive for his BMW.

"Don't you tell me to shut up." Christina's voice rose, loud enough to be heard back inside the dining tent.

It attracted the attention of the photographers drinking at a makeshift bar that had been set up near the catering generators.

"I know all about your fling with Lisa!" Christina shrieked.

Jason spun her around, bringing her face close to his, and for the first time in her marriage, Christina saw the depth of his anger and was afraid of what he might do.

In that moment, she knew he no longer had any love for her.

He clamped down on her arm so hard she gasped for breath. One silk strap of her dress slid off her shoulder, but she was helpless to do anything about it.

Jason held her in a vise grip. "Don't you talk to me." His voice shook with anger. "I'm finished with you." To prove his point, he twisted her arm back until she felt a sizzling bolt of pain.

Christina cried out. They had never gotten physical. Not like this.

When she came across a photo on some stupid Hamptons' party blog the next day, she realized this must have been the moment they had snapped her photo.

As it was, she never noticed the flash. She was too hurt, too angry. "Let me go." She stared into her husband's eyes with a determination that transcended all the wine she'd drunk. "Or I promise you'll regret it."

She had caught him off guard, she could tell by the way his eyes widened in surprise.

"You bitch," he snapped. But he let go of her arm like it was a hot potato.

Looking back, Jason had been less drunk that night than Christina but probably too drunk to drive. Normally, Jason took advantage of the dessert hour at parties to sober up by downing a few espressos so he could drive.

As it was, she just wanted to get the hell out of there, and so did he.

The sports coupe peeled off into the night, spinning loose gravel in its wake.

Christina and Jason Cardiff rarely spoke, even when they passed each other in the hall, from that point on.

These thoughts were with Christina on the first night of her widowhood as she fell into a troubled sleep on the living-room couch inside her house on an isolated stretch of East Hampton beach.

She woke up sometime later to discover she was not alone.

CHAPTER

5

Something was wrong.

Christina sensed it even before she opened her eyes.

Someone was there with her in the dark.

Close. Too close. Invading her personal space.

Looming above her. Blocking any chance of escape.

Shifting from sleep mode to full-scale panic, Christina's first instinct was to scream. But the sound withered in her lungs.

The intruder's hand clamped down hard on her mouth.

A strangling sound gurgled up from her throat.

Christina was alone with him, and no one to help.

She was awake enough now to remember she was in her living room, dark as a tomb under a moonless sky. She had left the back door open. She remembered the photographer at the end of the drive.

In the space of the seconds that passed while she recalled these facts, he lowered himself on top of her.

Tyler had already lost one parent. He couldn't afford to lose another.

Christina fought back, scrabbling with her fingernails until they caught the soft flesh of his face and neck.

He grunted with pain, and Christina seized the moment to raise her knees and curl into a protective ball.

It was no use.

He brushed her legs aside with little effort.

Leaving her open, vulnerable to attack.

"Christina! It's me. Stop it! Goddamn it, Christina!"

She knew that voice, knew that familiar scent of Old Spice and cigarettes.

The hands pinning her down in the darkness were not there to hurt her.

"Dan, oh my God, Dan." She went limp with relief.

Daniel Cunningham released his grip and rocked back onto the cushion next to her. "Jesus," he breathed, rubbing a hand across his face. He pulled it away and tested it with his tongue.

She was close enough to see him scowl in the dark.

"I'm bleeding."

Christina was too busy trying to figure out if she was having a heart attack to speak, so she reached to pat his shoulder with a hand that shook.

He shrugged her off, half-raising an arm. His hands were balled into fists.

"I'm sorry." She drew her hand away, pushing up to a sitting position. Every muscle in her body twitched. "You scared me."

He whipped his head around so fast she cringed. "*I* scared *you*?" He shook his head slowly from side to side, scowling at the tips of his fingers, which, she supposed, were wet with his blood.

Dan had a temper. He had lost his contracting business because of it. He hadn't told her that in so many words, but Christina remembered the story now. It was why he freelanced now, painting and plastering for other contractors around the East End during the summer months. He had told her he spent winters in West Palm.

She forced herself to reach out and pat his leg. "You scared me," she said again, keeping her tone soothing and low. Not whiny. Dan hated that. "And this day . . . oh, my God, Dan. I'm glad you're here."

His shoulders unhunched as he considered this, and she felt her own adrenaline begin to drain off.

Dan leaned against the back of the couch, angling his body so it faced her.

Christina allowed herself to relax now that the crisis had passed.

"The back door was open. I let myself in." He shrugged.

Christina nodded.

"There was a guy out there in front," he said by way of explanation.

"I know."

"Some prick with a camera. I didn't want to make things worse for you, so I parked a couple houses down. A friend of mine did a job there last week. They're gone for the summer. I left my car in their driveway and took the cut-through to the beach."

Officially, there was no public access to the ocean in this neighborhood. Unofficially, there was a path behind the movie producer's house for use exclusively by residents of Jonah's Path.

"I didn't want that guy to see me coming here." Dan's voice softened. "I didn't want to make things worse for us—you." He quickly corrected himself.

So he knew. And he was thinking of them as a couple.

Dan had never told her he loved her, but everything had changed now with Jason's death. Everything. "Thanks." Christina's voice broke.

Dan reached for a strand of her hair and started twirling it.

The act of tenderness melted Christina's insides, made her feel that everything was okay.

Dan was here now. Her Dan.

"So I just headed for the dunes," he said, his voice turning low, sexy.

Something inside Christina unlaced as Dan sidled over and pulled her close, his voice dropping to a whisper. "I snuck across on the beach and up into your yard."

Christina yielded, giddy when he dropped his fingers so they grazed her breasts. She was heating up.

"Then I let myself in," he whispered. "I am your backdoor man, after all."

It was their old joke. Christina arched her back in response to the small circles Dan was tracing on her nipples.

It was a short tumble into his arms.

She wanted more than anything to lose herself in his scent, the sound of his heart beating close to hers, the feel of his arms around her. She fell against him, practically passing out with the rush she got.

Lately, Christina's drug of choice was Daniel Cunningham.

"C'mon, baby." He used his mouth to urge her on.

She looked into his eyes, straining for some clue as to where he'd just been and with whom, but he gave nothing away. Despite this, something inside her unlocked like it always did, and Christina swung open, inviting Danny in . . .

His breath was hot, moving across her hair, her face, her skin.

Every square inch of Dan Cunningham's body was as Christina had remembered it all those hours she'd tossed in that narrow bed in rehab. She rubbed her face against his chest, breathing in the scent of barroom, Old Spice cologne, and pure man, through and through.

She lost herself in his heat. She felt like she had been cold for a million years. There were no words to describe the rush she felt. She was in the zone, right where she wanted to be.

Drunk on her drug of choice, Daniel Cunningham.

A sound escaped Christina's throat, a bubble of something between elation and desperation. She'd had nothing to eat or drink since a bottle of water on the plane this morning.

"You okay?" Dan whispered, his lips moving her hair so that Christina felt a trickle of heat, molten and liquid, race down through her stomach and spread along the insides of her legs.

"Great," she whispered in reply, shifting onto her side so her body pressed against his.

The move must have caught Dan off guard because he hesitated a beat or two.

Possibly out of respect, Christina wondered, for her new status of widow. Daniel Cunningham was not, as a rule, a respectful type of guy.

And that wasn't what they were about, anyway.

She whispered his name, tilting her face toward his in the dark until she caught his lips with hers.

If Dan had any reservations, they disappeared quickly. He kissed her softly at first, then, when she moaned, faster and deeper, until his mouth was bruising hard on hers.

He tasted of smoke and the Diet Coke he liked mixed with bourbon.

Christina sucked hard, savoring every drop.

If he was self-conscious about tasting of booze, he made no apologies for it now. He knew where she had gone. She'd left a message on his cell on her drive to JFK, saying she'd be in touch when she returned, probably in a month or so. If he questioned how she felt about coming back so soon, he kept that to himself as well. This relationship was not about talking.

Dan grunted and rolled on top of her.

This is what they were about.

Christina moaned, and that was all Dan needed to hear.

They went at it in a tangle of arms and legs and lips, sucking and seeking until their skin was hot and swollen.

"I'm gonna give you what you like," he said in that low voice he used in bed. "But you have to ask for it."

She did, spreading her legs where she was wet while he whispered things about her that she knew were true.

What she craved was the act of surrender, giving herself up to something or someone.

And that someone was Daniel Cunningham, and had been since the day he turned up to paint and replaster their pool house three months ago.

"That's right, baby, ask for it now," Dan ordered.

Christina surrendered to it, to him, in a swoon, and it felt so *good* after all those days in rehab, dreary and gray . . .

Dan pressed himself onto her, into her, and she closed her legs around him as their bodies pulsed together, faster and faster, harder and harder, and she felt she needed this more than anything in her life.

Crying out, she raked her fingernails across Dan's shirt, which they hadn't bothered to remove, and pounded her fists on his back.

Dan called her names that turned her on, pausing now and again to push his tongue to the back of her throat so that Christina was filled completely with Dan the way she wanted to be filled.

She begged for more the way he had coached her, and finally, when she was at the edge of where she needed to be, Christina let go . . .

She waited for the tidal wave that was Dan to crash over her.

What she got, in the end, was a tiny ripple.

Like a long-distance orgasm.

Dan didn't notice. He was heaving between her legs with sweat pouring off him so it soaked his T-shirt. Christina felt the wetness of his face, tasted salt on his lips.

The sex act was not so exciting now.

Keeping her legs in place, she rubbed his back and made sounds to encourage him. Her vagina was chafed and starting to sting.

He came at last, in a single great thrust, clenching his jaw and making that animal sound.

Normally, Christina found this sexy.

Tonight, she was aware only that her skin itched, and her neck was pressed against the couch at an odd angle.

Christina had been unable to come lots of times. She'd been drunk so much, she often fell asleep along the way, sometimes waking up when Jason or Dan was finishing the job, sometimes not. Other times, she woke up with no idea which one of them was on top of her.

But this was different. She wasn't drunk. Her body had gone through the motions, then seemed to just go on strike, like watching actors having sex in an X-rated movie, which she had done plenty of times.

But this was different. This was life on Planet Weird.

Dan planted one last kiss on her lips and slapped her bare thigh, hard enough to sting, before rolling off.

Christina rearranged her clothes, trying to cover her bare spots, hoping Dan couldn't see her frown in the dark.

He was too busy fumbling for his cigarettes and lighter to notice. "You mind?"

"No, go ahead." They had made love in the house and out by the pool any number of times when Jason wasn't around, but this was the first time Dan had lit up after. Christina didn't smoke, and Jason did so rarely, only very late at a party. Nobody smoked in their house.

There was a brief flare of orange when Dan lit up.

The room was so quiet she could make out individual sizzling sounds as each tiny shred of tobacco curled up and burned when he inhaled.

He blew smoke into the darkness. "Tough times."

Christina was silent. What was there to say?

"You okay?" He pulled on his cigarette again. The tip pulsed bright in the dark.

"I guess," she replied, then realized it would leave Dan no choice but to probe deeper. "I'm fine," she added quickly.

Taking her at her word, he continued to smoke.

There were no ashtrays around. Just when Christina

wondered what Dan would do with the ash, he tapped it onto the leg of his jeans and rubbed it into the denim.

The move, self-contained and resourceful, was pure Daniel Cunningham.

"Good." He sat up and switched on a light. "You hungry?"

Christina shook her head and blinked.

He squinted at her, the cigarette dangling from his mouth, his eyes narrowed through the smoke. "Did you eat today?"

She thought back to the bran muffin she'd shared with Sylphan in the break room this morning, a million years ago. The thought of food made her want to throw up. She shrugged.

"Just like I thought." He nodded. "'Cause you look—" He caught himself.

Theirs was a relationship based on mutual pleasure and convenience, mostly Christina's. At least until now.

Christina sensed things shifting slightly, away from her and toward him, and chose to ignore it. "I'm okay." Feeling self-conscious despite the fact he'd seen her naked on more than a dozen occasions, she busied herself with the zipper on her jeans, mumbling something about lunch on the plane.

He stood up, zipped his fly. "You need a drink or what?"

"No." Her voice was too loud. It came out sounding like the lie it was, and she knew it.

He watched her. "So this place you stayed at, they fixed you up that way?" His lips moved into a smirk.

But Dan always smirked. It had never bothered her before. "Yeah," she lied, looking down at the cotton rug and its pattern of dark green leaves and bright crimson berries.

"Shining sumac," the decorator had told her. "Very aggressive. If you're not careful, it will take over the whole garden."

Dan scratched his chest with one hand. "I'll check out what's in the fridge while you . . ." Jutting his chin in the direction of the powder room, he frowned. "You'll be okay. Tough day, that's all."

Mortified, Christina ran a hand through her hair and nodded.

He headed off to the kitchen, flipping on lights as he went, and she was struck by the incongruity of this, the final act of weirdness in a day that had been the strangest of her life.

Daniel Cunningham, whose activities in her house until now had been limited to applying plaster and paint to the walls, or humping her on the daybed in their pool house, was now methodically rummaging through the Cardiffs' kitchen cabinets.

And he was taking his time about it.

Rising to her feet was a struggle, as the combination of exhaustion, jet lag, and nerves finally got to Christina.

She leaned over, pressing her hands to her knees until the dizzy spell passed.

There was a whoop of triumph from the kitchen. "Eggs, we got eggs," Dan called. "And chives and Fontina cheese and Veuve Clicquot."

CHAPTER

6

Rain pelted the windows from every direction. The morning sky was the color of bruised fruit. They'd spent a sleepless night on the too-small double bed in the guest room. Dan had hesitated in the hallway at the top of the stairs after the supper of scrambled eggs that he had eaten and Christina had picked at. She left her champagne untouched, dumping it in the toilet finally when the smell got to her. Small victory, she knew, in a long war.

Dan had made no comment when Christina led the way to the guest room on the landside of the house, but she could tell by the way he tossed around trying to get comfortable that it wasn't what he'd had in mind.

The look on his face hadn't improved with lack of sleep. She wondered if he always woke up with dark circles under his eyes. "Hey." He flashed a quick smile and rolled away, reaching for the glass he'd left by the side of the bed. He took a swig, swished it around hard before swallowing, and took another before handing the glass to her.

"Hey." Christina forced herself to sit up and take a sip. As her lips closed over the rim of the glass, vapors rose from the liquid and stung her nostrils.

Wrinkling her nose, Christina lowered the glass and frowned. "Is this water?"

She knew the answer even before Danny smiled. "Go ahead. You need to relax, you know that?"

Christina set the glass down like it might explode, her nerve endings on fire. "No, I don't."

Dan was all movement now, stretching and yawning and keeping enough distance between them so they did not touch. "Happy Thursday." He winked.

Happy Thursday? Christina's world had come crashing down around her. Right now all she had was Dan. And an overwhelming urge to drain the glass of vodka on the nightstand. How could she tell him that, when their entire relationship was based on partying? Without vodka, she didn't know how they would fit together. But right now, Daniel Cunningham was all she had. "Right back atcha," she replied, aiming for a breezy tone.

"You okay?" Dan already had one foot on the floor, ready to bolt.

"Um, yeah," Christina began. Hope rose inside her. Maybe he was going to say now they could start their life together, like all those times they talked about it. Maybe he'd help her get through this, starting now. Maybe he'd tell her he loved her.

"Good," he said, not giving her a chance to tell him how scared she was, how much she needed him now. Dan cleared his throat, careful not to meet her eyes.

His next words caught her off guard.

"We need to hang back."

Something inside her shrank down into a tight little knot, making it hard to breathe. "What?" Christina's voice sounded small.

Dan shrugged. "Take five. Hang back. Lay low." He kept his gaze focused on the windows and the gray sky outside, flexing his arms, swinging them back and forth across his chest.

"You know what I'm saying," he said, when she made no reply.

Pure panic gripped her. Dan was all she had right now. And he was pulling away. All Christina could think of was that if she clung too tight now, she might lose him forever. "Yeah," she said finally, blinking back tears.

Feeling her entire world hung by a thread. It was an old feeling, one that traced its roots all the way back to when her father left, then her mother, then finally Nana died.

Praying Dan Cunningham wasn't about to tell her it was over between them.

"Good. Way to play it, baby."

She wanted to ask a million questions. Did he see a future for them together? Had he been seeing other women while she was in rehab? Did he love her? But Christina was afraid of what those answers might be.

More than anything, she was afraid of losing Dan Cunningham. So she uttered a silent prayer that he would spend more time with her after the funeral, that maybe he would love her.

He glanced at her. "We're good?"

She nodded. "We're good."

It was what he wanted to hear because relief washed over his face.

He gave her a brisk peck on the lips and slid off the bed.

She remembered a time on the chaise lounge out back when he was due back at work. His farewell kisses turned hotter than the midday sun while his fingers wiggled their way up inside her bikini bottom and he made her come with his thumb in a fit of giggles, knowing full well the landscapers would be back from lunch any minute.

He headed for the bathroom now. "I think a shower is in order." He turned on the water and used the toilet with the door wide open.

They had never spent a night together.

"Looks like another hot one," he called. "No sun, but muggy as hell."

The shower curtain rings jingled, and Christina wondered if she had enough time to grab her robe from the hook inside the door before he finished. She decided not to risk it.

She checked messages from the bedside phone instead. The ringer was off in here, but she'd heard it ring downstairs late into the night and start up again early this morning. She had lain still, keeping to her side of the bed so as not to disturb the large shadowy mound opposite that was Dan Cunningham.

There were condolence calls and people wanting to know about the arrangements. Another call from her sister-in-law in Southampton advising Christina that her parents and Tyler were in the Air France premium-class lounge at Charles de Gaulle Airport waiting to board their flight to JFK.

Dan emerged from the bathroom with a towel wrapped around his waist. "Yup, gonna be another steamy one. They say a tropical depression is moving in, whatever the fuck that is."

Christina did not move. Tropical depression sounded about right for this day.

Dan strode to the windows and snapped the blinds open.

The light stung her eyes.

"Not lookin' good." Danny flicked his damp towel on the bed.

Christina squinted one eye open to see if he meant her but he was staring out the window. She wished she had the nerve to reach for him, pull him back under the covers with her so they could hide from this day together, maybe lose themselves in sex since that was the only thing they shared. "It'll be a tough day for painting," she said, testing the waters.

He grunted. "I can work inside." He stepped into his boxers and jeans before leaning over with his hands on his knees the way an adult would in order to speak to a child. "Hey. I'm going downstairs to make us some coffee, while you . . ." He straightened up, letting his words hang there.

"Okay." Christina said quickly. She looked bad, and she knew it. The sides of her neck were beginning to lose heat as her pulse quickened. She was learning to spot the signs of a panic attack, and this one would be bad. She squeezed her eyes shut. "Dan," she whispered.

But he was busy working his head into his T-shirt. "You drink coffee in the morning, don't you?"

"Mmmmm." At the moment, she would just as soon pour battery acid down her throat.

"Comin' right up." He headed for the door. "I saved plenty of hot water for your shower," he called.

Christina allowed her eyes to flutter open, calculating how many movements would be required to cross the room and step into the shower. Because she felt like dying.

Dan passed the top of the stairs and continued on to the entrance to the master bedroom suite, where she heard him pause.

Taking it all in.

He gave a low whistle. "Nice."

She heard him head for the stairs. "Comfy-looking bed, too," he called.

The master bedroom had a platform custom-built to hold a California king.

She heard rummaging in the kitchen.

The bedside clock showed a few minutes after eight, which meant she didn't have much time before Señora Rosa and Marisol showed up.

They had strict orders never to disturb her. There were plenty of days when Christina rose late to find freshly laundered sheets and towels piled outside the guest-room door. But she couldn't risk them finding one of the subcontractors cooking breakfast, today of all days.

If she got up now, she could shower in peace and hopefully get the hell out before they arrived.

In the end, she had just enough time to get dressed.

The smell of coffee and frying bacon drifted up through the house, reminding Christina that she was still not hungry, when a car door slammed.

Moments later came a familiar voice in the living room.

Followed by a very few words, low and rumbling, from Dan.

Then silence.

"Shit." Christina met her own gaze in the mirror. Her skin was drawn, her eyes round with panic she'd seen once before. They'd left a wedding reception at Shinnecock Hills late one night. Jason rounded a curve too fast in the fog that was a fact of life on the seashore. In the dead center of the road was the biggest deer she'd ever seen.

An eight-point buck, Jason said later. He'd had no time to hit the brakes.

Christina braced herself for impact.

In the next instant the buck disappeared with a leap into the bayberry bushes and poverty grass that pressed against the sides of the road.

Saving them.

Christina had never forgotten the look of doom in that animal's eyes.

Her name rang out once, twice, from downstairs, in a tone of voice that promised the third time would sound even worse.

A glance out the front windows confirmed Christina's suspicion. A screaming yellow Land Rover was parked on the drive, a safari vehicle ready for the hunt.

Jason's sister had arrived.

Holy shit.

"Christi-*nuh!*" her sister-in-law screeched, twisting around the final syllable like a dentist's drill.

Christina winced. "I'm coming."

Pamela Cardiff Lofting waited at the bottom of the stairs, one sandal-clad foot planted on the lowest step, reedy arms folded tight across her tiny chest. Her eyes, dark brown like Jason's and set close together, flashed.

Christina knew that look. She probably could have gotten down without using the banister, but figured there was no harm playing every card she had. She leaned on the wood, lowering herself one step at a time.

Pamela did not look impressed. She didn't budge. "I let myself in."

They had spent a small fortune upgrading the security system, so things like this couldn't happen. "Um, how?" Christina frowned.

"I've always had a key. Jason gave me a copy of the new one when you changed the locks."

This was news to Christina. She made a mental note to get the locksmith out here. And choose a new three-digit code for the keypad at the gate, something they had never bothered to do in all the years they'd owned the house.

"What happened to the gate?" Pamela was not wearing any makeup. It was obvious she'd been crying.

Christina shrugged. "It just, I have to, ah, get that taken care of." She caught the look on Pamela's face. She knew that look. "I wasn't . . ." She started to tell Pamela she had quit drinking, once and for all, then stopped. Pamela wouldn't believe her. But that didn't matter anymore. The house, the yard, and even the gate belonged to Christina. For almost twenty years, she'd had to put up with stories about the Cardiff family history, the Cardiff family values, the Cardiff family wealth, until she was practically ready to throw up. And nobody had rammed it down her throat more than Jason's little sister, Pamela. Going all the way back to the stink she raised over the bridesmaids' dresses for Christina's wedding. And now it was over.

This realization lifted Christina's spirits.

Pamela scowled. Gooseflesh stood out on her suntanned arms, still crossed tight around her chest, as she kneaded the fabric of her Lily Pulitzer shift using her wiry little fingers.

Pamela had done her best to break up Jason and Christina from day one. Christina searched for something to say besides, "Get out." "Want coffee?"

Dan entered, carrying a tray loaded with mugs, padding across the room in his bare feet.

Pamela's face puckered in toward center, and her entire body quaked, moving from side to side.

Every instinct Christina had told her to duck and run.

Dan's hair was still gleaming wet from his shower. He set the tray down. Besides coffee, it contained paper towels he'd torn from the spool on the counter.

He'd no doubt chosen them in favor of the supply of Irish linens Señora Rosa kept, freshly ironed, in the glass-front cabinet above the coffeemaker.

"Ladies." Dan straightened up, giving an uneasy glance in Christina's direction.

Jason would have known what to do. Noticing that at a time like this was as petty as frowning at the permanent ring of yellow plaster around Dan's fingernails, which was exactly what Pamela Cardiff Lofting was doing at that very moment.

Pamela stared at Dan like he was something that had washed ashore and got stuck in the sand at high tide. She took a few steps back without bothering to uncross her arms, as her frown creased even deeper. She enunciated each syllable with care, as though she had no hope of being understood. "And, you, are?"

Dan leapt toward her, extending his right hand. "We saw each other. Before. In the kitchen, when you walked in. Daniel Cunningham."

Ignoring the outstretched hand, Pamela turned to Christina. "Who, is, he?"

The dentist drill tone had returned.

Dan's lips curved up ever so slightly. "A friend."

Pamela stared.

"He did some work here a while back," Christina added quickly.

Pamela wasn't buying it. Her little eyes were about to pop right out of her head.

"Dan was in charge of the part of the renovation project involving plasterwork," Christina blurted. "He oversaw all the refinishing of all the walls." Anything to avoid using the term house painter.

Pamela continued to avoid shaking Dan's hand, so he tucked it into the top pocket of his jeans. "You seen all that stucco work along the walls out by the pool and the cabana? I did that. That's me."

It came out sounding like a pitch for new business.

"Oh?" Pamela Cardiff Lofting's delicate jaw came a tiny bit unhinged. She glanced from Dan to Christina, where she let her gaze rest.

There was no warmth in that gaze. Caving under nearly two decades of Cardiff disapproval, Christina forgot for a moment that the scales had just tipped forever in her favor. "He did really good work and became a friend of mine."

Pamela blinked.

"And Jason's," Christina added, trying to gain traction.

Jason's name hung, supercharging the air until the room reeked of ozone.

Lightning followed. Pamela exploded with a fury that made even Dan take a step back. Standing no more than five feet in her Jack Rogers, she shot straight up, uncrossing her arms for the first time. Her hands were balled into fists. "I doubt that." She glared. "I really do."

Dan's voice was devoid of any formality. "You'll just have to take our say-so for that."

Pamela's response was to gasp for air, producing a sound that was truly awful.

Dan smiled.

Nobody had ever talked like that to Pamela Cardiff Lofting in her entire life, probably. It was enough to make Christina feel sorry for her. Almost.

"Oh, my God." Pamela raised a hand to her face, pressed a balled-up tissue to her nose, squeezed her eyes closed, and began to cry.

Christina blinked. This was awful.

Dan stood his ground.

"Pamela, look." Christina moved in close to pat Pamela on the shoulder.

Pamela's head popped up like a Jack-in-the-box, her dark eyes glowing black with rage. "I have no idea what's wrong with you," she hissed, placing heavy emphasis on the word "wrong," "but my poor brother has died . . ." The sentence ended with a squeak.

This tragic fact trumped everything else. Despite the fact that Pamela was scary on a good day, and that she was royally pissed off right now, Christina reached out to comfort her.

It was like hugging a tower of Legos.

But having Pamela break down in her living room was better than having Pamela scream at her, so Christina hung in there, patting Pamela's bony shoulder. "Things will be okay," Christina murmured, even though she knew this simply was not true.

Pamela allowed herself to be steered over to the couch. "I knew something was wrong," she sobbed. "I just knew it."

High drama was Pamela's MO. But she was giving Christina the creeps, carrying on about premonitions her brother wouldn't live to celebrate his fortieth birthday.

And he hadn't.

Christina sought Dan's gaze while continuing to rub little circles on Pamela's back.

"I'll call you," he mouthed, before ducking out.

Which didn't help Christina's creepy feeling, not even a little bit.

I came, or came to, or came as I came to. Whatever. It was great, absolutely fucking fantastic. Or fantastic fucking. I was in the zone, right where I wanted to be. That place you could spend your whole life trying to get to, the perfect mix of feeling and not, pleasure and nothingness.

My whole body twisted beneath Dan's weight, wave after wave moving through me of pleasure, nothing but pleasure, so I threw back my head and howled at the moon and the wind and the sand and the waves while my whole body rocked with it.

Dan thrust into me, deeper and deeper and maybe a little too rough but my pelvis had developed a life of its own, rocking with him, up and down, harder and harder, until I felt the sting of bits of sand that were working their way inside me but to be honest I didn't care about anything in that moment other than having the best orgasm I could, right along with Dan.

We went at it in a frenzy, both of us coming and howling in the sand at the top of our lungs and the beach that night was windy with nobody to hear us and we laughed and howled ourselves silly and I pounded him on the back, begged him to go harder and harder on me as fast as he could and he did till it seemed like even my lungs were vibrating with the force of it.

I don't know what happened exactly, but when I tried to use the toilet late that night my panties wouldn't come off at first and hurt like hell. They were caked through with dried black blood.

The wind picked up the way it always did along the coast at night, gathering moisture from the ocean waves. I felt it pelt my bare skin and knew I should feel its chill, like I should be bothered by the gritty sand underneath me.

But I wasn't.

I was still high on booze and Dan and fucking and right at that moment the moon and stars could have dropped out of the sky right down on top of us and I wouldn't have budged because right at that moment everything in my life was exactly where I wanted it to be.

I wanted more.

I reached out, sweeping an arm across the sand where I figured the bottle might be. I found it and raised it to my lips. Empty. "Shit!"

Dan laughed and slapped me on my thigh. Hard so it stung but I was drunk enough to like it and I just laughed.

He slapped me again, taking the empty bottle from my hand. "You love this shit, don't you?"

I said nothing. I was ashamed. I had never admitted anything to anybody about my drinking.

Dan's eyelids drooped shut and his lips curled up.

The effect was a cruel little smile.

He took the bottle and flung it far into the dunes.

I opened my mouth to protest.

He put a finger to my lips, smiling broadly in the moonlight, and he dug something from the pocket of his jeans. "Shhhh. I got something better."

"Christina?"

Rain gusted against the windows facing the ocean.

"Christina, are you okay?" Pamela frowned, still working the tissue across her nose and those tiny eyes now swollen almost shut with tears.

Still, she probably didn't miss much. "I'm fine," Christina murmured, edging away.

"You'll get through this," Pamela said, blowing her nose. "We'll get through this."

"Ummmm," Christina said, looking down at her feet. Her pedicure had worn away in rehab, the polish oxidizing from fire-engine red to something resembling rusted rebar.

Pamela gave one more swipe at her nose. "Let's get some things taken care of before my parents arrive." She pulled a leather-bound day planner from her purse, flipped it open.

Christina managed to get rid of her eventually, after pleading exhaustion (which was the truth), and promising to follow up on Pamela's list. They were back to pretending to like one another, this time for the memory of Jason, trading air kisses at the door to say good-bye. Pamela left.

In the living room, Pamela's yellow Post-it notes were arranged in a single tidy overlapping column. The number for Frank E. Campbell Funeral Home on Madison Avenue lay on top. Next one down listed the private cell phone number for the pastor of Towne Church on

East Eighty-third Street, and the one underneath that contained the cell phone and home numbers for the Sutton Place florist who had done the flowers for all the Cardiff weddings.

That florist had been rude to Christina, horrible to work with.

She peeled the yellow sticky notes from the table and crumpled them before tossing them in the trash.

Detective Frank McManus, phone hitched high against one ear, leaned all the way back in his seat so the caller on the other end could not hear the tapping sound his fingers made on his keyboard. Keeping most of his attention focused on his business call, he finished filling out the message for his daughter's gift and hesitated. For an extra seven bucks, he could use express shipping and guarantee his daughter's birthday present would arrive on time.

Decision made, he hit the PRINT button.

Outside, a bright yellow Land Rover pulled in, taking up the better part of two spaces reserved for visitors.

Ben Jackson appeared in the doorway and made an eating motion with his hands.

It was going on noon.

A blonde emerged from the Land Rover. A couple of tissues fluttered to the ground, but she paid them no mind. She was busy staring at the entrance. She dug in her pocketbook, probably looking for the tissues, but they were tumbling across the parking lot. Giving up, she swiped her nose with the back of her hand and made for the front door.

Jackson tapped his watch. On Thursdays, they always hit Subway for lunch.

McManus considered things. The blond woman with the Land Rover most certainly hadn't come in for a job interview. Which meant right now she was telling her story to the uniform at the desk.

Being a curious sort, McManus decided to skip lunch. Shaking his head, he mouthed the words, "Catch you later" to Jackson.

His gamble paid off less than a minute later, when the old-fashioned intercom on his desk flashed once and buzzed. He placed his call on hold and pressed the button.

"Good, you're there," the desk sergeant said. "I got someone out here who wants to talk about Jason Cardiff."

"No problem," McManus replied, pulling a box of Kleenex from his bottom drawer and placing it on his desk so it was in easy reach of the guest chair. "It's my new favorite subject. Send her in."

Jason and Christina had chosen the house for its location, two hundred feet of oceanfront property along the one of the world's most-sought-after stretches of shoreline, the southern coast of Long Island.

East Hampton is located approximately one hundred miles east of New York City. Its blood is not as blue as its neighbor to the west, Southampton (which was founded eight years earlier, in 1640), but its summer residents could fill the pages of *Vanity Fair*, and very often do. A trip for ice cream in town means waiting in line with Hollywood movie stars, network news anchors, or descendants of families whose names have been associated with everyday household products for generations.

But prime Hamptons real estate in the new millennium is only within grasp of today's American royalty: CEOs with stratospheric pay packages, hedge-fund operators, and owners of private equity funds.

Jason Cardiff's wealth fell into several of these categories. His pedigree reached back five generations. The name Cardiff graced a plaque on the headquarters of Wall Street's whitest white-shoe firm, with offices overlooking the bronze *Charging Bull* at the southern end of

Broadway. His forebears famously got their start earning a commission on every head of livestock bought or sold on Bowling Green.

Jason Cardiff's personal fortune, rooted in blue blood, had mushroomed in the wild nineties.

He talked nonstop on his cell phone during the Realtor's walkthrough.

"This house is a prime example of the Shingle Style of architecture." The Realtor directed his comments at a pregnant Christina.

Her allergies flared as soon as they crossed the wide plank porch to enter the old house.

Between sneezes, she eyed the thick knot of hickory and scrub oak that grew right up against the ivy-clad walls. Later in the car, she picked a tick off one leg of her Chaiken maternity capris.

They tore the place down after closing, replacing it with a postmodern abstraction of reinforced concrete and tinted glass. Living in this house, the architect promised, would be an interactive experience, like installation art. The new structure had soaring geometric angles and walls of glass with computerized blinds that popped up from a slit in the floor with the touch of the controls. There was a chef's kitchen, underground media room, wine cellar, humidor, and a small butler's pantry tucked inside the master bedroom suite. There was a minimalist sculpture garden and a koi pond (in constant need of restocking) on the lawn where the trees used to be. The entire south-facing wall was glass, looking out over the ocean from every room, "to integrate the lives of those inside with their natural surroundings."

Christina, Midwestern in her soul, never latched on to

the Atlantic. Unlike the freshwater lakes she had visited only rarely as a child, the ocean was loud and messy, crisscrossed with powerful currents, brimming with strange animals that stung and bit, or worse. Her son Tyler, native New Yorker that he was, grew up loving the sea. And so Christina had learned to swim in the briny heaving surf, keeping always to the shallows well inside the line of breakers, and even taking a water-safety class for the sake of her son.

She had developed an uneasy alliance with the watery wilderness that began at her doorstep and stretched for thousands of miles.

On this day, Christina wanted to get away. The pounding sea reminded her too much of the thoughts tumbling, dangerous and untamed, through her mind.

It was enough, almost, to make her grateful for the arrival of Señora Rosa and Marisol.

Almost.

Christina heard them before she saw them, speaking quietly in Spanish out by the pool. They were dressed in their gray work uniforms and dark sunglasses. The landscapers joined them on the patio, following suit when Señora Rosa and Marisol dropped to their knees and crossed themselves. The group prayed for a few moments before lowering a small bouquet of flowers into the deep end of the pool.

The group watched as the flowers, tied with yellow ribbon, bobbed along the surface..

That ribbon would clog the filter system. Christina made a mental note to fish the bouquet from the pool before Tyler got home tonight.

Señora Rosa was still sniffling when they entered the

house. At the sight of Christina she cried, *"¡Dios mío!"* and grabbed Marisol for support.

Whether Señora Rosa was expressing sympathy for Christina's new status as widow, or was simply taken aback by Christina's appearance, was difficult to tell.

The answer was evident within a few seconds.

Señora Rosa ripped off her sunglasses for a closer look and cried out even louder, this time in English.

"Oh, my God, no! Oh, no, Señora Christina! No, no, no!" Sobbing, Señora Rosa collapsed onto Marisol, who made the sign of the cross three times.

So much for the beautifying benefit of detoxification, Christina thought.

Her cell phone rang. She grabbed it, hoping it was Dan.

Caller ID revealed it was a call from area code 651. Shit. Minnesota.

"How's it going, Christina?" Her counselor always sounded like he was bench-pressing a heavy weight, and today he sounded as though he were lifting more than usual.

There was simply no way to reply.

Peter, to his credit, did not ask whether there was anything wrong. "Have you been drinking today?"

"No."

"Good for you. You're a winner."

She didn't tell him she planned to check on her cache of Grey Goose in the freezer as soon as she got a minute to herself. "I guess."

"All you need to do today is not drink." Peter's voice was firm. "You know, Christina, everyone here is praying for you and asking about you and thinking about you."

It was hard to imagine anybody praying for her. Christina's eyes, already sore and aching from lack of sleep, boiled over with tears. The sides of her throat narrowed, squeezed in tight around something hot that wouldn't budge when she tried to swallow. A sob bubbled up.

Peter picked up on it from all the way out in the Central Time Zone. "It's okay, Christina. Go ahead and cry. Crying is an appropriate response to what you're going through."

Christina nodded even though he couldn't see, lowering herself onto a couch. The tears came hot and fast.

Señora Rosa hurried over to press a glass of ice water into Christina's hand. "Drink, *señora,*" she implored, waving her hands through the air as if to sweep the liquid into Christina's throat.

Christina managed a tiny sip.

Peter was following her progress from his end of the phone. "Have you had anything to eat or drink today?"

"A little." It was a lie. She hadn't had enough to eat or drink even to merit a visit to the bathroom since yesterday.

"H.A.L.T., Christina. You remember H.A.L.T.?" When she didn't reply, he filled in the blanks. "Don't get too hungry, angry, lonely, or tired."

Again with the slogans, Christina thought. "I'm trying."

"It's so important to stay hydrated and eat whatever you can," Peter continued. "Early on in sobriety, especially during times of stress, we need to make a special effort to eat."

Rosa must have been on the same wavelength because she was heating something in the microwave.

The odor made Christina's stomach heave. "I'm trying."

Peter changed tacks. "Have you been to an AA meeting yet?"

When was she supposed to have gone to an AA meeting? "I'm working on that," Christina responded tightly.

There was silence on the line.

"Really." Christina wondered how to change the subject.

"I can help. Let me pull up something on my computer here."

Ever ready to be of service.

The timer on the microwave went off.

Señora Rosa rushed in with a steamy plate of something piled on rice.

Christina gagged.

"How about Westhampton Beach? There's a step meeting there at eleven."

Christina frowned. He must have access to a list of every AA meeting in the country. "That won't work."

"Why not? It's got to be fairly close. Westhampton Beach. And you're in a Hampton, right? It's right there on Montauk Highway." He pronounced it Mon-toke.

She did not bother to correct him. "Long Island is big. I'm in East Hampton, which is not really that close."

"Okay," he said in a tone that told her he would stick with this all day.

She heard clacking noises. He was a fast typist. She sighed.

Señora Rosa removed plastic film from the plate, releasing a lardy cloud.

Christina tried to narrow her nostrils to block the smell. She squeezed her eyes shut.

"It's a 'We' program," Peter was saying on the other end of the phone.

"Please, señora, if you would only try." Rosa's voice was pleading.

Christina cracked one eye open.

Señora Rosa stood, hands clasped as though in prayer, beseeching her. "Only to try."

Peter was still working on her through the phone. "Meeting makers make it."

Another slogan. He could shove it up his ass.

Marisol was making her way through the living room, a feather duster and furniture spray in hand. She slowed to get a look at Christina.

Their eyes met, and Christina did not like what she saw.

She and Marisol were about the same age.

Christina remembered one time, Labor Day weekend before last, the morning after a big party. She'd come down early in search of aspirin. They had run out of Tylenol in the master bathroom.

Jason was there, dressed to play golf, standing very close to Marisol.

Marisol was smiling.

They both turned, startled, as Christina approached, and moved away from each other.

Not before Christina saw something in Marisol's hand. A thick wad of green bills. She had asked Jason about it later.

He turned quiet. "She's got a kid back home, retarded or something."

Jason was not the softhearted type. "We pay them

plenty of money," Christina had protested. "They get paid better than half the people who work in town."

Jason shrugged. "You ever take a look at this place sometimes?" He had looked around the giant space that encompassed the living area, entryway, dining area, and eat-in kitchen. It was spotless now, but Christina knew what he was getting at. "Do you have any idea the shit they clean up after one of our parties?"

Now it was Christina's turn to shrug.

"Yeah, well neither do I."

"They're probably not even supposed to be in this country," she had sniffed. Truth be told, she had no idea whether they were here legally. Jason handled the household accounts.

He shook his head. "Yeah, well at least they both know how to keep their mouths shut. I like to keep our private lives private. Once in a while, a little extra for them doesn't hurt."

But it was Marisol he had given the cash to, and not her aunt Rosa, who had worked here longer.

And now it was Christina who looked away first. Christ, she felt like a stranger in her own home.

Marisol headed upstairs to dust.

Señora Rosa backed off at last, leaving the plate of food behind.

Within retching range.

Peter did not back down. "You know, Christina, you can't do this on your own. Not without help. Especially not with all you're going through right now."

All she was "going through" was a mild way of putting it. Just hearing the words made her crumble inside. All the breath blew out of her lungs in a whoosh. Too late, she realized he heard it.

Peter changed tacks. "How's Tyler?"

Christina's shoulders hunched with guilt. The fact was she had no idea. "Fine." Her voice was small with the effort of holding the floodgates closed. She hated to cry.

Peter's voice no longer flowed like syrup. It had hardened into something else. "You know, Christina, you will not be able to help your son get through this if you don't stay sober."

Meaning, Christina supposed, she was useless as a mother. The tears welled up now, hot and bitter. These were not tears for Tyler, who had just lost his father, any more than they were for Jason, who was dead. No, the tears were for Christina.

For the failure she had been in the past and the failure she would be in the future.

She doubled over and moaned.

Peter heard it. "Our problem is self-centeredness. Self-centeredness and self-pity."

How dare he accuse her of self-pity at a time like this? "Excuse me," she said, icing him. "But I don't think you have any idea what it's like to lose your *husband*." She spat out the final word for emphasis.

There was a moment of silence on Peter's end. "Not to mention your best friend, alcohol."

It was a cheap shot. And true. "Shit," Christina moaned. "What am I going to do?"

Peter's tone was brisk. "You'll get through this. You don't need alcohol, Christina. It wasn't working for you anyway."

She blinked. That much was true.

"The thing is, we can change our lives anytime we want. It's never too late to start over. You can turn this around, Christina. You can get through this sober."

She wanted to believe him. She really did.

It was like he could read her mind. "Fear is the enemy, Christina. Don't let it rule your life. Fight it. You can do it."

"How?" Her voice was small and weak, the insides of her mouth coated with glue.

Peter was back to business now. "We need to find you a good AA meeting. What about Amagansett?"

Amagansett was practically next door.

"There's a meeting in less than half an hour. Think you can make it?"

"Yeah." She couldn't believe she was agreeing to this. But it would give her a place to go, safe from Marisol's sly glances and Señora Rosa's fried pork bellies or whatever they were. Christina checked her watch and grabbed her car keys.

Paparazzi at the gate be damned.

At the moment, AA was the least of all evils.

Jason Cardiff's life ran smoothly, a well-oiled machine with him as the central cog. His self-regard was of the very highest caliber and was innate, a core part of his being from birth. Like most people who are born into tremendous privilege, Jason Cardiff lacked any insight into the source of his superior confidence (unearned), which of course was due only to his vast wealth.

What this translated to in the day-to-day conduct of Jason Cardiff's life was an unquestioning acceptance that money was his ultimate servant, there to spin the wheels that revolved, always, with him in the center.

Money was the number one tool in Jason Cardiff's Life Toolbox, the first one he reached for to solve any problem.

It was the Cardiff way.

So it did not require any stretch of the imagination to use money to solve Jason Cardiff's single problem early that summer: how to end his marriage.

The idea came to him one afternoon as he mounted the cleaning girl from behind on the cellar steps.

She was nice in a spicy, dirty, Latin way, with smooth dark skin and a good attitude, he'd seen that from the start. Cheeky.

"I don't know this word," Marisol giggled, pronouncing it "sheeky." She waited until she heard him zipping his fly before turning over and hoisting herself into a sitting position on the steps.

Jason wiped his hands on his golf shorts and took a seat beside her to catch his breath on the bare wooden steps. He made a mental note to tell Christina they needed carpeting. Not some custom imported wool she'd spend weeks on, arguing with some fag decorator, just something plush that could be wiped up.

Marisol was careful to arrange her skirt underneath her, no doubt to avoid getting a splinter in those soft, juicy thighs.

Jason looked into his wallet, peeled a bill off, and tossed it onto the step between them.

Marisol was bent over, straightening her thigh-highs, which had slipped a bit.

Sexy. Jason felt himself getting hard again.

She picked up the bill and tucked it inside her bra. She smiled. "So, what does 'sheeky' mean?"

Jason smiled back. "It means," he said, reaching one hand up under the folds of her skirt and helping himself to a generous handful of flesh, "you have a nice ass."

Marisol leaned back against the steps, giggling now. "So much to learn."

In the shadows he could see a thin film of sweat on her face. It was a warm day.

There were footsteps in the kitchen above, passing within inches of the cellar door.

"Ees only my aunt," Marisol said, giggling harder now.

Jason nodded. It was just after eleven. Christina never got up this early. And even if she did . . . "Hey," he said, working his hand up Marisol's thigh, "want to do something for me?"

"*Sí,*" Marisol whispered, hiking her skirt up again.

Jason stayed where he was. "I want you to watch things."

Marisol gave him a questioning glance.

"My wife," Jason explained. "I need to know who comes here when I'm not around."

Marisol's eyes narrowed, losing the playful look.

She'd be good in business, Jason thought. "I mean it," he said. "I need to know if men come here."

Marisol nodded. "I understand."

And it was clear by the look on her face she did understand. "I'll make it worth your while," Jason said, digging his wallet out once more. This time he handed the bills directly to her.

Marisol's eyes flickered when she saw how much, stowing the bills with the rest. "Okay," she said, nodding vigorously. "No problem."

*T*he First Presbyterian Church of Amagansett looked the same as Christina remembered it from a wedding ten years ago. Manicured grounds and a tidy blue sign proclaiming in gold letters that the church had been established in 1860. Her spirits rose when she pulled in to park and found a spot between a brand-new Lexus and a Rolls Royce.

AA, Hamptons style.

Inside was another story. The meeting was in the basement of an outbuilding, all fluorescent lights and dropped ceilings. The place smelled like a high-school gym.

Christina shivered, wishing she had worn something warmer than a sleeveless gold-mesh tank top. She turned to leave, and practically toppled over an old lady in a snowy white cardigan and blue gingham sundress. Like Aunt Bea from *Mayberry R.F.D.*

"I'm Lois. Welcome to the Amagansett group of AA," she said, grabbing Christina's hand.

Christina backed away. "I'm sorry. I think I'm in the wrong place."

Old Lady Lois had a grip like Bruce Lee. "Nobody gets here by accident, my dear." She yanked Christina up to the front of the room, to the first row of metal chairs, which were set up facing a Formica table with microphones. "Come and meet the girls."

Christina didn't want to meet the girls, who materialized clutching styrofoam cups.

"Coffee's done," one of them announced.

"Hey, Stan," another called. "You hear that? The coffee's done."

One of the biggest men Christina had ever seen appeared with an armload of books. "Hallelujah!" he roared. "The coffee's done."

This was greeted with a round of raucous laughter from the crowd that by now had almost filled the room. There was a general stampede for the coffee urn.

Lois steered Christina by the elbow. "Girls, we have a newcomer, and her name is . . ." Lois fixed Christina with a gaze from eyes that were blue like her dress but piercing like lasers.

There was no time to lie. "Christina," she mumbled.

"Christina," several of the women repeated in unison, trying it out.

Like the Moonies. Christina glanced back at the door.

Someone pressed a meeting list into her hands.

At least three of them asked if she wanted coffee.

Old Lady Lois never let go of her elbow.

Big Stan came over. "Congratulations." He clapped her on the shoulder as though she had just won a 10k race.

Christina couldn't stop shaking. She longed to run out to her car and grab a hoodie. Or better still, leave.

But there was no chance of that. Stan took one of the seats at the Formica table and banged his gavel so loud it made Christina jump.

Lois pushed her down into a metal chair in the first row and lowered herself into the seat next to it.

A man she didn't know raced over and pressed a cup of black coffee into Christina's hands. "Welcome, Christina," he whispered, smiling. "You're in the right place."

Stunned, Christina took the cup.

How come everyone knew her name? And what was it with these people and coffee?

She couldn't stop shaking.

Next to her, Lois smiled and patted Christina's leg. "You're okay," she whispered. "Just ride it out."

Christina didn't know what the old lady was talking about, so she kept her eyes straight ahead, to where Stan banged his gavel again. "Welcome to the Amagansett open meeting of Alcoholics Anonymous," he hollered, smiling directly at Christina. "If you don't want to drink today, you're in the right place."

The meeting had begun.

"First of all, I want you to know my brother was afraid of the water. He almost drowned once when we were young. He never would have gone into his pool for a swim at night." Pamela Cardiff Lofting, a miniature feminized version of her old man, placed one dainty hand on Frank McManus's desk for emphasis. "Never."

There were so many jewels mounted in platinum on that hand it would take a detective's salary for an entire year to pay for them, McManus thought. "What are you implying, ma'am? That your brother's death was not an accident?"

"I'm not implying anything," she said hastily. "I just want you to be aware of certain things."

McManus nodded. It was not unusual in the case of a violent, wrongful death for families to go to war. The depressing truth was you could almost count on a divorce within a year, two at most, following any sudden tragic death.

Instinct told him lines were already drawn between the patrician Cardiffs and their nouveau riche daughter-in-law Christina, who as of this time yesterday stood to inherit quite a chunk of the family's cash.

All it took was one look at the smooth planes of Pamela Cardiff Lofting's face, harmonious in that way of the überrich, to see which side of the line she straddled.

"Detective McManus, I am here today on behalf of the entire Cardiff family because I want you to be aware of certain things. First, my brother was planning to file for divorce." She took in a deep breath. "And second, I saw something this morning that I find shocking." She grabbed another Kleenex from the box on McManus's desk and swiped at her nose, which was beet red compared with the rest of her tanned face. "Absolutely shocking."

Except Jason Cardiff's sister didn't look shocked, Frank McManus thought. She looked pissed.

"I went over to Jonah's Path this morning to help his wife, Christina," and here Pamela Cardiff Lofting interrupted herself and looked at McManus. "You know Christina?"

McManus nodded to indicate he did know Christina. This was going to be worth skipping lunch for.

"Well, I went over there this morning and used my key to go in. My brother, my poor brother"—Pamela Cardiff Lofting dissolved into tears here—"made sure

I had a key even after they got the locks changed." She swiped her nose again and looked up.

McManus caught a flash of something on her face. Shock, anger, and grief mixed with something else he couldn't identify right away.

"She didn't know this, but Jason always made sure I had a key to his house so I could always get in."

His house. Not "their house," even after sixteen years of marriage. Yup, something there. A kind of smugness. "So, you had access to the Cardiff residence on Jonah's Path?" McManus said, to keep things moving.

Pamela Cardiff Lofting nodded, shaking the precisely trimmed ends of her bob. "I let myself in this morning, and Christina was there, with a man." She shook her head in disbelief, glancing around to see whether anyone else was listening.

The only person within range was Detective Pete Cardillo, who was intent on peeling back a layer of cellophane from the top of an Indian entrée he had just removed from the microwave, a task McManus knew would require all of Cardillo's dubious powers of concentration and furthermore would presently fill the office with the stench of curry.

As if on cue, Cardillo uttered a four-letter word and began waving his hand through the air like he did every day at this time.

Pamela Cardiff Lofting, apparently reassured that Cardillo was not eavesdropping, leaned in closer. "She'd obviously spent the night with this man"—Pamela's voice trailed off again—"right after my poor brother . . ." Jason Cardiff's sister dissolved into tears once more. "He didn't deserve that, he never should have married her. She married up when she married my brother."

McManus glanced surreptitiously at his watch.

"A lot of people might have things to say about my poor brother, Jason, but he was a good person," Pamela Cardiff Lofting said through her tears. "In his own way," she added after a tiny hesitation. "He was good to his staff. He was helping support one of the maids, who has a son with special needs. He told me so himself." She closed her eyes and swiped at them again. "Not that that wife of his would appreciate it. But he was a good person, and he didn't deserve what he got."

Pamela Cardiff Lofting's eyes blazed. "When I walked into that house this morning, and I saw that man half-naked." She frowned, squeezing her eyes shut like she really was in pain. "Disgraceful."

She was pissed.

McManus cleared his throat. "Any idea who this guy is?"

Pamela Cardiff Lofting's eyes sprang open once more. "Oh, yes," she said firmly. "It was the painter who worked on their pool house. That's unbelievable, don't you think?"

McManus decided to treat that like a rhetorical question. "Do you know his name?"

She nodded. "Dan Cunningham."

"Road trip."

A short while later, Detective Ben Jackson stood in front of McManus's desk and drained what was left of his Subway soda. "Let me guess? Back to Jonah's Path?"

Detective Frank McManus nodded, eyeing the chocolate chip cookie his partner was finishing. "Let's hit a drive-through on the way."

Jackson tsk-tsked. "You shoulda come to Subway when I asked."

McManus's stomach was rumbling like the percussion section of a high-school band. "I had a visitor."

Jackson's eyebrow rose.

"Jason Cardiff's sister."

"And? How are things with the in-laws?"

"Like the Hatfields and the McCoys. Let's just say the good widow Cardiff is bouncing back pretty quick, based on what the sister-in-law saw this morning.

Jackson dropped his jaw in mock horror. "You don't say."

"Sad but true." McManus suppressed a shudder. His own marriage had ended shortly after just such an incident.

Jackson grinned. "You're killing me, dawg."

They riffed like this all day long. It helped them parse a situation. Separate fact from fiction. See where the bullshit lay.

Because the basic fact of every cop's life was that everybody lied to you, all the time.

They saved the biggest, most whopping lies of all for members of the homicide squad.

They needed to. A lot was at stake. New York had been flirting with the death penalty since 1890, when it became the first state to use the electric chair. The Empire State had no death penalty currently, but McManus had toured the maximum-security Clinton State Prison for men at Dannemora.

Given a choice between life in Dannemora and a needle in his arm, Frank McManus would opt for the needle.

Jackson was already heading for the car.

McManus fell into step behind him. "Jonah's Path, here we come."

"'Last night, I dreamt I went to Manderley again. It seemed to me I stood by the iron gate leading to the drive . . .'"

McManus smiled. See, that was the thing. Just when you thought everybody under forty was a waste of time, along came a guy like Ben Jackson, who had not only read the classics but knew most of the lyrics to Black Sabbath's "Paranoid."

It was forty-four miles from Yaphank to East Hampton. They made decent time. Frank's breath caught in his throat the way it always did when they emerged from the tree-lined portion of Dunemere onto the rolling open plain that was home to the Maidstone Club. The ground here pressed right up against sky, edged by a wilderness of dunes and ocean, a reminder even on an overcast day like this one that it was still God's country.

They followed Dunemere for a short distance before making the right onto Jonah's Path. The lane was short and narrow, with privet hedges that were eighteen feet tall on both sides. It was like barreling down a green tunnel that dead-ended at the ocean.

The Cardiff gate looked the worse for wear since yesterday.

Señora Rosa's accent sounded thicker on the intercom than it had in person. "Meessus Cardiff ees no here now."

A happy smile lit Ben Jackson's face. "That's okay, ma'am. We're here to speak with you."

The voice on the other end grew fainter. "Bye, bye."

The intercom went dead.

McManus chuckled.

Jackson buzzed again.

No reply.

Jackson buzzed again.

No reply.

Jackson held the buzzer down for a long time.

"¿*Sí*?" Señora Rosa's voice held a note of exasperation now.

Jackson let his voice run cold. "Suffolk County Police Department, ma'am." He flashed his badge at the electronic eye. "We need to speak with you about Jason Cardiff."

"You come back." The intercom clicked off abruptly once more, which pissed Ben Jackson off.

McManus laughed hard enough to blow the dregs of his Big Gulp into his nose. Whatever Jason Cardiff's character flaws had been, underpaying his staff had not been one of them.

Jackson threw the Crown Vic into park, got out and leaned on the buzzer a good long time. He drew up to his full height, which was substantial. "You need to open the gate, ma'am," he said, scowling into the electronic eye. "Right now."

There was no reply, but the gate swung open at a tilted angle.

Jackson drove through. "This'll be good."

The landscapers kept their heads down except for one, who stopped work and walked over when they parked and got out.

McManus had a hunch who it was before even before he opened his mouth.

Roberto Torres of Costa Rica, lately of Shirley, a hardscrabble town on eastern Long Island, had powerful ropy arms and wary brown eyes that flickered at something over Frank's shoulder while he gave his statement.

McManus caught movement at the windows out of the corner of his eye.

They checked IDs and headed inside, where the reception from the housekeepers was just as lukewarm.

"So sad," Señora Rosa said, more than once, "so very sad."

McManus didn't doubt the sincerity of the woman's sentiment. She had calmed down a lot since the day before. A dry uniform helped, as did the fact that the man of the house was no longer floating facedown in the swimming pool. But she was pretty broken up about it, you could tell by the way she kept glancing through the French doors to the pool.

"Please sit," she said with a sweeping gesture that took in most of the sprawling room that looked straight from the pages of a spread in *Architectural Digest*.

They waved off her offer of drinks and seated themselves at two of the twelve chairs around an enormous glass-topped dining-room table.

The table was spotless like the rest of the room. The place had been put to rights since yesterday, swept clean since McManus and Jackson had first visited approximately twenty-seven hours ago.

He wondered what their day rate was.

Señora Rosa and her niece pulled out chairs and sat. Both looked like they wished they were anywhere but here.

Señora Rosa gave it one more try. "Meessus Cardiff, she return soon, you talk to her."

They assured her they would do that, but that right now they appreciated her time and cooperation.

Jackson pulled out his pad and pen and got the ball rolling with simple questions about where the women resided (in a ratty-ass converted garage apartment in Patchogue, judging by the address), how long they had worked for the Cardiffs (eight years for Señora Rosa, and two for her niece, Marisol), and who else resided with the Cardiffs in the house during the summer months.

This brought the first smile of the day to Señora Rosa's face. "One son, Tyler. I know him since he was this high." She motioned with one hand slightly above the chrome back of the chair she was seated in. "And now he almost as big as *su padre*." Beaming, she raised her hand as high as it would go toward the vaulted ceiling.

And then it hit her, you could tell, that Tyler's height was not going to be measured any longer in terms of where the top of his head reached when he stood next to his *padre*. Her face crumpled.

Marisol whispered something McManus couldn't make out. A high-school Regents diploma in Spanish, and McManus could recall just about enough of the language to order Mexican takeout.

Whatever the younger woman whispered, it did not have the intended effect of soothing her aunt.

Just the opposite, in fact.

Señora Rosa dissolved into tears, fingering her crucifix with one hand while extracting a rumpled tissue from her pocket with the other, and to tell you the truth, this was, many times, when Frank McManus choked up.

Death was sad.

But Frank had trained himself over the years to use the emotion in the interview process to his advantage. He couldn't bring anyone back from the Great Beyond once they crossed over, but if they had been helped across before their natural time—maybe in the form of a one-way ticket on the River Styx Express—Frank McManus sure as hell could figure out whodunit.

"It's too bad," he began in an agreeable way.

"*Sí, sí.*" Señora Rosa continued to weep. "Very sad."

Marisol nodded in a somber way while managing, Frank noticed, to remain dry-eyed herself. If you took away the stiff nylon uniform and its unbecoming shade of battleship gray, she would be a looker. And if you undid the tightly coiled bun at the base of her neck, he'd bet anything a long thick mane of shiny dark hair would tumble free. In which case, she would turn heads.

Jason Cardiff had most likely taken note at some point.

McManus's eyes met Marisol's, and he saw something similar to what, he imagined, she was reading in his own gaze. Watchful. Cautious. Wary.

Marisol looked away first.

Frank eased into things. "Do you like working here?"

Both women nodded vigorously.

"Oh, yes," Señora Rosa said, making a sweeping motion with her hand. "*Es* beautiful."

Frank McManus followed her gesture and nodded. It *was* beautiful, even with dunes the color of new-poured cement from the tropical storm that was churning up the coast from Capes Hatteras to Cod.

"And the Cardiffs? You like them?"

The nodding stopped and there was the merest beat.

"*Sí,*" Señora Rosa said quickly.

Marisol stared down at the glass surface of the table. "*Sí,*" she echoed.

"So," McManus said slowly, "you like them both?"

Señora Rosa frowned. She gave a quick look at her niece, who continued to stare at the glass tabletop.

Marisol and Auntie Rosa were not, apparently, going to do any heavy lifting today. Frank and his partner exchanged glances. McManus leaned forward trying again. "Do you like working for both of them, Mr. and Mrs. Cardiff?"

"*Sí.*" Señora Rosa nodded. "Yes, of course." She allowed her crucifix to fall back onto her chest for emphasis. Frowning, she folded her hands in her lap.

"*Sí,*" Marisol echoed.

"And do you get along well with the other employees here?" Frank used a neighborly tone as the women exchanged a quick glance. "Are you friends with Roberto and the men who work outside?"

This hit home. Marisol stiffened at the mention of Roberto's name.

Señora Rosa's lower lip came out. She gave a quick glance at her niece and shook her head. "No problem."

"Right." Marisol shifted in her seat and kept her glance firmly fixed on the tabletop.

If she'd been wearing a watch, she probably would have made a point of checking it right now.

As it was, her lips tightened, and she brushed away imaginary crumbs from the top of the table.

Frank changed tacks. "Do the Cardiffs have a lot of friends?"

Señora Rosa perked up, and even Marisol seemed to loosen up a bit. This question, apparently, was more to their liking.

"*Sí.*" Señora Rosa nodded.

"Do they have friends come over to the house?"

Again, nods. "Parties?"

More nods.

"Do they have a lot of parties?"

"In summer, *sí, muchas fiestas,*" Señora Rosa replied.

"How about night before last?"

The two women glanced at each other.

The place had been trashed when McManus first got here yesterday morning.

"Yes, sir," Señora Rosa replied.

"Do you know who was here?"

Both women shook their heads.

"No," said Señora Rosa.

McManus leaned in closer to Marisol, who met his gaze. "And you," he asked. "Do you have any idea who was here?"

"No, señor," she said, still shaking her head. "*Yo no sé.*" There was a pause. "The Cardiffs have *muchas fiestas.*"

It was true. Jason Cardiff's blood was loaded with more than alcohol at the time of his death. The medical examiner said preliminary findings indicated Cardiff probably had a fair amount of cocaine and marijuana in his system, and other things besides. Cardiff had been known around the East End as a party boy.

"Any idea who came to Mr. Cardiff's party the other night?" Frank directed the question at Señora Rosa.

She shook her head. "Sorry."

Her regret seemed genuine.

"Do you know what his plans were for the night?"

"He met his friend for dinner at the club. Señor Stanton." Rosa brightened up now that she had, at last, supplied McManus with some information. "Gil Stanton."

"Gil Stanton. Is he a friend from around here or the city?"

Señora Rosa glanced at her niece.

"From the city," Marisol replied. "Gil Stanton is Mr. Cardiff's attorney."

Attorney. Not lawyer and definitely not *abogado*. It was an American way of describing that most cherished American relationship, the one between a client and his legal representative.

Ben Jackson glanced up.

He had caught it, too.

"They went to dinner sometimes," Marisol said with a quick shrug, as though by giving them more information she could retract the fact that she had just revealed she knew much more about the business dealings of the master of the house than she had intended to let on.

Señora Rosa stared straight ahead, twisting her gold wedding band in her lap.

Frank rested one hand on the table so that everything in his body language said this-is-all-good. "So"—he directed his question at Marisol—"Gil Stanton. Do you know what law firm he's at?"

"No."

It was a Park Avenue firm. Cardiff's sister had mentioned it during her visit to the station earlier today.

"Do you know where they went for dinner?" Pamela Cardiff Lofting had been most helpful on that score as well.

"The Dunes."

The Dunes was a new members-only golf club that catered to the nouveau riche set. There were no dress codes and no admissions committee. It cost one cool million to join.

"Around what time was that?"

"Meester Cardiff leave here around six," Rosa said.

"Do you know if Mr. Stanton came back here with him after?"

"No." Both women spoke in unison.

"I don't think so," Marisol added. When her eyes met McManus's, he believed she was telling the truth.

"Do you know if anyone else was here with him that night?"

Señora Rosa stopped toying with her wedding ring.

Marisol shook her head without looking up.

"Anyone at all?" Frank waited, tapping his fingers on the tabletop. He'd bet anything the smudges would be Windexed away before Señora Cardiff returned, or there'd be hell to pay.

Señora Rosa's response was firm. "No."

Marisol's answer came out as no more than a whisper. "No."

McManus and Jackson exchanged glances.

McManus changed tacks again. "Did you like Mr. Cardiff? Was he a good boss?"

"*Sí,* yes, yes," Señora Rosa replied, her voice cottony with tears. "*Es muy terrible.*"

But it was Marisol he wanted to hear from.

It took the younger woman a moment to raise her eyes, and she reddened when she realized the question was intended for her. "He was a good boss."

"Did you like him?"

"*Sí,* nice man. Good boss," Señora Rosa said.

"Yes, of course," Marisol replied.

McManus shifted gears. "What about Mrs. Cardiff?"

"Señora Cardeeff, poor woman," Señora Rosa burst out. "And her son, now . . ." Her voice trailed off in a fresh round of tears.

Marisol blinked. "She is a good boss."

"Easy to work for?"

"Sure."

"Is she fair?"

The young woman frowned, and her aunt lifted her head. "*¿Qué?*"

McManus leaned forward slightly. "I mean, is she a fair boss? Is she good to work for?"

Señora Rosa sniffed. "*Sí*, yes of course."

Marisol nodded.

"Do they pay you on a regular basis?"

Señora Rosa frowned, and Marisol nodded again.

McManus stated the question another way. "Who gives you money and when?"

"Meester Jason does on Friday," Señora Rosa replied.

Her niece nodded in agreement.

"Does he ever pay you extra?"

Bingo. His question was greeted with silence. But something passed between the two women, nothing you could see. Blink and you'd miss it. But McManus could tell.

Across the table, Jackson sensed it, too, because he raised an eyebrow. But he kept writing.

They had worked out long ago that it was best for the interview if whoever was taking notes just kept writing. Too much stopping and starting was a distraction and worse, reminded the interviewee that anything they said could be used in Suffolk County's investigation into the possible commission of a crime.

Most likely, McManus knew, his partner was jotting a list of things he needed to get at Costco early Saturday morning. Ben did the bulk of the Jackson family shopping. Once in a blue moon Frank joined him when he was running low on soap or paper products.

Ben Jackson, he knew, was listening as intently as he was.

Señora Rosa frowned and shook her head. "No."

"No," Marisol said in a quiet voice.

"Never? They don't pay anything extra?"

Both women shook their heads.

"Not at Christmas?"

There was silence during which the women glanced at each other.

Señora Rosa responded. "*Sí*, at Christmas *un regalo* . . ." She looked uncertainly at her niece.

"We get extra at Christmas," Marisol explained.

"Any other time?"

She shook her head quickly.

"What about after a party?"

Marisol looked away.

McManus looked at Señora Rosa. "They gave parties, big parties, right?" He waited.

They both nodded.

"Did they pay you extra to clean up after a big party?"

There was a silence. McManus waited.

Señora Rosa shrugged at last. "No, señor," she said firmly.

McManus frowned. "Never any extra money?"

Señora Rosa leveled her gaze at McManus as she fingered her crucifix. "No, señor," she replied.

Marisol stared sullenly down at the center of the dining room table. She looked up. Her dark eyes glinted when she met Frank's gaze. "No," she said evenly. "Nothing."

CHAPTER

9

There was something familiar about the man telling his story from the table at the front of the room.

All it took was one smile for Christina to place him. She knew in an instant how his face would move and arrange itself even before it happened.

"I'm Matt," he said. "And I'm a grateful alcoholic."

"Hi, Matt," the group replied, just like in the movies.

This was surreal. Until two seconds ago, she had planned to bolt for the exit once the meeting got under way.

Now, she didn't dare. She ducked her head, praying she wouldn't be recognized by the handsome man telling his life story into the microphone, going back to when he was thirteen and began sneaking Scotch from his father's liquor cabinet and watering the bottles down.

The room roared with laughter.

It was sick.

Familiar pieces began to emerge such as how he got a job bartending while working his way through Hofstra at night. "I made good money, stole from the house, and felt like a big man." He grinned. "I got a summer share in the Hamptons."

Christina sank down lower in her chair. *Summer share in the Hamptons.*

"I was hanging out with kids who had gone to Ivy League schools, thinking I had it made. I was kidding myself," he said quietly. "I still remember the beautiful women I met there, girls who knew better than to waste their time with a drunk like me."

Christina snuck a look at him, and their eyes met.

Close to two decades disappeared in the space of one second.

Those eyes were still blue, the color of a tall sky on a windswept day, lined now with crow's-feet around a nose that was big, almost hooked. Too ethnic in an Irish way to be movie-star handsome but on him, it all worked.

It always had.

With a jolt she realized Matthew Wallace was even more attractive now, well into his thirties, than she remembered. Now there was something else.

He looked happy.

Matt's smile broadened. "I have no regrets. Everything I did got me here today. And this"—he placed both hands palms down on the Formica tabletop to make a point—"is the best place for me. I owe everything I have to AA."

Christina blinked. Memories flooded back of that summer long ago. Sundowner cocktails on a deck overlooking Shinnecock Inlet and the rickety old wooden Ponquogue Bridge they used to fish from. Matt was sweet and good-natured, down-to-earth and affectionate, something Christina didn't appreciate at the time.

He had big dreams. But they were nothing more than dreams, and Christina Banaczjek had not used her meager savings to leave Hamtramck, Michigan, behind so she could live on Long Island as a bartender's wife. Not when she had just met an up-and-coming equities trader named Jason Cardiff.

Christina played it cool on the weekends with Jason that summer, dropping hints she'd had a coming-out party in Grosse Pointe. During the week, she hung out with Matt Wallace and his friends in Hampton Bays.

When Labor Day came, she dumped Matt. He was sweet, but no match for Christina's ambitions. She'd never seen or heard from him again.

He finished his story. "I love you all, and I want to thank you for keeping me sober today."

She didn't have the nerve to look at him when he said that.

The room exploded with applause.

A man at the back yelled, "I love you, too, Matt!"

It was bizarre.

Christina wondered if Matt had turned gay.

A skinny young man no older than Tyler, with bright red hair combed straight up like a rooster's comb and tattoos lining his arms, yelled, "Thanks for being my sponsor, Matt! You saved my life!"

As the applause continued, Big Stan clapped the kid with the rooster comb on the shoulder, hard enough to knock him off his chair.

Matt Wallace called to him, "Hey, Jake, how much time do you have?"

Jake jumped to his feet like he had just won the lottery. "Forty-three days clean."

The room turned quiet.

"And that's one day more than yesterday." Jake's voice broke.

To Christina's horror, he began to cry.

Applause thundered through the room.

Someone yelled. "How'd you do it, Jake?"

Jake swiped at his eyes with one tattooed wrist, his voice low and ragged with emotion. "One day at a time."

Christina looked away, embarrassed.

There were hoots and hollers and calls of "Go, Jake!"

Tiny elderly Lois bellowed, "Don't drink even if your ass falls off."

Peals of laughter rang out.

It was getting weirder by the second.

People tossed dollar bills into straw baskets that were coming around.

Matt stretched his long legs out in front of him. "Who else is counting days?" He scanned the audience. "Christina, how about you?"

Just like that, he spoke her name. But there was something careful in his voice.

Like talking to her, even across a crowded room, might batter his heart all over again.

The way hers felt right now. She opened her mouth, but there was no voice.

The room got very quiet. People turned in their seats to get a better look.

Christina remembered now how she had dumped Matt without any warning. It was cruel. She managed to get her voice working through a mighty effort. "Um."

The laughter and lighthearted banter of a few moments ago was gone. In its place was a profound silence. Christina wracked her brain trying to come up with an answer to Matt's question. She remembered puking into the tiny airsick bag on the god-awful plane ride to Minneapolis, peeing into a cup during her intake exam at rehab. "I, ah . . ." Christina's voice faded and, to her horror, the corners of her mouth yanked down. "I'm not sure," she whispered.

When Matt spoke, his voice held no edge at all. "I'm glad you got here."

She nodded, miserable.

He smiled, oozing sincerity, which just made her feel worse.

Christina had had the upper hand in their relationship. He had been devoted to her like a puppy dog, once jumping off a bridge late at night into Shinnecock Canal to prove it. Looking back, she was too busy climbing from the wreckage of her so-called childhood to have returned anybody's love, even a love as pure as his.

Matt Wallace watched her now with the measured gaze of someone trying to decide whether or not to call an ambulance.

Christina winced. She wanted to curl up and die.

Lois patted her arm. "Keep coming back."

How hateful. "Ten days," Christina blurted, pieces meshing together in the fog that was drifting through her brain. "I'm pretty sure my last drink was ten days ago."

"Well, all right," Matt said.

There was applause, but just a smattering. As though people couldn't make up their minds whether to believe her, Christina decided. She didn't blame them. She had left rehab early—not her fault—but if the truth were known, Christina Cardiff did not have a very good track record. Her marriage, over now—not her fault—was on its way out, and had been for a long time. Her son chose to spend most of his time away from home. And she had no friends to speak of.

So she wasn't feeling all that strong about quitting cold turkey the way these people had.

"Get a sponsor," someone yelled.

Christina felt as though she'd been slapped.

Announcements followed about a potluck dinner and God knows what, but Christina wasn't listening.

When it was over, Jake ran up and threw his arms around her. "You can do it," he said, smiling like she was his favorite aunt. "Just don't drink and go to meetings. Stay tight with Lois. She'd make a great sponsor. I've got the best one in the world, but you can't have him 'cause he's a guy."

This last remark was intended in part for the benefit of Matt Wallace, who had finished taking congratulations and walked over. He stood, larger than life, smiling like no time had passed.

He grabbed young Jake in a man hug. "Good to see you got another day, kid."

Jake grinned up at Matt, hero worship all over his face. "I'm giving it my best shot. I'm making meetings every day, and I plan to go to bed sober tonight." He beamed at Christina. "Matt's keeping me on the right track."

"Nope," Matt said. "You're doing that for yourself. And you're keeping me sober while you're at it."

Christina blinked. She'd never heard men talk like this.

Now Matt turned his high-wattage smile on her along with those eyes, which were exactly the way she remembered.

Like laser beams into her heart. How could that be,

after all the years and all the living (and dying) that had happened to her?

"How 'bout you, Christina? How are you doing today?"

Coming from someone else, it would have been a straightforward question. Christina's face collapsed toward center, and a big sob rose in her throat. She knew she looked like shit. Crying wouldn't help. But she burst into tears anyway.

Matt Wallace dug a handkerchief from his pocket and handed it to her. "It's clean."

It took a minute or two for Christina to cry herself out. She mopped at her face after the sobs subsided, pretty sure if Matt had any regrets about being dumped so long ago, he'd be losing them now. She blew her nose, honking long and loud.

Matt Wallace and young Jake watched as if they had all the time in the world.

"I have to get groceries," she said when she managed to regain control of her voice. "My son is coming." She hiccuped. "I have no food." She dissolved into tears again.

Matt Wallace and Jake exchanged a look.

"We'll go with you," Matt said quickly.

"Sure." Jake smiled, revealing a wide gap between his front teeth. "We love Waldbaum's."

Finished with their interviews of the Cardiffs' domestic staff, Detectives Jackson and McManus climbed back into the Crown Vic and headed down the long, winding drive past the lawn that was dotted with landscapers intent on keeping the grass in putting-green shape.

Nobody waved good-bye.

Detective Ben Jackson sighed. "I feel like a mushroom."

It was an old one, but Frank McManus took the bait. "Why's that?"

" 'Cause I work in the dark and get fed nothing but shit."

"You don't mean to imply that Señorita Marisol—?"

"Is holding out on us?" Jackson grinned. "Could be," he said, proceeding to answer his own question. "What do you think? Who do you like?"

Frank let loose a mock-deep sigh. "I hate when you talk about things like this. I really do."

"I know, dawg." Jackson gave a solemn nod. "All those years of Catholic school, down the tubes. But give it a try."

It was a corny routine, but it passed the time.

"There's something there with Marisol," McManus offered.

"No question," Jackson agreed. "We know she was getting it on with Roberto because Christina Cardiff told us so." He paused. "If you can believe her."

"Big if," McManus said.

"But did you see the look on her face?"

McManus nodded to indicate he had.

"I'm thinking maybe there was something with Jason Cardiff, something going on there with Marisol."

"Could be," Frank replied. "No love lost between the cleaning women and the lady of the house."

Ben Jackson snorted. "I'll say."

They slowed near the exit.

Roberto Torres paused in his work long enough to watch the gate swing wide, his strong hands wrapped around the worn handle of a spade.

"Catch you one day soon, *hombre*," Jackson muttered under his breath.

The case was turning out to be more interesting than McManus would have guessed. A lot went on behind the privet hedges at the Cardiff estate. It was a regular ol' *Peyton Place,* in fact. But there you go, Frank McManus reflected. Too much money and too many drugs did not make for a happy home. This was a truth that played out, over and over, in his line of work.

They pulled onto Jonah's Path, where Happy Dick was in place once more with his camera.

He saluted.

Frank scowled.

They pulled in at the very next drive, one up from the ocean along Jonah's Path. According to the cleaning ladies, it was the only house on the block that was occupied this week.

"Now this," Frank said, "is what you picture when you think of a beach house." A drive consisting of crushed white shells wound past old-growth linden trees to a snug Cape with cedar shingles.

There were hydrangea bushes with blooms the size of soup bowls alongside hollies and rhododendrons that were taller than McManus. All native shrubs, none of that twisting topiary they charged an arm and a leg for at the garden center in Amagansett. The porch was an explosion of color. Everywhere you looked were containers brimming with flowers and vines that trailed in a leafy curtain down past the railings. Ceramic pots of every shape and size were crammed with color. The humid air hung heavy with a perfumed mix of spice and fruit and tang. A wind chime tinkled with the breeze.

A pair of weathered Adirondack chairs competed for space with a collection of garden gnomes.

A flag held by a giant frog fluttered in the onshore breeze.

The place was like one big welcome mat.

The animal that launched itself at Frank was not.

A black Scottie, which McManus had mistaken for a lawn ornament, sprang to life. Its jaws made a snapping sound as it rushed the car.

"What the f–?" Jackson was half-out of the driver's seat when he reversed direction, yanking the door closed just in time.

The Scottie went up on its hind legs and continued barking its oversized head off.

Frank McManus laughed out loud. Ben Jackson, who was approximately the size and shape of a Giants quarterback, was afraid of dogs.

So was Frank McManus. Dogs, like people, could pick out a cop at fifty paces. "It's okay," McManus said, keeping his voice easy breezy for the dog's benefit. He cracked his door open and attempted to exit the passenger side, taking his time.

The dog dropped back down onto all fours and came around to McManus's side of the car. The animal wasn't very big, after all.

"It's okay, pal," McManus murmured, reaching down with one hand.

The dog skidded to a halt and cocked its head. A thick fringe of eyebrows covered most of its face, trailing right down into a long black beard.

"Doggie needs a haircut," Jackson said.

"Don't be critical," McManus murmured. He was closer to the dog. "You'll piss him off."

But it was too late. The dog's head was large, out of proportion to its tanklike body and stubby legs. It bared its fangs, revealing a set of teeth that would have been at home inside the jaws of a German shepherd.

A loud rumbling came from deep inside its chest.

"Jesus," Jackson muttered.

McManus kept one hand on the car door. He tried again in a light, friendly tone. "How ya doin', fella?"

The Scottie charged, barreling at him in a blur of black fur.

Frank McManus dove back into the car.

Ben Jackson roared with laughter.

McManus muttered an oath.

The Scottie parked itself near the grillwork in the front of the cruiser, keeping up a steady, shrill bark.

For a little dog with stubby legs, he was loud.

McManus watched the screen door, one of those old-fashioned ones with a wooden frame, the kind that would slam shut in a classic sound of summer.

Nobody came to the door.

"Anybody home?" Jackson gave the horn a couple of quick toots.

One blast from the Mace they carried would solve the problem, but that would piss off the dog's owner. And that would not get things off on the right foot. However tempting it was to blast Fido in the snout.

The dog kept up its steady barking, actually rising to stand up again on its hind legs.

The better to terrorize them.

"Cujo lives." Jackson tooted the horn again. "Hello," he said through the loudspeaker. "Anybody home? Suffolk County PD."

"I'm coming." A woman's voice came from the direction of the yard. "I'm coming."

And the woman herself appeared a moment later. Barefoot, wearing a linen blouse and plaid shorts that were on the longish side but still showed she had great legs. She wore gardening gloves, not the cutesy canvas kind but the serious ones with chamois leather reaching halfway up her shapely arms. She carried an honest-to-goodness wicker basket filled with fresh-cut roses, and looked straight out of a centerfold from *Hamptons Life*.

"Shep," she yelled, giving a cheery wave to the car.

As though police cruisers showed up in her yard all the time.

"Shep," she yelled at the dog, who finally lowered his volume to somewhere around earsplitting. "You miserable beast," she said happily. "Where are your manners?"

Shep's mother pulled off one glove and extended her hand, still smiling in that sunny way she had. "I'm Biz Brooks."

Biz. Short for something preppy and elegant to match the melodious voice, the million-dollar smile, and the house to match.

"Come and sit down." She headed up the porch stairs without waiting for an answer.

Ben Jackson glanced uneasily at the dog, which kept its snout pointed their way, like a cruise missile ready to launch.

Biz Brooks motioned for them to sit.

The choices ranged from Adirondack chairs to a porch swing with faded floral cushions.

"Can I get you some iced tea?"

A cold glass of iced tea sounded great.

"No, thanks," both men said in unison.

"Let me know if you change your mind," Biz said, dropping into the swing.

The Adirondack chairs did not lend themselves to any sort of official pose, so Frank settled on perching at the edge.

Ben Jackson did the same.

Biz Brooks ran a hand through her blond hair, which she wore in a short blunt cut.

Usually, blondes had masses of tumbling thick curls, like McManus's ex-wife, but Biz Brooks's hair was pin straight. The overall effect was refined. McManus cleared his throat. "We're here to talk about your neighbor, Jason Cardiff."

Biz's eyebrows skipped in close together.

"He died," Frank said.

"Oh." Biz Brooks's eyes widened.

And that was it. Which pretty much told you the Brookses and the Cardiffs had never traded gardening tips through the privet hedge.

"That's too bad," she said. "He was young, wasn't he?"

Younger than two out of the three of them on her porch. Frank nodded. "Thirty-eight."

Biz's shoulders dropped, and she shook her head, her mouth settling into lines that didn't exist when she smiled. "That's terrible."

Ben Jackson shifted so the Adirondack chair gave off a sharp cracking sound.

Shep let out a low rumble.

"We were hoping you could help us with some information."

"Sure." Biz Brooks frowned at the wall of green separating her yard from the Cardiffs'.

Ben Jackson flipped out his notepad and pen.

"Mr. Cardiff's body was discovered in his swimming pool yesterday morning by the housekeepers," Frank said. "Apparently, he drowned sometime during the night.

"That's awful." Biz shook her head sadly and looked at Frank.

Her eyes were hazel, intelligent. "Were you at home night before last?"

She nodded.

Frank glanced through the screen door to the living room, where you could just make out an overstuffed couch and a couple of easy chairs gathered around a fieldstone fireplace.

Overall, the effect was cozy.

"Was anyone in the house with you, ma'am?"

"Um, no. Only Shep."

The phone was listed under Brooks, Edward.

"It's just us."

Frank ignored the tiny tha-rump inside his chest as Biz flashed a rueful little smile. "I'm a widow," she said quickly. "My husband passed two years ago."

Shit.

"I'm sorry," Frank said.

"It's okay," Biz said, focusing on a spot somewhere past the hydrangeas. "I'm okay."

Which meant it wasn't, she wasn't, and that she'd had a lot of experience with people telling her they were sorry.

"I'm sorry," Frank repeated, as Ben Jackson chimed in, because no matter how long they'd worked homicide, there was never anything else to say.

"I wasn't home yesterday," Biz said briskly.

Moving things along. Frank liked her, everything about her.

"I got up early to meet friends and play golf. I started taking lessons last summer. My husband always wanted me to." She gave a little smile that held a big dose of rue.

Widows did things a lot to please their dead husbands. Frank wanted to take them by the shoulders and tell them to yuk it up, spend the inheritance however they pleased. If there was an afterlife, the poor bastard was in the strings section learning to play the harp. Not looking down to keep tabs on the Missus.

But Frank McManus didn't believe there was any sort of afterlife. What he believed in was justice for wrongs done in this one. "Where do you play?"

"Over at the Maidstone," she said casually. Okay, maybe Mr. Brooks was nodding approval somewhere. The Maidstone was a challenging course, besides being one of the most elite clubs around. "I did notice a van coming down Dunemere as I returned home," she added.

The County wagon carting off the earthly remains of Jason Cardiff, a fact Frank McManus did not spell out. "What about the night before? Did you notice anything or hear anything out of the ordinary?"

She gave the same answer everyone did when he asked this question, ten times out of ten. "No."

A little prodding always helped.

"The weather was still calm Wednesday night, not too windy," Jackson said. "Do you sleep with the windows open?"

"Usually," Biz replied. "We had A.C. installed, but I hate to use it. I love the sound of the ocean at night."

"So, you can hear the Cardiffs as well. Say, sounds of a party?"

Biz's frown returned. "They entertain a lot."

Records showed a series of noise complaints had been phoned in from the Brooks residence over the years, two in the last eighteen months.

"I'm a really light sleeper, I guess, especially since my husband died." Biz shifted around in her seat, self-conscious.

Widows and insomnia went together, after all, like a hand in a glove.

But, from what they were learning, the Cardiff house shook, rattled, and rolled many nights.

"What about him?" Ben Jackson motioned with his chin to where the dog lay motionless in the hydrangea beds under the porch. "Is he a light sleeper?"

Biz Brooks smiled.

They had returned to a subject of her liking.

"Shep?"

At the sound of its name, the dog stirred.

"Yeah," Jackson replied quickly. No doubt hoping ol' Shep would go back to his union break. "Does he ever hear things at night?"

"He sure does. I had to cancel my *New York Times* subscription because he kept waking up when they came to deliver. Now I've got to buy it in town," Biz said with a shake of her head.

And who said the überrich had it easy? Frank exchanged glances with his partner. Frank knew what Jackson was thinking. If Shep were his dog, he'd be sent somewhere nice and quiet so Jackson could enjoy a peaceful night's sleep.

"What about Wednesday night? Did Shep hear anything?"

Biz let her gaze drift from the dog's napping spot to

the skyscraper of a hedge separating her property from the Cardiffs. "You know," she said thoughtfully, "come to think of it, he did."

McManus and Jackson waited.

"I went up to bed early for my golf game Thursday morning. There was nothing on TV."

McManus knew what she meant. Even *Survivorman* was in reruns till fall. Living alone was evil. "Nothing wrong with TV," he pointed out.

Biz smiled. "Anyway, the wind picked up, and I just couldn't sleep. I tried to read. After a while I got tired of the book and came out here to sit for a while."

Jackson looked up from his notepad. "Approximately what time was that?"

"Oh, I'd have to think." Biz let out a breath.

McManus thought of his own weeknight routine, downing a bottle of Bud on the back deck while the Weber heated up. "The sun sets around half past eight," he said, trying to be helpful.

"Way later, close to eleven thirty. I saw a bunch of cars pass on their way to the Cardiffs."

Jackson glanced up from his notes. "A bunch of cars?"

Biz frowned. "I don't know. A few, I'd say."

"Two?" Jackson pressed. "Or more like three or four, or more?"

She considered this. "I'd say four, counting Jason's. He drives a sports coupe. It's smaller than the others and lower to the ground. I definitely saw that one first. There were two or three others following that one. One of them was loud, like it needs a muffler."

She wrinkled her nose in a girlish way that was fairly

attractive, and Frank would just bet she drove a nice, pricey ecofriendly hybrid that was quiet and great on gas. "Sounds like a party," Frank commented.

"Nothing unusual for that house." Biz's frown deepened.

Frank nodded, all ears. "They entertain a lot?"

She rolled her eyes. "Um, yeah."

He waited.

"I don't really know what goes on there." But you could tell by the way she said it that Biz Brooks had a fairly good idea of what went on there. "There are lots of cars coming and going from that house, especially at night." She paused. "How is their son doing? Tyler." Her concern appeared to be genuine.

Not a good side path for this interview.

"He's good," Frank said quickly. "With relatives, at the moment. He's in good hands."

"The Cardiffs?"

McManus gave a quick nod.

Biz's face lightened. "That's good."

Frank pressed on. "So, is it busy around here at night in summer? Or quiet?"

Biz made another face. "Pretty quiet. The neighbors across from me don't come till August. The house across from Cardiffs is owned by a film producer. He only comes in June." There was a pause while she completed her mental inventory of Jonah's Path. "There's a retired couple just off Dunemere who are visiting their daughter out of state."

Which pretty much accounted for anyone who might have seen or heard anything night before last. Frank nodded.

"Things were pretty quiet after the Cardiffs finished redoing their pool house a few weeks back." Biz hesitated. "Well, fairly quiet."

McManus shifted in his Adirondack chair again, trying to get comfortable. His butt cheeks were numb. "Fairly quiet?"

Biz hesitated. "Pretty much," she said at last.

Jackson looked up. "Meaning?"

"Meaning only one of them was there at a time. When Jason was around, there'd be lots of cars at night. With her, not so much." She paused. "Just one car that needs a muffler." She plucked at the roses in the basket at her feet, fidgeted in her seat.

Trying to get comfortable with the fact that she was engaging in the good old American pastime of ratting out the neighbors.

McManus and Jackson exchanged a glance, and Frank did the asking this time. "Would you say it's the same car?"

You could tell by the look on her face it wasn't the first time she'd considered this. She looked Frank in the eye, and her gaze was startlingly direct. She was, he could tell, the type that wanted to get everything right. "I don't know," she said. "Honestly, I just don't know that much about cars. But maybe."

"This is good," Jackson said quietly. "What you've told us is already a big help."

Biz frowned. "Are you here because . . ." She let her voice trail off. "I mean, it was an accident, right?"

Frank chose his words with care. "At some point during the night, Jason Cardiff went swimming in his pool. He drowned. We're trying to put together a time line for the events of that night."

And if Biz Brooks was correct, there was a gap of several hours that needed accounting between the time Jason Cardiff dined with his attorney and when he returned home to Jonah's Path.

The new chef at the Dunes was supposed to be pretty good. In fact, he had made it all the way to the finals last season on *Top Chef*. Still, nobody spent five hours over dinner with his attorney. No matter how good the crab-cake appetizer was.

Jason Cardiff had made another stop on the last night of his life.

"So," Frank said, "you noticed headlights and cars heading toward Cardiffs around eleven, maybe eleven thirty. Then what?"

"I went up to bed."

Jackson nodded, his gaze drifting down into the hydrangeas bushes. "And Scottie here, he went up to bed with you?"

"Things aren't that bad." Biz grinned.

This simple fact warmed Frank's heart.

"He sleeps downstairs in a crate by the back door. Kind of like a backup to my alarm system."

"Good," Frank said, realizing he had known her for all of twenty minutes, and he was already concerned about her.

"You sound just like my husband," Biz remarked.

Something about this statement pleased Frank, though he didn't want to admit it. He cleared his throat. "So, you see the cars, and after a while, you go up to bed. Scottie goes down to bed, and that's it till morning?"

"Not exactly," Biz said. "I heard engines again later. Much later. There were cars headed back out Jonah's Path to Dunemere."

Jackson looked up from his pad. "What time?"

Biz shook her head. "I don't know. I just noticed the engines, especially the loud one, then I went back to sleep.

"That must have been when the party broke up." She was ready to say more but changed her mind.

"And then?" Jackson looked up.

"Well, it was nothing really." Biz frowned. "But it must have been much later when something woke me. Or rather, something woke him." She motioned with her chin to where the dog was napping. "I don't know what it was."

Jackson waited, pen poised. "When was this?"

"Later," Biz said. "Much later; I don't know the time, but I had been in a deep sleep, so it must have been at least an hour after the cars pulled out."

Which would make it two or three. Frank inched forward, forgetting that the edge of the chair was cutting off the circulation in his legs. "What kind of sound was it?"

Biz shook her head. "I couldn't say. Shep was the one who heard it. Not me. He's the one who woke me. He barked."

They all considered this.

"Did he bark a lot," Frank asked, "or just a little?"

Biz Brooks laughed out loud. "Shep only barks one way."

"Got it," Ben Jackson said. "What'd you do then?"

She smiled. "I yelled down and told him to shut up."

No arguing with that. "And?"

"He wouldn't stop. Something was bothering him." She crossed her arms instinctively in a protective gesture.

Whatever it was, it was bothering her as well, Frank thought.

"Anyhow, he doesn't normally bark at night unless it's something unusual. I took a look out the window, but it was pitch-dark. I didn't see anything. I listened for a minute or two." She paused.

Both detectives watched her. "Did you hear anything?" Jackson's pen was poised.

She hesitated. "Not exactly."

Frank leaned forward. "What does that mean, not exactly?"

Biz Brooks chewed her lip. "Well, it's hard to say. I went back to bed, and I must have dozed off. Sometime later, I thought I heard an engine again."

Frank frowned. "Can you describe it?"

"I really can't." She glanced toward the one-lane road, invisible behind the tall privet hedge. "It was not close by but in the distance, out toward Dunemere. I can't be sure, but I think it was the one that sounds as though it needs a new muffler. But with the wind . . ." She shrugged. "I'm not really sure."

Jackson frowned. "You think it might be the same car as the one you heard earlier in the night?"

Biz shook her head. "It's hard to say. I wasn't really awake or asleep. But something definitely woke my dog at some point. Not a car. A car on the road wouldn't have bothered him."

"Were you concerned?" Frank asked.

She hesitated. "Not really, not too much."

Frank would bet anything the late Mr. Brooks, liberal ideologue that he was, had kept a trusty semiautomatic handgun stashed somewhere in his house and, further, that he had bequeathed it to his wife who, despite her

Martha Stewart penchant for gardening, was well-versed in its use.

Biz Brooks glanced placidly around her yard. "I'm never afraid here at night."

Frank McManus nodded.

"After that, I went downstairs, got a drink of water, told Shep to settle down, and came back up." She shrugged. "That was it till the alarm rang Thursday morning."

They thanked her for her time.

She walked them to the car, which was good because Shep woke from his nap.

The hydrangeas practically vibrated with a low rumbling sound.

It was the B–52 of dog growls.

Frank checked his watch. Lunchtime for Fido. A good time to exit.

Biz shushed the dog in that proud-mama tone of voice.

Cirie Jackson was always telling McManus to get a puppy, and now he wondered whether he should. Women dug dogs.

CHAPTER

10

The frozen foods section of the East Hampton Waldbaum's was gripped in an arctic blast.

Christina huddled inside a sweatshirt with a faded NYAC logo. Someone had wrapped it around her shoulders at the AA meeting, and she was grateful they hadn't asked for it back. She scanned the freezer shelves, reading from her list for Jake's benefit. "Let's see . . . there. That one." She used her fingernail to tap the glass, indicating a box of pizza-topped Bagel Bites.

"Coming right up, Christina. Allow me." Jake reached in, grabbed a box, and placed it in Christina's cart, which was already overflowing.

"Thanks. Tyler loves those."

"They are good, especially with a cold beer," Jake said with a laugh. "Don't tell Matt I said that." Jake leaned in close. "He'll kick my ass. We're not supposed to glamorize our drinking, you know?"

"Glamorize our drinking?" What the heck did that mean?

Jake was watching her like a big puppy.

Happy, she supposed, to be helping out. "Uh-huh." Christina nodded to show she got the point.

Except she didn't. She might as well be walking on the surface of the moon. Because right now she was on Planet Weird, where she could chat about cold beer in the frozen-foods section of the supermarket with a recovering heroin addict, while the man she had loved and hurt a million years ago was off in search of the Horizon Organic 2% Chocolate Milk that Tyler liked. Not to mention the fact that she had just attended her first meeting of Alcoholics Anonymous. Oh, and her to-do list today consisted of planning her husband's funeral.

Just another day on Planet Weird.

Christina Cardiff, Long Island's most jittery new widow, gripped the handle of her Waldbaum's shopping cart and held on for dear life.

"Got it." Matt Wallace reappeared. Placing the container of milk inside the shopping cart, he gently nudged Christina's hands to one side and took charge of the cart. "Your hands are like ice," he observed. "How're you doing, Christina?"

She heard his words as if from a great distance. She just couldn't come up with any meaningful reply. Planet Weird had a thick atmosphere that made conversation difficult.

Matt looked at Jake, who answered for her. "She's taking it one minute at a time."

"Sometimes, that's how it goes." Matt slowed his pace to match Christina's. "Hang in there." He gave her shoulder a squeeze.

His face swam out of focus. Christina nodded and pretended to scan the freezer shelves. She knew she would start blubbering again if she looked too long into those caring eyes. It had been a million years since anyone outside of the rehab center had been kind to her.

"You think we got all of Tyler's favorite foods?"

She nodded.

Matt smiled. "Great."

Christina had told them only that she needed to stock up on groceries for her son's return from Europe this afternoon, nothing more. She'd been shocked when they offered to shop with her. Who does that?

Matt kept the cart rolling. "Jake-O, which way to baked goods?"

"Right this way, chief," Jake replied. They kept up a steady banter through the aisles until they found what Matt wanted.

He picked up a long white box. "Entenmann's Cheese Danish. This is for you." Matt smiled at Christina.

She stared. It was hoi polloi food, loaded with empty calories.

Matt grinned. "It's the only thing I could hold down when I was detoxing."

"Tasty," Jake remarked.

Christina ducked her head in embarrassment. She wished detoxing were her biggest problem.

Matt steered them to checkout.

"Paper or plastic?" The clerk directed her question at Christina.

Deciding, no doubt, they were a basic family out doing the grocery shopping. Except they weren't, and Christina couldn't make up her mind. "Ummmm . . ."

"Paper's fine," Matt said, as he and Jake began bagging.

Something on the newsstand caught Christina's eye. The cover of *The Hampton Wave,* a weekly tabloid, featured a photo of her and Jason on their wedding day ripped down the center. The headline screamed, WAS IT OVER EVEN BEFORE HIS DEATH?

The contents of Christina's gut heated up and turned to hot, molten liquid. The noises of the checkout line faded away, replaced by a whooshing sound in her ears.

There was a second, smaller headline running across the bottom of the page:

SLAIN BANKER WANTED OUT! Details Inside.

Christina shook her head in disbelief. She grabbed the paper with fingers that shook and opened it.

Pages 2 and 3 were devoted to Jason:

DROWNED BANKER JASON CARDIFF CONSULTED WITH FAMED NY DIVORCE ATTORNEY MAURICE GOLD, blared a headline stretching across the top of both pages.

There were a series of other, shorter articles quoting unnamed sources with information about the way Jason had drowned in their pool. Halfway down Page 2 was another article with its own headline:

CARDIFF'S WIDOW LEARNED THE NEWS IN REHAB—IS SHE DRINKING? Beside it was a photo of the mangled gate.

There was even a sidebar listing famous clients of Maurice Gold.

"Oh, my God." Christina's head was spinning. Maurice Gold was the most vicious divorce lawyer in the country. Did Jason know about her affair with Dan Cunningham? The printed words blurred before her eyes as the pounding in her ears grew more intense. How could *The Hampton Wave* know all this? She stared at the picture of the rumpled gate. IS SHE DRINKING?

What if Tyler saw this?

The tabloid slipped from her hands and fell into the basket in a crumpled heap.

"Want me to ring that up?" The clerk's voice sounded far away.

Her in-laws were behind this. Christina squeezed her eyes shut in an attempt to stop the throbbing in her head.

"Just add it to the bill." Matt paid while Jake loaded the cart.

Matt grabbed her hand. "Let's go."

Christina's eyes fluttered open. The clerk was staring. So were the customers waiting to check out all around her.

They knew.

This was just the beginning. Jason's death would probably turn up on a future segment *20/20* or *American Justice*.

A gray cloud swirled through Christina's vision, and she squeezed her eyes shut. But it was no use. The cloud was still there inside, haunting her. She moaned.

Matt Wallace caught her. "Come on, Christina, let's go."

"You okay, miss?" The clerk's voice sounded more curious than concerned. "Do you want me to call a doctor?"

"No," Matt and Jake both chimed at once.

Christina allowed Matt to half carry her to the exit as Jake pushed the cart ahead. She didn't bother opening her eyes.

If she had, she would have seen everyone in Waldbaum's checkout stop to get a closer look.

* * *

Half an hour later, Christina sat on a stool in her kitchen, toying with a slice of Entenmann's Cheese Danish.

Matt Wallace was stowing groceries.

The kettle was heating on the stove.

Young Jake had helped Matt load the groceries into Christina's trunk at Waldbaum's. He directed his question at Matt. "How 'bout I follow you?"

Matt gave a quick nod. He was already steering Christina around to the passenger door of her Mercedes.

As though they were in complete agreement on the fact that she was in no shape to drive. She had been too grateful to protest.

Like now, taking tiny nibbles of pastry at Matt's urging.

He was rummaging through cabinets, passing over the numbered Limoges tea set they kept out for show in favor of two sturdy mugs that didn't match. "Where do you keep tea bags?"

Christina hesitated. "I don't drink tea." The truth was, she had no idea. They ate out a lot or ordered in.

"Now's a good time to start," Matt said cheerfully.

Christina had never actually sat on one of these stools. Only the cleaning ladies used them, and sometimes Tyler. The stools were comfortable, she decided, and she felt okay watching Matt Wallace whip around her kitchen. She wished she could freeze this moment in time, not go forward and not go back.

Just for right this moment, she was okay.

"Look at that, my favorite." Matt located an unopened box of Twinings Earl Grey that Señora Rosa must have bought. He let the bags steep before adding plenty of milk and a heaping spoonful of honey. He set one of the mugs down in front of her. "This will do you some good."

Christina forced some down. It was warm and too sweet and thankfully did not make her gag.

Matt stowed groceries away, setting baked goods, fruits, and snacks out on the counter.

When he was finished, the place looked lived in. Tyler would be happy.

Matt opened the refrigerator and frowned. "You have beer and open bottles of wine in here."

The housekeepers had strict orders to save open bottles of wine using special stoppers Christina had ordered from Cook's Illustrated. Jason's collection was extremely valuable.

"It's best to dump this stuff so you're not tempted to drink it."

Jason had bought those French reds at a Christie's auction. He'd be rolling in his grave right now. She thought of the tabloid article about Maurice Gold, the divorce lawyer Jason had hired, and shrugged. "Go ahead."

With the faucet running full blast, Matt dumped out all the wine. He placed the empties into Waldbaum's bags. "I'll take them with me so they don't stink the place up."

He'd have a heart attack if he saw the contents of the wine cellar beneath their feet.

Matt slid onto the stool next to hers and nudged the cake plate. "Good," he said, after she managed a tiny bite.

As though he spent every day coaxing old girlfriends to eat something. Maybe he did.

"You know, Christina, they say you should not let yourself get too hungry, angry, lonely, or tired."

Another zippy slogan from AA.

Matt saw her eyes roll. He took her hand and held it in both of his, smiling as he let out a long slow breath.

As though he felt it, too. As though for the space of that single moment they were the couple they might have been.

Christina closed her eyes. She wished he would say something, like he would stop at a farm stand for corn on the cob after Tyler finished his soccer game. He'd call her so she could heat up the grill. Maybe later they'd head into town for ice cream and a movie.

It was a glimpse at life in a parallel universe, where she and Matt would have been quiet and content and married forever, easing toward middle age.

Happy.

She chose wrong. And now look.

"Oh, Matt," she whispered, squeezing her eyes shut against tears that scalded with regret. She buried her face in her hands, miserable.

"I'm sorry." His voice dropped to a whisper, and she realized he was crying, too. He wrapped his arms around her and pulled her toward him, and it was a crazy thing to notice but he smelled the same as she remembered.

Christina breathed deep.

"Chrissie," he whispered, "I'm so sorry."

It was her old nickname, one she hadn't heard in over a decade. And she literally sobbed on Matt's shoulder, for all of it, for everything she had lost, while he held her.

"Look," he said, handing her a luncheon napkin.

Christina mopped at her face, and this simple act calmed her.

Matt rubbed her shoulder until she straightened up. "I'm sorry you're going through . . ." He searched for the right word. "All of this."

"Me too," Christina said with a wan smile. One thing she had noticed since she quit drinking was that crying helped. For a little while, at least. It was like loosening the valve on a pressure cooker so the steam could escape.

Matt took her hand in his once more and smiled back at her.

The weight of his hand on hers felt good.

"I do know one thing," he said, turning to face her. "Everything that happens is meant to be."

More AA talk, she suspected. But the way he said it, and the comforting feeling she got just having him near her, solid and sane and close enough to touch, reminded her for that one single instant of something she used to know and forgot.

Deep down inside, she was okay.

It was a feeling she hadn't had in years and years.

Christina nodded before she even realized what she was doing. She was not, nor had she ever been, the type to put a brave face on things. And yet here she was, in her kitchen with Matt Wallace, of all people, acting like everything was going to be okay.

As if he could read her mind, Matt said, "Everything is going to be okay."

"I know," she murmured, and the crazy thing was she believed it.

She wished she could hold on to this feeling forever.

"You can do this. Just don't drink, Chrissie." Matt

gave her hand a final hard squeeze and stood. "I'm on your side." He winked. "I owe you."

Christina's eyes widened. What did he mean, exactly? She was the one who had dumped him that summer, so how did he figure he owed her? Her mind raced back to the time they'd shared, endless days and nights at the beach, full of laughter and full of fun. Was her drinking already out of hand? Or was she simply such a mess right now that he pitied her? She didn't want to ponder that question.

But he didn't look like he felt pity. He was smiling at her like he was just, well, happy. The Matt she remembered.

He pulled a business card from his back pocket and jotted something on it before pressing it into her hands. "Here."

The card had all his pertinent information. Underneath his name in tidy block letters were the words, ATTORNEY AT LAW.

He had achieved his childhood dream. Christina beamed at him. "Good for you." She meant it.

He was beaming right back at her. "The most important part is on the back."

She turned the card over. On the back was his cell phone along with a note. "Free rides to AA. Call 24 hours a day."

"Thanks," she said, uttering a silent prayer she could stay sober through the days ahead.

Matt's eyes were dark with intent. "I mean it. Call me before you do anything you'll regret later."

The day would come, looking back, when she would wish she had taken his advice.

"Tyler needs a sober mother," Matt continued. "That's the most important thing."

He hit pay dirt with that statement, and Christina ducked her head so he wouldn't see her tears. More than life itself, she wanted to stay sober for the sake of her son. "Thanks," she whispered, not even trusting her voice.

She was grateful when the intercom buzzed on the security panel in the foyer.

One of the screens showed an aging Jeep Wrangler idling outside the front gate.

"That's Jake," Matt Wallace said. "My ride."

Christina buzzed the car in. She did not want to be alone. "Jake can come in. I can make him some tea."

"Thanks," Matt replied with a check of his watch. "He's got to get to his job in less than an hour. He can drop me at Waldbaum's on his way."

She was about to offer to drop him back at Waldbaum's or say anything she could think of to keep him from leaving her alone to face the mess she was in.

Without warning, Matt leaned down and grabbed her in a bear hug.

And in that one moment, in the crush of those arms that had always been so safe and warm, it all came tumbling back. A summer full of happy, carefree times. Nights spent dancing on the beach under the light of a moon that in her memory was always full, or just lying in the dunes, trading secrets and dreams for the future. It was the first and only time in Christina's life she had experienced real joy.

One night in particular stood out. They had swum far out past the breakers on Sand Bar Beach, floating on their backs in the warm sea, beneath a sky brimming over with stars, and Christina felt her heart tumble inside her chest with a supernatural certainty that Matt

Wallace would be the great love of her life. Somehow, she just knew.

It all came back now, right down to the smell of the brine mixed with the warm spice of the cologne he wore, and the scent of honeysuckle in bloom, drifting across the waves on a gentle June breeze.

Maybe it was just wishful thinking, but Christina felt a tremor in Matt's arms as though he didn't want to let go, either.

"Wow." Matt straightened up and held her at arm's length. "You could use a few good meals, girl."

Jason had insisted she stay thin, a size 0. Embarrassed, Christina wrinkled her nose.

Matt grinned. "Sorry, I forgot. Never talk about weight with a beautiful woman."

It was a glimpse of the old Matt, whose mother used to say he could sell coals in Newcastle. But he always told it the way it was. The Matt Wallace she remembered would probably ask her out for a steak dinner right about now.

Christina smiled expectantly.

No invite came.

Instead, Matt shifted gears. "You have Lois's number, don't you?"

Christina nodded, ducking her head so her disappointment wouldn't show. The old lady from the meeting had scrawled her number inside the AA directory she had thrust into Christina's hands.

"Good. Hang in there, Christina."

And with that, Matt Wallace was gone.

The house felt empty. It *was* empty. Not just empty as though nobody was home, but empty as though nobody had ever lived there and never would. As though the walls had never echoed with music and laughter from the parties they gave. She remembered so many sunny days here, a clambake on the beach for Tyler's tenth birthday. They had hired a magician, and there were pony rides out front. A big pool party the following year, with kids screaming and splashing. A water-balloon fight that went on and on.

When had it changed? Sending Tyler off to sleepaway camp that year had been the turning point. She had stopped being Mommy, Christina reflected. There was no longer any need to slow her drinking down because there was no reason to get up early the next morning, nobody to serve breakfast to. And, she cringed when she thought of this, no reason to hold back at those parties. They went on all night, deep into the hours toward dawn.

And the next day there was no one to face but herself. Jason always left early to play golf or tennis or meet friends for breakfast or go back into the city. By tacit agreement, they never discussed what had gone on the night before.

He had handled the change better than she had, Christina reflected. Jason still had the strength and resilience of a young man, able to bounce back the next day from any kind of hangover.

While she, Christina, came to slowly only after many hours, struggling her way to consciousness through a dull haze of pain. She was wretched, sad to look at, and she knew it. "You disgust me," Jason had finally told her.

She had moved into the spare bedroom soon after.

Looking through the French doors now to where wind was moving little ripples across the surface of the pool, which today was the color of wet slate, she thought how ironic it was that Jason was the one whose drinking had finally killed him.

Not hers.

She looked through the open windows at the dun-colored surface of the swimming pool, whipping around in the afternoon breeze, and shuddered.

Jason, in the end, was the one whose fast-lane lifestyle had finally overtaken him.

Not Christina's.

A dove cooed, over and over, the sound working its way deep into Christina's heart, making her wish she could find her way back to a fork in the road long ago and do things over.

But she could not.

Doves, she knew, often nested on the ground. She'd leave a note telling the landscapers to search for nests and remove them.

Tyler would be home soon, bringing the house back to life.

She would spend the hours until his return making the place feel like home again. She started by listening to phone messages.

There were a few condolence calls from friends she and Jason saw perhaps once every year or two. But not many. In fact, she hadn't heard from Jason's relatives.

Most, she thought sourly, had probably called her sister-in-law, Pamela.

There was a call laced with static and the sound of rushing air.

She wondered for one wild instant whether it was Jason calling from beyond the grave.

But it was her father-in-law calling from on board the Air France jet. The only words Christina could make out were "Jason" and "reception," before he hung up. The whooshing noise continued for a few seconds more, followed by a series of clicks.

And, finally, there was a call from the Medical Examiner's Office in Hauppauge. Jason's autopsy was complete, and they were waiting for instructions concerning Jason's remains.

The ME's next words chilled Christina to the bone.

"Please don't be concerned, Mrs. Cardiff. I've explained to your in-laws that you are the next of kin, and I will not release your husband's remains to anyone but you."

The call ended with a click.

Christina sat, stunned.

Next of kin. The term was foreign. She'd had no need of that phrase during her entire life.

Until now.

Because her in-laws had been calling the Suffolk County Medical Examiner's Office without her knowledge to try to have Jason's body released to them.

The drumming started up inside Christina's ears again, accompanied by a burning heat that grew steadily hotter until she practically smelled smoke.

The Cardiffs were trying to take control of Jason's funeral the same way they had taken control of her wedding and Tyler's baptism, the same way they had attempted to control everything in her life.

Because in their eyes she would always be the poor girl from Hamtramck who had married up, hitting it big-time the day she met their son and married her way into the fabled Family Cardiff.

She thought of the pile of Post-its Pamela had left with step-by-step instructions for planning a glorious sendoff worthy of a Cardiff.

And yet they had gone behind her back to do it themselves.

This meant war.

Christina felt a tingle of victory. The State of New York, at least, recognized a fact the Cardiffs refused to accept about her even after nearly sixteen years of marriage.

She was their son's next of kin.

Christina reached for the South Fork Yellow Pages, scanning the Amagansett listings till she found the number for the only church she'd been near in years.

A receptionist answered on the second ring. "Good afternoon. First Presbyterian Church. How may I help you?"

"My husband . . ." Christina's voice trailed off. Words failed her. She forced herself to try again. "My husband, um, has died." There, she'd said it.

The person on the other end of the phone made some sort of reply that did not involve falling to pieces.

Thank God.

"And I need to plan a memorial service as soon as possible," Christina continued. "Something small and simple."

They left Biz Brooks's place, and Frank placed a call to Jason Cardiff's lawyer on the private cell phone number Pamela Cardiff Lofting had given him earlier today.

Gil Stanton picked up on the first ring.

It was, Frank thought, one of the good things about lawyers. The only thing.

Stanton, it turned out, was just down the road a piece, finishing up a round of golf at the Dunes. They agreed to meet in the clubhouse bar in half an hour's time.

Stanton was easy to spot. Tall and wiry with silver hair, a golfer's tan, and the patrician face of a man who, well into the middle of his life, knew he was at the top of his game.

"Gil Stanton," he said, rising as they introduced themselves.

His handshake was firm, in control. All part of the package when you shelled out a thousand dollars an hour for a Park Avenue law firm.

He motioned for them to sit, ordering a round of Perriers when they declined his offer of cold beer.

Stanton followed Jackson's gaze to the eighteenth hole, where the last of the day's foursomes were playing through. "Challenging game out there today. Lotta wind. Tough on a player like me," he said with a pleasant smile.

McManus was pretty sure it was false modesty. "Thank you for meeting with us on short notice."

"No problem. Terrible thing." Stanton looked down at the table's surface of smooth polished wood. "How's Jason's wife?"

"Christina Cardiff?" Working her way through the contents of that mammoth wine cellar would be McManus's best guess. "She's holding up."

"And Tyler, the son?"

"Holding up."

Jackson scraped his feet noisily and looked up from his pad, which was open and ready for business.

Like McManus, Jackson did not care much for lawyers.

"Tell us about your relationship with Jason Cardiff," McManus said, before Stanton got a chance to ask another question of his own.

"My firm has represented the Cardiff family in various business dealings over the years. I took Jason Cardiff on as a client, oh, about fifteen years ago."

About the time Jason could have begun tapping into his trust fund to pay those stratospheric hourly fees, McManus figured. "And how would you characterize the nature of your dealings with him? Were they of a business nature?"

"Yes, they were," Stanton replied.

"And he paid his bills on time?"

"Yup." Stanton shrugged. "He was a good client."

"How did things go night before last, when you met him here for dinner?"

Stanton hesitated.

McManus cut to the chase. "You were one of the last people to see him alive. How did he seem?"

"He seemed okay. It was a quick dinner. I had to leave early, in fact."

The ME's report stated Cardiff's blood alcohol level was 0.18 percent. Sloppy drunk. Plus traces of cocaine and the Ecstasy. "Did he drink a lot, any more than usual?"

"No. Just a glass of wine or two."

McManus believed him. Stanton didn't look like a drinker.

The attorney continued. "But Jason didn't leave when I did. We said good-bye at the table. He headed for the bar." Stanton glanced in that direction. "Arthur's been here every night since I became a member."

The man working the bar, like every bartender worth his salt, looked like a walking billboard for "What Happens in Vegas Stays in Vegas."

At least there was no such thing as bartender-client privilege. McManus gulped his Perrier. "Did Jason Cardiff discuss anything out of the ordinary?"

Stanton was quiet.

"Any problems? Anything he hadn't mentioned before?"

Stanton sipped his Perrier and gave the glass a little shake so the ice shifted. He set the glass down. "Jason came to me a while ago with something I couldn't help him with. I referred him to outside counsel."

"You got a name?"

Stanton's reply changed up the game. "Maurice Gold."

Detectives Jackson and McManus exchanged a Things-Just-Got-Interesting look.

Maurice Gold's number came preprogrammed in the BlackBerry of every trophy wife from Palm Beach to Beverly Hills, and every suburb in between. Gold had made a name for himself by going to the mat for a roster of clients who had included the founder of America's premier cosmetics company, whose wife had discovered his penchant for teenage boys, the heiress to a media empire who claimed her husband forced her to engage in oral sex with the family Shih Tzu, and—it was rumored—drew up the prenup for a now-deceased member of a certain royal family.

Maurice Gold didn't just sling mud. He supplied the dirt.

Gil Stanton drained his Perrier and set the glass down. "That's all I have."

It was plenty.

Christina was in Tyler's room when the phone rang.

She had decided that tonight they would order in pizza, Tyler's favorite, and had gone upstairs to make sure his room was ready for his return.

She hoped, more than anything, he would notice she wasn't drinking.

She wanted to be, for once, the mother he deserved.

Señora Rosa and Marisol had left the room spotless, with fresh linens and pajamas lying out and ready to wear on top of the bedspread.

Christina hadn't been in this room all summer. She looked at the bookshelf, lined with trophies for swimming and soccer and Little League and (her favorite) best chess player in third grade.

In a place of honor on the top shelf was Humpy, an oversized camel that had gone everywhere with Tyler once upon a time. The special thing about the plush toy was its hump, which actually was a secret compartment in the back that opened and closed with a hidden piece of Velcro.

Once upon a time, Humpy had been fat with special things that mattered to a little boy.

These days, Humpy was threadbare thin, missing an eye with its matching fringed eyelash. The toy sat winking down at her like an aging veteran from a forgotten war.

Christina reached for Humpy and squeezed him tight in search of a whiff of Tyler. Not the way he smelled now, on the edge of manhood in ninth grade, but the way he'd smelled when he was her little boy, warm like baking bread and sweet like the yard on a summer's day.

The phone rang, shrill inside the empty house.

Still clutching the threadbare camel, Christina hurried to the guest bedroom to answer.

"Hi, Mom."

The sound of Tyler's voice raised a storm surge of love inside her. "Hi, sweetie. You landed." The connection was too good to be coming from her in-laws' car. She glanced at caller ID. It was a 212 area code. Bullshit. Hackles rose on the back of Christina's neck.

"I'm with Granddad and Grandmère."

Grandmère. An affectation Christina had never liked. Her own grandmother had been Nana. Good enough, she supposed, for a woman who had lived out her final days struggling to raise the granddaughter whose parents had walked out on her.

"We're at the house in town."

"Oh." Christina frowned. "House in town" was

shorthand for the Gilded Age home on Fifth Avenue, built at the same time the Astors and Commodore Vanderbilt were building theirs. "How was the flight?" She was stalling. Why wasn't Tyler in the car right now headed for the Hamptons?

"Okay, I guess. Are you coming in with Aunt Pamela and Uncle Richard?"

Tyler's voice was tight with nerves. Christina's heart ached for him. But she had been married to the Cardiffs long enough to detect a setup when she saw one. "I might," she said, taking care to keep her voice steady.

Her son cut her off, trying to help. "You can ride with them if you don't feel good enough to drive."

The bastards. They were using him for their dirty work. "Yeah, I could. Um, may I speak with your granddad?"

"Okay." Tyler's voice shrank.

As though he already knew she wasn't going to come. Meaning he assumed she was "tired." Code, in his world, for too drunk to leave the house.

"Ty, hold on a sec." Christina struggled to keep her voice neutral for his sake. She clutched Humpy the camel tight to her chest.

There was silence.

"Ty?"

"I'm still here, Mom."

She wanted to tell him she hadn't had a drink in ten days, and that from now on things would be different. They would make a new life now. How do you tell that to a kid? "Ty, I love you." Her voice broke. "More than anybody in the whole, wide world. I'm going to see you really soon, okay?" The rest of the words came out in a squeak. Like when she was drinking. She was kneading Humpy so tight now he was squashed almost flat.

"Yeah, Mom. I love you, too." He sounded like Bambi, lost in the woods.

"Stay strong, Tyler. Your father would want that." It sounded awful, like a cliché from a crummy movie. But it was the best she could come up with. "I'll see you soon."

"Yeah, Mom. Bye."

She had let him down. Like she always did. What was left of her heart cranked through a grinder and spilled out the other end in pulpy little slivers.

Her father-in-law got on. "Christina," he said in his usual controlled tone. "How are you bearing up?"

"What the fuck are you doing with my son?" she wanted to yell. "Fine," she said. Nobody messed with Jason Colbert Cardiff III.

"I'm glad to hear that."

He was oozing sincerity.

"Um, are you driving out here tonight, or should I come in and get Tyler?" Simple enough. But every instinct Christina had told her something bad was about to happen. Her heart began to hammer in her chest.

"There's been a change in plans, Christina."

She frowned. "Oh?"

"Pamela and Richard are driving in with their children . . ."

Her father-in-law was still speaking, but Christina couldn't concentrate. She was hung up on the "change in plans." What the fuck was he talking about?

"I can well imagine you're not up for the drive," he was saying on the other end of the phone.

"Um, excuse me?" Christina gripped the phone in one hand, Humpy in the other.

He continued on smoothly. "Tyler is where he needs to be, where we all need to be, safe and together with family."

"What do you mean? What do you mean?" Christina's voice climbed into the shrill zone, not a good tactic with her father-in-law. She didn't care. "I want to be with my son."

"He's here with us now." A yawning silence opened around those words.

Christina's heart pounded harder. What the fuck did he think he was doing? But she knew the answer to that. "I want to see my son," she repeated, allowing an edge to come through.

"We're staying in town, Christina, because there has been a change." Her father-in-law allowed a note of weariness to creep into his voice. "I have decided it's best we all stay together now at our family home."

Which had stood, stalwart and stern, its gargoyles glaring down their noses at the people of midtown Manhattan for the last hundred years. Like the Cardiffs themselves.

"We need to be a family now, not just for Jason's sake," his voice rose a notch to drown out Christina's protest, "but for Tyler."

"Aren't you coming out here for the funeral?" Christina's voice climbed toward hysteria.

"As I told you, there has been a change." His response was slow and measured, wrapped in a voice like tempered steel.

Jason had once told her he and his sister had never been yelled at when they did something wrong. They had to write essays for their father on behavior that was more befitting of a Cardiff.

"Planning is under way for a memorial," he continued, "to take place next week at Towne Church where, as you know, all Cardiff family memorials are held."

She noticed the words he chose to distance himself from taking responsibility for his actions. "You can't do that," she sputtered. "Jason's memorial is tomorrow, out here in Amagansett."

He went on as though he hadn't heard. "I did want to check the spelling of your grandmother's name for the obituary. It will run in the *Times* on Sunday, with details for visitation at Campbell's on Madison Avenue."

Christina's panic turned to just plain rage. She didn't want the *New York Times* printing their version of Christina's life with Jason. She thought of Nana, who had taken her in and raised her, working extra shifts at a bakery until she was too sick to leave the house. Christina rushed home every day after school, afraid of what she'd find. Feeding Nana soup and praying for a miracle.

But no miracle came.

On her wedding day, with no male relative on hand to give her away, her father-in-law offered a toast in honor of Christina's proud Midwestern heritage.

He butchered Nana's name, which was long and Polish, and everyone laughed.

"You can't do this!" Christina screamed into the phone.

"Christina, our family is grieving. We knew him far longer than you did," her father-in-law replied. "We need closure, and we need to do it our way."

"You can't do this!" Her voice came out in gritty, hysterical spurts. "I want to see my son. Tonight."

Mr. Cardiff allowed his voice to soften. "How are you feeling, Christina?"

She knew what he was getting at. "How dare you?"

But he cut her off. "I've spoken to my daughter. Several times today, in fact, and she's quite upset."

This was too much. "Your daughter is always upset," Christina spat.

His voice dropped a notch, sending shivers down her spine. "We all know this is a difficult time for you."

"I'm fine." She was on the defensive, and she knew it.

"Use this time, Christina." His voice was still fakey soothing. "Sit back, let the dust settle, and work some things out. You can rest assured that Tyler is right where he needs to be."

With them. It was too much. "I want my son back!" Christina pounded the bedside table with her fist.

Her father-in-law's voice dropped lower, menacing. "Use this time to get your affairs in order."

It was not a random choice of words. The muscles in Christina's neck contracted in shame. He should know the way his own son carried on. Christina was about to tell him, but his next words stopped her.

"And keep them out of the tabloids. Such as today's *New York Post*."

"What?" The answer to that question, Christina knew, had everything to do with the English bastard parked at the end of her driveway.

Mr. Cardiff's fakey soothing tone was back. "Just get yourself through this."

This was a role he had been born and bred for, she

thought. Stomping all over people when they were at their weakest. She considered the Wall Street legend of the Cardiff brothers helping early colonists with their cattle trades, and wondered how many Dutch boys got dumped in the harbor with their throats slit.

"Just get yourself through this," he repeated.

She was about to scream that she was going to drive in there and get her son, but the line went dead.

He had already hung up.

Turning left from the Dunes onto Montauk was tricky in rush hour. The road had been widened over the years until it sprawled across four lanes, not counting the so-called suicide lane down the center for turns. Even with the new 30 mph speed limit (which everyone ignored), this section of highway was so primed for fender benders that tow trucks parked here all summer, waiting for new business.

Ben Jackson activated the flashers, hit the siren, and they were out, heading east.

Frank McManus rang Maurice Gold's office in Manhattan. A real human answered, despite the fact it was after six.

Impressive. Frank left a message.

Arthur the bartender had been, per the job requirement, reticent. His answers regarding Jason Cardiff's activities two nights earlier had been of the single-syllable variety. Frank McManus made a mental note to hire him to bartend at the squad's Christmas party.

Arthur gave them a good solid lead as to where Cardiff had gone when he left the Dunes on the night of his death. "Hang Ten."

The up-to-the-minute Southampton night spot that

had gained notoriety when one of its pretty young patrons yelled a not-so-pretty racial slur before ramming her daddy's SUV into the crowd.

Business had skyrocketed since then.

Go figure.

They thanked Arthur and left him polishing glasses.

It was a short ride to Hang Ten.

The massive field that served as parking lot was nearly empty at this hour. A gleaming red Jaguar parked near the front entrance had vanity plates that read, HANG10.

A few battered Fords and Chevys were parked way out back, no doubt owned by staff hoping not to get creamed if there was a repeat of the SUV episode.

The scene at a place like this did not start rocking till eleven, way past Frank McManus's bedtime.

They parked around back and followed a sandy path to the kitchen door, which was propped open with a brick.

Jackson had to pound for a while before they heard a shout from somewhere deep inside the club. "Yeah?"

"Suffolk County Police," Jackson yelled.

Someone pulled the plug on the Bare Naked Ladies.

Quick footsteps approached.

"Can I help you?" A young man skidded to a halt, breathless. His hair was short on the sides and spiked up at the front, like Caesar if he'd caught his finger in a light socket.

The expression on the kid's face when he saw their badges added to the effect.

Despite the fact he looked about twelve years old, Frank guessed by the number of diamond studs lining the kid's ears that the Jag outside belonged to him.

"Ross Middleton. I own the club. Partially," he added hastily. "There are seven of us."

McManus did not imagine Ross Middleton usually spelled this fact out.

The kid's eyes were wide with nervous energy behind flashy white-framed glasses that were about ten sizes too big. "Come in. Can I get you anything?" He ushered them down a hallway into a dark cavernous room that reeked of beer and sour cherries.

The floor was sticky the way floors in bars always were.

"Tell us what you know about this guy." Jackson pulled a photo of Jason Cardiff from his breast pocket.

"That guy who drowned. He came here a lot." The kid looked from McManus to Jackson, relief washing over his face. You could tell he had decided this was going to be easy. They hadn't come to pull permits or check working papers.

Arthur at the Dunes could take a lesson.

"How often?" Jackson flipped open his pad.

"Once a week, maybe more. He had a place out here and a place in the city." The kid shrugged. "Like most people."

Most people who were millionaires. "Except Jason Cardiff wound up dead after a night in your club," McManus pointed out.

The kid pushed his glasses up and rubbed the bridge of his nose.

Those glasses looked heavy.

The kid stopped rubbing his nose and pointed a finger at Jackson, who was taking notes. "He usually took a table in our VIP room."

McManus raised an eyebrow. "Big spender."

"Five hundred to get a table, drinks are extra. Five-hundred-dollar minimum on drinks," the kid said without missing a beat.

McManus blinked. Jackson gave him a look, the kind that said, *Must be nice.*

There was no way Jason Cardiff dropped that kind of money so he could sit and listen to shitty music by himself. "Who was with him?"

The kid hesitated.

McManus leaned in close, dropping his voice into the danger zone. "I understand there's illegal substances being bought and sold here at night, right here on your premises. The DA can shut you down for that, for an indefinite period of time while we look into it."

The kid swallowed. The other six owners were not going to like this, the way he was about to rat out some of their loyal customers to the Man. It was practically flashing in superscript across his forehead.

But the other owners did not have their six collective asses in a sling the way Ross Middleton's was at that moment.

"I can point them out." He pulled off his glasses and knuckled the red spot on his nose. "Come back around ten thirty."

CHAPTER 12

Christina pressed the END CALL button as fury built inside her.

"How dare you?" she screamed at the phone.

But her father-in-law would not hear her. He had hung up.

"Who do you think you are?" she screamed, slamming her fist onto the nightstand in rage.

But Christina knew the answer to that. They were the Cardiffs, the same people who had been telling her what to do since the day they'd first met. Walking all over her as though she didn't matter. She remembered now how they'd gone behind her back to the caterer for her wedding reception, changing the menu items at the last minute.

Christina hadn't realized it till she sat down and took a nibble, taking care not to drop any on her gown. She had been shocked when she tasted veal.

She had ordered chicken.

Jason had shrugged. "They probably got the order screwed up."

But Christina remembered the way her mother-in-law had turned up her nose. "Veal is elegant" was all she had said.

The Cardiffs were not going to do this to her anymore.

Christina would leave now, drive into the city, bang on their door, and not leave until they answered. She would get Tyler and take him home with her where he belonged. Right now.

She'd show them.

Christina set the stuffed camel down and headed off in search of the keys to her car.

What she found was her cache of Grey Goose in the freezer.

"Come on." Dan was impatient now, prowling the living room while I stopped to pee in our downstairs bathroom.

I had heard him talking on his cell phone in short, urgent sentences. I did not realize this at the time, or even when the memory first floated back to me. Only when I replayed the events of that night, over and over, after more time had passed, did I remember that fact. That Dan had stopped to call someone on his cell phone from the living room of our beach house while I used the bathroom.

"C'mon, Christina." Dan's voice echoed through the cavernous great room. The house was empty, with Tyler away and Jason in the city until tomorrow.

"Let's go!" Dan's voice rose on the last syllable, in a way that reminded me of my high-school gym teacher when he urged us to do something we didn't want to do. I laughed, not seeing what the big rush was about, or even why we needed to leave.

There was plenty of vodka, my beverage of choice, right here.

Dan rapped sharply on the bathroom door. "Christina." He pushed the door open a crack.

I stopped laughing.

He pressed his face into the crack. "Come on."

I was pretty drunk, but I didn't appreciate him following me into the bathroom and telling me what to do. I wiped and stood, ready to tell him off, but I got tangled in my panties and lost my footing on the sand I had tracked in. I went down, hitting my cheekbone hard against the counter as I fell.

That cracked me up.

"Bullshit." Dan stepped inside.

I lay on the floor. Try as I might, I could not untangle either my panties from my ankles or my sundress, which was twisted around me like a pretzel. Bits of sand clung to my bare skin.

"You're all fucked up."

Dan was disappointed, I could tell. "You're a fuckin' alcoholic, you know that?"

We were crossing a line, and I knew it. He had never talked to me that way before.

"Get up." He grabbed my arm and yanked. "Get up."

I tried to wrench my arm away, but it was no use.

He was strong. His fingers bit into the soft flesh of my arm.

I had four round bruises there for a week.

He yanked me to my feet with just one hand.

"C'mon, we gotta go." He pulled my panties up and snapped them into place.

I reached one hand out for balance as he pulled my wrap dress into place and cinched the belt. Rough.

I felt really hot all of a sudden. "I change my mind,"

I said. "I don't want to go." But the words came out jumbled.

He grabbed me by the shoulders and spun me around so I faced the door. "Road trip."

"No," I protested. My voice was thick. The act of standing was tough. I was really thirsty. I wanted to stay here, drink a gallon of water, and finish what we started on the beach. Here, in my own bed.

Danny still had me by the shoulders.

I shook my head. "No."

His mouth was set, the muscles in his jaw working, and for a minute, this was not the playful Dan Cunningham I knew. His eyes narrowed.

I was afraid.

He smiled, but it was a fake smile, I could tell.

The look in his eyes did not match that smile.

An eerie little sliver of something like cold water slid down my spine, and I sobered up a bit without realizing it.

I stepped back, away from him.

Danny stepped forward, so close that when he exhaled I had no choice but to breathe it in.

"You're gonna like this." Sticking two of his fingers and his thumb inside his mouth, he rolled his tongue across them until they were wet. Quick as lightning, he slid his hand inside the top of my dress, peeled back my bra, and began rubbing my nipple with his fingers. Hard and then harder.

Heat came on me in a rush, burning me up from the inside out, and I had never felt anything so good in my life, I swear to God. I was crazy for it and I wanted him to fuck me right then and there like I have never wanted it in my life and I begged him.

But Dan just laughed, his mouth relaxing into a real smile now like the Dan I knew and when I think back that was because he knew things were going to work out his way. "C'mon." He pulled his hand away even though I begged him not to stop, and yanked me along by the hand. "This is gonna blow your fuckin' mind."

I followed, so thirsty I made him stop for a bottle of water from the kitchen and I wanted a whole case but he said it would make me pee too much.

He wouldn't even let me drink the bottle till we got in his car.

He said nothing about where we were going, only that I would like it. I was so horny I couldn't wait to get there, sliding around in the passenger seat with my knees up so he could finger-fuck me while he drove.

Familiar landmarks slid by. We took the Springs Fireplace Road across the island, past East Hampton Wines & Liquors (a place I knew well) and into the Springs, past the sign for the Cagramar Farms stable.

"We're going to my place," Dan said.

I had never seen where he lived.

He pulled into a subdivision of small ranch houses packed in close together on small lots. We parked on a rutted blacktop drive next to an aging pickup truck. There were a few more beater cars parked out front.

I remember thinking there must be a party.

Dan put the car into park, his eyes glinting in the light from the dash. "Now you get to see how the other half lives."

B en Jackson and his wife, Cirie, lived with their three young children in a tidy brown ranch with mustard-colored trim in Sayville, a town of working families not far from the squad headquarters in Yaphank.

The house was, like Frank McManus, vintage early sixties with some updates such as new windows and shrubs. Overall, the effect was cozy.

In the warm months, the Jacksons spent most of their family time out back on the cedar deck McManus had helped build. His reward had been more barbecued dinners than he could count.

Cirie and the kids were in the middle of one when McManus and Jackson arrived.

The mist that had been blowing all day had stopped, at least for a little while.

McManus followed Jackson around the side of the house and the aging yews Cirie wanted to replace (the sight of which made McManus's back ache) into the yard.

Cirie was serving dinner on the deck to three "Mini-Me" versions of their old man.

Janice, age three, the only girl and the youngest, dropped her fork and squealed with delight. "Unca Fwank, you hewe!"

Her Elmer Fudd accent got to Frank like it always did, and he tried not to laugh. Ben had told him the speech therapist had advised it was best not to react.

But everyone was laughing a little, so Frank didn't feel so bad, scooping her up when she flung herself at him. "Hello, princess."

Her big brothers, Dale and Drew, piled on their old man. "Daddy's home!"

"You made it." Cirie nosed her way in to give her husband a peck on the cheek. "Lucky for you, I haven't turned off the grill." She smiled at Frank. "Hey, Frank, hope you haven't eaten. It's only hamburgers and hot dogs."

"Hot dogs ah my fay-vuh-wit," Janice announced, and they snickered again.

Cirie turned to her husband. "I thought you said you were working late?"

"I am. We're just here for dinner. We've got one more stop in Southampton, but not till later." Ben Jackson pulled a small brown bag from his pocket with a flourish. "Bought you a present, babe." He pulled out a Bic fire starter and brandished it as though it was a dozen roses.

"Just what I wanted." Cirie grinned. "Look, kids."
The kids stared.

"You missed it, Daddy," Dale piped. He was older, and the man of the house when his father wasn't around. "Mommy started a fire in the kitchen. The smoke detector went off, and we all ran outside."

"I did not start a fire in the kitchen," Cirie protested.

"There's burn marks on the ceiling," Drew yelled.

Cirie rolled her eyes. "There are no burn marks on the ceiling."

"Mommy had to climb on a chair to make the alarm go off," Dale added.

"Mommy started a fire in the kitchen?" Ben let his eyes widen in surprise, which was all the encouragement the kids needed.

All three yelled to get their version heard above the others.

Ben egged them on, asking questions of each in turn, making a show of getting every detail down so they could be sure their father heard the story just right.

They took turns flinging themselves at him while their dinner turned cold.

On the whole, it was a typical dinner at the Jacksons.

Frank McManus looked at Cirie over the din and smiled. "You got the grill going, I see."

Cirie nodded happily. "Pull up a seat, and I'll get you something cold to drink."

Frank did, choosing the place with the least amount of ketchup blobs.

Something bit him.

"How 'bout a Diet Coke?" Cirie was headed inside, yelling at the kids to finish eating.

"Sure," Frank shouted in reply.

Nobody else paid her any mind.

He could already feel goo from the seat of his chair seeping through his pants. Frank McManus leaned back, thinking as he always did that Ben Jackson's place was the one place in the world where he always felt at home.

"So?" Jackson did a half turn.

Smoke from the grill swirled around him.

"I'm thinking a lot about Torres." Frank had called

the squad earlier, using the ancient Princess-line phone on the cluttered desk in a corner of the playroom that served as Jackson's home office.

Their admin ran a background check on the Cardiffs' head landscaper, Roberto Torres.

McManus hadn't had to wait long for the results. "Señor Torres has had some brushes with the law," he said now.

Jackson tipped up the edge of one burger, checked it, and let it drop back down to cook some more.

Frank's mood sank a bit. Jackson always overcooked the burgers. "Buncha small stuff, and a couple of disorderly conducts."

"Really?" The volume of smoke from the grill increased.

Frank resisted the urge to grab the spatula and rescue the burgers. The Jacksons liked their meat well done. "One for resisting arrest."

"Was he drunk?"

It was a good question. "Nope."

Jackson let out a low whistle before, thankfully, turning his attention back to the burgers. "Sounds like our man has a temper."

"That's what I'm thinking." Frank watched as Jackson moved the patties from one spot on the grill to another. To his dismay, he left them cooking and turned back to Frank.

"I don't see how that fits in anywhere."

"Agreed. But there's something." Frank thought back to the warning looks Marisol had exchanged with her aunt. "Definitely something.

Jackson nodded.

The burgers were turning a dark, hockey-puck shade

of brown. Frank couldn't take any more. He got up and walked across to the grill. "Can I give you hand with those?"

Things were heating up later that night when they returned to Hang Ten. The line of cars waiting to get in spilled out onto Montauk Highway.

A threesome of goons, keepers of the red velvet ropes, gave Detectives McManus and Jackson the once-over as they approached.

One of them spoke into the tiny mouthpiece that hung down over his powerful jaw.

"The word," Jackson muttered, "is 'Thunderbird.'"

McManus snorted, even though he knew he had nothing to laugh about. They had picked over the contents of Jackson's closet for their visit to the nightclub.

Of the two, Jackson had fared better, squeezing himself—just barely—into a pair of black denim jeans left over from what his wife termed his Mr. Soave Bolla days when he was single and on the prowl. He topped it off with a T-shirt of black metallic mesh that highlighted the portion of his gut that hung over his belt.

Cirie covered her mouth with her hands at the sight of him, which set the Jackson progeny racing through the house in gales of laughter.

"Hey, you kids, stop!" Ben Jackson used the same tone of voice he used on the job. "Or you will all go to bed right now!"

This only added to the merriment.

Frank McManus didn't fare as well. None of Jackson's hot-young-blood duds were suitable for Frank, who was only an inch shorter than his partner but fourteen years older. And twenty pounds heavier.

In the end, they settled on a surfer-dude look for Frank, using a Hawaiian luau shirt Cirie's father had left in a closet. A pair of flip-flops, one size too big, completed the getup.

Frank allowed Cirie to apply a dollop of hair mousse to his head.

They had been aiming for Charlie Sheen's character on *Two and a Half Men*.

The result more closely resembled Fred Flintstone.

Little Janice fixed Frank with a look that was a dead ringer for her old man's. "Unka Fwank, you come back faw Halloween."

It was too much.

Ben Jackson roared until his metallic-enrobed belly practically fell off.

Cirie laughed until her eyes turned wet with tears.

The boys stopped pelting each other with hair-mousse snowballs and joined in.

"I wasn't hired for my looks, you know," Frank grumbled.

Dale found the camera, and they posed for pictures.

Cirie and the kids waved good-bye from the doorway. "Happy cruising," she called merrily.

Jackson made a hissing noise through his teeth. He threw the Crown Vic into reverse and pulled out.

Getting old is tough, McManus thought.

He was reminded of that fact now, when the Hang Ten bouncers parted the velvet ropes to let them in.

"Enjoy yourselves," one of them called, not bothering to hide the smirk on his face.

Frank wondered whether a high-and-fast left hook would knock that pompous mouthpiece from his face.

Inside, surf-guitar music blared so loud Frank felt his large intestine re-coil itself.

Jackson turned to Frank. "Revels."

Frank responded with the title. ' "Church Key.' "

It had been a monster hit for the Revels in 1961, well before Jackson's birth. Frank gave his partner a nod of approval.

Earlier this afternoon, the place had reeked of stale beer. Now it smelled of the real thing (Southampton W on tap, brewed right up the road at Don Sullivan's Publick House, and that, at least, showed good taste) mixed with a flowery cloud of cologne and sweat hovering above several hundred gyrating young bodies.

Ross Middleton, Boy Owner, stood at the base of a recessed staircase on the far side of the room. He motioned them over, wearing a pair of Flavor Flav rhinestone-studded glasses.

His evening look, Frank decided.

While Jackson took the circuitous route around the edge of the dance floor, Frank plowed right in.

It was like the parting of the Red Sea. Dancers twisted, shook, and shimmied as far away from Detective Frank McManus as they could get.

He couldn't blame it on the department's regulation sport-coat dress code this time.

They followed Middleton upstairs to a small room with windows overlooking the dance floor. Security screens mounted on the opposite wall relayed flickering images from a variety of locations both inside and out.

Once Frank's eyes adjusted to the gloom, the crowd below appeared less chaotic and freewheeling. Patterns emerged. Groups of dancers clustered around an alpha male. Interspersed were dancers in pairs, groups of girls dancing together (a phenomenon that had puzzled Frank since he had attended his first dance in junior high), and even a weirdo or two waltzing solo.

The crowd at the bar was three deep, like any place in the Hamptons.

A line of girls waited to use the bathroom.

An indoor beach-hut stand sold popcorn and hot dogs.

Couples made out in booths and, in a sign that times had changed, some of the kids going at it were boy-on-boy and even girl-on-girl.

High on a huge screen on the opposite wall, Annette Funicello and Frankie Avalon were leading their friends in a soundless Technicolor sing-along from *Beach Blanket Bingo*.

If you liked music loud enough to rattle your porcelain crowns, Hang Ten was the place to be.

The group that caught McManus's attention was positioned along the wall at the entrance to the men's room. At ground level, they would hardly be noticeable.

"Your guys." Ross Middleton pointed. "They're here most nights."

These were not your typical frat boys crammed into an overpriced summer share. No J. Crew, for one thing. If they were first- or second-year associates at a Park Avenue law firm, then it was one that offered free tattoos.

The tallest, who wore a Mets cap in the rally position, was approached by a potential customer as they watched.

After a whispered exchange, the Mets guy led the way into the men's room.

The kid from the dance floor followed, digging for his wallet.

"Looks like steady business," Jackson remarked drily.

Business in which Ross Middleton and his six partners most certainly shared a stake.

In the spirit of cooperation, Middleton began spilling his guts as fast as his boy mouth could form words. "The guy with the Mets cap is Bobby Baldwin. And the guy standing outside the bathroom door right now, the one who's uh—"

"Standing watch?" Frank supplied helpfully.

"Yeah." Middleton kept his gaze steady, aimed down below. "That's Bruce Zachari. I can spell it."

"Good." Ben Jackson flipped open his pad.

"They're both local guys, from around here, both graduated from Westhampton Beach High School," Middleton pointed out.

Like it mattered.

Frank McManus scowled, which had the intended effect of further loosening Ross Middleton's tongue.

The Boy Owner fingered another guy whom, he said, had left the club two nights ago in the company of Jason Cardiff. "Plus another guy who isn't here." He checked his watch. "He moved in on things at the beginning of the summer, and now he's a ringleader. He'll show up. It's still early."

Frank checked his watch. He was usually on the couch by now.

Middleton tapped his finger on the glass excitedly.

Three women had arrived. All blond, the type that could be in an ad for cosmetic surgery.

"That one there, that's Jason Cardiff's girlfriend from

the city, Lisa-something. The one with the big . . ." Middleton's voice trailed off.

But there was no mistaking what he meant.

Lisa was dressed in a skintight white leather miniskirt that didn't leave much to the imagination.

Her friends shimmied in time to the music.

In the next instant, everything changed.

A thundering sound shook the club's floorboards.

"Get ready for the special effects," Middleton murmured.

McManus braced himself.

White lights strobed, throwing the dance floor into bas-relief. The sound system surged impossibly higher into the unmistakable drum intro to "Wipe Out"

Jackson looked at McManus. "Surfaris," he mouthed.

Impressive. McManus gave an approving wink. Another sixties jewel.

A ton of glittering confetti rained down on the crowd, whipping it into a fever pitch.

Lisa threw back her head and let out a war whoop, opening her mouth wide enough to show off her back molars, before launching herself onto the dance floor.

Her Barbie Doll posse followed suit.

Detectives McManus and Jackson exchanged a look.

Everybody grieved in her own way.

"Things will wind down soon." Ross Middleton proceeded to tell them all he knew about Lisa's girlfriends. They showed up for the first time the other night, leaving with Lisa, Jason Cardiff, Mets cap guy, and his cronies. "One of them told my bartender they were on their way to a party at a mansion in East Hampton." Middleton saw something down on the dance floor that made him tap the glass excitedly.

"There. That's the other guy who hung around with Jason Cardiff."

Down below, Hang Ten's latest arrival picked his way through the crowd. He was built like a panther, tall and narrow, with powerful shoulders and biceps you could make out from up here. He wore his dark hair slicked back on the sides and pulled forward on top. Vintage greaser from *West Side Story*.

He was older than the average Hang Ten patron by five years, maybe more. If this was a frat guy home from college for the summer, he was a member of the Alpha Delta San Quentin chapter.

As they watched, he plowed into someone deliberately, causing the guy to spill most of his ten-dollar beer.

The guy whipped around and, when he got an up-close look at Tarzan, backed away.

"That's him," Ross Middleton said. "Daniel Cunningham."

Christina Cardiff's barefoot brunch chef. McManus exchanged a quick glance with his partner.

Cunningham chose that very moment to look up at the one-way mirror high on the wall above his head.

As if he knew.

Their eyes met, and something tugged McManus's gut. He remembered taking his kids to the Atlantis Marine World in Riverhead. A shark had swum up to the floor-to-ceiling glass right in front of Frank and hung there, treading water, staring at him with those lifeless black eyes until everyone around them noticed.

McManus shuddered, grateful now as he had been then for the heavy glass in front of him.

Jackson stopped writing. "So," he said in a low voice.

Which meant Jackson felt it, too. "Is he a local?" McManus asked, knowing the answer.

Ross Middleton shrugged. "I have no idea. He started hanging around at the beginning of the summer, sometimes with Cardiff. Sometimes, not. Popular with the ladies." The Boy Owner pushed his forefingers up under the rhinestone frames and rubbed that sore spot on the bridge of his nose. "That's all I got."

McManus waited.

"He's a rough guy. I mean, I don't know that for a fact, but the bartenders heard some things. I don't know." Middleton spoke rapidly now, his words tumbling out.

You could tell he didn't want to go down on record as having said Daniel Cunningham was trouble. Even though he was.

"Look, that's about all I know." Spoken in the pleading tone of someone who hoped that Detectives McManus and Jackson would get the hell out before his clients realized that cops had moved in.

That hope just wasn't realistic.

A short time later, Detectives McManus and Jackson had set up shop in a storage area in the club's basement, with McManus taking statements on two old metal chairs they dragged into a dark corner surrounded by shelves of liquor and paper supplies, while Ben Jackson stood watch over the group they had corralled waiting in the dim hallway.

Like a shepherd tending a jittery flock of sheep.

The girls were haughtiest, which was not surprising since Frank suspected they weren't guilty of much of anything.

The thinner of the two Barbie-Doll types went so far

as to suggest she wanted to wait for her attorney before answering their questions.

City girl. "Fine," McManus replied. "Call him, tell him to drive out to Yaphank and wait there. We should get there by"—he checked his watch—"oh, say, two or three in the morning, latest." Enough to run up a thousand-dollar tab, easy. "Could be later," he added, "depending on how much cooperation we get here."

Sounds from the dance floor thundered overhead.

The girl rolled her eyes. "Okay. We work together at Brenner & Colt in the city."

It was a big PR firm.

She shrugged. "We're friends. Lisa found a place in Montauk, and we went in on it for a couple weeks."

The second girl told a similar version, stumbling when McManus asked how they could afford a place in Montauk on an AE's salary. She chewed her pink-glossed lips. "I'm bad with numbers."

Lisa, when it was her turn, aimed for something closer to the truth.

"We got it for free," she said coolly. "Friend of my uncle's."

"Must be nice to have friends with money," McManus remarked, making a mental note to keep his daughter out of clubs until she turned thirty. "What's his name?"

"I don't remember."

"What's your uncle's name?"

Lisa shrugged her perfectly tanned shoulders. "I'd have to look that up when I get home and get back to you."

McManus cut to the chase. "How well did you know Jason Cardiff?"

Lisa blinked. "I don't know." She twisted one of her heavy diamond-stud earrings.

The studs looked like platinum. Impressive on an account executive's salary.

"Did you know him well enough to be invited to parties at his house?"

Lisa recrossed her smooth legs, gave the diamond post in her ear another half turn. "Sometimes."

McManus stared. "Was his wife at any of the parties you attended?"

"I can't remember."

If she twisted that diamond stud any harder, Frank thought, her earlobe would twist right off. "You were at the Cardiffs' two nights ago, when Jason drowned. Is that correct?"

She said nothing.

She was, McManus reflected, the perfect girlfriend for a married guy. "It was quite a way to go, drowning all alone in his own pool."

That shook things loose a bit.

Lisa allowed her blue eyes to flutter shut and sank back against the back of her folding chair.

"Was he okay when you left?"

She shrugged again, not opening her eyes. "He'd been partying a lot, but he was okay."

McManus waited.

Lisa gave her blond head a tiny shake, opened her eyes, and gave a small sniff. "We argued, sort of, you know? And I left with my friends. That's it."

McManus watched her. "How'd you hear about his death?"

She sighed. "I heard it on the news, like everyone else." She sighed again. "I tried to call him the next morning."

Twice, according to Jason Cardiff's phone records. Which was two times more than his wife. "But you got no answer," McManus said, stating the obvious.

Lisa's tanned shoulders heaved a little bit. "That wasn't so strange. The way we had it set up, he called me."

It made sense. McManus nodded. "Did you meet him sometimes in the city?"

She nodded. "It was no big deal with us." She pressed the tips of her manicured fingers into the flesh beneath her eyes, and Frank saw for the first time that she was trying not to cry. "It was just, you know, a casual fling."

"How often did you see him?"

"Not often. Maybe once or twice a month. We'd meet at my place in the city when his wife was out here, you know, or sometimes I'd meet him out here if she was in the city."

And maybe Cardiff would take out a lease on a place in Montauk so Lisa was handy while his wife was safely tucked away in rehab for sixty days.

"Was it serious with you two?"

"No." Lisa tossed her highlighted mane from side to side, giving her nose a dainty swipe with an index finger. "There was nothing between us. Not really, besides you-know-what," she said delicately.

By the looks of things, Jason Cardiff had been getting himself some very good and righteous you-know-what. "How'd you meet?"

If he'd thought about it, Jason Cardiff could have pinpointed the moment that ended his marriage.

A light snow was tying things up on Central Park South. Rush-hour traffic crept along Fifth slower than usual, thanks to the weather. Horns blared.

Jason Cardiff, freshly showered after his workout, stood in the lobby of New York's most elite private club. Weighing his options. He wished he had thought to reserve a car. There was no point calling for a limo now that it was snowing, even if his name was Cardiff.

"Good evening, Mr. Cardiff." Bailey, the club's doorman, bounded into the lobby. "Wonderful weather we're having, sir. Shall I find you a cab?"

"Only if you're hiding one in your pocket," Jason cracked.

Bailey laughed his booming laugh until the snow shook from his epaulets.

Job requirement, Jason thought. "Thanks anyway." He checked his watch. If he started walking now, he'd get there in time to grab a drink before dinner. He pulled up the collar of his Paul Stuart coat. "I'll walk."

Bailey frowned. "Where are you headed this evening, Mr. Cardiff?"

"Up Fifth," Jason said, giving the name of the foundation named for his great-great-uncle that was located twenty blocks north.

"Have you got an umbrella, Mr. Cardiff?" Without waiting for an answer, the doorman handed Jason an oversized canvas umbrella that bore the club logo. "Take mine, sir, I insist."

"Good man, Bailey." Jason handed the man a twenty and headed into the night. It wouldn't look good if he was late to his uncle's awards ceremony for work he'd done to establish a center in the South Bronx for children with special needs. The mayor was scheduled to speak, followed by a young senator who was a likely GOP nominee for the US presidency.

The reception was in full swing when Jason arrived. Lights blazed inside the limestone town house that had been constructed when the Central Park skyline was level except for the improbable new high-rise that had been dubbed The Dakota for its outrageous location so far from the center of commerce.

The giant lobby chandelier, built in County Waterford and shipped from Ireland, glittered powerfully, its light spilling outside onto the red-carpeted sidewalk, dry even tonight thanks to heating elements embedded in the concrete.

Inside, great-great-uncle Stuart Cardiff kept a stern eye on the proceedings from his perch in a giant gilt frame hanging at the apex of the town house's famous twin curving staircases.

Liveried footmen rushed across the marble foyer to take Jason's overcoat and umbrella from him. They had known Jason since he was a little boy, a fact neither of them would dare mention. "Your parents are seated with the mayor, along with your sister and her husband, at the first table, sir. When you are ready, I will announce you."

Jason nodded. "Very good."

"Will Mrs. Cardiff join you, sir?"

But Jason Cardiff was preoccupied, staring at the press table that had been set up across the large foyer. Specifically, at the young woman who was working it.

The footman repeated his question.

Jason Cardiff frowned. "My wife's not coming."

"Very good, sir. We will rearrange the head table accordingly."

Jason turned his attention back to the press table.

The blonde with the clipboard bent over, revealing the outlines of a nice ass.

She glanced up, caught Jason watching, and smiled. She leaned lower, giving him a good view of the contents of her push-up bra.

Jason Cardiff crossed the foyer in a few long strides while the blonde held her pose, tits and all. His smile broadened. It was going to be a good night.

Giggling, the blonde straightened up, clipboard forgotten. She looked him over, letting her gaze linger at his crotch. "Sorry," she said sweetly. "The press seats are all taken."

Jason's dinner jacket had been fitted to his body and hand-sewn by the lead designer at a workshop in Milan. Not your average working journalist's gear, and they both knew it. Jason played along. "I need to make a call."

"This is a private affair, sir." She flicked her hair extensions behind one shoulder, releasing a burst of perfume that smelled like figs.

Jason breathed in deep. "Can I borrow yours?" He hitched the waistband of his trousers and, while his gaze flickered up and down her tight little business suit, he used one hand to shift his balls.

She caught it. "Borrow my . . . what?" She let her head sort of loll back on her neck a bit and laughed.

He could see the points of her nipples pushing through the thin fabric of her suit. Leaning forward so he was halfway across her check-in table, he stared pointedly at her chest. Jason Cardiff licked his lips. "It all looks good."

She giggled some more and was about to say something but changed her mind.

Jason heard the rat-a-tat of dainty footsteps moving fast, making straight for him.

"Jason! There you are."

His little sister, Pamela Cardiff Lofting, launched herself at him like he was still nine years old and she was seven. She didn't so much as glance at the blonde. "Kiss, kiss." She offered her cheek. "Do you like the dress? It's a Herrera."

"Bunny, you look great," he murmured, using her childhood nickname. He barely brushed his cheek with hers so as not to muss her makeup, which she got professionally done for nights like this.

"Thank God you're here," she whispered, wheeling him toward the entrance to the grand hall. "I'm between your empty seat and the senator, who's a complete bore." She pressed one dainty hand to her mouth in a faux-yawn. "Daddy's not on till dessert."

Jason gave one last glance over his shoulder at the blonde, who blew him a kiss. He felt his hard-on come back for an encore.

Pamela was chattering on. "Fair warning: Maman's in a snit."

Maman was their pet name for their mother. *"Comment ça va?"* But Jason already knew.

"Your other half called a while ago. She's a no-show." Pamela didn't bother looking to gauge his reaction. She was busy fussing at a strand of hair in the gilt-framed mirror.

The footmen waited for Jason's signal to pull open the oak doors that had been hand carved in Florence more than a century ago. Latecomers, as a rule, would not be announced after the Cardiffs had been seated. The arrival of more Cardiffs was the exception to that rule.

"Too bad," Jason commented. In fact, it was great news. He turned once more and winked at the PR tart.

She winked back.

Pamela pretended not to notice. She hated Jason's wife. "Let's do this." She gave Jason's arm a squeeze.

The footmen threw open the doors, and a hush fell over the dining room as Jason and his sister made their entrance.

Inside, another liveried man had been waiting. He drew in a deep breath before bellowing their introduction. "Presenting Mister Jason Cardiff of the city of New York, and his sister, Mrs. Pamela Cardiff Lofting, also of the city of New York."

The pair stood, smiling, on the very same spot where they had been presented countless times before.

"Whatever you do," Pamela whispered, "don't get the senator started on standardized tests for children."

"Got it." Jason Cardiff was grateful that his wife was a no-show.

He left dinner at his first opportunity, spending the remainder of the night in the Helmsley, watching porn while the blond PR girl named Lisa sucked his dick.

CHAPTER 1

The pounding bass and laughter from the dance floor vibrated down into the basement of Hang Ten, reminding Frank McManus of something he'd learned on his honeymoon during a tour of Alcatraz. The inmates had been tormented by the sounds of life going on without them across San Francisco Bay. If the wind was right, they could smell chocolate from the Ghirardelli factory.

The young man sitting on the folding chair had the wistful look about him that those inmates must have had. He swallowed for the tenth time, fingering the Mets cap he had removed in a fit of nervous energy.

The spot on the top of his head where his hair was thinning was now clearly visible.

Bobby Baldwin cleared his throat. "That was the first time and only time I ever went to Jason Cardiff's house." He shook his head. "Just my luck the guy winds up dead, right?"

"It could always get worse." McManus let that statement hang while Baldwin attempted to twirl his Mets cap on one finger. Baldwin fumbled, and the cap fell.

Someone should tell the kid about body language. "How well did you know him?"

"Not too much, you know, just to say hello."

Lie. "You're a friendly guy," McManus remarked in a tight voice.

The kid cracked a sarcastic grin before thinking better of it. "I guess."

McManus shifted forward, quick as lightning, quick enough to make Bobby Baldwin flinch. "Helps to meet new people in your line of work, doesn't it?"

Bobby Baldwin said nothing, swallowing so his Adam's apple rose high on his throat before dropping again.

Keeping his voice tight and low, McManus kept his face close to the kid's. "I know that when I get back to my office in Yaphank and turn on my computer and look in my database, your name will pop up. And when it does, I will know in two seconds how much time you'll spend in prison, based on your priors, if we go after you for selling illegal substances." He waited.

It was a bluff, but it worked.

Bobby Baldwin took the bait, his eyes wet with tears. He swallowed audibly. "I swear, I didn't know Cardiff. I dealt with someone else who made the calls for him."

"Who was that?"

"Some asshole, Daniel Cunningham." Bobby Baldwin was bitter. "And I'll betcha it's a fake name."

McManus was in complete agreement on that score. "Did Cunningham do a lot of buying for Jason Cardiff?"

Baldwin nodded. "Fair amount."

"Like what?"

Baldwin blew a short, derisive breath out through his nose. "Cardiff was a regular garbage can, man. He wanted anything. Pot. Coke. Chicks go for that shit, keeps the weight off." He paused. "He was into E."

Ecstasy.

"Cardiff was a steady customer," McManus observed.

Bobby Baldwin shrugged. "I guess."

"He invited you back to his place the other night?"

"No way, man." Baldwin glared.

The kid knew what McManus was getting at. Ecstasy was known for inspiring users to screw anything that moved. A regular Love Potion Number Nine.

"I'm not into that shit, man." Bobby Baldwin scowled.

"Was Cardiff?"

"Probably." Baldwin shrugged. "Guy was a freak, if you ask me."

Baldwin seemed sincere. "So how did you wind up at the Cardiff place two nights ago?"

"We got invited by one of those girls." Baldwin shook his head, balling the Mets cap with his fist. "I wish I had never laid eyes on them. That chick Lisa and her friends, you know who I mean?" He glanced at McManus, who nodded.

"Supposedly, Cardiff rented a place for her out in Montauk while his wife's in rehab or some shit. Must be nice, huh?" Baldwin paused.

Probably calculating how long it would take to square away that kind of money on a petty dealer's salary. Dream on, McManus thought. "So, Lisa told you all this?"

"That bitch wouldn't give me the time of day." Baldwin spat. "She's stuck-up. She was all over Cardiff, moving in to be wife number two. Acting like she already was, if you ask me. Her friends weren't so bad, though. One of them was kind of nice." He stopped, embarrassed to talk about a girl he had a crush on.

McManus waited.

"The one was okay, the blonde." He stopped. "The bigger of the other two, I mean, 'cause they're all blond. Coulda been triplets, you know?"

McManus did know.

"Anyway, the kind of chubbier one talked to me a little. We danced." He shrugged. "She told me about Jason Cardiff dating her friend, Lisa, how he has a big mansion out in East Hampton. Guy's got serious bucks." He studied his Mets cap. "Guys like that, they don't even have to try. Chicks are all over guys like that."

"So, he'd come out here and invite people to parties back at his place?"

"Sometimes. Guess he liked to show off his mansion, you know?" Bobby Baldwin's voice was soaked through with bitterness.

"And that's what he did night before last, invited you back to his place so he could show off?"

"Pretty much." Bobby Baldwin shrugged, stared sullenly down at his Mets cap.

"Nothing out of the ordinary happened?" McManus let his skepticism show.

"Nope."

"Just some friends getting together by the pool?"

Bobby Baldwin twisted his Mets cap some more. "That's right."

Two nights earlier, the one that would become his last on earth, Jason Cardiff was tired. The late-night scene at Hang Ten was beginning to bore him. He'd put in a half day at work in his office on lower Broadway that morning, and was now feeling every bit of the fifteen-year age difference that separated him from Lisa and her friends.

His sister Pamela had called his office that morning, inviting him to a barbecue at their place in Southampton over the weekend. It was, in unspoken terms, something she would not have done if Christina had been with him. "Richard is doing some kind of fishing rodeo with the boys for charity. We're having people over after. Nothing fancy, just friends from Southampton Bathing Corporation."

The über-WASPy beach club Jason's family belonged to. Jason and Christina had applied when they first bought out here. Jason had gotten admitted for membership. Christina had not.

Jason flashed back to blind dates Pamela had arranged with her sorority sisters from Wellesley, right up to the weekend before his wedding. He laughed now. "I'll see." Lisa was bringing two friends out with her for the weekend at the place he'd rented for her in Montauk. She had assured him they could look after themselves or join in the fun if that was what Jason wanted. The place had a hot tub.

Jason liked the sound of that.

His sister's voice took on a note of concern. "Don't tell me you're going to rattle around in that house on your own this Saturday night?"

He'd told his family the truth—that Christina had gone away to rehab.

Jason's mother absorbed the news in the kind of silence that made you wonder about symptoms for stroke.

His father shook his head. "I pray Tyler doesn't find out."

Jason didn't point out that Tyler had been bringing his mother ice chips in bed since preschool.

In the end, Jason told his sister he'd let her know about the weekend.

He didn't live to make that call.

Jason Cardiff drove out to East Hampton alone in late morning, making plans to hook up later that night with Lisa and her friends. He spent Wednesday afternoon lying by his pool checking e-mails.

He showered and changed for an early dinner at the Dunes with his attorney, Gil Stanton.

"How are things going for Christina?" Gil Stanton asked in a voice that was, as usual, low and discreet. "Out there?"

Meaning "out there in rehab," Christina's latest "stunt." The timing was terrible, considering Jason was preparing to sue for divorce. He was fed up with his wife, drunk or sober. Jason shrugged. "No news is good news. I mean, what the fuck." He shook his head. "I don't give a shit what she does anymore."

Gil Stanton was an elegant man, a gentleman's gentleman. Harvard undergrad, followed by Harvard Law. And a roster of clients whose names came right from the Social Register, including but not limited to, the Cardiff family.

If Gil Stanton was of the opinion that Jason Cardiff IV was a spoiled and cruder version of Jason Cardiff III, whom Stanton represented and held in high esteem, he had always been careful to hide that fact. He concentrated on his plate of seared tuna, the specialty of the day. "Has Maurice Gold been helpful?"

Jason brightened. "Gold's a genius." He was about to say more, but Gil Stanton stopped him with a warning look.

A waiter approached, asking if their entrées had been prepared to their liking.

Without giving the waiter a glance, both men assured him they were.

Gil Stanton waited till they were alone. "Maurice Gold is a creative thinker."

Jason Cardiff chewed through a mouthful of filet mignon. "He found a way around my prenup."

"Good." Stanton swallowed his tuna and dabbed at his lips before making a reply. "I never liked that prenup. As I recall, she's entitled to thirty percent of your assets after ten years. More as time goes on."

"Yeah." Jason's jaw tightened. "We've been married almost sixteen years."

"You'd have been better off to marry Christina in her home state of Michigan, which I advised at the time," Gil Stanton pointed out.

They had discussed it before. "Uh-huh." Jason made a quick, deep cut into his beef.

"What's done is done," Gil Stanton added quickly. "Maurice Gold is the right man to correct mistakes of the past."

"True." Jason Cardiff's lips curled into a smile. "He came up with a bold plan. It doesn't matter what Christina does now. Her free ride is about to end."

They parted ways after dinner on what was to become Jason's final night.

Lisa called later from her friend's borrowed car.

Jason heard giggling in the background.

"We're heading east on Montauk with the windows down," Lisa trilled. "Your baby wants to go dancing."

Jason agreed to meet them at Hang Ten.

He placed a call to Dan Cunningham, his "go-to" man in the Hamptons, and placed his order for the night.

And now here he was, bored with the view from his private booth, which the owners kept ready in case he decided to drop in. One of them, the kid with the goofy glasses, boasted they'd turned away Lindsay Lohan's mother to hold the booth for him. Lisa had practically wet herself.

Money talked in this world, and Jason Cardiff liked what it said.

He checked his Rolex. A few minutes to eleven. He yawned.

Lisa was dancing with her two friends.

He couldn't remember their names. They both had big tits. One of them had a horsey laugh.

They were dancing right in front of Jason's table now, rubbing up against each other.

Jason Cardiff knew he was living out the wet dream of every guy in this place. But he was bored. Downing the remains of his Bacardi and soda, he raised one suntanned hand in the air and snapped his fingers.

Lisa rushed over.

The other two kept gyrating for his benefit.

"What, baby?" She nuzzled him.

Jason stood, watching Lisa's friends dry-hump one another.

"Let's go," Jason said.

"Let's go to your house and have a pool party." Lisa had a tendency to whine.

Jason scowled. They had done lines of coke in the booth a while ago, but the effects were wearing off. He shook his head. "I got business to take care of."

Dan Cunningham watched from across the dance floor. Ready, Jason knew, to supply whatever Jason required. And waiting to be paid for services already rendered.

"Please," Lisa said in her little girl voice.

It was irritating.

The girls on the dance floor were still at it. When the horsey one saw Jason glance their way, she put her hand up the other girl's skirt.

"Please." Lisa flicked her tongue in Jason's ear. "I told them about your house, how big it is." She rubbed her hand on Jason's arm. "They really want to swim in the pool."

Jason pulled his arm away, exasperated. "Okay," he snapped, swiping at his ear. "Just quit whining."

Lisa rode in the coupe with him.

Her friends rode in their borrowed car.

Dan Cunningham followed in his car.

Zachari and Baldwin rode in a fourth car.

A short time later, they held their own private rave on Jonah's Path.

The underwater lighting system for the pool pulsed on and off in time to the music.

Dan Cunningham tended bar, serving up drinks with a side of Ecstasy.

The girls took turns doing a striptease on the diving board.

Somewhere in the darkness, Jason heard the shrill barking of his neighbor's dog.

He turned up the volume to drown out the sound.

*   *   *

Detectives McManus and Jackson held off questioning Daniel Cunningham until last.

He sat in stony silence, looking too big for the battered metal folding chair.

Frank McManus watched him. Everyone he came across in his line of work was having a bad day, to put it mildly. The men and women he questioned had just stepped in a pile of shit the size of Texas, and most times they reeked of it.

Not this guy. Daniel Cunningham was not giving anything away, not so much as a twitch of his arms, which were the size and shape of Dearborn hams (bone-in), to his eyes, which held as much warmth as wrought iron.

A true sociopath. McManus kept his right hand in the ready position above his gun belt.

Ben Jackson stood, arms akimbo, just behind McManus's chair. Blocking Cunningham's path to the door.

If he was tired of standing, Jackson didn't show it. On the contrary, his wide jaw was working, and he appeared to be fighting the impulse to rip the veins from Cunningham's thick tree stump of a neck.

The club upstairs was quiet, the sound system off. Everyone had gone home, except Ross Middleton, upstairs closing the till. His responsibilities as one-seventh owner of Hang Ten included the risky job of counting cash and closing up.

Jackson and McManus were finished taking statements from the others, who had gone home. Bobby Baldwin and Bruce Zachari, Lisa and her friends, racing up the stairs so fast one of them tripped and nearly tumbled back down.

Which left Daniel Cunningham to face the law alone. "I told you, we partied a little and went home."

"Just an ordinary night," McManus said.

Jackson shifted his stance, which made a scratching noise on the bare concrete cellar floor.

Cunningham shrugged. "Pretty much."

"Except Jason Cardiff wound up dead."

Dan Cunningham stared at a spot on the shelf near McManus's head. "Too bad."

"Another customer bites the dust," Jackson remarked softly.

It begged the question that this sort of thing happened a lot in Cunningham's sphere.

Cunningham did not so much as glance Jackson's way. "It's late," McManus observed. "We're all tired." It was as close to the good cop routine as Cunningham was going to get. "Let's finish up, so we can all go home and call it a night."

Cunningham lifted an eyebrow. Nothing else moved on his stone face.

Waiting to see what, if anything, would be put on the table. Frank didn't need his Spidey sense to tell him this was a guy with prior convictions, who knew the value of cutting a deal. "You reside in the Springs?"

Cunningham nodded. The Springs was located north of East Hampton along the Island's South Fork, a modest neighborhood of aging ranches rented out each summer to the migrant workers from Ecuador, the Dominican Republic, and Guatemala, who cleaned houses, cleared tables, and harvested the vineyards.

"You spend the winter months in Florida?"

Cunningham gave another tight nod, staring straight ahead.

"And your primary occupation is painting houses?"

"Plastering," Cunningham corrected him in a sullen tone. "I do high-end restoration. All custom jobs."

Jackson spoke. "That's what you did for the Cardiffs, a custom job?"

Cunningham shrugged, not bothering to take the bait.

McManus watched him. "No trouble with the law, Mr. Cunningham, is that correct?"

This time there was a tiny pause.

Cunningham gave a tight nod. "That's right."

Lie. McManus and Jackson looked at each other.

"Just some unpaid parking violations, according to what you've told us," McManus said. "That's all we'll see when we run your name through our nationwide database, Mr. Cunningham. Is that correct?"

"Yeah."

Jackson and McManus exchanged another "my ass" look.

The hard steel of the folding chair was causing McManus's back to stiffen up. He changed position and leaned forward. "And you were subcontracted to do some plaster repair at the Cardiff home back in early spring, is that correct?"

"Correct," Cunningham replied.

"You completed that work to the satisfaction of Mr. and Mrs. Cardiff?"

A flicker of something tripped across the sharp planes of Daniel Cunningham's face. Blink and you'd miss it.

McManus did not blink.

"Right," came Cunningham's reply.

"And you finished that work, you said, about a month ago? Is that right?"

"Right."

"And after that, you went on to work at other locations and undertook other jobs?"

Daniel Cunningham's powerful shoulders hiked in a small shrug. "Yeah."

"You were paid, and that was the extent of your financial dealings with Mr. Jason Cardiff?"

There it was again. That flicker on Cunningham's face. He swallowed. "Right."

Tsk, tsk, another whopper. McManus allowed his voice to turn sharp as a saw blade. "What about the drug deals you arranged, up to and including the night of Mr. Cardiff's death?"

Daniel Cunningham stared straight ahead.

The basement was so quiet you could practically hear the boards of the dance floor settling overhead.

A stray mosquito must have worked its way inside and landed on Jackson's arm because he slapped it. Hard.

It was enough to make McManus's gun hand twitch.

This time Cunningham flinched.

"Give us a break, Dan," McManus said softly. "Bobby Baldwin already gave you up."

Cunningham jutted his chin the way McManus's son did when he was young, after he'd been caught doing something wrong. "I wouldn't know about that."

Lie number three. McManus was grateful for every time he'd ever put his son in a time-out. Spare the rod and spoil the child, he thought. The proof was sitting right in front of him.

Jackson leaned over and propped his hands on his knees.

He was a big man, and when he did that, it had the effect of lowering his face, along with his massive shoulders, down to Cunningham's eye level. He hung there, like some bogeyman and when he spoke the tone in his voice left no doubt that it was a role he could play. "We have you on dealing." Jackson paused to let that sink in. "We'll get you on more, much more."

"Like sleeping with Jason Cardiff's wife." A mosquito whined, zeroing in on McManus's neck. He swatted it a moment too late.

The slapping sound bounced around in the small space.

The bite was worth it, because this time Cunningham twitched.

"I don't know what you're talking about." Cunningham shifted around, so the folding chair let out a metal cracking sound.

"You were at Cardiff's house the night he died," McManus pointed out. "You procured drugs for him. You have a known record of trouble with the law. You were sleeping with his wife. And you expect us to believe you had nothing to do with it?" McManus let incredulity show in his voice.

Cunningham blinked.

Jackson's voice was a low growl. "Why in hell should we think you left when everyone else did?"

Daniel Cunningham's jaw was working hard now.

It was enough to give Frank McManus his second wind. He loved his job, he really did.

"There were other people there, man," Cunningham burst. "Ask them."

"One's dead, so he ain't talking," Jackson said softly, leaning in closer to Cunningham, so his big frame was well inside Cunningham's zone of personal space.

Blocking Cunningham's light.

"That leaves five. We talked to them," McManus pointed out. "Now we're talking to you."

"We just hung out." Cunningham swallowed. "I left with everyone else."

McManus let out a long breath to give the impression of a weariness he did not feel. "So, you did some work for the man, a multimillionaire, who gets to like you so much he invites you back to his house?"

"Yeah." An arrogant little smile formed on Cunningham's lips.

As sociopaths went, this guy rated right up there with O.J. "Two nights ago, he has you over for a party," McManus stressed the word "party" so it sounded ridiculous, out of place. "And he winds up floating facedown in his pool with enough drugs in his belly to put him under." McManus's version of events had the intended effect.

The smile faded from Cunningham's face.

"You scored drugs for him all summer, we hear you were doing his wife," McManus continued, "you were one of the last people to see him alive, and you expect us to believe Cardiff's death was an accident?"

Jackson stood up, shifting his weight from one foot to the other, like a bull waiting to be released into the ring.

"That's right." Despite the damp cool air of the basement, a thin sheen of sweat was forming on Daniel Cunningham's face.

"I doubt it, bro," Jackson said softly.

"I'm telling you." At last, Cunningham's voice had lost its Joe Cool edge. "I had a few beers by the pool and went home. That's all."

*   *   *

The night was turning out okay. Jason's headache was gone, thanks to the Tylenol he'd washed down with champagne and the premium-grade cocaine Dan Cunningham had cut into lines on the glass-topped table inside the pool house.

Jason didn't want to do more if he could avoid it. Coke gave him rubber dick.

Things were going swimmingly in the shallow end of the pool, where all three girls were going at each other.

"Jason, come on." They took turns calling his name.

Bobby Baldwin and his friend tried to pile on and were rebuffed. One of them disappeared into the bathroom, probably to jerk off.

Dan Cunningham had better luck, sliding off his jockey shorts to reveal what had to be the world's biggest cock.

The girls tittered nervously while Jason rose to his feet, interested now.

Dan Cunningham looked at Jason and smiled. He stood on the top step in the shallow end, fondling himself. He took a step down.

The girls squealed.

Bobby Baldwin at the other end of the patio grew quiet.

Cunningham lowered himself into the pool and waded over to Lisa.

Jason Cardiff's girl.

Lisa stopped giggling.

She glanced at Jason, uneasy now.

A silence hung over the pool.

Dan Cunningham glanced at Jason.

Jason nodded.

Dan Cunningham smiled. Without missing a beat, he reached down and grabbed Lisa by the chin.

She gave a little shriek. "Hey."

Cunningham tapped her on the cheek with two of his thick fingers, hard.

"What?" Lisa frowned, tried to get up.

The other girls were quiet.

Cunningham grabbed her firmly under the chin and yanked her mouth around to his cock.

Lisa opened her mouth to protest but all she got was a mouthful of Dan Cunningham's dick.

Jason Cardiff grabbed his crotch and crossed the steps to the edge of the pool, where he dropped his swim trunks.

The two girls smiled nervously.

Daniel Cunningham smiled.

Even Bobby Baldwin and his friend, back now from the john, were smiling. Waiting for a show.

The only person not smiling was Lisa. She bared her lips and gasped for air.

Jason Cardiff stroked himself while the girls frolicked, vying for his attention.

But Dan Cunningham was the one Jason watched as he teased his erection.

Dan Cunningham chuckled softly.

Jason Cardiff stepped swiftly down into the pool and positioned himself at Lisa's ass.

Dan Cunningham rocked up and down on the balls of his feet, pulsing slowly in and out of Lisa's mouth.

Jason Cardiff, panting now with excitement, dropped low.

Lisa managed to give off a squeal of protest that was cut short when Dan Cunningham squeezed her jaw with his fist. Only the muscles in his forearm moved, nothing more. "Hold still," he ordered.

Jason Cardiff mounted Lisa from behind.

Lisa's eyes bulged so the whites showed. She squirmed.

Jason Cardiff slapped her. Hard.

Dan Cunningham gave another little chuckle, his eyes never leaving Jason's.

Jason eased himself in.

Now Lisa was holding very still.

Jason pumped faster and deeper as his excitement grew.

Lisa gasped with pain.

Her friends looked away, scared.

The pool was quiet now, except for small splashes and grunting sounds from the two men.

Bottles of Grey Goose were lined up in the freezer like soldiers ready for battle.

"No!"

Christina slammed the freezer door shut.

The sound echoed hollowly around the empty kitchen.

She had never felt so alone in her life.

The humming sound inside Christina's brain grew louder.

In the living room, the answering machine picked up. The phone had been ringing all afternoon and into the night.

There had been calls from TMZ and The Insider. Now it was a reporter from the *New York Post*, seeking comment about her husband's death.

Christina stuck her fingers in her ear and slid down the counter till she came to rest on the floor.

The freezer beckoned from six feet away.

"No," she murmured. "No."

"Everything is okay the way it is," Matt had told her earlier.

Christina tried desperately to remember how good it felt to believe that, but she couldn't muster her faith again now no matter how hard she tried.

There had been calls from the rehab in Minnesota. Peter, her counselor, reminding her to take it one day at a time.

A message from Sylphan, her roommate from rehab. "This whole thing sucks. Big-time," the young girl said. "Look on the bright side. You don't have to be nice to anybody or even wash your hair if you don't feel like it. Nobody's going to expect you to act normal anyway. You can sit around in pajamas all day, and nobody will stop you."

Christina smiled. The rest of Sylphan's message pierced through to the center of Christina's heart.

"I've been through some tough times myself." Sylphan's voice, so young and girlish, combined with the understatement of her words to bring tears to Christina's eyes. "Just know that no matter what, Christina, we're all here for you. I can't say I can truly relate to exactly what you're going through, but there were times when I hurt so bad, I didn't want to live." Sylphan's voice broke, and there was a pause while she collected herself. "Just hang on," she continued. "We're all on your side, thinking about you. Call me anytime you need a shoulder to cry on."

"I want to be you when I grow up," Christina whispered. She would save that message.

There were a couple of more messages from patients in rehab, wishing her well and telling her to hang in there. Don't drink and go to meetings.

Not a word from her in-laws.

She was angry, angry and ashamed that her in-laws were treating her as though she was a criminal.

She should call someone. Lois or Peter or Sylphan or Matt. But she was too embarrassed to ask for help.

The humming noise inside her head grew worse.

A drink would help.

The freezer was right there, within arm's reach.

She couldn't stay here.

Christina stood, went to the living room, and picked up the phone.

She dialed her in-laws' town house.

Nobody answered.

She left a message, demanding that Tyler call her back.

She pressed the END CALL button. Then called again, telling them she was coming in to get him.

Christina sat on the couch, felt the humming noise grow louder until the couch started to spin.

The beginnings of another panic attack.

She was not capable of driving anywhere in this condition, she knew that. Defeated, she curled up against the couch cushions and began to cry.

Detectives Jackson and McManus were ready to call it a night.

The pine forest at the edge of Hang Ten's parking lot twisted and moved under a steady rain as they headed for the Crown Vic.

The parking lot was deserted. The place was silent as a tomb.

Except for Daniel Cunningham, sitting alone in the dark inside his late-model Toyota.

Even Ross Middleton and his red Jaguar were gone.

Jackson checked his watch. It was late.

Still, Cunningham did not move.

Muttering something under his breath, Jackson angled the Crown Vic so its strobe lights hit Dan Cunningham and his Toyota full on. "You're free to leave now, Mr. Cunningham," he boomed over the loudspeaker.

This prompted Dan Cunningham to make a move.

The Toyota's engine sputtered and caught in an explosion of sound.

"Ouch," said Jackson.

"Midasize!" McManus called.

"Loud enough to wake the neighbors," Jackson remarked.

"Or at least the neighbor's dog."

The Toyota rumbled inside Frank's head for a long time when he tried to fall asleep that night.

Christina Cardiff lay curled in a fetal position on her couch while her mind raced, turning over the news that her husband had been planning to divorce her. Jason had cheated on her many times over the years. He had been discreet, at least, until recently.

Christina, on the other hand, would have lost everything if she had cheated on him, and so she hadn't. Until she met Daniel Cunningham . . .

Sex had never electrified her the way it did with Dan. There was something scary and wrong about it. Not just the fact that she was married to someone else, but the way they were with each other. And yet Christina gave herself over to being what Dan called his fuck buddy in a way she never had before.

Dan had taught her a whole new language, made her ask for it. "Dan," she would say, "fuck me harder . . ."

Dan urged her forward, making fun of her when she protested at the start of their affair.

"I'll make you beg for it." Dan pinched her thighs and slapped her. " 'Fuck me, Danny,' " he said in a falsetto

voice. "'Please, please, baby, I want your big cock!'"
He wouldn't let up until she said the things he wanted
her to say so he could get off.

And Christina had gone along with anything Dan
suggested, discovering she liked it. Every time in bed
with him was different, exciting. Christina had imagined she was falling for him, whatever that was, a fact
she kept to herself.

Because she knew Dan Cunningham would never
allow that.

Instead, he moved them further along each time they
had sex, changing things so she never knew what to
expect, bringing them closer to something she refused
to think about.

It seemed to Christina now, curled on her couch in
her living room at the edge of the storm-swollen Atlantic, that she and her lover had indeed crossed a line.

The realization caused her panic attack to worsen.
She should call someone, she knew that. But who?

"Shit," Christina said out loud.

Her voice sounded like a radio with the volume
turned up too loud, reminding her she was alone in a
house whose owner had just died.

"Shit, shit, shit."

Snatches of thought and bits of memory spun through
her mind like a wheel of chance at a carnival.

A carnival from hell.

The wheel slowed. Random pieces coalesced into
images that were, mercifully, blurred around the edges.

Images she dared not bring into focus.

Christina Cardiff was having, in the parlance of Alcoholics Anonymous, a moment of clarity. A moment,
looking back, when every drunk sees just how far down

the scale of human depravity they've slid. It's enough, most would agree, to scare them sober.

Christina grabbed one of the throw pillows on the couch and kneaded it, holding on for dear life. She was trapped in the house with her worst enemy: her thoughts. She couldn't take even one more minute of this. The paparazzi, in all likelihood, were still parked outside the front gate. She was in no shape to drive anyway. Looking out at the heavy darkness that pressed up against the dripping windows, Christina Cardiff opted for Plan B.

She headed out into the storm.

Wind whipped her hair into strands that clung to her face and neck.

Christina shivered.

It felt good to be cold, more alive than sitting alone in that house.

She picked her way across the wet stones of the patio, careful to steer clear of the pool's inky surface, which beckoned like a siren's call at the gates of the netherworld.

She forced herself to look away.

Her feet were soaked by the time she reached the back gate, hewn from thick cedar planks. She pushed it open and stepped through.

The wind was much stronger here. It whipped around her in gusts, pushing at her every which way.

What she noticed most was the ocean, thundering and pounding in the darkness just across the dunes.

It sounded closer than usual.

Christina hesitated. She hadn't listened to a weather report, hadn't done anything as mundane as that for as long as she could remember.

A hard gust of wind slammed the gate shut, and she

jumped, propelled forward along the narrow path that wound its way through the grass to the top of the dunes.

Here she paused, buffeted by the forces of the night.

The temperature was twenty degrees lower out here.

She shivered as raindrops pelted her bare skin, pushed by the gusting wind.

Unseen waves pounded nearby, shaking the ground beneath her feet.

Spray flew through the air, mixed with rain.

Christina opened her mouth to catch her breath and tasted salt.

She squinted her eyes shut against the spray and the foam that pelted her.

There was no moon.

It was impossible to see where sky met water, or waves met sand.

She should go back.

Something slithered across the sand and wrapped around her bare ankle.

Christina hopped around from one foot to another, trying to get the thing off. It wouldn't let go. She screamed.

The sound was lost to the night and the wind.

She forced herself to reach down and pull the thing off. It was a long strand of wet saw grass.

She couldn't shake the feeling that snakes were slithering around her bare feet. She ran, leaving the relative shelter of the dunes behind, emerging onto the open expanse that was the strand.

Normally, the strand stretched forty feet, from the bottom of the dune to the tide's edge.

Not tonight. Something was wrong. Her feet landed in water mere steps below the dune.

The waves shouldn't have been breaking so close to shore.

The wind and the rain made it too dark to see.

Breathing heavily, Christina retreated a few steps into the soft heavy sand at the base of the dune.

The beach moved and groaned with shifting shadows and wind. Bits of white flashed on top of the line of breakers, close by in the dark.

Too close.

Cold spray flew through the air, stinging her eyes.

The beach was alive with sound and blowing, twisting sand.

A shape emerged from the darkness, looming large and moving fast.

Fear gripped the base of her neck and fired through her nerve endings with the sizzling heat of an electric current.

The shadow moved, coming swiftly at her across the sand.

She opened her mouth to scream, but instinct warned against it.

The sound would make it easy for the thing to find her.

Christina's breath stalled in her lungs. Her feet grew wings, propelling her back up into the rising dune. She scrambled through the thick sand, calculating how many steps there were to the cedar gate and its landside lock.

At least twenty feet, all of it uphill.

And she was no match for the form moving swiftly across the sand along the high-water mark.

Coming straight for her.

She stumbled and fell.

This time she screamed.

CHAPTER

16

The figure moved swiftly through the night, closing in on her.

Christina's breath caught high in her throat. There was no time to scream. Scrambling frantically onto all fours, she fought to keep her footing in the heavy, wet sand.

In the back of her mind, she was aware that if something horrible happened to her now, Tyler would be an orphan.

She pushed with all her might, willing her legs to sprint faster across the heavy sand.

But it was no use.

She heard panting, felt hot breath on her neck as arms swung down to catch her in a vise grip.

Time slowed the way it does in nightmares.

"Christina!"

The sound of Dan Cunningham's voice, labored and short of breath, worked on her like a drug.

He was back. Daniel Cunningham had come to her. Relief made her giddy. All the fight went out of her. Christina stopped struggling and landed in a heap.

Swearing, Dan dropped down beside her on the wet sand. "Goddamned photographers are still there." He was panting. "What the fuck are you doing out here?"

But he didn't say it in an angry way. His voice was soft, his tone warm with concern. Thank God. Christina tried to explain, but words would not come. Just a wave of relief that she wasn't alone anymore on this awful night. "Hi," she finally managed.

"Come on," Dan replied. "Let's get the fuck outta the rain at least." He stood and reached down to pull her up.

It must have been a trick of the night, with no moon and all, but he didn't look like the Dan Cunningham she knew.

He looked for one instant like a thing with a face and black holes for eyes.

Christina stiffened, opened her mouth to scream.

He took that as his opening and leaned down to kiss her.

Dan kissed her long and deep, and, despite everything, Christina felt something stir in her solar plexus and knew that the roller-coaster ride that was Dan Cunningham was about to start up again.

The feel of his mouth, hard and deep, his lips moving against hers, transported her the way a shot of vodka would have, the shot she had been fighting all night.

Dan tasted of booze.

Christina kissed him back, felt herself grow giddy with the drug that was Dan.

It was the polar opposite of the way she had felt just a few short hours ago, calm and serene and working hard to believe Matt Wallace when he said everything would be okay.

This was easier.

Dan pulled his mouth away and smacked his lips. "I missed you, baby," he said, his voice hoarse, and if Christina had any resolve to heed the advice she'd heard at the AA meeting to avoid people, places, and things that might lead her back to her old ways, it evaporated in the chill rain.

They went back up to the house then, picking their way across the dunes and through the back gate.

This time, with Dan to lean on, Christina did not even glance at the pool.

Christina went into the bathroom to get towels, leaving a trail of wet sand on the floor, while Dan headed straight for the kitchen.

He was holding two highballs on ice when she came back. Ignoring the towel she offered, he pressed a glass into her hand.

It felt cold and heavy and familiar, snug against her palm.

The ice tinkled.

Christina tried to hand the glass back. It required a mighty effort.

Dan wouldn't accept it. He tapped the rim of his glass against hers. "*Cin, cin,*" he said, his eyes glinting.

She watched, mesmerized, as he took a large swallow. "Come on," he said, his voice still soft but commanding now, "this will do you a world of good."

And, in one of those moments that should seem significant but felt as natural as can be, Christina raised the glass to her lips and took a sip.

Every molecule in her body came screaming to attention as the vodka flowed past her lips.

Waking up to rework itself around the alcohol.

She took another sip.

And then one more, and one more after that.

Dan smiled at her and took another sip of his drink. "To us."

See, Christina told herself, the earth did not move. The tide did not shift. The planets did not spin out of alignment.

The humming sound inside Christina's brain died down for the first time in what seemed like hours.

She gulped down most of it, unable to stop. She knew she should be embarrassed but couldn't help herself.

Dan didn't care. He smiled. "You're back," he said, taking her glass and setting it with his on the counter. He pulled her roughly to him as the towels tumbled from her grasp onto the floor, forgotten. He covered her mouth with his so the vodka on his tongue swirled into her, and she swallowed it greedily while he kissed her. He pulled away, taking her glass and pressing it to her lips, tipping it up high so she had no choice but to drink it down fast in one swallow. "You're back," he said, his voice hoarse.

And she was.

He pulled the glass away when she was out of breath and set it down on the counter with a loud clank. He pushed her onto the counter with it, pushing her legs apart and pressing himself onto her, flicking his tongue down to the top of her V-neck leaving a long wet trail across her chest. He bit her nipple through her blouse and raised his head to look at her.

Christina felt the cold tiles beneath her neck while inside the vodka burned a trail down her throat.

"Welcome back," he whispered, smiling wide so his teeth gleamed.

Christina could not manage a reply. Her brain was fogging over, disappearing and sinking down into the old, familiar vodka haze.

"You," he said, fumbling with the zipper on her pants, "are no fun at all when you're not drinking."

Warmth spread through her insides as the alcohol kicked in like jet fuel, while Dan Cunningham got down to business right there on the tiled kitchen counter, pulling her panties down over her hips and undoing his jeans while Christina Cardiff propped herself up on one elbow. Her glass was empty, so she reached for his.

The sound of the phone ringing, far off downstairs, woke her.

Christina cracked one eye open. She was hungover. Memories of last night came back. She drank. Or, in the parlance of AA, picked up. She was no longer sober.

She wanted to die.

The room was dim. The sky outside was overcast. A smattering of rain hit the windows. Surf raged on the other side of the dunes, today the color of wet cement, landing on the sand with a steady pounding.

The sea view was one she hadn't woken up to in a long time.

They had spent the night in Jason's room.

"The master bedroom," Dan had corrected her.

Which was true, of course. It was the master bedroom suite, with a wall of windows facing their private stretch of beach. It had been hers as well as Jason's until she had moved into the guest room last fall.

The room belonged to her now.

Christina stretched and her hand brushed against the sleeping form of Daniel Cunningham and it all came tumbling back. She should have driven into the city to collect her son by now.

Christina blinked and sat up too fast.

Her head pounded so she could hardly see straight.

Daniel Cunningham stretched and rolled to face her from his side of the California king. "'Morning," he said with a sleepy smile.

Christina wished he were someplace else. "Hi."

He moved with lightning speed to close the space between them. One of his arms shot out from beneath the covers and closed on hers, pulling her down.

Christina resisted.

"What?" He let his lips form into a sexy pout. "You don't love me today?"

Love. They had never used that word, and even though she would have given anything to hear it up until a few days ago, now it hung between them. Wrong. Like a solitary Christmas ornament on a fir tree in July.

Dan watched her, letting his brown eyes turn soft and beseeching, like a puppy.

The phone downstairs continued to bleat.

Christina glanced at Jason's alarm clock. Quarter past eight.

His memorial service would begin in less than two hours.

She frowned and pulled her arm away. "I need to go." What she meant was, "You need to go."

Dan sidled closer. "C'mon, baby, take it easy." He reached out and began massaging one of her breasts.

Probably any day until today, Christina would have given anything to wake up this way. She had told him so lots of times after they made love, when they whispered about how it would be when they were together. She had said it again last night when, finally, Dan had half carried and half pulled her up the stairs, steering her left and not right when they reached the top.

Snatches of last night came tumbling back.

"Move over little dog," Dan had sung. "The big ol' dog is movin' in."

Christina winced. Shrugging Dan's hand away, she climbed out of bed and stood, waiting for a wave of nausea to pass.

She wanted aspirin.

Dan rolled out of bed and followed her into the bathroom. "Nice," he said, taking in the Jacuzzi tub and its raised tile platform. He stepped inside the floor-to-ceiling glass shower stall and turned on the hot water while she fumbled in the medicine cabinet for the Tylenol.

"We could shower together and save water," he said playfully as the steam rose.

Trying again.

"No." Christina gulped down three of the pills and pushed Dan's hands away. "Jason's memorial is at ten."

"Oh," Dan said, sounding wounded.

His next words did nothing to settle her stomach. "I can come to that, you know."

"No! I'm expecting a lot of people." Her voice trailed off as she thought of the detective, the old one. The white guy who had left a message on her machine. One of the messages she had ignored along with all the others. "Shit," she breathed. "I think some cops will be there."

Dan took his hands away and backed off. "I can take a shower in the other room," he said, all business now. "I'll just get my jeans."

Hers had been left in a wet, sandy heap on the kitchen floor.

There were sounds from downstairs.

"Shit," Christina exclaimed.

Dan froze. "Who the fuck is that?"

Christina saw a strange look on Dan's face, one she had never seen before.

Fear.

"It's just Señora Rosa and Marisol," Christina explained. "I asked them to come help the caterers set up."

The funeral home had released Jason's obit with details for the memorial service to *Newsday* and had even made sure a piece would run in the brand-new edition of *Dan's Paper*, out today.

"Right. I can skip the shower."

The room was filling with steam.

He stepped in close and pecked her on the cheek. He kept his face there, just centimeters away from hers. "You hang tight," he said softly, "you hear me?" He put his hands on her shoulders and squeezed.

Hard.

"Hey? You hear me?"

It was impossible to see his eyes. His heavy lids had dropped low, closing them off to her.

Christina winced. "Yeah, I got it."

Dan released his grip and stepped back. "Good."

Christina rubbed her shoulders and frowned.

"Call me if you need . . ." He paused to let out a breath and run a hand through his hair. "You know, if you need me."

Christina nodded.

They heard a commotion from the front of the house where, judging by the sounds, the housekeepers had gone out to meet the caterers.

Dan put his finger to his lips. "I'll let myself out the back way."

And he was gone.

Mist swirled in his wake like smoke.

Christina spotted orange traffic cones and wooden barricades as her limo neared Amagansett's First Presbyterian Church.

She had advised Sprague Funeral Home to work with local police on crowd control for Jason's memorial service, to handle the mourners who always showed up to pay their respects at Cardiff funerals.

But there were no crowds today.

There was only a smattering of tourists clad in shorts and rain ponchos, such as you'd see on any Hamptons street on a summer morning. A little boy perched on his father's shoulders, eating an ice-cream cone.

A group of paparazzi, clustered behind one of the barricades, trained their lenses her way.

Thank God for tinted windows. Christina smoothed her hair, which she had set in hot rollers and sprayed as protection against the humidity. Glancing around at the near-empty street and parking lot, she wondered for one awful moment if she had got the date wrong.

But Gil Stanton, waiting to deliver the eulogy as she had asked, stood oblivious to the rain that was soaking him as he waited at the entrance to the church. And she glimpsed her sister-in-law's neon yellow Land Rover.

Nope, there was no mistake.

So, where were all the mourners?

The list of possible answers to that question made Christina queasy. She and Jason had barely spoken for months, but she had never considered she would come home to this.

Jason's funeral.

Dan, his bare chest slick after sex, staring up at the sky with his dark eyes. "We could buy a place in Florida someday," he'd said.

"We'd be tan all year." Christina played along. "You could do the cooking, since I hate to cook."

"I'd cook," he said thoughtfully. "If you got a good settlement, I wouldn't have to work." His voice shifted into falsetto, imitating the housewives who were his clients. " 'I thought the finish would be lighter when it dried. Can you come back and do it over?' "

Christina giggled until Dan's voice suddenly took on an angry edge. "I don't want to do this shitty work until I'm old," he'd burst.

Christina had looked away, embarrassed for Daniel Cunningham and his failed ambitions.

She squeezed her eyes shut tight against the memory now, leaning back against the headrest.

A soft rap on the limo's back window made her jump out of her skin.

It was the funeral director from Sprague, huddling from the rain beneath an oversized golf umbrella of jet black.

"May I join you?" he mouthed.

When Christina signaled, he opened the door and slid into the seat beside her.

This sent the paparazzi into action.

She could hear the click and whir of their cameras.

"How are you doing, Mrs. Cardiff?"

Christina thought of the pint bottle she had debated bringing, deciding at the last minute not to risk it with her son close by. She had stashed it for emergency use in the downstairs powder room. The memory of the bottle's smooth weight in her hands and its easy screw-off cap, made her break out in a cold sweat. "Fine," she said, avoiding the undertaker's gaze. "Did the obituaries run?"

"I've got copies." He pulled news clippings from the slim leather portfolio he carried.

The clips had full details of this memorial service with the date and time, from *Long Island Newsday* and even *Dan's Paper,* as she had instructed. Christina frowned. "Why are there so few people?"

"Your in-laws are already inside with your son," he said helpfully. "Your family attorney is here to deliver the eulogy. The flowers are set up, and the soloist is here to perform the hymn you selected."

Christina had envisioned a brief simple service followed by a reception at their house on Jonah's Path where, away from the prying eyes of the crowds and media, Jason's friends and family could commemorate him privately.

Señora Rosa and Marisol had arrived early this morning to oversee preparations, enough to accommodate several hundred guests, including an outdoor kitchen with two gas-powered generators to handle the overflow.

"But there should be a lot more people," Christina pointed out.

The little boy on his father's shoulders was beginning to whine. His ice-cream cone was starting to drip.

The man from Sprague cleared his throat delicately. "There may be some confusion about what appeared in the *Times*."

Something heavy landed in the bottom of Christina's stomach with a thunk. "What do you mean?"

"Um, there was an item that mentioned another memorial, one that will be held next week at Towne Church," he said.

Towne Church on Manhattan's Upper East Side had been the preferred venue to bid farewell to Cardiffs practically since they landed on the *Mayflower*.

The thing in the bottom of Christina's stomach doubled in weight, settling lower and heavier. Pulling everything inside her down along with it. "Let me see," she demanded.

"I tried calling the *Times* to find out what the confusion was, but I couldn't get anyone on the phone." The man from Sprague toyed nervously with his portfolio.

Christina Cardiff had a pretty good idea.

The twisty feeling in the bottom of her stomach increased when she saw the article.

It was an entire half-page obituary devoted to Jason Cardiff, complete with a photo of him at the helm of a sailboat standing beside a very young gap-toothed Tyler. The sky was a brilliant blue. They were skimming the surface of a whitecapped sea.

The sea was Narragansett Bay.

She knew every detail about that photo. She had taken it during an afternoon sail on their last visit with Jason's family up in Rhode Island six summers ago.

The invited guests at that night's dinner party included Jason's ex-girlfriend, who had recently divorced. She had been seated to Jason's right, and spent the evening fawning all over him while his mother and sister smiled to each other.

They had been in charge of the guest list.

It was the last Cardiff family reunion Christina attended.

She scanned the obituary. It was an account of Jason Cardiff's life according to her in-laws. There was no mention of Christina, or even the fact that he had been married, unless you read all the way to the end. And there, after mentioning that Jason was survived by his beloved son Tyler, parents, sister, and her husband and brood who would always miss their beloved "Uncle Jase," was mention of his wife, Christiane.

Christiane.

Jason's mother had made up that name after they got engaged. Christina had corrected her once or twice before giving up, embarrassed.

Her sister-in-law, Pamela Cardiff Lofting, tipped her off. "It's less ethnicky-sounding than Christina," she'd said after too many cocktails.

This was no typo.

Just like there was no misunderstanding about the memorial service, which the *Times* stated would take place next week at Towne Church.

"They can't do this!" Christina crumpled the paper into a tiny ball. Her in-laws didn't like the funeral Christina had planned, so they had planned one of their own.

Without so much as inviting her.

The man from Sprague looked as though he wished he were someplace else.

Christina wished she had a match so she could burn the obit. "How dare they?" She stared at the funeral director. "I mean, have you ever in your life heard of anything like this?"

"I'm very sorry, ma'am," said the man from Sprague, turning to look out the window.

An icy little quiver of something moved through Christina, dousing her anger. "I never heard of anything like this," she stammered, less sure of herself now.

The man from Sprague made no reply. He was busy examining the seam on his leather portfolio.

The limo driver had not looked her in the eye this morning, and neither had Señora Rosa and Marisol. Not even once.

The icy quiver in Christina's gut broadened into something bigger, which turned her anger into unease. She frowned. "Sorry," she said, taking a deep breath. "My son is waiting. Let's go."

The shouts of the paparazzi told the whole story. "Christina," they cried. "How did your husband really die?"

The implication made her glad for the funeral director's arm, glad for the umbrella and the rain, glad for the oversized dark glasses she had thought to wear.

"Have the police ruled his death an accident?"

"Did he OD?"

"Are you going back to rehab?"

Jesus Christ, she thought, had Tyler been subjected to this?

"That's not a Cheetah girl," the little boy shrieked from atop his father's shoulders.

Disappointed, the family of tourists turned away.

Gil Stanton gave Christina his usual smooth greeting at the church entrance. "How are you, my dear?"

After the most fleeting of glances he, too, looked away.

She accepted his arm but tried not to lean on it too heavily.

Gil Stanton was the attorney of record for the Cardiff family and, by virtue of that connection, Christina as well.

But she had never trusted him.

Gil Stanton held the door.

Entering, she gasped out loud.

As churches went, the First Presbyterian Church of Amagansett was not large. It had, after all, been built 310 years ago to house a tiny congregation.

Even taking that fact into consideration, the place looked empty with only a few people seated here and there in the gleaming wooden pews.

So few, in fact, it was positively pathetic.

Her in-laws were there, stone-faced and staring straight ahead from their front pew. Matt Wallace, who caught her eye and winked. Young Jake at his side, his hair swept up in a fresh cockscomb for the occasion, flashed her a thumbs-up. Lois from AA sat in a prim black cardigan for the occasion, looking like she could last all day. Two rows back was a suntanned woman, smartly dressed in a tailored navy suit, who smiled when Christina looked her way. Without the straw hat she always wore in her garden, it was difficult to place her as Biz Brooks, the neighbor she and Jason had been poking fun at for years.

There were Marisol and Señora Rosa, dressed in their gray uniforms, sobbing loudly.

That was all.

Christina shriveled with shame against Gil Stanton's arm. Not wanting to give him that satisfaction, she straightened up.

She'd give anything for that pint bottle now.

"Hi, Mom." Tyler was waiting for her at the back of the church. His eyes held sadness mixed with the old uncertainty.

Christina scooped him into her arms and squeezed with all her might. "Tyler," she whispered.

He still smelled of a mix of boy and soap and soccer fields, reminding her of the way she had sung to him when she tucked him into his crib at night.

"Mom." His voice was muffled.

Christina had him in a vise grip and couldn't let go.

Tyler hated public displays of affection, but Christina didn't care.

She held him like she had when he had been her baby and she could still lift him, not towering over her like he did now. "Tyler," she breathed, closing her eyes against everything else in the world.

"Mom," he said in a voice that croaked and broke at the same time, and she ruffled his hair.

The tension in his narrow shoulders gave way, and he was her boy again, leaning on her.

But Christina couldn't make this trouble go away with a dish of his favorite ice cream.

"Mom," he said again, holding back a sob.

Christina gathered her son, if it was possible, even closer, and in that one second she remembered the fact that there was one single thing in her whole life of mistakes and missteps and messes that she had done right, and that was give birth to Tyler.

More than anything, Christina Cardiff wanted to be the mother he deserved. Reluctantly, she loosened her grip and stood back to look at him.

He had inherited his father's refined looks, with a

mix, perhaps, of the strong jaw from her father's side of the family. The result, in Christina's eyes, was utter perfection.

Embarrassed to be seen crying, Tyler, ducked his head.

She might have told him things would be okay, but she did not. Her relationship with Ty was the only one she'd ever had that was honest, and she wasn't about to start screwing it up with platitudes.

She rooted through her pocketbook, grateful there was no telltale pint bottle in it, and came up with a rumpled tissue. "Here."

Tyler stared. "Ma, this already has boogers."

"Ty, it's all I have right now."

He raised one eyebrow to make sure she knew he was annoyed by this lack of preparedness on her part.

Their eyes met in a mother-child moment that was just like a million other moments that had passed between them. There was something so normal about it, so run-of-the-mill ordinary about it that Christina didn't want it to end. She felt okay for the first and only time on this day from hell. Something uncorked inside her chest, and she felt a hundred pounds lighter. She grinned. "It's all you're going to get, kiddo. So take it or leave it."

"Gross."

Tyler scowled, but it was a fake scowl. Christina had never been the mommy who came prepared with tissues or juice boxes or crayons. It was an old joke between them, going all the way back to the first time she volunteered to bake cookies for his nursery-school class and burned them. Tyler never held it against her. He'd been happy to slather the brown edges with extra frosting.

Tyler, like Nana, loved Christina just the way she was. He squeezed his eyes shut and gave a good long honk into the tissue, holding it out between his thumb and forefinger when he was done. "In case you want to use it again." He couldn't hide a smile.

"Thank you." Christina stowed the tissue in her bag with care.

They both started to giggle.

Tyler had inherited his looks and his trust fund from his father's side, but he got his sense of humor from her.

As always when they were together, it was easy to laugh. The combination of nerves and relentless sadness of the past few days got to her. Once Christina started, she couldn't stop. She threw her head back and laughed until she thought her ribs would break, not caring how loud she was.

From a pew nearby, Detectives McManus and Jackson watched.

*T*he service had been brief and, as Jackson pointed out, there was barely a wet eye in the house.

The sole exception was Marisol, the young and beautiful housekeeper, who was sobbing so hard she needed to lean on her aunt's arm for support on her way out.

Her boyfriend, Roberto Torres, was nowhere to be seen.

The detectives stood as Christina Cardiff approached, walking with her son, and it was a curious thing, but of the two you would swear Marisol was the one who had been widowed, she was that broken up about it.

McManus nudged his partner.

Jackson dipped his chin to show that he had noticed it, too.

Christina walked past, arm in arm with her son. She had that same quality to her she'd had when they first saw her getting off the plane at JFK, like an oversized doll neglected by its little-girl owner, in need of a hot bath, a good meal, and some comfortable clothes. Her skin retained the pallor that was common to addicts, but she wasn't shaking today.

Frank McManus wondered whether she was back on the sauce.

Of the two, her son appeared to be taking it harder.

"Tough times," Ben Jackson murmured, watching the kid steer his mother up the center aisle.

Frank McManus nodded.

Tyler Cardiff appeared to be a nice enough kid, about the same age as Frank's daughter, who had called early this morning to thank him for the birthday gift.

"Daddy, it's great. I love it, and I needed it. I used to have one just like it and it got worn-out and I was hoping I'd get another one because I loved it so much and my friend Stacey, do you remember Stacey? Well, she had the same one even though she didn't get it down here in Florida, she got it at her grandparents' house when she went to visit last spring in New Jersey . . ."

Frank hit the MUTE button and ran an electric razor over his face. He tried to concentrate as his daughter went on about this and that, her friends and school and things that mattered in her life. He zoned out, checking his watch, knowing he had to leave soon for Jason Cardiff's memorial service.

Looking at the Cardiff kid now, his face the color of a sheet of loose-leaf paper, McManus remembered how he'd felt looking down at his old man stretched out flat and still inside a casket. His father was quiet, for once, with nothing more to say. Ever. His lips had been sewn shut. Despite the fact that Frank had been thirty-three years old when his father died, with kids of his own and a job that gave him more than a passing acquaintance with death, Frank McManus had spent that night sobbing like a baby.

Tyler Cardiff was struggling to hold it together now, muscles jumping along the lines of his jaw so that his thin face twisted up in knots. He was taking it like a man, though, throwing his thin shoulders back as he led his mother by the arm.

"Sucks," Ben Jackson muttered, as they passed.

Christina Cardiff's day was about to suck worse. She was about to be informed her lover had been with her husband the night of his death. A fact which, and this was the fun part of McManus's job, she might have known all along. They were about to find out. "Mrs. Cardiff?" McManus stepped quickly out of the pew, blocking her path.

Christina Cardiff stared straight ahead.

"May we have a word with you?"

They had formed a little traffic jam in the aisle, but the few mourners filing past gave them wide berth. Including Old Man Cardiff and his wife, who dipped his patrician chin at McManus and kept right on going.

McManus wasn't fooled. He'd already received two messages on his BlackBerry this morning from the assistant DA, wanting status updates for Cardiff.

The old man didn't stop now to offer any assistance to their daughter-in-law, McManus noticed.

Young Tyler shifted his arm from his mother's elbow to her shoulders in a protective move. He swung around to face the detectives squarely. "Can we help you?"

You could tell he knew on some level who they were and why they were there, same as everyone else who hurried past. "Mrs. Cardiff," McManus said in his most respectful voice, "we'd like a moment of your time."

The dim light of the church made it impossible to see her eyes behind those shades, but there was no mistaking the dismissive wave of her hand. "I'm busy now."

The kid scowled.

There is a strong family resemblance, Frank thought.

Ben Jackson nodded. "We understand, ma'am, but there is some information we'd like to share with you."

Such as the fact they wanted to judge her reaction to the news that Lover Boy had been partying at her house the night her husband bought the farm. Heads, Christina Cardiff sent him there. Tails, she had no idea she was bedding down with someone who posed a danger to her and her son.

Christina Cardiff's response was to give a little wave, motioning to them to move out of her way.

McManus and Jackson exchanged glances.

Frank tried again. "Mrs. Cardiff, we do have some new information about your husband's death which you need to know." He looked at the kid. "We want to share that with you now, in private."

Young Tyler hesitated. "Mom?"

Showing the kid, thank God, had inherited some brains from somewhere. Apparently not from his mother.

She tightened her grip on her son's arm and shook her head, pointing those dark shades at McManus for the first time. "Not now," she said firmly. "Leave a message on my cell."

And with that, she swept past.

Jackson gave Frank his Are-You-Getting-This? look.

Frank gave a quick nod that yes, he was.

They turned to go and got waylaid by Pamela Cardiff Lofting, who had hung back and witnessed the whole thing.

"Detectives, I'm glad you came." Her eyes were puffy, sans makeup. "Because this"—her voice dropped to a hiss—"is an outrage."

Her hand, when Frank shook it, was like a block of

ice with jewels stuck to it. He and his partner offered condolences.

Her puffy eyes focused on Frank with the same laser-beam intensity you'd get from her old man. "What sort of progress have you made?"

By progress, of course, she wanted to know whether they were close to slinging anyone's sorry ass in jail in connection with her brother's death. "We're exploring all avenues," McManus replied, using the company line.

"We're checking out all the information you provided us with, ma'am," Jackson added.

"Good." Pamela Cardiff Lofting gave a sad shake of her head. "Because this"—her lips tightened with fury around the words—"needs a quick resolution." Her eyes flashed with anger.

Gil Stanton, the Cardiff family attorney, had been standing a respectful distance away. He moved in now, placing a fatherly hand on Pamela's linen-clad shoulder. "I trust these gentlemen are doing all they can. I know the DA is providing them all the resources they need."

Stanton flashed them a tight little professional smile that pretty much implied he and the DA were BFFs.

Detectives McManus and Jackson watched impassively.

"My parents, my entire family," Pamela said, pushing the words out in a voice that was choked with tears, "are just so devastated by this, this, this . . ." She paused, searching for the right words. "Disaster," she said at last. "Most of them were too upset even to attend this memorial today."

"I see," Frank said. Based on the Cardiff family reputation, they were too busy double-checking the findings of the team of forensic accountants they had no doubt put on the trail of their son's estate.

Because Jason Cardiff's untimely and wrongful death had resulted in one very large honking transfer of dough from the Cardiff family trust into the hands of Christina Banaczjek Cardiff.

Based on her swollen, makeupless eyes, Pamela Cardiff Lofting must have been up half the night thinking about that very thing. "This is an outrage," she repeated. "Pure and simple."

Gil Stanton gave Pamela's shoulder another fatherly pat.

"Stay calm, my dear," the lawyer murmured, "and let these men do their job."

His words seemed to have the intended effect on Pamela Cardiff Lofting, whose very DNA was programmed to respect the great American work ethic.

She tightened her grip on her black pashmina shawl and sniffed. "You'll call as soon as you have news, won't you?"

Detectives Jackson and McManus nodded.

As next of kin to the decedent, Christina Cardiff was the point person to inform about any developments. And if the assistant DA in his infinite wisdom wanted to keep a line open to Old Man Cardiff, that was his prerogative. Frank McManus, for his part, was not going to spoil anyone's brunch by telling the dead guy's sister he had been sleeping with one of the maids, thereby pissing off the maid's bad-ass boyfriend.

It was enough to make you lose your appetite for the egg strata.

Not to mention it was raining cats and dogs. Frank wished he had thought to bring an umbrella.

The wind had picked up quite a bit, tossing the tree branches around like toys. The weather service had been forecasting this for days, as some tropical storm off the Southern coast had picked up speed and begun rotating north toward Long Island. Two swimmers had drowned off Rockaway Beach in Queens, according to 1010 WINS. That was nothing new. Swimmers were always drowning off Rockaway.

"An umbrella would come in handy right now." A feminine voice, pleasant and familiar, echoed McManus's thoughts.

Biz Brooks stood, looking very put together in a trim suit that showed off her legs to good advantage. She flashed a smile. "I've been standing here, waiting for a break in the rain, but it could take days."

"Yeah." Frank smiled back. He couldn't think of anything to say.

"We've got an umbrella in the car," Jackson offered. "Wait here. I'll get it." Before McManus had time to protest, his partner dashed out into the rain.

Leaving Frank to wonder just how much worrying Ben Jackson and his wife did about whether McManus would spend his twilight years in their guest bedroom.

The church was empty now.

Frank scraped his feet, jangled his change, and searched for something to say.

"They've been forecasting this for days. A tropical storm, I think." Biz Brooks smiled again and, for the second time in as many days, the word "fetching" leapt to Frank's mind.

Frank cleared his throat. "Tropical depression." Wrong word, he thought. Never say the word "depression" to a beautiful woman.

"An umbrella is just the thing," Biz remarked.

She looked like she could drip-dry no problem. "Yup," said Frank.

The old church was silent.

"So, um, how are things going?" Biz Brooks turned those hazel eyes on Frank. She caught herself. "I mean, I guess you can't say much about your job, in your line of work."

"Not too much." Frank's natural shyness engulfed him. "Other times," he began, "we can."

"That's fascinating," Biz Brooks said.

She actually batted her eyes at him, which made him stand up a little taller. Note to self, he thought, switch to light beer.

Biz tucked a strand of hair behind one delicate ear.

The motion tugged at something in Frank's gut.

"I just think your job is fascinating," she said. "I mean, you help people and solve crimes and figure things out when bad things happen."

She smiled again, and Frank wondered if her hazel eyes changed color depending on her mood. "It's my job," he said, but not before his voice croaked. Jesus Christ, her dead husband had been some big-time writer, and here he was sounding like a tongue-tied idiot. "I think what you do is great," he blurted.

Biz Brooks frowned. "And what, exactly, do I do?"

Frank felt sweat beading on his forehead. "Your garden. Flowers. They make the world a better place."

Oh, crap, what was next? Peace and love and reducing her carbon footprint?

Biz Brooks watched him, probably trying to decide if he was sane.

"Thanks," she said at last. "I enjoy it. I don't have

too much time for it these days. I've been donating most of my time and resources to a project based at Shinnecock," she explained, referring to the US Coast Guard facility in Hampton Bays. "I'm helping fund a new program developed by the state university system dedicated to improving the water quality and marine life in and around the local bays and the Long Island Sound."

McManus braced himself for a spiel on global warming, and how powerboats and the vast agro-military-industrial complex was ruining the earth and the legacy we leave for our children, but it didn't come.

"I grew up spending summers out here," she said simply. "Fishing with my dad off Montauk. I love it."

"Yeah," Frank McManus added. "Me too." He was certain a rainbow was blooming above the church rafters.

Biz Brooks smiled at him, and Frank smiled back.

The parking lot behind the Presbyterian Church was deserted when they walked her out to her car. It was a sleek top-of-the-line BMW, not some sputtering hybrid, or worse, a Volvo.

"Thanks again," she called to Ben Jackson, who had thrust the umbrella into Frank's hands before racing head down through the rain to the Crown Vic.

Which left Frank McManus holding the umbrella over Biz while she slid behind the wheel. "Drive safe," he said, patting the door.

Biz Brooks had yet to start her engine. "It was nice chatting with you."

Frank McManus smiled. Or rather, kept smiling. He realized he'd been smiling for five minutes at least, long enough to make his face hurt. "Nice chatting with you, too."

Biz sat.

The rain fell in sheets around them.

It was against policy to ask someone out during an investigation. Not to mention he was a humble civil servant, and she was a wealthy widow living in a prime piece of Hamptons real estate.

Biz Brooks had been fingering her keys. She stopped now and dug something out of her purse. "Here," she blurted, cheeks flaming as she pushed a business card at him and fired up the BMW. "Keep it, you know, if you're ever in the neighborhood and want to give a call."

Frank McManus was not the sort of cop to go against department policy, nor was there any way to explain this without sounding like a complete dweeb. So he simply shoved her card into his pocket without saying a word.

Biz Brooks drove off, flashing a smile that made Frank McManus forget his ankles were soaked through to his skin.

"So, dawg," Ben Jackson said when they were back in the car. "Who do you like?"

"Torres," Frank replied. "I still like Señor Torres for this." He was bent over his BlackBerry, which had hummed to alert him to incoming messages during the service.

"Okay," Jackson said thoughtfully. "I'll ride that train with you."

"Hold on." There were two messages, both flagged URGENT, asking him to call the office right away.

Rain lashed the windshield as Frank waited for the call to go through.

His admin picked up on the first ring. "I did some checking like you asked on your man Daniel Cunningham," she began.

What she told him next was enough to warrant using the flashers despite the light traffic.

Jackson shot him a questioning look. But he had already guessed. "The Springs, right?"

Frank nodded as Jackson threw the Crown Vic into drive. He jotted down the name and number of the officer on duty in Deer Park, a rough town in central Suffolk.

"Desk sergeant says he wants to speak with you personally," the admin explained.

"Let me guess," Ben Jackson said, when Frank signed off. "We need to pay a visit to Daniel Cunningham." He swung the car east onto Amagansett's Main Street, which looked like a Currier & Ives print, even today in the soaking rain.

Traffic was at a crawl in the westbound lane, bumper-to-bumper with city folk heading back to Manhattan. The village streets were empty except for a long line at the Jitney, the overpriced bus that ran between the city and the East End.

Thereby proving Frank's theory that your average New Yorker had all the staying power of a hothouse flower when it came to weekends in the suburbs.

"Rise and shine, Daniel Cunningham," Jackson said cheerily.

"Not his real name, by the way."

"You don't say?"

"Danny Cisco, aka plain ol' D.C."

"D.C.," Jackson said. "I like it. It has a certain felonious ring to it."

"He's an enterprising man," McManus commented. "I do hope we catch him at home."

"I'm sure he's got places to go and people to see."

The rain continued to blow in strong gusts. Maybe the summer people had the right idea. The radio was tuned to the National Weather Service, which was predicting conditions would worsen as the tropical depression rotated onto the south shore of Long Island.

It was anybody's guess when or if the storm would blow out to sea.

They headed east against the flow of traffic, making a quick left for the journey due north along Stony Hill Road, which dated to colonial times and cut across the open farmland that led to the South Fork hamlets of Kingstown and the Springs.

A flash of lightning lit the sky. It was, despite the mess on the roads, breathtakingly beautiful.

"Biz Brooks could be very happening for you," Jackson said out of nowhere, changing back to his favorite subject.

Fact was, Frank McManus agreed. He'd dated a bit since his wife left, but nothing serious. Nothing that ever came close to filling in the giant sinkhole that had opened inside him when she took his kids and moved to Florida. McManus had hated that sinkhole at first. But after a while he got used to it, living with pain.

Like most of the people he met in the course of his work, Frank McManus learned to accept the fact that he had lost his one and only best shot at a happy life.

And then one day, out of nowhere, someone like Biz Brooks showed up and, Bam!

Just like that, McManus remembered how it felt not to have a sinkhole inside him. Whole and happy like everyone else.

He wasn't about to admit that, so he changed the subject. "I wonder what the honorable Danny Cisco has planned for this fine morning."

Ben Jackson took the hint. He had been partnered with McManus through most of the sinkhole years, after all. "Worth a looky-see. Nothin' better than paying a social visit after a funeral, I always say."

McManus grinned. "Seeing as how we were left off Christina Cardiff's guest list for the reception."

"Must have been an oversight."

"No doubt."

Jackson headed onto Springs Fireplace Road, taking it slow through the massive puddles that were filling with storm runoff. He slowed for the turnoff into the subdivision of homes between County Road 41 and Three Mile Harbor.

The Springs.

"Did you get her number, at least?" Ben Jackson slowed while they checked house numbers.

Frank let that one pass.

Jackson grinned. "Good. I like it."

The roads here, chock-full at night with pickup trucks parked alongside minivans and sedans (most were domestic, and most designed to handle a crowd), was like any working-class neighborhood in the middle of the day. So deserted it looked like the day after the big one had hit.

Except for one house, where a lone individual appeared to be making up for lost time and heading for the hills.

Daniel Cunningham was attempting to wrestle a large canvas duffel bag into the trunk of his car.

"Well, well, what have we here?" Jackson swung the Crown Vic into the drive and gave the horn two quick toots.

Cisco didn't turn around, just kept wrestling with that bag. The Toyota's trunk was so jam-packed, it wouldn't close.

Jackson parked the cruiser, and they got out.

It was raining pretty hard. Frank's feet were already damp, but he didn't care. "Shitty day for a road trip," he remarked.

"Good morning, Mr. Cisco," Jackson called.

Cisco did not answer. He was busy rearranging his stuff.

"Hope you're not planning to go far in this weather," Frank said.

Successful at last, Cisco slammed the trunk. He took his time, and when he turned to face them, he was scowling. "You looking for something?"

"You, Mr. Cisco," Jackson replied softly.

Cisco showed no reaction to their use of his real name.

"We know your true identity, Mr. Cisco, which you neglected to tell us last night," McManus added.

Cisco's scowl deepened, but he said nothing.

"It must have slipped his mind. He's got a lot to worry about." Ben Jackson's voice slipped into hard-ass mode, and he moved forward an inch or two, no more.

Enough to make Cisco flinch, which was nice to see.

"You got a list of convictions and charges going all the way back to 1991," McManus said.

Cisco shrugged.

"The sergeant on duty in Deer Park didn't have anything nice to say about you, Danny."

Stone-faced, Cisco tugged at a lock of hair that had fallen onto his forehead and was plastered, wet with rain.

"Neither did the officer on duty in Fort Lauderdale, Florida," Jackson added.

Cisco said nothing, but his eyes had shrunk to tiny little slits. And the tapping of his left foot gave him away. "I wouldn't know anything about that." Cisco's mouth stretched into a sneer that made McManus picture Cisco's mother slapping him a lot when he was a kid.

Or, more likely, Cisco didn't get slapped often enough.

"That's over now," Cisco said. "I'm finished with that."

"I doubt that, Danny." Ben Jackson stood his ground, not budging an inch. "Bad luck follows you around. Several clients in Florida claim they lost a great deal of money after you did some work for them."

Cisco ground his left foot down to stop the tapping.

At last, Frank McManus thought, a suspect who knew a little something about body language.

"The problem is," Jackson continued, "two of them went missing. Nobody's heard from them since you got involved. Why is that, Mr. Cisco?"

The driveway was filled with the sound of falling rain and the tapping of Danny Cisco's foot, which had started up again.

Cisco shrugged. "I have no freakin' idea. That's too bad."

"You know what else is too bad? Your record," Frank shot back. "Turns out you have a list of convictions going back years in Deer Park. When you do a job for people, bad things happen. They lose money, or . . ."

"They just disappear." Ben Jackson finished the sentence. "Like that couple in Fort Lauderdale, Danny."

"Like Jason Cardiff," Frank added.

Cisco stared down at his feet. The tapping stopped again.

"There's one basic truth about our line of work, Danny," McManus said in a conversational tone. "Any cop will tell you. The last person to see a guy alive always had something to do with it."

Cisco's left foot started up again. "I don't think so. And I got five people who will tell you I left that night when they did."

"You know, you're talking like someone who's got a lot to hide," Jackson commented.

Cisco shook his head, keeping his eyes on his feet. "Whatever."

"We didn't see you at Cardiff's memorial today. Why is that?" McManus stared.

"Seeing as you said you were such a close friend and all," Jackson added.

Cisco made no reply.

The Toyota was hanging low to the ground thanks to the weight in its trunk. "Planning a vacation?"

Ben Jackson didn't give Cisco a chance to reply. "You run into some extra cash lately?"

But Danny Cisco had heard enough. He looked up at them and glared. "Unless you got a warrant, I'm headed out now."

"I'll bet any money our forensic accountants will find a trail straight from Christina Cardiff's account to yours, Cisco," McManus said.

Cisco's sneer widened. "I'll take that as a no. If you don't have a warrant, you'll excuse me." He turned to go back into the house.

"We're working on it. Twenty-four/seven," McManus said evenly.

"Don't plan any trips to Florida, Cisco," Ben Jackson said. "Because the officer we spoke with down there says if he sees you in his jurisdiction again, he'll make sure you serve out your full sentence this time."

"Thanks for the tip," Cisco muttered.

The flash of anger in his eyes left little doubt that Cisco's temper had pushed him down the road to ruin.

It was a theory worth testing.

"Good luck with Christina Cardiff," Frank said softly. "She got what she wanted, and my guess is she's done with you."

Cisco's shoulders hunched, but that could be nothing more than an attempt to shake off the rain. Frank gave it one more try. "She's not gonna waste her time with a piece of garbage like you."

Bingo.

Cisco wheeled around.

Blink and you'd miss it, he was that fast. His eyes had gone blank. Cold, dark, and empty.

Shark time again. Frank's training kicked in. His gun hand was steady. In position and steady. Ready.

"You f- . . ." Cisco started to say something that Frank knew he would enjoy hearing.

So it was a disappointment when Cisco snapped his mouth shut.

Ben Jackson held out a business card. "Don't leave Suffolk County. You check with us before you leave town. Got it?"

Every muscle in McManus's body twitched, on high alert.

Cisco's only answer was to take the card from Jackson's hand. His movements were slow and deliberate.

This small act of self-control reinforced McManus's opinion that Cisco was ruthless, capable of anything that would serve his own interests.

The only sound now was the tiny ping of raindrops landing on the Toyota.

Cisco stepped back slowly, in the manner of someone who understands just how delicate his situation is.

The sneer on his face made Frank's parting shot that much sweeter. "Hey, Cisco," he said softly, "don't go far. We won't stop till we find out how Jason Cardiff died."

"I keep tellin' you I left with everyone else." Cisco shook his head as his eyelids drooped low over those blank dark eyes. "It was just a couple friends at a pool party."

It was late. The moon faded away when the wind picked up, blowing gusts that prodded even the heaviest tree branches with a constant rustling noise. Ocean waves pounded hard against the sand, landing closer together as the closing hours of the day just ended merged with the earliest hours of the day still to come, creating the long, dark nameless hours of night.

Rave music thumped at full volume.

The neighbor's dog barked.

Jason Cardiff barely noticed. He'd done more coke after everyone left, draining the remains of a bottle of champagne while he thumbed through porn magazines at the side of the pool.

He had rubber dick, hadn't been able to get off even inside Lisa's tight ass.

She left, clutching her clothes to her stomach, shuffling slowly out the side gate. She barely said good-bye, rubbing her jaw and sniffling.

Jason Cardiff could find a piece of ass like hers whenever he wanted. Any girl would give her right tit to be in Lisa's shoes, and she knew it.

Her friends both kissed him good-bye, all smiles. The prettier one, the one with the better boob job, had slipped her card into the waistband of his swim trunks, caressing his balls while she was at it. "Call me," she whispered, not giving a shit if her good friend Lisa noticed. "I like to do everything."

Daniel Cunningham had departed, too, without obtaining payment for services rendered. "We got things to discuss," he'd said at one point. "We need to settle."

"Not yet," Jason replied.

The others were too wasted to hear.

But Daniel Cunningham pressed on, careful to keep his voice low. "I want my money."

"Couple of more weeks, like I said." Jason Cardiff's new attorney, Maurice Gold, had warned him not to pay until they had filed a motion in divorce court.

"It keeps things cleaner," Gold had said.

Jason Cardiff had learned early on what successful businessmen knew. If you were going to pay for legal advice, you should act on it.

"Hang in there," Jason Cardiff said, out of earshot of Lisa and her friends.

Daniel Cunningham looked ready to argue, but Jason cut him off. "Not till my wife gets back. It'll be a couple of weeks." Gold had advised against serving Christina in rehab. It would look bad to a judge. With any luck, she'd start drinking again after she came home. One look at the evidence against her, and it would be a slam dunk.

"I need it now," Cunningham said. His voice was low, but something about him stiffened, making him seem bigger than he was. The look in his eyes was cold, harder even than when they had first come up with their plan early last summer.

Jason Cardiff had known at that time he was dealing with a very different sort of man than anyone he had grown up with or dealt with on Wall Street, but he was still unprepared for the look he saw now in Daniel Cunningham's eyes.

Jason Cardiff was afraid. "Soon. You'll see."

Daniel Cunningham stared at him, considering things. And when Jason had almost given up hope, he backed off. "Okay," he said. "We'll see."

Jason couldn't shake the feeling it hadn't really put things to rest, other than put a damper on the party, which had been winding down since its high on the pool steps.

Sometime after one, Jason Cardiff told them all to leave.

Bobby Baldwin and his dealer friend had gone home after realizing the group by the pool was not performing for their benefit.

Lisa left without a peep, despite the fact she'd been begging since Christina left to stay overnight so she could sleep in the master bedroom to the sound of the ocean waves.

Getting fucked up the ass by two men cured her of that desire.

Now they were gone, and Jason Cardiff sat by his pool, alone with his rubber dick and his porn magazines and a new round of barking from his neighbor's backyard.

And, suddenly, he was no longer alone.

A movement by the back gate caught Jason's eye.

In an instant, it swung open.

Daniel Cunningham stepped into the yard.

Jason Cardiff frowned. "What the fuck?"

Closing the gate behind him, Cunningham moved swiftly across the yard, moving soundlessly in his bare feet.

He reached the patio before Jason had time to move.

"What the fuck?" Jason sat up.

Cunningham padded around the edge of the pool, his glance taking it all in. The empty champagne bottle, the porn magazine, and the rolled-up dollar bill.

In the dim patio lights, Jason could see the sneer on Cunningham's face. "Still up, I see."

Jason didn't like any of this. He stood. The movement required effort. "What do you want?"

"My money." Cunningham's face lacked the "can-do" expression he'd shown months back when Jason first proposed his plan. In fact, Cunningham's face didn't look human. When he spoke, Jason was aware that his voice sounded plaintive, which was dangerous with a thug like Cunningham. "I told you, I'll pay you when things shake out."

Cunningham moved closer. "Things need to shake out right now."

Jason tried to ignore the tingle of fear that settled in around the base of his spine. He felt naked now, helpless in his swim trunks.

Cunningham was now fully dressed except for his bare feet.

"I can't pay you tonight," Jason said. "I don't have cash." It was a lie. He had a wad of five-hundred-dollar and thousand-dollar bills upstairs in his closet safe, fifty thousand dollars in all, which was exactly double the amount they had agreed on.

Cunningham saw through it and shook his head.

Jason's thoughts turned to the panic button they had installed just outside the pool house entrance, behind a boxwood topiary in a cement urn. Without meaning to, he glanced that way.

Cunningham had applied wet plaster around that button.

He looked that way now, too. "The price just went up," he said softly.

"No." Jason kept his voice level. "We had a deal. You'll get your money in a couple of weeks, like we said."

"I want more." Daniel Cunningham took another step closer. "And I want it now."

Jason Cardiff inched back a step. Immediately, he realized his mistake.

Sensing weakness, Daniel Cunningham moved in like a leopard at a kill. "I gave you what you wanted. On time."

"So what?" Jason Cardiff shrugged in an attempt to cover his fear, which was growing. "I said I'll pay you the money we agreed to, and I will."

Daniel Cunningham's eyes glinted like light flashing on the barrel of a gun. "That price is no good. I want more."

"Bullshit." Jason Cardiff scowled. "Leave now, and

you'll be lucky to get the money we agreed on. Nobody talks to me this way in my own backyard, and definitely not a two-bit piece of shit like you."

But something was wrong. Daniel Cunningham refused to budge. "No," he said. "New terms."

The wind, which had been building steadily all night, suddenly let up. In the silence of that moment, a wave crashed onto shore, landing harder and louder than the others.

There was an instant of pure silence, as though the ocean had blown its wad and was holding its breath.

And then all hell broke loose. There was a ground-shaking rumble as the rogue wave devoured everything in its path.

Daniel Cunningham smiled.

"Okay." Jason tried not to sound like he was giving in. "I'll give you fifteen."

Cunningham snorted. "The new price is a hundred thousand."

Jason Cardiff blinked, trying to make sense of what Cunningham had just said.

"One hundred thousand dollars," Cunningham repeated.

"Fuck you." Jason Cardiff straightened up to his full height. He had several inches on Cunningham, but even in his disoriented state, he was no match, and he knew it. Cardiff's years on Wall Street had taught him one important lesson, and that was cut your losses and move on as quickly as possible. Every instinct he had told him this meeting needed to end. "Get out of my yard." For good measure, and because he'd had a lifetime of coddling to give him a false sense of self-importance, he added, "you fucking low-life loser."

It was a critical mistake.

Daniel Cunningham moved, fast as a shadow, to block Jason Cardiff's path to the house. "Pay up. Now. Before I raise the price again."

Jason Cardiff stared. It took him a minute to find words, and when he did, they came in angry little bursts. "What the fuck," he said with a brittle laugh, "makes you think I'm going to give you a hundred thousand dollars?"

"Because." Cunningham's reply came in short little bursts to match Jason's. "There's another DVD now, one I shot tonight."

"What?" The wind turned colder on Jason's bare skin, and he shivered. "Fuck you," he said, frowning. But he had a feeling Cunningham wasn't bluffing.

"No, fuck you," Cunningham sneered. "I filmed you tonight, and I think your wife is gonna like it. Watching her husband fuck his girlfriend up the ass."

Jason knew instantly it was the truth. Cunningham had been gone a long time in the pool house, supposedly mixing drinks and cutting lines. In reality, he'd been setting his digital camcorder with its zoom lens on autofocus. "You greedy bastard," Jason said, shaking his head in disbelief.

"I'm a businessman," Cunningham said in that same taunting tone. "Trying to make a living, that's all."

"You're a lying, cheating scum," Jason shot back.

"Some of us"—Cunningham waved his hand to take in the house, the yard and the pool with its imported Italian tiles—"didn't inherit all this. You did nothing to deserve it." His voice was bitter.

Jason Cardiff had heard enough. "Fuck you," he snarled, taking a swing at Cunningham.

Cunningham easily dodged the blow. "Pay me." He grinned, enjoying this. "Before I double the price."

Jason Cardiff drew his arm back for another swing, but Cunningham easily sidestepped the blow.

They had edged much closer to the deep end of the pool.

Cardiff's voice was ragged with rage, louder now. "I don't give a shit what you have."

Cunningham's smile broadened. "Your wife will like it. And so will her lawyer."

Rage boiled up inside Jason Cardiff, mixing with the alcohol and drugs in his system, clouding his judgment. "You piece of shit. You were nothing but a house painter, till I cut you a deal." He inched closer to Cunningham. "And now the deal's off." He glared. "I hired you to catch her cheating. I got the DVD inside. And now I don't need you. The deal's off."

Daniel Cunningham's eyes glinted in a way that made Jason Cardiff wish he had kept the back gate locked.

"I got a new deal," Cunningham said, his voice dangerous and low. "With your wife." His lips curled around the word "wife." "I'll get a piece of everything that's yours, Cardiff."

Rage made Jason Cardiff bold, foolhardy. He took a giant step toward Cunningham. "You stay the fuck away from my wife."

Cunningham laughed. "That's a switch, isn't it? You hired me to fuck her, remember?"

Jason took another swing and missed again. He swore and wheeled around for another shot.

Cunningham continued to taunt him, enjoying it now. "Hey, Cardiff, your wife got off on it. She told me it's the best cock she's ever seen. And she's seen a lot."

Jason Cardiff lunged at Cunningham and missed. "I'm calling the cops."

Lightning quick on his feet, Cunningham skipped closer to the pool's edge. "Your wife won't like that. She's in love with me."

Jason Cardiff was angry now. "If you think my stupid, drunk wife would go for a low-life piece of shit like you, you are out of your fucking mind." He had the satisfaction of seeing his words hit home.

Daniel Cunningham raised a fist, ready to throw a punch. And then stopped himself. "Oh, you're wrong about that," he said, shifting gears. "She wants me. And in fact, I'll bet she wants you gone."

Cunningham's words contained a terrible possibility. Jason Cardiff simply could not grasp the full implication of Cunningham's words. So he pushed it from his mind in what was to be his final, critical mistake. Instead, he acted like the spoiled, arrogant man he was. "You," Jason said, jabbing his finger in the air and looking down his nose at Cunningham, "are a worthless piece of shit. You are nothing more than the hired help, do you realize that?" He paused to take a breath. "You're a dick for hire, Cunningham. Do you know how low that is?" Cardiff laughed, warming to his subject. "You're a male prostitute."

In the next instant, Jason Cardiff at least had the satisfaction of watching his words hit home.

Daniel Cunningham's face twisted with anger. "I'll tell you what, I'll take everything that's yours." He lunged at Cardiff.

Cardiff ducked. Scrambling to maintain his balance, he landed in a crouch mere inches from the pool's edge.

With lightning speed, Cunningham repositioned himself, landing on the balls of his feet in the classic warrior stance.

What happened next required very little effort on Cunningham's part.

Daniel Cunningham took one giant step in the direction of Jason Cardiff's retreating back. Cunningham lunged, arms outstretched with palms open and facing out, landing dead center of Jason's swim trunks. Cunningham pushed.

Jason Cardiff landed in the pool with a splash.

Daniel Cunningham watched and laughed.

His derision turned to incredulity, however, as Jason Cardiff sank.

Everything that followed happened in slow motion.

Jason Cardiff cartwheeled to the bottom, his mouth open in a silent scream.

Daniel Cunningham watched.

Their eyes met briefly.

Jason Cardiff's were round with panic. He fought mightily for the surface, clawing his way until he broke free at last, sputtering and coughing.

Daniel Cunningham stood, uncertain, careful to stay out of reach.

Tilting his head back, eyes wide with terror, Cardiff took in gulps of air with ragged sucking noises. "Help," he managed.

Daniel Cunningham did not move.

Cardiff sank below the surface once more.

Cunningham stayed where he was.

Jason Cardiff used the last of his strength to propel himself to the surface once more. Having a pool in the Hamptons was status quo, but he rarely used it. Christina was the swimmer. He got his head above water and managed another breath.

Staring, Daniel Cunningham moved back.

"Help," Jason Cardiff begged. "Help."

Daniel Cunningham did not move.

Jason Cardiff's mouth stayed open in a futile attempt to get air as he slipped below the surface. He took in water instead. He tried to spit it out but could not.

Water filled his nostrils and his mouth. He pushed his arms and legs in one last desperate attempt to reach the surface, but he failed. Winded, he pulled the water deeper into his lungs and began to choke.

It was like the time when he was a boy at Candlewood Lake but worse.

This time, Jason Cardiff felt himself slipping away beyond help, and he knew these were the final moments of his life. Memories of his past did not come tumbling back, regressing him through his life of privilege.

Rather, he watched the colors flashing by of the halogen lights they had installed last spring, winking at him in red and yellow and blue and green as he slid past.

And the shadowy figure standing high above at the water's edge, laughing down at him as Jason Cardiff sank to his death.

A steady rain lashed Jonah's Path, carried on a wind that blew in fits and starts.

Perfect weather for a funeral.

The smattering of people who came back after the church service walked through the near-empty house, pretending not to notice they were outnumbered five to one by catering and household staff.

Biz Brooks, who it turned out was also a widow, stood on the porch with elderly Lois from AA. Oblivious to the rain, they pointed and gestured at various shrubs and grasses and God knows what. Christina had no idea what the attraction was. It had all been designed by a landscape architect whose hourly rate, Jason had fumed, was about the same as that of an attorney.

Señora Rosa and Marisol were in the kitchen, over-seeing trays of food that would go uneaten.

Señora Rosa shook her head sadly as though she had just lost her best friend.

Marisol tsk-tsked under her breath, sneaking smug glances at Christina when she thought the new boss wasn't looking.

Christina made a mental note to fire Marisol's ass as soon as this was over.

Matt Wallace sat with Jake on a couch, sipping coffee. Tyler had gone directly to his room and stayed there. Nobody went near the pool.

The only one of Christina's in-laws who came was Jason's sister, Pamela Cardiff Lofting, who made it clear she was here solely to keep tabs on Tyler. "Perhaps I'd better go upstairs and check on him," she said after ten minutes had passed.

Christina blocked her path. "Where are your parents? Why didn't anybody else in your family show up?"

"Oh, Christina." Pamela shook her head slowly, curling her lips up sadly into something that was half smile and half sneer.

It was a look Christina knew well.

Pamela Cardiff Lofting sighed. "You're not the only one hurting today."

Christina wondered how that triple strand of Mikimoto pearls would look if it were knotted up tight around Pamela's skinny neck. "What the hell does that mean?"

Pamela flinched. She took a big sip of her Bloody Mary to collect herself. "I'm sorry," she said, tapping the side of her glass with a fingernail. "Are you okay with this?"

The meaty aroma of tomato mixed with horseradish from Pamela's drink was boring a hole into Christina's brain. "Don't give it a thought," Christina said evenly.

"Are you sure?" Pamela raised her glass, practically fanning the fumes into Christina's face.

The back of Christina's throat itched. "Look, I saw the obit from the *New York Times*. What the hell do you people think you're doing, planning a separate memorial for Jason?" She tried not to sputter. "Without even asking me?"

One of Pamela's eyebrows lifted lazily, all innocence. "As I said earlier, Christina, you are not the only one who grieves."

Christina's voice was climbing into the anger zone, but she didn't care. "And as I said earlier, Pamela, what the hell does that mean?"

"Our family needs closure."

Christina stared. "Closure?"

"We need to say good-bye to Jason in our own way, in the place that holds meaning for us. Towne Church in Manhattan. The church that meant so much to Jason and means so much to our family."

Our family. Christina frowned. "So, you planned a memorial service to make yourselves feel better even though you knew it would hurt his wife and son?"

"Our family needs closure," Pamela repeated with a sniff.

Christina inched forward, her hand itching to wipe that smug look off Pamela's face.

Sensing it, Pamela's eyes widened in alarm. "Christina, get control of yourself," she chided.

But, Christina noticed, she backed away pretty fast in her heels,

Pamela's eyes darted, birdlike, around the room in search of help. She found it, settling on a spot just behind Christina's shoulder. "Oh, hello," she breathed, her relief palpable. "Please join us. I don't believe we've met."

"Nope. I don't believe we have. I'm Matt Wallace. I'm sorry to meet you on such a sad occasion." Matt positioned himself at Christina's side and gave Pamela's hand a warm shake. He directed his next question at Christina. "How are you holding up?"

"Okay," she murmured.

"Liar," Matt said in a low voice.

Christina felt tension drain from the air. Even Pamela looked more relaxed.

"How did you know my brother?" She directed her question at Matt, evidently deciding he'd be a safe bet for small talk.

And she was right. Christina watched Matt as the pair chatted, remembering the good looks he had possessed when he was young. Not flashy-movie-star handsome, more like a star athlete on a box of Wheaties. His looks had mellowed, not diminished, with time. And he oozed sincerity.

Pamela Cardiff Lofting, incredibly, felt it, too. "I'm glad I met you," she said, excusing herself and going off like a lamb without a peep.

Leaving Christina alone with Matt. "So." He looked at her, really looked at her. "You holding up okay?"

It was impossible to lie to a guy like him. "It's all too weird," she said with a shake of her head. "Bizarre."

"No argument there," Matt said with a quick nod. "When I saw you at the AA meeting yesterday, I knew you were going through a bad time." He smiled. "Nobody just wanders into AA, I guess."

You can say that again, Christina thought.

"I figured you had just left rehab," he continued, "but I had no idea about everything else."

By "everything else," he meant her husband's sudden death and—if you believed the tabloids—pending divorce and feuding in-laws. "I suppose it's all part of the process," she said, parroting another AA slogan. She sounded bitter and she knew it but was beyond caring.

Matt caught one of her hands in his and squeezed. "Listen to me, Chrissie."

Chrissie. Just hearing him say it made her hand turn warm inside his.

He bent his head low near hers, his gaze full of concern.

Snarky comments she could take. But kindness was too much. Hot tears sprang to Christina's eyes. "What?" She worked at stopping her lower lip from quivering.

"You're going to be okay." He pressed both hands around hers, giving them a sort of hug inside his.

She remembered now that hugs had been Matt's specialty, big bear hugs that went on forever. The memory sent more tears spilling down her cheeks. Christina hated to cry.

Matt squeezed her shoulder. "Look, Chrissie, I'm really sorry about Jason's death. I don't know what you're going through, but I want you to know I'm here for you."

His eyes were the same as she remembered. Kind, matter-of-fact, and with a hint of a twinkle waiting to happen. "Thanks," she murmured.

He gave her hand another squeeze. "This will pass. So long as you don't drink, things will get better."

Christina cringed. Would he be there for her if he knew how much she'd drunk last night? "Maybe." She sighed.

"Every day is a new day, and you can start over anytime." Matt's eyes were brimming with the sincerity she had once found boring.

But that was because she had wanted the thrill and excitement of a drinking life, Christina realized with a pang.

Matt Wallace had wanted to set the world on fire and be the first member of his family to earn a college degree even though he was proud of his father, who'd emigrated

from Ireland and served proudly as a firefighter on
Staten Island. Christina found herself wondering now
whether he had ever found the true partner he had once
told her he sought. She shook her head sadly. "Matt, I
don't think I handle things as well as you do."

He didn't rush to tell her she was mistaken, or worse,
spout off some dopey AA bumper-sticker slogan.

It would have been easy to write him off if he had.

Keeping her hand tight inside his, he gave her shoulder another squeeze. "Give it your best shot, Chrissie."
He winked. "I think you'll do fine."

Nobody had placed any bets on Christina, not since
she could remember. Touched by the warmth in Matt's
eyes, Christina managed a brave smile. A tiny spark of
hope sputtered to life inside her. Maybe she could turn
things around. Maybe she could turn into the mother
she wanted to be. Maybe.

A loud familiar rumbling came up the drive, louder
and louder.

Christina froze. This couldn't be happening. But it
was.

The sound reverberated over the wind and the rain,
then stopped, close to the front door.

Oh, no.

Pamela had a clear view of outside. Her voice rang
out, overly loud, echoing through the near-empty
room. "How fortunate, Christina, that you have special
friends to help you through this terrible time."

Emphasis on "special friends." The words buzzed
around like angry horseflies.

Matt Wallace tightened his grip on Christina's shoulder. "What?"

Pamela Cardiff Lofting was perched in her tiny black

pumps, glaring at the front door. Her birdlike eyes flashed like two angry exclamation points.

"Wouldn't my brother be pleased?"

Pamela's tone was acid.

There were footsteps and voices on the porch.

One voice was deeper than the others.

"Oh, no," Christina murmured, shrinking against Matt for support.

He gave her a questioning frown, but there was no time to explain. She wished she could disappear.

Lois entered first, looked ruffled for once. "Maybe I should be going," she said to no one in particular.

Biz Brooks followed. "It's this way," she said over her shoulder, brushing raindrops from her hair, which didn't need tidying. "Everyone's inside because of the rain." Her voice died when she saw everyone staring.

"I know the way," said a male voice from the porch.

Christina closed her eyes and prayed everyone would disappear.

No such luck.

Pamela Cardiff Lofting was visibly shaking, shifting her weight from one dainty black slingback to the other. "I don't believe this," she exploded.

Neither could anyone else, based on the hush that fell over the room.

Señora Rosa and her niece came to the kitchen doorway. *"Dios mío!"* Señora Rosa whispered, clutching her crucifix.

A deep voice boomed across the threshold and ricocheted around the room, too loud. "Sorry I'm late."

Daniel Cunningham had arrived.

The air inside the Cardiff living room was so still and so heavy it felt as if the barometric pressure were falling through the floor.

Dan came in from the storm, jet hair soaked with rain and clinging to the sides of his head. His dark suit, puckered with raindrops, was obviously a loaner. His gaze swept the room and landed on Christina. He gave an apologetic smile. "I got here as soon as I could."

As though she had asked him to come, which she hadn't. For all the times Christina had wanted out of her marriage, she had never imagined this. Helpless, she watched Dan cross the room and plant a kiss on her cheek.

He let his lips linger a moment too long.

Christina shrank back.

"You okay?" Matt Wallace slid a hand protectively under Christina's arm.

"She's fine," Dan answered, reaching for Christina's other arm.

Christina felt like the rope in a tug-of-war. She was grateful when Daniel Cunningham let go and swung around to face Matt Wallace head-on. "I'm sorry." His voice was still overloud. "Have we met?"

Ignoring the question, Matt introduced himself.

Dan pumped Matt's hand too hard. He looked at Christina. "Have I met him before?"

Christina wanted to die. At a backyard barbecue, spoken by a husband to his wife, the question would have been friendly.

Matt Wallace's eyes narrowed.

"I don't think so." Christina tried not to sound simpering and failed.

Daniel refused to let the moment pass. "Has he been to the house?"

It was another husband-to-wife question, and it hit home.

"Dear God." Pamela Cardiff Lofting popped straight up from her tiny black shoes. Raising the back of one small hand to her forehead, she staggered off to the staircase.

Nobody made any attempt to stop her.

Biz Brooks, who seemed the type that soaked up other people's excess emotion like a sponge, looked ready to faint. She rallied, though, directing a question at Dan. "Is that your car?"

The look on Dan's face was that of a man who has just stepped in something he knows will be tough to scrape from the bottom of his shoe. "What?"

The air felt heavy.

"I was wondering about the car you're driving," Biz said slowly. "It sounds like it needs a new muffler."

Dan rolled his shoulders back. "Yeah?"

"I mean, I was just wondering about, um, if you're happy with it." The color rose in Biz's cheeks.

But Christina had the feeling she wasn't wondering whether Dan was happy with his car or not.

Biz cleared her throat. "Because I'm kind of shopping around for a new car, and I was thinking of getting one just like it."

Not likely, considering Biz had pulled up earlier behind the wheel of next year's 700 series BMW.

Dan stared. "Really?"

"Yes, um, you know, I was wondering if you'd recommend it. You know, in spite of the, um, problem with the muffler and all."

Dan continued to stare at her.

It was rude. "Dan," Christina said, trying to break up the tension, "I'm not sure you've met Biz Brooks, my neighbor."

"You live there." Danny motioned with his chin to the privet hedge on the landside that separated the two houses. He stopped short of adding alone, but the word dangled like a loose power line.

"With my dog," Biz said.

"The one that barks all the time."

Biz Brooks had a way of keeping her gaze level, and she did so now. "He's a good watchdog."

Dan started tapping his foot, and somehow it was very noticeable even though they were standing on a wool rug. Christina searched for something, anything to make this strange little moment pass.

"I've seen that dog," Dan said at last.

Biz nodded. Clearing her throat, she shifted gears and went with the only safe bet remaining in the room. "Lois, can I get you some hot tea?"

"I'd love some," Lois said from the couch.

"Great." Biz headed off to the kitchen.

Which left Christina alone with Dan and Matt Wallace.

"So, how do you know Christina?"

The question was phrased like a challenge. Dan's lips were curled in a tiny, controlled smile.

Frowning, Christina laid a hand on Dan's arm.

His muscles were coiled and tight inside his suit jacket.

Ready to spring.

He flexed his hands open and closed, open and closed.

"Friends of friends, from a while back," Matt said, keeping his tone mild.

But he had straightened up to his full height, Christina noticed, reminding her of the fact that he had played football in college. Despite the fact he had two inches and at least fifteen pounds on Daniel Cunningham, it was clear who had the upper hand, physically.

There was nothing relaxed about Daniel Cunningham, ever. He had a narrow frame, but it was coiled like a cougar, ready to pounce.

Dan's eyes narrowed. "Is that right?"

Christina prayed something would happen, and it did.

Young Jake, who had been watching all this from the couch, got up now and walked over. "I don't believe this," he said, stretching out his hand with a big grin. "Danny Cisco."

Dan stared.

Nonplussed, Jake held his hand out. "Man, I can't believe you're here. I figured you were dead or behind bars."

Dan said nothing.

Still grinning widely with his hand outstretched, Jake tried again. "Just kidding, man. I didn't mean that the way it sounded." He glanced at Matt, his AA mentor, for reassurance. "Hey, D.C., I'm glad you're here."

Daniel Cunningham said nothing.

Jake's grin faded as a tinge of pink began to work its way up his cheeks and across his forehead to where his rooster comb up do began. "Don't you remember me? Jake Warren from Deer Park." He named a hardscrabble town in western Suffolk that was better known for factories than shoreline. "I used to see you around, got into the same scene you did." He gave a nervous laugh. "I know you. You're Danny Cisco."

"We've never met." The only thing moving on Cisco's head were the tiny muscles just below his ears that worked his jaw. He shook his head. "I'm Daniel Cunningham."

Jake frowned. "Danny, it's me. Jake Warren. From Deer Park." He looked from Matt Wallace to Christina and back to Danny Cisco. "Same as you."

"You must have me confused with someone else," Danny Cisco said firmly.

The room was quiet except for rain lashing the windows.

Everyone looked at Christina, who felt her nerves stretching thin like rubber bands about to snap. "This is Daniel Cunningham," she said at last. "He did some work for us earlier this summer. He's ah, our friend."

The man known as both Danny Cisco and Daniel Cunningham smiled.

"Wow." Jake looked ready to say more, but Danny Cisco cut him off.

"Excuse me," he said, draping his arm across Christina's shoulder.

She fought the urge to shrug it off.

"I'm going to fix myself a drink," he continued. "Anybody else want one?"

He raised an eyebrow at the round of no's, repeating the offer to Christina. "How 'bout some Grey Goose on the rocks?"

Christina tried not to flinch. "I'm okay," she said quietly.

Danny raised an eyebrow.

"None for me," she repeated, miserable now. "I'm good."

Matt Wallace and Jake exchanged glances when Danny finally headed for the kitchen.

"That's odd." Jake frowned. "I know him. From places where you don't forget how you know people. Know what I mean?" He directed his question at Matt, who winked.

"Gotcha," Matt replied.

Christina glared at Jake. "He's from West Palm. He did some work for us early this summer." Jake couldn't be right, could he? That would make Dan a liar. "His name is Daniel Cunningham."

Jake's cheeks were now the same carrot shade as his hair. He swallowed, his Adam's apple bobbing up and down on his skinny throat. "I'm sorry, Christina, I don't want to make things any tougher for you today than they already are." He surprised her with a hug that was brief and fierce.

It was something Tyler would do. Christina blinked back tears even though she had no idea why she felt like crying.

"I think," Matt said slowly, "it's time for us to go."

Jake nodded. "Hang in there, Christina. I hope things turn out good for you and your son."

Christina shook the hand he offered, but was taken aback by his next words. "Keep good people around you, Christina, only good people." He gave her hand a final squeeze, directing his next words at Matt. "I'll catch up with you outside. I have something I need to do."

Matt nodded. "Go for it."

Jake headed for the kitchen.

Daniel was in there, fixing himself a drink. Christina frowned. "What's that about?"

"Don't worry about it," Matt replied.

He obviously didn't know how short Danny's temper was. "If he needs to talk to Dan, I should go with him," Christina began.

"Nope." Matt grinned. "Jake's a big boy. He can take care of himself." He lowered his voice. "Jake is probably doing a ninth step with Danny." He saw Christina's quizzical look. "He's making amends. It's one of the twelve steps from AA."

"Oh." Christina learned in rehab that AA members needed to perform twelve steps in order to stay sober. The first step was admitting they needed to quit drinking. The twelfth step called for members to help other alcoholics any way they could. She couldn't remember any of the others. She looked toward the kitchen, scared. "What do you think Jake's doing?"

"Probably apologizing," Matt said cheerfully. "My guess is Jake screwed Danny in a drug deal. I've heard him mention names from Deer Park. One of them is Danny Cisco."

Christina shook her head. "His name is Daniel Cunningham." It was beginning to sound like a lie.

"Whoever he is, he's about to hear Jake's amends." Matt smiled.

Christina frowned. "What?"

"His amends. If Jake wants to stay clean and sober, he has to set right his wrongs from the past. By Jake's own account, he did some bad things." Matt shrugged. "Deer Park's a rough town."

"I wouldn't know," Christina replied crisply. She'd heard enough about weird AA rituals for one day. Her nerves were shot. And she was still trying to figure whether to believe Jake or Daniel or Danny, if that was what his real name was.

Christina was beginning to have her doubts. She had never really believed Danny's story that he had grown up in West Palm, the only child of a homemaker and a CPA. Or that he had dropped out of the University of Miami to care for them when they both developed Alzheimer's. He didn't have a Florida accent, for one thing. And he barely knew how to swim.

Matt Wallace didn't argue. He flashed a smile instead. "You have a lot to think about."

"I guess I do," Christina said slowly.

"I'll let you get to it." He pulled his car keys from his pocket.

Christina's eyes widened in surprise. She was used to people arguing with her, not giving her space to think things through. "You're leaving?"

"I'm not going far." He winked. "Just to Hampton Bays. I have a law office there."

It was the one bright spot in this awful day. Christina smiled. "Good for you. Sounds like all your dreams have come true."

Matt grinned. "Most of them."

A tiny flutter of hope took flight inside her. She didn't have the nerve to ask if he had someone special in his life.

"Guess what? Dreams come true."

By the look on his face, she could tell he believed what he was saying. "I guess," she said heavily.

"It's your turn now."

Christina couldn't hold back a short, brittle laugh. "Yeah, right." She sounded like her teenage son, having a bad day, and she knew it.

"Just you wait, Christina." Matt grabbed her shoulder and squeezed, earnest now. "It's your turn now."

He must be good in front of a jury, she thought.

"Recovering alcoholics like us get a chance to start life over any day we choose. Other people don't get that opportunity," he said. "That's a miracle for a former drunk like me."

Looking at him now, handsome and clean-cut and happy, talking about miracles, Christina almost believed him. Almost. "Well," she said at last, "I could use a miracle right about now."

Grinning, Matt gave her shoulder one last squeeze. "Quit drinking. Trust God. Clean house." Glancing around, he winked again. "I mean that figuratively, not literally, since I see you've got staff to do that."

She couldn't help but smile. "You know, when I was growing up I wished for a big house with staff to clean up after me. Now, I have those things. And look where they got me." She hung her head and shrugged, miserable.

"Sounds like you're already gaining a new perspective on life," Matt observed.

When she snuck a look at his face, he was beaming at her like she was a star pupil. "So, that's the miracle?"

"It's a start," Matt replied. "But you have some work to do." He glanced in the direction of the kitchen. "I'll leave you to it. Take it easy, Christina."

A long, slow swell rolled through her stomach. Panic rising. She did not want him to leave. He was her rock.

Matt must have read the look on her face. "I'm glad we met again," he said in a gentle voice. "You're going through a rough time."

She nodded, ready to tell him just how rough, but he didn't wait to hear it.

He squeezed her shoulder instead. "You have a lot of things you need to sort out, Christina. I can't help you with this. I know you can do it." His voice dropped, low and husky. "I'll be waiting." The hug he gave her was fierce and his lips brushed her hair. "You have my number if things get really rough." And then he let her go.

Moments later, Lois told her the same thing, giving Christina's hand a firm good-bye squeeze for a woman her age. "This will pass, my dear, I promise you that." Her blue eyes were lively. "I've buried three husbands, I should know."

That was it. No admonitions not to drink or go to every meeting listed in the AA directory Lois had pressed into her hands after the meeting the other day. They simply left.

Biz Brooks followed suit, promising to drop by one day when things quieted down a bit. She glanced uneasily in the direction of the kitchen. "I mean, I'll call in a few days and hopefully we can have lunch if you're feeling up to it."

"Thanks," Christina murmured. Biz's grumpy husband, *The New Republic* writer they had made fun of, had died two years ago, and the Cardiffs hadn't even noticed. Christina felt sorry for Biz Brooks, living in her isolated beach house all alone while she, Christina, had

Danny to love. "We could meet for drinks," Christina said, feeling charitable.

Jake emerged from the kitchen, flashing a peace sign. "Thanks again," he called. "You helped me a lot today, more than you know." He grinned. "I hope I get to return the favor."

And with that, they were all gone.

Danny emerged from the kitchen, scowling.

For she thought of him now as Danny, not Daniel. That's how he had introduced himself when he showed up with the construction crew last spring to work on their pool house renovation.

"Daniel Cunningham," he had said, extending a hand roped with veins and muscle as his gaze slid across Christina's body.

The other men on the crew had greeted her shyly and looked away.

But Danny had held her hand long enough to make her blush while he looked around. "I love what you've done with the place."

Now Danny held two highball glasses, full to the brim. "Your little friend is gone."

"You mean Jake?" But Christina knew he meant Jake.

Danny shrugged. "Kid's a freak." He thrust one of the highball glasses her way.

The room reeked of vodka. Before she knew it, Christina was gripping the frosty glass.

Tyler was upstairs with Pamela, out of sight.

Saliva was already pooling inside Christina's mouth, and she swallowed.

It was loud.

"Cheers." Danny hoisted his glass, waiting.

The walls felt like they were collapsing in around her.

Danny took a deep sip of his drink, keeping his eyes locked on hers. "Damn, that's good." He took another, letting out a satisfied little sigh.

Christina needed a drink so bad she could taste it.

Tyler would be heartbroken if she drank, today of all days.

Danny took another swallow. "Baby, you gonna drink that or watch it melt?" He jerked his chin up, signaling it was okay.

He of all people understood what she was going through. Christina could see that now. It was all the encouragement she needed. She raised the glass to her lips, closed her eyes, and swallowed.

The Grey Goose filled her mouth with its cool promise, wafting up into her nostrils, sliding down her throat with a slow, steady burn.

Christina tried not to gulp. She downed half the glass before coming up for air.

Danny watched. Smiling. "What a day." He set his glass down and made a move for her with a chuckle. "What a fucking day, huh?"

In the next instant Christina was in his arms, powerless over the fact that her hateful sister-in-law and even her son were upstairs and could walk in on them any minute.

"I'm here for you, babe," Danny growled in her ear. "Don't forget that."

For one single solitary moment the only thing Christina was aware of was the thump-thumping of her heart, as the weirdness of the entire day and her whole entire life faded, and she allowed herself to lean in to Danny's broad chest, breathing in his musky scent, and she wanted to lose herself. She allowed herself to be folded inside his arms, giving herself up to the high she always got off the drug that was Danny.

A small noise caught her attention. Christina stiffened, opened her eyes.

Señora Rosa and Marisol were there.

Señora Rosa's mouth fell open in dismay.

Her niece Marisol stared, eyes narrow with disapproval.

Christina felt her cheeks go hot. "I didn't think you were still here."

Danny slowly pulled away before leaning lazily back against the counter. He reached for his glass and took another sip.

"I'm sorry, Meessus Cardiff," Señora Rosa said. "We were outside with the catering . . ." She hesitated. "We came to tidy up." She looked around.

There wasn't much to tidy up.

Marisol said nothing. Just continued to stare at Christina with a spiteful little look on her face. Like she'd finally won. She had caught Christina in the act.

Christina looked away. Her gaze landed on her highball glass, half-drained now.

"I think it's time for the girls to call it a day." Danny set his glass down.

Señora Rosa's eyes widened.

Marisol's lips tightened.

"Load up the dishwasher and vamoose." Danny motioned toward the door with his chin.

The housekeepers looked her way, and Christina nodded. Jason was the one who had hired them, but it was her house now. She turned away. "I'm going upstairs to check on things."

The truth was there was an open bottle of vodka left

in the master bedroom from last night. She knew just where it was, tucked away under her side of the bed where no one could find it. A few more hits would calm her nerves, and no one would know.

"You go ahead," Danny said, all business now. "Check on Tyler. We'll get things squared away down here." Ignoring the looks the housekeepers were exchanging, he started gathering dirty dishes. "This won't take long."

Christina fled upstairs.

Tyler's door was closed. Pamela was probably in there with him.

Christina couldn't face them, not yet. Not with her nerves jangling out of control. She'd feel better in a few minutes, once she was calmer. She walked quietly past Tyler's door, down the hall to the master bedroom.

She slipped inside, closing the door soundlessly behind her. Relieved that help was within reach. She made a beeline for the bed, which the housekeepers had remade, uttering a silent prayer as she reached underneath that nobody had moved her stash since last night.

Christina's fingers closed around the smooth cool neck of the bottle, and she gave thanks.

Dropping to her knees, she felt a surge of elation when she saw how much was left. She unscrewed the cap, raised it to her lips and drank. Not giving a shit whether she gulped or not.

The Grey Goose went down smooth and easy, sliding into her stomach with a welcome burn. Once upon a time, Christina had drunk it on ice, mixed with orange juice. She graduated to a curl of lime peel. Then discovered it was better straight up. She took to storing it in the freezer so she no longer required ice.

She no longer needed her vodka chilled.

Nor did she require a glass.

Christina Cardiff crouched on her knees, waiting for the heat in the pit of her stomach to spread until it eased the jangling of her nerves.

It required a mighty act of willpower to pull the bottle from her lips. She wanted to drink enough to take the edge off, not enough for Tyler to notice she'd been drinking.

Christina screwed the cap on carefully, ready to stash the bottle back in its hiding place.

There were at least half a dozen others around the house where she could get to them easily.

She drew in a deep breath, to aid the vodka along its journey. There was mouthwash in the bathroom. She'd use some before knocking on Tyler's door for their mother-and-son chat.

Christina stood, still clutching the Grey Goose.

The door to Jason's closet was partly ajar.

She frowned.

The cleaning women never left it that way.

There were small noises coming from inside.

She tiptoed over and nudged the door all the way open, afraid of what she'd find.

Her sister-in-law, Pamela Cardiff Lofting, knelt in front of Jason's in-wall safe.

"What do you think you're doing?" Fueled by vodka, Christina's voice rang out strong, accusing.

Caught off guard, Pamela rocked back on her heels. She lost her balance and went over, losing her grip on the manila envelopes she was holding.

A sheaf of official-looking papers spilled on the carpet, along with a good-sized wad of U.S. currency.

Pamela's eyes widened in alarm when she saw Christina. "Ooh!" She made a frantic grab for the papers which, presumably, she had just removed from the safe.

Christina had never known the combination to that safe. She took one giant step forward, planting one foot firmly on the stack of papers Pamela was making a grab for. "What do you think you're doing?"

Pamela looked up, shaken and scared for once. "Nothing," she stammered. But she made one final grab for the papers, which were pretty much not going anywhere unless Christina moved her heel.

Christina had no intention of doing that. Eyes blazing, she dropped to a crouch and grabbed the contents of the manila envelope, brushing Pamela's hand away. "You have no right to be here," she snapped. "Get out."

Pamela scrambled to her feet, her eyes still focused on the manila envelopes Christina was now clutching to her chest. "You're being childish," she said in her best Cardiff tone.

But her cheeks flamed with guilt.

Christina stood, drawing herself up to her full height. "You're not welcome here." Her mind was reeling.

Jason had provided his sister with the combination to his safe.

Something he had refused to give her. His wife. Rage boiled up inside her. Her grip tightened around the neck of the Grey Goose bottle. "Get out."

Pamela's eyes widened, and she took a step back. "Really, Christina," she huffed. But her gaze returned to all that cash scattered at their feet.

Christina took a menacing step toward her. "Don't even think about it," she growled.

Pamela Cardiff Lofting was no fool. She backed up but made one last grab, this time with one dainty foot, for a slim DVD jewel case that had fallen to the floor. Covering it with one of her Manolo Blahniks, she slid it across the carpet until it was within reach, revealing all the instincts of a street urchin.

Christina grabbed Pamela's bony little wrist and squeezed. "That's mine."

Pamela dropped the DVD, her mouth opening and closing like a fish. "Well," she huffed, "my brother—"

Christina cut her off. "Is dead," she snapped.

Pamela's eyes widened. "My brother wanted me to have the combination to his safe—"

Christina cut her off again. "It's mine now." She'd had a lifetime of Pamela's misplaced jealousy of her brother.

Especially when it seemed that even beyond the grave, Jason chose his sister over his wife. "Get out," Christina growled.

Pamela was angry now and self-righteous as always. She stamped her foot. "How dare you? My brother didn't trust you with the contents of his safe, any more than he trusted you with his belongings or his son."

Christina took another step forward. "I was Jason's wife," she said through clenched teeth. "I know everything about him."

"My brother was planning to divorce you, Christina. The proof was all in there." Pamela motioned at the safe. "Looks like you are the last to know."

Her sister-in-law's voice had a triumphant ring to it. More than anything, Christina wanted to wipe that smug look off Pamela's face. She played the one card she had that trumped all others. "Everything your brother had is mine now."

Christina's words hit home. Pamela grew very still, tilting her head to one side as she considered this statement.

The way a bird watches wet grass on a rainy day, knowing if it sits long enough, the right moment will come.

"I wouldn't bet on that," she said in a quiet voice.

Christina plunged on, reckless and spiteful, into dangerous waters. "You wish," she hissed. "Jason died before he had a chance to divorce me."

Even as the words left her mouth, Christina suddenly understood. This didn't look right. A wealthy man in a bad marriage, ready to divorce his wife, found dead.

Something cold and small snaked its way up from the pit of Christina's stomach, leaving a trail of ice in its wake. Like a Roto-Rooter worming through her veins, sucking up all the blood. Christina clutched the bottle with both hands now so Pamela wouldn't see them tremble.

Pamela's deep-set little eyes flashed with something darker than simple anger. "Based on what we know, he had good reason to leave you."

"Based on what we know," my ass, Christina thought. Pamela was just trying to scare her. But truth be told, Christina was frightened. "What's done is done now," Christina said, wanting to end this. It was lame, but all she could come up with.

"Oh, yeah? Then what was that man doing at your house early yesterday morning?" Pamela, getting her mojo back, straightened up, eyes blazing. "The man who was barely dressed." She snapped her fingers in the air for emphasis.

It was an angry sound.

Pamela didn't wait for any reply.

She seemed to know it wasn't coming.

"We all know the answer to that, Christina. You're sleeping with him!" Pamela's eyes blazed and she leaned forward, warming to her subject. "You might want to ask yourself why my parents aren't here right now. Why nobody in the entire Cardiff family will come near you. Why practically nobody showed up for you today." She paused, allowing the meaning of her words time to sink in. "You are a disgrace."

Christina wondered how it would feel to smash the Grey Goose bottle across Pamela's skull, maybe knock that skinny black headband out of kilter. She tightened her grip without knowing she did so.

Pamela moved back out of swinging range. "You're insane," she said, shaking her head.

It was enough, combined with the Grey Goose she'd downed, to push Christina over the edge. She was about to draw back her swinging arm, the one holding the Grey Goose bottle, when she heard movement from the bedroom.

Tyler appeared in the doorway. "Mom? Aunt Pamela? Is everything okay?"

Christina's heart melted in the space of a second. "Ty, it's okay," she began, letting her arm fall to her side.

"Tyler, your mother and I were just having a grown-up discussion," Pamela began in the fakey "Everything's okay" voice she used for her own children.

But everything was not.

Tyler's eyes, red-rimmed from crying, took in the whole scene from the pile of papers and cash on the floor to the open safe door, to the bottle in his mother's hand.

"Oh, Tyler!" Christina dropped the bottle so it landed with a loud thunk, and rushed at her son with arms outstretched. She wanted to explain. But the vodka was already kicking in. She was drunker than she realized, and unsteady on her feet.

"Mom." His voice was small and sad. Instead of returning her embrace, he tried to steady her.

It felt to Christina that her son was pushing her away.

"You said you weren't going to drink anymore." Tyler's sweet little-boy eyes swam with tears.

More than anything, Christina wanted to make Tyler's tears go away. She reached for him.

Tyler resisted.

In her semidrunk state, it was enough to throw her off-balance. She tumbled over and landed in a heap on the floor.

"My God," Pamela shrieked.

"Mom, Mom, are you okay?" Tyler fell to his knees and tried with all his might to pull her back up.

"I'm fine," Christina mumbled, rolling onto all fours to get her balance. She struggled to her feet, leaning heavily on her son's arm. "I'm fine, don't worry."

Pamela looked ready to throw up. "I think it's best if we leave," she said stiffly.

We. Christina glared. "I don't think so."

She would have said more, but Tyler cut her short. "Okay, Aunt Pamela," he said, his voice cracking. "I'll grab some stuff from my room." He turned to his mother.

The look on his face was pleading, pure torture.

"I want to go to Grandmère and Granddad. I'm sorry, Mom."

The closet shrank around them until it was no bigger than a tomb and deathly quiet except for the pounding inside Christina's head, which she understood to be the sound of her heart breaking.

"Okay." Christina nodded. She had failed again. Tyler deserved to leave without a messy scene. "Go ahead, Ty." She kept her voice steady. "I'll see you in a few days."

He gave her a peck on the cheek, without looking at her, and was gone.

To her credit, Pamela didn't look so smug for once. In fact, she was choking back sobs. "Good luck, Christina," was all she managed as she brushed past.

Christina was unable to move for a full minute after they'd gone.

"Dammit," she said aloud, kicking the safe door.

It slammed and bounced back open, hitting her in the shins.

Which hurt.

"Dammit," Christina said again.

There were wads and wads of cash.

Why would Jason, a banker, keep so much cash around?

Christina frowned. She dropped to her knees and began gathering stuff. There were thousands of dollars here, along with the DVD and a stack of papers. She stuffed it all back inside the manila envelopes.

Both envelopes bore the return address for the law offices of Maurice Gold in Rockefeller Center.

The icy thing from deep inside her gut returned, slithering through her veins, telling her to stash the envelope someplace where even the cleaning ladies wouldn't find it.

If Jason had wanted to keep it hidden from her, then she wanted it to stay hidden.

But where?

She didn't know the combination for the safe, so that was no use.

She heard movements downstairs. The front door slammed, followed moments by the deep rumble of Pamela's Land Rover starting up.

Pamela and Tyler were gone.

Time was running out.

She looked around in search of a hiding place. The master bedroom suite had never felt comfortable to her. It belonged to Jason. And the guest room where Christina had been sleeping felt like, well, like a guest room.

Danny's footsteps rang out on the bare wood floor of the living room downstairs.

Christina clutched the envelopes and tried to think.

Tyler's room. She hurried down the hall, taking care to tread softly.

The single twin bed was mussed where Tyler must have lain. Christina fought the urge to crawl into it the way he had, pull the covers up over her head, and try to go to sleep to make this awful day go away. The way Tyler had tried.

The rumpled pillow still bore the imprint of Tyler's head. The blanket and spread were rumpled.

Most heartbreaking of all was Humpy lying there, abandoned.

Tyler had left in such a hurry he hadn't bothered to take his old friend.

Humpy was a poor substitute for a mother's love, but it was all Tyler had right now. And he'd left him behind.

Christina went to the bed and gathered the old camel in her arms, cradling it, and decided she deserved to die.

Danny's voice echoed up the stairs. "Christina?"

Startled, Christina remembered the envelopes. She needed to hide them. Fast.

Her gaze came to rest on the empty space at the top of the bookcase. Humpy's space.

"Christina?" Danny's voice got louder as he moved up the stairs. "You okay? Your sister-in-law and your son just left."

Christina tightened her grip on the envelopes. Whatever that paperwork contained, every instinct she had told her to hide it. Even from Danny.

Humpy's space would do just fine.

"Christina? Where are you?" Danny was in the upstairs hall now.

Christina stuffed the envelopes into Humpy's hump, careful to close the Velcro around the opening.

She walked over to the hutch, stood on tiptoes, and placed the animal back on his shelf. She stepped away to check.

"Where are you at?" Danny, impatient now, walked down the hall to the master bedroom suite.

Humpy keeled over on his side, off-kilter now, with an empty space next to him like a neon sign.

The stuffed camel looked drunk like Christina, trying but not able to fit in with the tennis trophies and snow-globe paperweights and whatnot.

"Christina?" Danny, exasperated, was heading this way. "Christina?"

Christina stepped up on tiptoes once more and righted Humpy with hands that shook. She pushed together the snow globe and one of the trophies, grabbing another stuffed animal from a different shelf at the last second before springing away from the bookshelf. There was no time to check.

"There you are." Danny appeared in the doorway.

Heart pounding, Christina turned back to the bed and began smoothing the covers.

"What?" Danny frowned, one hand on the knob. "You don't answer when I call you?"

CHAPTER

21

Christina came to in late afternoon or early evening, she wasn't sure which.

The phone was ringing, and she knew it had been for some time, so that she had made it a part of her dreams. Dreams of loss. Nana was there, alive but not, in a place of noise and darkness, shaking her head sadly while Christina searched for something that was already gone.

Christina's head bounced in the ruts on the road between drunk and hungover.

The sharp, high scent of vodka swam up into her nostrils. A glass on the nightstand was half-full. Groaning, she turned her head away.

The bed beside her was empty.

Rain splashed the windows in horizontal sheets. Waves pounded the shore like giant wrecking balls.

The plasma-screen TV was tuned to the weather station. A forecaster stood outlined in eerie bas-relief against a man-sized map of Long Island, while a giant fur ball slowly spun toward the south shore.

These images did nothing to ease the throbbing in Christina's skull.

"A tropical storm warning is in effect from the Jersey

shore all the way to Montauk and Block Island," the forecaster said. "If you're on the coast, you can expect tides surging up to six feet above normal. You should also be on the lookout for riptides, which are extremely dangerous and unpredictable."

The forecaster droned on, but Christina couldn't focus. Sitting up required all her concentration. Too fast, she knew based on long experience, and she would vomit.

The dress she had worn this morning to Jason's memorial service lay on the floor like a crow with crumpled wings. She stepped around it, heading for the guest room, where she kept her clothes now.

There were sounds from Jason's walk-in closet.

Danny was in there on a step stool, running his hands along the high shelves, so intent he didn't notice Christina at first.

Christina cleared her throat. "Did you lose something?"

Danny whirled around. He was dressed in Jason's robe, one Tyler had given him last Christmas. "Just checking."

"Checking?"

Jason's hats, usually lined up in neat rows, were off-kilter. Golf hats, tennis visors, ski hats, and even a fedora from Brooks Brothers he'd bought and never wore.

"You never know what you might find." Danny shrugged.

Christina said nothing. She needed Tylenol.

"After my father died, it was years before my mother got around to going through the closets. When she finally did, she found a pile of old savings bonds that woulda come in handy early on. You know?"

Christina did know. "We have lawyers for that." Hadn't he told her that both his parents died within weeks of each other? She frowned, her gaze went automatically to the safe, its door hanging open, useless.

She didn't know the combination.

Danny followed her gaze. "Looks like someone cleaned you out."

Christina shook her head and looked away. "It's okay." The pounding inside her head moved down into her shoulders.

"So, you kept important stuff in there?" Danny's tone was casual, helpful.

Christina shrugged. "No, not really."

"Is that right?" Danny said, keeping his tone light.

But he stared at her long enough that Christina became aware that she was still naked.

They had had sex again after Pamela and Tyler had left. Danny had held Christina at first while she cried, comforting her in Tyler's room. It was a new role for him, for them, and it felt awkward.

He had kissed her, slowly and comforting at first, then deeper, tasting the vodka she'd downed.

"Takes the edge off," he'd said with a knowing little smile.

Before Christina had a chance to feel embarrassed, he snapped his fingers. "I have an idea." He dragged her out of Tyler's room and into the hall, giving her a push toward the master bedroom.

Jason's room.

"You go cozy up. I'll be back in a sec." He returned

with two tumblers of Grey Goose on ice and a spare bottle from the freezer. They passed the rest of the afternoon in a blur on the California king bed.

Christina's experiment with the sober life was officially over. She had returned to the two things she could always count on, no matter what.

This time, however, she was off her game.

She couldn't get a buzz no matter how much she drank.

And she couldn't climax.

"You okay?" Danny raised his head from between her legs, wiped his mouth, and did a long, slow neck roll.

He looked haggard. They had never spent so much time together. Danny always went back to his place in the Springs after one of their afternoon fuck sessions.

"I'm good." Christina shifted her weight, trying to get comfortable.

"Good." Danny got back down to business. "Because Operation Cheer Up is under way."

Christina fell back against the pillows but her climax, when it came, was pale and faint.

Like her vodka buzz.

As opposed to her current hangover, which was pounding at her full strength.

Her cell phone chirped.

She squeezed her eyes shut.

"Whoever it is, fuck them." Danny was off his step stool and across the closet in the blink of an eye. He snapped his fingers. "I got just the thing for a hangover. Let's get out."

Rain lashed the bedroom windows, so it was impossible to see across the yard to the tops of the dune.

"I don't know," Christina began.

Danny smiled, warming to his idea. "Let's go to the best restaurant in the Hamptons, just you and me. No more sneaking around."

She opened her mouth to tell him she felt sick, but he put a finger to her lips. "No excuses." He raced off. "I got something that will perk you right up," he called.

There was no use arguing with Danny when he got his mind set, so Christina headed for the guest room. She was reaching for a pair of designer jeans when Danny burst into the room, a ball of energy now, holding a leather bag the size of a shaving kit. "You're gonna like this."

Christina tried again. "I'm kind of tired."

Danny was bent over the contents of his bag. "You got a handheld makeup mirror?"

Wearily, Christina got one for him.

When she returned, Danny handed her a rolled-up crisp new bill. Swiping the mirror with the sleeve of Jason's robe, he measured out white powder and used a razor blade to cut it into thin rows. "This is the best shit to leave Colombia."

"Danny," Christina began. She had used cocaine only rarely, and not recently.

"No ifs, ands, or buts." Danny grabbed her by the wrist.

She hesitated.

He guided her hand, the one with the rolled-up bill to one of the lines of powder, and pushed her down by the back of her neck. "It'll make your hangover go away."

And a short time later, she had to agree. She sipped her Grey Goose cocktail, modeling outfits in a fit of giggles.

They settled on a short pink cocktail dress she'd bought on a whim and never worn.

Danny used his teeth to nibble the tags off, nuzzling her breasts along the way. "My bitch is ready to go."

Christina surveyed herself in the mirror and frowned. He had never called her his "bitch" before. The dress was lower cut than she remembered. "Maybe it's too much," her voice unsteady thanks to the cocaine and vodka.

Danny stood behind her, cupped a breast in each hand, and squeezed. "You know, you could go even bigger."

This set Christina to giggling.

"Come on." Danny led the way back to Jason's room. "My turn."

Christina followed. Seeing Danny wearing Jason's robe that was a size too large had been macabre just a short time ago. But the cocaine had made her feel alive again, like she had been living her life in black and white and suddenly stepped into Technicolor.

At the entrance to Jason's walk-in closet with its three-way mirror, Danny wheeled around and pulled her to him. Kissing her full on the lips so it made a smacking sound, he watched their reflection in the full-length mirror. "Let's find something classy for me."

And they did, shoving aside hangers until they found a sport jacket spun from a fine weave Irish linen and made to order. Christina had purchased the fabric many years ago on Jermyn Street and had the jacket made, but Jason hadn't liked it.

Danny stood, preening and slicking his dark hair back till it gleamed. Under the jacket, he wore a plain white dress shirt that was too big, but he kept it open at the neck so it wasn't noticeable. He settled for his own black denim jeans.

All of Jason's pants were too big.

They were almost ready to go.

Danny watched Christina don a pair of Cartier diamond drop earrings that Jason had given her when Tyler was born. He let out a low whistle. "Nice ice."

"I worked hard for it," Christina replied. She had suffered with morning sickness throughout her second trimester. But it was during the first, she recalled, that Jason began staying out till the wee hours.

Danny went through her jewelry box, examining its contents. "Is all this shit real?"

Christina nodded, not bothering to tell him about the safe-deposit drawer at the bank on Park.

He fingered a heavy platinum necklace with a large sapphire pendant nesting in diamonds. "Wear this," he ordered.

The necklace was over-the-top with the earrings, and both were too much with the sleeveless summer shift. Christina was about to tell him that, but Danny was working the clasp at the back of her neck.

He stepped back to admire his choice. "Works your cleavage." He licked his lips wolfishly.

Christina was unsteady, working her feet into silver slingback sandals.

Danny surveyed himself in the mirror and scowled. "I need something." He pulled off the black plastic watch he always wore, even when he was plastering. "I can't wear this piece of shit."

Christina thought of Jason's Rolex, sealed inside the plastic bag from the coroner's office, down in the garage. Even in her cocaine-fueled state, that would be pushing the envelope.

Danny pouted. "Now I got nothing."

The Rolex was going to sit there, go to waste. So what if Danny wore it for a couple of hours? Nobody would know. And Christina Cardiff had not had a night out in about a million years.

A million and one years, to be exact.

"I have just the thing," she said playfully.

Danny's pout faded.

She experienced no more than a passing twinge when she used Danny's penknife to slit open the Suffolk County seal on the evidence bag inside the garage. Not even a twinge. They had stopped to do more lines with a chaser of champagne before leaving the house.

She reached inside the bag, feeling her way past the swim trunks, now dry, to the small baggie at the bottom that contained the Rolex and Jason's wedding ring. She fished out the Rolex, leaving the baggie and ring where they were. "Here," she said, "now you're as good as me."

Christina made for the old Suburban, which would make the most sense in a storm like this.

Danny held back, eyeing Jason's sports coupe. "You know, I've always wanted to drive a car like this."

In the end, they took Jason's car.

The station was bustling despite the fact that it was after five on a Friday, the time most people would be heading home for a barbecue or, on Long Island in the summer, off to the beach. Police stations, like firehouses, bus depots, and emergency rooms, never slowed down.

The scent of coffee permeated the conference room, thanks to the ancient Mr. Coffee setup that had been brewing in one corner for as long as Frank McManus could remember. He offered some to his guests, who took one look and shook their heads.

Señora Rosa and her niece, Marisol, sat across the table from him, clutching their pocketbooks.

They looked like they'd rather be having root canals. In hell. Still, something had prompted them to drive over here unannounced. He'd been surprised when the sergeant on duty had buzzed to say he had visitors. "Thank you for coming out in the rain," McManus said to get the ball rolling.

The women exchanged nervous glances.

Waiting to see whether INS agents were going to leap out from the men's room next door. Based on the loud flushing coming through the wall, you could only hope they'd stop to wash their hands.

"It's good," Frank said. "No problem for you to be here." He gave a nod that was meant to reassure them. New York State remained a safe haven, meaning undocumented aliens could contact law enforcement or seek medical treatment without any risk of arrest. Which made McManus's job easier, so people could speak up to help solve a crime without fear they'd land in jail.

Like now. "No problem." McManus put some body language into it this time, leaning all the way back in his chair till it gave a warning squeak.

The term "conference room" gave the place too much credit. It was nothing more than a battered steel table surrounded by a graveyard of chairs no longer suitable for desk use.

"So?" McManus said, using his best it's-all-good tone.

The two women exchanged nervous glances.

Marisol prepared to speak, leaning in close to the table.

Her voice was soft, but the look in her eyes was not.

"I have some information about Meessus Christina Cardiff."

Langdon's Roadhouse was an East End legend, hidden at the end of a narrow lane that twisted through wild marshes before opening onto a sandy bay. The path to the front door wound past mounds of shells from little neck clams six inches deep in places, castoffs from generations of diners on the back deck.

A sign behind the scarred oak bar advised no drinks would be served before six. Next to the sign was a battered clock with hands permanently fixed at five minutes past six.

Jason Cardiff had been a regular.

The lone valet on duty, huddled in a windbreaker that was no match for the storm, recognized Jason's Porsche and sprang into action with an oversized umbrella. His smile faded when he saw Danny at the wheel. "Good evening, Mrs. Cardiff." He rushed around to her side.

"Good evening," she murmured, accepting his hand to pull herself out of the car.

"Hey, sport," Danny called. "Leave it right here in front."

The kid stared. "No problem."

The place was deserted inside.

"Good evening, folks. You've got your choice of seats tonight." The maitre d's face fell when he got a look at Christina. "Good evening, Mrs. Cardiff." His voice lost some of its booming quality. "And you, sir."

"Cunningham." Danny, unsmiling, extended his hand. "Daniel Cunningham."

"Right." The maitre d' shook hands while giving an

uneasy glance at Christina, who was feeling the effects of the last few lines of coke.

She rubbed her nose and sniffed, shifting her dress around. Her skin was crawling.

Danny Cisco rubbed his nose and sniffed. "You got a table for us or what?"

"But of course, sir." The maitre d's voice was overloud as he grabbed two menus and swept his arm across, taking in the empty room. "Your choice, sir."

Danny swept past and Christina followed, unsteady on her feet.

Rain lashed the windows, shut tight. Normally, there would be a beautiful sunset over the bay.

Tonight, the wood-paneled room felt desolate as a tomb.

"Bring us a bottle of French champagne, your good stuff," Danny ordered.

Christina winced. All champagne was French.

The maitre d' frowned. "What type of champagne would you prefer?"

There was silence.

Both men turned to Christina, who was attempting to push a lock of hair into place. The wind had mussed it. She looked, she knew, a mess. "Huh?"

The maitre d' cleared his throat. "Do you have any preference as to which type of champagne?" The question was directed at Danny, who in turn stared at Christina.

Christina shrugged. Jason always chose the wine. "You pick," she said to Danny, scratching her arms.

Danny looked down and began tapping his left foot.

A moment passed.

The maitre d' developed a smirk.

Another second or two passed.

Christina felt dumb, standing in the center of an empty dining room unable to choose where to sit or what to drink. She wasn't used to this, and worse, she was starting to sway.

"Mrs. Cardiff?" The maitre d' took a step in her direction.

"Got it," Danny said brusquely, grabbing her arm. "She just needs a little something."

The maitre d' gave a knowing look.

Christina had had enough of this. "You pick," she told the maitre d', making a beeline for the nearest table.

The man raced past to pull a chair away from the table she was aiming for.

She tottered, ready to sink down.

"No." Danny's voice rang out. "This one's no good."

Christina struggled to stay upright as the maitre d' frowned. "Sir?"

Danny glared. "Place is empty. Why should we sit near the door?"

"Of course." The man backed off, waiting with his menus. "Whatever you would like, Mr. Cunningham."

"Pick one," Christina said at last. "Pick two." She laughed at her own joke, then couldn't stop.

One look at Danny's face silenced her.

He was quiet and still except for the muscles in his jaw, which were working overtime.

She remembered an argument he'd had over a parking spot with one of the landscapers last summer. After, Danny had backed the white construction van up over the man's Toro edging machine while the man gestured and shouted wildly in Spanish.

"Sorry," Danny had said.

But the Toro machine was crumpled beyond repair.

"That one." Danny pointed at a table in front of the windows. "I want that one."

"Very good. Please follow me." The man led the way, pulling both chairs away from the table Danny had indicated.

Danny made a show of pushing Christina's chair in before seating himself and grabbing both menus. "Get the champagne," he said, waving the man off.

"I'll send your waiter at once," the maitre d' replied.

Christina did not tell Danny how rude he was being because she knew it would provoke him. So she pretended it wasn't happening, the same way she ignored the cooking staff who peeked at them through the kitchen doors.

They clinked glasses in a toast when the champagne arrived.

"To us," Danny said.

"To us," Christina echoed.

He kept his glass aloft. "To a good partnership."

It was an odd choice of words.

Christina's Grey Goose buzz was almost gone. She downed her glass, and Danny refilled it.

Dinner passed in a haze.

They picked over the steaks they ordered and sent back, after Danny insisted neither of them was truly rare enough, concentrating instead on polishing off a second bottle of champagne.

When the plates were cleared, Danny raised his glass once more. "Time for another toast." He smiled.

Christina hoisted her glass, spilling a little. She was pretty wasted. But it was okay. Danny never cared about that.

"To the future." There was a light in the depths of Danny's eyes. "To us." He clinked his glass against hers, which caused her to spill more.

She laughed, covering her mouth with one hand.

"Christina." Danny leaned forward. "I want this to be the beginning of us, our lives." He grabbed her hand across the table as she nodded, not quite following.

"Sure," she mumbled.

"Together."

Christina clinked her glass and took another swallow, closing her eyes as the bubbles bit the back of her throat. What she wanted was vodka, cold and clean. Because this champagne was only giving her a mild hit. Her buzz from earlier was fading.

Danny was saying something, squeezing her fingers.

It took a moment for his words to sink in.

"Married . . ." he said. "A fresh start . . . fuck everyone else."

The word "married" had a sobering effect. Christina sat up straight and began to pull her hand away.

Danny tightened his grip.

"What?" Christina struggled to focus.

He kept on smiling. "You and me. We're good. Fuck everything that happened before. We'll get married, live however we want." He paused, lowered his voice. "Like we said."

Christina looked out the window.

The night was black. There was nothing to see but raindrops glistening on the glass like silver bullets. And her own face staring back at her. She turned away.

From across the table, Danny watched. "Now's the time," he said quietly.

The room seemed to shift, like some unseen hand had

rotated the walls a quarter turn. Christina's stomach turned queasy. She shook her head, trying to take it in, her voice came out barely above a whisper. "It's just way soon."

Danny's gaze did not waver. "This is what we wanted."

"Yeah," she said slowly. "But these last few weeks . . ."

There was a small pucker in the tablecloth, and she gathered it now, making little folds of fabric and pressing them against the base of her champagne flute over and over again.

It gave her fingers something to do.

Danny grabbed her hands. He didn't wait for her to finish. "Fuck these last few weeks. That place you went to was bullshit." He spat the words out. "Bullshit," he repeated. "You don't need that psycho crap. You just need to live how you want to live. With me."

Christina looked at him uncertainly.

He squeezed her hands, leaned forward across the table. "Just you and me, like we said. From now on, we do whatever the fuck we want with nobody to tell us what to do." His eyes were penetrating, his voice intent. "All this"—he hesitated, looked around for the right word—"all this bullshit is over, starting now.

"We get hooked up, we go down to the Bahamas, have some laughs, party, and get all this bullshit behind us. Starting now. Tonight."

Christina nodded uncertainly. She couldn't think straight with him holding her hand.

But he was not loosening his grip.

She hesitated. "There's Tyler."

"Tyler's fine," Danny burst out.

Christina stared, her eyes widening with alarm.

Danny stroked her hand, lowering his voice a notch. "You know what I mean. He's fine. He's got his place at school, he's busy with his grandparents and his friends. You know how kids are."

Christina nodded slowly. "Yeah." But she didn't see it that way.

Danny hunched even closer. "Listen, doll. We talked about this a lot, and I know it's tough for you. I know that." His voice was warm now and sweet.

Christina nodded.

"But I live my life with a plan. And one thing I've learned"—here Danny loosened his grip long enough to stab his index finger onto the table to make his point—"is you stick to the plan. You don't abandon the plan because times get tough. You stick to it and ride it out." He made a sliding motion sideways through the air with his fingers. "You ride it out." He paused. "You see what I'm saying?"

Christina had been holding her breath. She let it out now.

Danny watched her intently. Waiting.

"I get it."

"Good," he said. "Because now's the time to ride it out. Like I said."

He picked up her champagne flute and pressed it into her hands. "That bullshit they told you at that place you went. You don't need that." He picked up his own glass. "You don't need to go cold turkey on anything." He lowered his voice again. "Don't listen to these bullshit people. You got money, you go live your life. Don't try to do so much at once."

Their eyes met.

"You see what I'm saying?"

Christina, weary and wobbly and confused, nodded.

Danny smiled. "Good." He clinked his champagne flute against hers. "To us."

Christina closed her eyes and drank. The rest of her life stretched out before her, empty and uncertain. Her old life was gone. Jason was gone. And Tyler might be gone as well.

Danny was talking again. "We've had laughs," he was saying. "Good times. We'll have more."

Christina nodded. She didn't know what else to do.

"Good." Danny beamed. As though that settled it.

Christina was about to say more, but he jumped out of his chair and came around the table. He picked her up, sweeping her off her feet so fast she lost one of her sandals under the table.

He kissed her right there, long and hard and deep, bending her over backwards like a rag doll.

When he released her at last, he made a loud smacking sound with his lips.

Christina had a bad landing, with one shoe on and one shoe off. She grabbed the edge of the table for balance. She had lost weight since purchasing her dress last spring, and one of the straps slid off her shoulder, exposing most of her breast.

A flash exploded outside, then another and another.

Christina fumbled for her strap, but Danny was moving much faster than she.

He hiked her arm high overhead in a victory flourish. "She said yes," he shouted. "Yes!"

Christina heard a smattering of applause from the staff gathered at the kitchen door.

Danny bowed, pulling her down with him, and she fell.

Danny helped her up.

She blinked in the glare of flashing lights as Danny hoisted her up and put her sandal back onto her foot.

"Don't worry," he said. "You're beautiful no matter what, dollface." He clapped a hand on her buttocks, hard, and planted another big kiss on her mouth.

There was more applause from the kitchen.

The waiter insisted dinner was on Jimmy Langdon, waving off her credit card.

Danny, Christina noticed, made no attempt to pay.

They left, stepping directly into a maelstrom Christina never could have anticipated.

At least a dozen flashbulbs exploded as a crowd of paparazzi closed in, oblivious to the howling wind and lashing rain.

"Christina! Christina!" they cried, closing in.

Langdon's must have tipped them off. Christina remembered how rude Danny had been to the maitre d' when they arrived. She shrank against Danny now, uttering a cry of fright as the pack closed in on them.

"Is it true you're engaged?"

"Who's the lucky man?"

"How'd you two meet?"

"Is it true your husband wanted a divorce?"

"When's the wedding?"

Danny answered this last, skidding to a halt while the rain drenched Christina's new dress. "Soon, boys," he called with a smile. "Real soon." He kissed her again while the cameras clicked and whirred. "C'mon, baby, give 'em what they want."

Christina felt too trapped to argue. Squinting in the glare, she did as he asked. "Please," she whispered through gritted teeth. "Please, can we go?"

"Sure." He grinned from ear to ear. "We're done now. Fuck them."

They ran to the car.

Danny gunned the engine, taking off in a squeal of tires and a chorus of shouts from the paparazzi, some of whom had to jump out of his way.

Danny just laughed, slapping his free hand on the flesh of Christina's bare leg. "It's official."

CHAPTER

22

It was going on two in the morning, and Frank McManus could not sleep. The storm kept him up.

He rolled over, grabbed the clicker, and switched on The Weather Channel. The tropical storm that had been looming changed its rotation and was now spinning away from Long Island, out to sea. The storm surge was probably at its peak right about now, although the surf would remain rough for days.

Long Island had dodged a bullet.

He got out of bed and padded down the center hall of the small ranch, into the kitchen for a cold beer. Twisting the top, he opened the back door and got hit full on with a wet wind.

There wasn't much to see, what with the wind blowing in sideways gusts, blowing rain every which way against the asbestos shingles outside the house.

Frank took a swig of his tall boy. He could probably fall asleep again if he put his mind to it. But there was no joy in returning to an empty bed and, truth be told, Frank McManus loved a good storm. His plan was to spend tomorrow, his day off, at the ocean to see what the storm had washed up.

At the moment his mind churned with the events surrounding Jason Cardiff's death.

His thoughts kept returning to Biz Brooks and her noisy little dog.

She had left a message on Frank's machine earlier today, just back from the reception at Christina Cardiff's house.

"Shep barked at something in the woods the night Jason Cardiff died," Biz said in her message.

Even on a machine, her voice sounded nice.

"I know the car I heard belonged to Daniel Cunningham," she said firmly. "Or Danny Cisco. Whatever his name is. It's his car, and it's a Toyota that needs a new muffler. He drove up our road the night Jason died. I know it was Danny Cisco's car because I saw him drive it to Christina's house for the reception after the memorial service today."

Frank McManus didn't doubt Biz was right.

Her observations fit the time line he and Ben Jackson had constructed for the night of Jason Cardiff's death. The way they figured it, the group from Hang Ten left Cardiff's place sometime around midnight. Danny Cisco returned later, parking his noisy Toyota at one of the empty houses close to Dunemere and returning on foot for a private meeting with Jason Cardiff.

A meeting that had resulted in Cardiff's death.

He thought about Biz Brooks alone in her tidy Cape way out on Jonah's Path. Alone near the ocean in a storm, except for her crazy neighbors and that yappy dog. He hoped that yappy dog was too high-strung to sleep through storms like the one that was brewing out there tonight.

So Biz would have some warning if that scumbag Cisco was driving around in the rain near her house.

"Here's to you, Shep," Frank muttered as he took another swig of his beer.

"Our man Cisco was planning a runner," Ben Jackson had observed as they pulled out of Cisco's driveway in the Springs this morning.

" 'Fraid so," Frank had agreed.

"He ain't getting far now."

"Nope."

Ben Jackson had grinned. "Confucius say, 'The journey of a thousand miles begins with a single step.' "

"More like six miles," Frank mused, "due north to Jonah's Path."

Biz Brooks's call confirmed that Danny Cisco had, indeed, headed straight for Christina Cardiff after their meeting with him on his driveway this morning.

So had Frank's impromptu visit late in the afternoon from the Cardiffs' cleaning ladies, Señora Rosa and her niece, Marisol.

Marisol had done most of the talking. "She is with that man. Daniel." She spat the name out and looked at her aunt Rosa, who was clenching her gold crucifix like it might leap off her necklace. "The house painter," Marisol added, to make sure Frank got it.

Frank nodded to show he got it.

"Those two," Marisol leaned forward, raising her index fingers to illustrate her point, "together are no good." She pushed her index fingers together, dark eyes flashing. "No good."

"No good," Señora Rosa had echoed.

Frank McManus agreed, despite his hunch that Marisol's motive for hauling in here in the rain today was the simple fact that she was jealous of her late boss's widow because she, Marisol, had been sleeping with him.

Or perhaps Marisol had been collecting overtime on Jason Cardiff's payroll, keeping an eye on things while Jason was out and about with his gal pal, Lisa.

Or maybe she just wanted to throw them off the scent of her Dream Date. Roberto Torres.

Or option D), All of the above.

The wind shifted, sending a heavy dose of spray through the screen.

Frank closed the door, grabbed a kitchen towel to mop at his arms before swiping it across the floor with his foot.

Floor could use a washing anyway.

There was still half a Bud remaining.

He headed for the living room, whose main décor consisted of a giant Hi-Def flat-screen TV and a desk with a hutch that contained his computer. He switched the computer on and settled in his chair while it flashed through start-up screens, flipping on the lamp while he waited to sign on to Google.

Google, as any widowed or divorced person could tell you, was the insomniac's best friend.

He had long ago tracked the marital status of every girl he'd had a crush on since junior high, even Mary Jean McCoy who he played spin the bottle with in seventh grade. She had decked him hard after his turn. She never married and was living in Santa Fe, New Mexico.

Frank McManus typed in Christina Cardiff. Nothing new. The same photos, now almost forty-eight hours old, of the Mercedes ramming her front gate on Jonah's Path.

Sometimes it took a while for his Mac to get cached pages.

He went directly to a popular Hamptons gossip site and was rewarded with photos barely three hours old.

"Wow." Frank stared at the screen. He reached for the phone and hit speed dial, checking the time as the call was being placed. Just after 2:00 A.M. Oops. Frank dropped the receiver back into place before the call went through. It was Ben Jackson's loss. These photos were worth a look-see.

A grainy one, shot with a telephoto lens showing the inside of Jimmy Langdon's Roadhouse, a place Frank knew well and liked, of Christina Cardiff clinking champagne glasses high in the air with none other than Danny Cisco.

Everyone grieves in their own way. "My ass," Frank muttered, draining the last of his beer.

There was another of the couple leaving the restaurant, with Cisco holding Christina's thin arm high overhead like he was hoisting the Stanley Cup after a playoff win.

The caption underneath read, "Cardiff widow to wed mystery man."

"You gotta be kidding me," Frank said out loud. He set the empty bottle down on the desk with a clank and kept reading. "Sources at Langdon's Roadhouse tonight confirmed Christina Cardiff, brand-new widow of Wall Streeter Jason Cardiff, whose drowning death just days ago has shocked the East End, was out celebrating her engagement to the mystery man (pictured here)."

There was a photo of Cisco with his tongue halfway down Christina Cardiff's throat.

Frank McManus frowned.

"It was gross, according to one witness, who said the pair were both pretty wasted."

Unbelievably, there was another series taken later at a jewelry store on East Hampton's Main Street, which reportedly stayed open late for their benefit. In one, Christina Cardiff waved her left hand in the air so she and her "mystery man" could admire the ring while the salespeople looked on.

There were more, but they were overkill. Frank McManus didn't need to see any more to know that Danny Cisco was directly involved in Jason Cardiff's death.

McManus kept playing the crime scene over and over in his mind. Jason Cardiff's body showed no sign of bruising, according to the ME's report. Meaning he hadn't been pushed into the pool. At least not hard enough to lacerate Cardiff's bare skin.

Frank McManus stared at the screen. If he wanted to push someone overboard, he'd be damned careful not to leave any marks. He'd be careful not to use enough force to cause bruising, which wouldn't be much of a problem if the guy was as wasted as Jason Cardiff had been.

He'd push him squarely in the seat of his pants, so as not to scratch the skin or scoop any of the guy's DNA under his fingernails by accident.

Swim trunks didn't collect fingerprints.

Frank McManus squinted his eyes shut. They were sore now. He rubbed his eyes, knew he should probably go back to bed.

Something he'd read came back to him, headlines from the not-too-distant past.

Frank's eyes sprang open.

Grabbing the mouse, he directed the browser back to Google and JonBenet Ramsey. There were close to half a million hits on the tragic strangulation of a little girl in Colorado in her own home on Christmas morning. Frank scrolled past the most-viewed cached pages with details of the 1996 crime, the autopsy photos and the gooey cyberspace tributes to the slain beauty-pageant queen, till he found the link he wanted.

CNBC reports that Jon and Patsy Ramsey, parents of the little girl, had been exonerated following discovery of evidence that a stranger had touched the little girl's pajamas, using brand-new technology that hadn't been available at the time of JonBenet's murder.

None of which changed the fact that Frank McManus, like most of America, believed the Ramseys were guilty as hell.

The cached pages contained the information he sought.

The Suffolk County DA, he knew, would welcome his request for a warrant with open arms. The district court judge on call for the weekend would consider their request, and if things went Frank's way, sometime tomorrow he'd go back to Jonah's Path to collect Jason Cardiff's swim trunks for complete testing.

Frank McManus directed his browser to the Google home page once more.

He entered "DNA touch technology."

Behind the low cover of storm clouds, dawn came to Long Island's East End as sudden and fast as ever. The change in light woke her, the steady brightening of the room from pitch to dark gray.

Christina Cardiff had spent a fitful night, caught in the state that was neither sleeping nor awake thanks to the drugs and alcohol coursing through her system and the storm that lashed the shore just steps from where she slept. She'd dreamed noisy dreams, dreams that echoed with the sound of rooms devoid of color, only shadows in shades of gray that flitted around corners and doors that opened and closed, opened and closed.

The rain, for now, had stopped. She saw this through the dull dishwater haze that had seeped into her brain and would not leave.

They had drunk quite a bit. Not enough for Christina to get off. Just enough to produce that dull haze.

She and Danny had had sex when they came home. Raucous and bordering on rough, the way they used to before Christina went to rehab.

She had fallen into a deep sleep immediately after, as the coke's effects faded, leaving her nervous system drained and exhausted.

But she couldn't sleep for long. Furtive noises roused her. The bed beside her was empty each time. She was too exhausted and too sick to get up to investigate. Once, she noticed lights on and tried to sit up, but her stomach heaved. She fell back into fitful slumber.

She must have slept through the dark hours till dawn, when she finally felt strong enough to sit up.

There was a glass of clear liquid on the nightstand and she reached for it. The sharp scent of vodka filled her nostrils, and she set it back down with a shudder.

Water. Christina needed water. And aspirin.

The bed next to her was empty.

She raised herself slowly on one elbow, willing the room to stop spinning, and swung her feet cautiously over the side of the bed. Her head felt like it was going to split right down the middle. She became aware of a weight on her left hand, familiar but not.

Christina raised her hand to look and groaned out loud.

"No!" She closed her eyes. When she opened them again, the ring was still there.

A brand-new diamond ring, on the fourth finger of her left hand.

"No," she moaned again.

The thing weighed three carats at least, and looked to be machine-cut like that stuff they sold on the shopping network. The stone was set in a gaudy hunk of what looked to be white gold. No handiwork there, none of the intricate scrollwork carved in platinum that formed the base of her other engagement ring, the one that had belonged to Jason's maternal grandmother.

The one Christina hadn't paid for with her own Visa card.

She slumped back against the covers.

Snatches of last night came back, like snapshots torn from an album.

She had agreed to marry Daniel Cunningham.

"Ugh." The pounding in her head intensified. Squeezing her eyes shut, Christina curled into a ball and dragged the covers over her head, willing herself back to sleep.

The sound of heavy footsteps in the hall ruled that out.

"Good morning, dollface!" Danny Cisco entered carrying a tray. "Breakfast."

The scent of coffee hit her. Hard. Christina wrinkled her nose and tried to ignore the pull it had on the insides of her stomach.

Danny plopped the tray on the bed. "I got coffee. I got toast. I got orange juice. I got ice-cold Grey Goose."

"Ugh." Christina clutched the sides of her stomach and fought the urge to be sick right there.

"Little hair of the dog, that's all." Danny landed on the bed next to her, his movements jerky. Unsteady.

Christina opened one eye to squint at him. What she saw made her open the other for a better look.

She had never seen him like this. His skin was several shades paler than normal, with dark hollows under his eyes. His hair stuck straight up on top of his head. He reached up and ran a hand through it, for what must have been the thousandth time. He smiled at her crookedly. One side of his mouth yanked down in a kind of nervous tic.

Christina frowned. "How are you?"

"Any better, and I'd be twins." Danny smiled. The pupils of his eyes were dilated so wide they looked black, the lids rimmed red like blood. "Real good." He kissed her, so she got a strong whiff of something metallic. Sweat mixed with . . . she didn't know what. "Got you here, and that's all I need."

Christina struggled to sit up once more, swinging around to get a better look at him. He didn't look good. For the first time she noticed that everything in the room, from the bookshelves the decorator had filled with objets d'art in varying sizes, to the drawers of the built-ins just inside the closet, to the antique lingerie chest near the mirrors, was off-kilter. Everything had been touched. Christina frowned. "Did you sleep?"

He was swirling lots of sugar into his coffee, stirring it too fast. He shrugged, smiled, and raised the cup to his lips. "Little bit, how about you?"

"A little."

He took a sip of his coffee and offered the cup to her.

Christina wrinkled her nose and looked away. "No, thanks. I never drink it first thing."

Danny smiled, and the effect only intensified the hollow look of his cheeks in the weak light of morning. "Guess I'll have to get to know those things about you."

Bile rose at the back of her throat, and she swallowed. Christina was afraid she was going to be sick.

He pulled her left hand out to admire the ring, and more snatches of last night came to her.

The manager of the jewelry store in East Hampton pulling out one ring at a time so she could try them on. Saying something to his staff while he rang up the sale. Laughing out loud.

"Quite a rock," Danny observed.

Christina nodded.

A memory from rehab floated back. Her counselor, Peter, with his watery blue altar-boy eyes pointing at the closed door to their therapy room.

"Remember," he'd said, "your disease is doing push-ups right outside that door. No matter how much time you spend in here doing the work, your disease is waiting for you outside this room. Waiting for you to drink again. It wants you dead."

Christina realized that in the space of a single day she had once again turned into a blackout drinker. Wary with that knowledge and sick with her hangover, she searched for words. "I don't think," she began.

Danny cut her off. "First step is getting a marriage license." He gave her another quick peck on the cheek. "I'm sure we can find someone working in Hauppauge today," he said, naming the county seat. "It's Saturday, but they should be there till noon." He ran his hand across his scalp, then rolled across the king-sized bed, scratching himself. Unable to sit still.

Christina twisted the ring on her finger. It was too big, and all wrong. "Danny," she said quietly, "I don't think I can do this."

He sat up. "You can," he said simply.

His eyes were dark with shadows, deep spaces with no light inside. Christina thought again how little she knew of him. Jake had called him Danny Cisco. Jake, with his track marks and the well-worn sheet of paper he'd brought to the AA meeting that needed to be signed as proof of attendance for his probation officer, had insisted he knew Danny Cisco from Deer Park, a place Christina had never been. "I think—" she tried again.

Danny cut her off. " 'I think,' " he said in a loud falsetto imitation of her.

And then, with no warning, his arm shot out and knocked her over.

Christina tumbled back onto the covers. "Danny!"

Her protest was of no use. He was on top of her in an instant, pinning her arms and smiling, trying to make it seem like foreplay.

But it didn't feel that way to Christina.

"I think," he repeated, leaning in close so his breath filled her nostrils, "that we should just do it. Today."

Christina felt her breath leave her lungs in a whoosh. She longed to squirm, try to wriggle out from under him, but something warned her not to.

Danny Cisco had a bad temper.

"Too much talk is no good. You understand?" He gave her hands one final squeeze, and this time it was too much.

Christina couldn't hold back a squeal of pain. "Okay."

"Good." He let go, but he leaned in closer and kissed her, forcing her mouth open and moving his tongue inside her.

Fighting the urge to wriggle out from under him, Christina lay there. Passive.

Rolling off her at last, he propped up on one elbow. "We got a lot to do. You clean yourself up. Find your birth certificate. Then we'll go."

He ran a finger slowly, possessively, down the length of her arm.

Christina nodded.

"I got a couple things to do while you get ready."

She nodded again.

"Good." He stood, walking to a suitcase propped open in a corner of the room, and pulled out a T-shirt.

She didn't remember seeing it last night. It was black with vinyl trim and battered wheels, a world of difference from the brown-and-tan Louis Vuitton set she and Jason used.

Christina headed for the bathroom.

Everything—*everything*—was askew, as though it had been moved sometime during the night.

She was sitting on the toilet when Danny poked his head in.

Christina looked down, embarrassed.

"I'll be back in a minute," he announced.

"Okay," Christina mumbled.

"Hey." His voice was loud in the tiled bathroom.

He waited until Christina looked up, forcing a smile to her lips. "Sounds good."

"Good," he replied.

After he had gone, she searched the medicine cabinet for something to stop the pounding in her head.

Here, too, everything had been gone through.

She filled a Dixie cup and downed three Tylenol. The water felt good on the back of her throat, which was hot and raw like a hamburger on the grill.

She went back out to the bedroom and took the phone from its handset charger. The ringer here was always set to silent, but she was certain some of the sounds in her dreams had been the ringing of the phone downstairs.

Scrolling through the RECEIVED CALLS list, she saw a number of attempts had been made throughout the night from a number that was blocked. Keying in her security code, the one she and Jason had shared, she got her messages.

Despite all the attempts to connect, there were only two messages.

Both from the blocked caller, Detective Frank McManus of the Suffolk County Homicide Squad. The older, white cop, the one with the stern Irish face.

In the first, he sounded pissed off. "Mrs. Cardiff, we need to speak with you at your earliest convenience. I realize you're busy today, but we have some information we need to share with you about your husband's death. We now know who he was with and how he spent his time. Call me as soon as possible. Thank you." McManus left his cell-phone number. That call had been placed late yesterday afternoon.

The next message left her throat dry and her heart pounding. It had come in while they were at Langdon's.

McManus's tone held more of an edge, lots more. "Mrs. Cardiff, we've attempted to contact you several times. We have information that is very important for you to know. We need to speak with you, in person."

McManus stressed the words "in person," before continuing. "As soon as possible. We have learned that your companion, Danny Cisco, whom you have identified as Daniel Cunningham, was at your house the night of your husband's death."

Blood was pounding through Christina's temples, loud enough to make it difficult to hear McManus's voice.

A bluish gray mist swam up out of nowhere, clouding her vision.

She reached a hand out to steady herself and knocked over the glass.

It tumbled over, splashing vodka onto the bed, the wall, the rug.

For once in her life, Christina ignored a glass of vodka.

The detective's message continued. "We know for a fact that Danny Cisco was among those present with your husband immediately before his death. We have some information to share with you. I urge you to call as soon as possible." McManus repeated his cell-phone number and hung up.

Christina stood, too numb to move, while the recorded voice from the answering service listed the various options for subscribers who wished to dial another mailbox number or change personal greetings.

Danny had been here with Jason the night of his death.

Icy fingers of dread walked up her spine, fanning out across her shoulders and arms.

He had lied to her about his real name.

She stood, frozen, trying to take it all in.

Outside, the rain had stopped. The weak dawn revealed a sky heavy and swollen with low-hanging clouds. Wind tossed the wet trees. The grass was battered, littered with leaves as though autumn had come.

A movement caught her eye.

She frowned.

A jeans-clad leg disappeared around the corner of the garage.

What was Danny doing out there?

It was Saturday, the landscapers' day off.

There was nobody on the grounds.

He passed back into her line of sight, lugging a can of gasoline Jason kept for the lawn mower he'd bought years ago and used once.

Danny held something in his other hand that tightened the panic's icy grip.

A white plastic bag, one with the Suffolk County seal.

It contained the swim trunks Jason had been wearing when he drowned.

"What?" Christina breathed the question out loud.

There was, however, no one to hear.

Danny disappeared around the side of the garage.

She'd have a better view of that section of yard from Tyler's room.

She grabbed her robe and headed down the hall.

The guest-room door was closed. She stuck her head in, knowing what she'd find. The room had been gone through. The closet door was open and she could see the drawers of the built-in were out of order, some half-closed with sweater sleeves and pant legs hanging over the edges. Christina wasn't much of a housekeeper, so it was nothing that would attract attention on an average day.

Except that Señora Rosa kept the closets in apple-pie order. That's how this closet had looked last night, when Christina and Danny came in, tearing dresses off hangers and modeling them until they settled on the pink one she wore to Langdon's. But they hadn't touched the built-in drawers.

The hairs on the back of Christina's neck were waving wildly now. She crossed the hall to Tyler's room.

Things here were the same. The bedspread hung off-kilter.

Someone had pulled off the covers and remade the bed.

The desk had been gone through, with some drawers closed and some open a fraction of an inch.

Tyler's paperweight cube and pencil case had been dumped, their contents strewn on the desk blotter.

The entire place appeared to have been burgled by someone moving fast, with no time to spare.

Christina hurried to the window.

Danny was pouring gasoline onto something in the fire pit.

Her heart started to pound. She was surprised it wasn't pushing the terry robe open. She cinched the belt tighter in an effort to stop shivering.

It was no use.

She turned back to the room.

The bookshelves had been gone through but not, she prayed, as thoroughly as the rest of the place. The books on the lower shelves had been moved. Hoppy, Humpy the camel, and Clown still sat up top where they always did.

She reached up and grabbed Humpy, pulling the Velcro apart.

Her shaking fingers felt paper.

The manila envelopes were still stuffed inside.

Thank God.

Her knees practically buckled with relief.

She pulled the envelopes out and tossed Humpy on the desk, certain these were what Danny was after.

Just as Pamela Lofting Cardiff had been.

One of the envelopes had a familiar heft in its center. It was the one containing the DVD.

Christina fumbled for the maroon string with fingers that shook while she walked to the window.

A thin plume of smoke was rising through the air.

Danny watched, arms crossed over his muscular chest.

She got the envelope open.

Inside was a sheaf of papers from the law offices of Maurice Gold, pertaining to the filing of divorce proceedings in the State of New York.

The words Cardiff vs. Cardiff swam into focus.

Christina's pulse raced. Her breaths came in short, shallow bursts.

The *New York Post* had it right. Jason had been about to file for divorce.

But she didn't have time to read through those papers now.

Not with the DVD weighing heavy in her hand. A distant thrumming noise started in Christina's ears as she stared down at it, plain and white.

The thrumming noise in Christina's head intensified into a hammering. Her hands turned slick, so each finger left a small, humid print on the side of the plastic case.

Which made it difficult to pry the case open.

But she managed.

Christina switched on the plasma-screen TV they'd given Tyler for his thirteenth birthday.

She slid the DVD into the slit at the side, and it seemed to take forever to start scanning, but it was only a few seconds.

Enough time for Christina to realize she knew what it contained.

Waking up the day after was like finding myself in a pit at the bottom of hell.

Memories of that night come back to me in bits and

pieces. I don't know what I can't remember until something else comes back to fill in the gaps. Big, empty gaps.

There is a word for what happened that night, and the word is too ugly even to think.

I remember there was music coming from Danny's boom box. I know I liked it, and we were dancing.

Other people were waiting for us in the little basement apartment he rented in the Springs. They were partying when we got there and everyone laughed and clapped when we walked down into this cave of a room he lived in.

There was a mattress on the floor in a corner.

I smelled pot right away, I do remember that. I don't like it, I never have, but once you smell it, you can always recognize it.

A couple was on the bed making out. The girl had her top off. She looked at me and smiled.

Danny kind of pushed me into the center of the living room, and said, "We're here. It's ladies' night."

Everyone started laughing, and so did I.

I remember being thirsty, so thirsty I ran to the sink for water. I was on my second glass when Danny took it from me. "You don't want too much of that," he said. "It's the E, do you get it?"

I didn't really get it, but I said I did. I knew those tablets we dropped in the car were something like that, Ecstasy. He had talked about it before and I resisted but right then I was glad we did it. Ecstasy does that to you, you know what I mean? I guess I shouldn't say this, but I felt better that night than I ever had in my entire life, like I loved every single one of those people more than anyone I had ever met.

We started dancing, Danny and I, and everyone joined in. Everyone was laughing. We were all in a big circle like a square dance and I wanted it to go on and on forever.

The couple from the bed got up and she was dancing topless and really getting off on it, you know, touching herself and letting her boyfriend touch her boobs and then Danny started touching them, and it didn't even bother me. I mean, if you really want to know, it turned me on. I wanted them to touch ME that way and I must have said it out loud because Danny came right over to me.

"Come on, baby," he said, smiling that way he has. "You could, too, you know." He put his hands up inside my shirt and next thing you know it was off and we were all laughing and I felt hands on me, all over me, and it was wild.

Christina stared at the screen in Tyler's room with its flickering scenes from hell.

She watched a version of herself, Christina the Porn Queen, star of the movies Jason liked to watch, bobbing her head up and down like a rubber doll to keep time with the rhythm of the men and women taking turns with her.

At one point, Porn Queen Christina squinted drunkenly at the camera. "Are you filming this?"

There was laughter, then Danny's thick hands coming up to pull her down . . .

She had taken part in an orgy.

The clicker slid from Christina's hand to the floor as a wave of hot shame crashed over her, swamping her in memories of that night.

She gasped for air. It was difficult to breathe.

Christina raised her hands to her throat to clear a passage, but it did no good.

What would Nana say? Nana, who'd lit a candle before Mass every Sunday in memory of her own long-dead husband, the smiling young man in military garb whose photo had been lovingly preserved next to Christina's inside a plastic sleeve in Nana's frayed wallet.

Christina's ears filled with the mighty roaring sound of that wave of shame.

How did the DVD get here? How? How? How? *How?*

A memory came back. Danny sliding his hand high up inside Christina's short skirt while Jason leaned over, steps away, peering at something the head contractor pointed to down near the floorboards.

Realization hit home in another deep wave.

Danny didn't care if Jason saw the flirtations between them because he knew Jason was in on it.

Another memory came back. She had returned home early from a canceled tennis lesson to find Danny and Jason on the lawn, out of earshot of the other workers, deep in conversation. Seeing her, they sprang apart . . .

The awful significance of the DVD swirled through Christina's mind like a funnel cloud.

Danny had made the DVD, and it wound up in Jason's safe.

Why? Why? Why? *Why?*

Christina knew the answer would be spelled out in the papers from the law offices of Maurice Gold, LLC.

Jason planned to use the DVD as evidence against her in divorce proceedings.

Danny, *her* Danny, the one she imagined she was in love with, had videotaped their sex play.

At Jason's request.

Another realization, just as awful, followed the first.

Her mind recoiled from it, even though she knew it was true. What if Danny had pursued her, initiated their entire affair, because Jason had hired him to do it?

Another memory. Danny, half-joking, asking if the Storm dealership in Southampton would give him a good deal on a Mercedes like hers.

"I might be in the market. Business is good this year," he'd said, "Better than ever."

Their affair had been tumultuous and wild, building finally to that night barely two weeks ago.

Not just any night, the night that had left her too sick and too ashamed to look at her own reflection in the mirror the next day.

The day Christina Cardiff woke up so sick and so desperate she packed herself off to rehab.

She must have thrown a monkey wrench into her husband's plans.

Jason Cardiff had told her many times that he'd leave her penniless, the way he found her, if she cheated. But that wasn't the part that scared Christina. It was Jason's cool resolve that he would take Tyler from her.

Christina had never doubted that Jason would keep his word.

New York's archaic divorce laws would have made it easy for Jason to walk away with his precious Cardiff family trust intact, taking his son—*their* son, with him. It would be easy to do if he had proof that Christina's behavior was immoral.

The images she'd just viewed, complete with sounds

that would have been at home in a barnyard, were all the proof he needed.

Her sister-in-law, Pamela Lofting Cardiff, had told the truth. The tabloids had got it right.

Jason *had* been planning to divorce her, and she was the last to know, on terms so ugly Christina would have had no choice but to walk away.

But Christina had thrown a curveball Jason's way.

Checking herself into rehab made it less likely Jason's mud would stick.

There was another curveball, however. Her growing feelings for Danny as the summer wore on. She thought back to the game they played so many times after they had sex.

Danny and she would take turns imagining what life would be like if they were married.

"If you got a good settlement," Danny said, "I wouldn't have to work so freakin' hard."

When had their pillow talk turned to talk of divorce settlements, she wondered?

It had been Danny's doing, not hers.

Because he had known what Jason was planning.

"Oh, my God," Christina whispered, pressing her fingers to her mouth to keep from throwing up. But there was nothing she could do to stop the pounding in her heart.

Danny had been hired to trap her. By Jason.

And now Jason was dead.

Young Jake had tried to warn her. So had Frank McManus, the Suffolk County Homicide detective. He had come to the church yesterday morning, and later through the day he'd left two messages on her cell phone. Urging her to call him.

But she hadn't.

There was a click from the TV as the DVD played to the end.

"My God," Christina breathed.

The bedroom walls were spinning like a Tilt-A-Whirl.

Her stomach heaved.

Jason rarely swam in the pool. Especially not at night.

Never when he was alone.

Now she suspected he hadn't been alone. More than likely, Danny had been there.

Downstairs, the screen door slammed.

"Christina!" Danny's voice boomed.

Christina made no reply; her only thought was to find someplace to hide.

"Christina!" Danny crossed the wood floor of the main room and began climbing the stairs. "You outta the shower yet?"

Heart pounding, she picked up the remote from the floor and fumbled for the OFF button. Her palms were slick with sweat, her fingers shaking so bad she fumbled and dropped it.

Danny was climbing the stairs.

Christina made a frantic grab for the clicker, sweeping it under Tyler's bed along with the manila envelopes from Maurice Gold's office.

"Christina?" Danny's voice was sharp now. A moment later he appeared in the doorway. "There you are," he said softly, scanning the room.

Too late, Christina realized she had left Humpy lying on the desk, upended with his Velcro compartment hanging open.

Empty and glaring.

She had been in the midst of tightening the belt on her robe but she froze, watching Danny take it all in with those dark eyes, hooded now.

The DVD player whirred and clicked the way the newest models did even after they were switched off. Resetting itself.

The sound cracked through the room like a gunshot.

The screen flashed, PLAYER READY, across the bottom and went dark.

Christina's heart sank.

"So"—Danny turned his gaze on Christina with eyes that were laser-sharp—"you found it."

There was something there, in the words he left unsaid. A challenge, perhaps.

Christina sensed that her world hung in the balance. She tried to speak and failed. Her mouth was so dry her tongue stuck to the roof of her mouth.

He stepped inside.

It was a small move that made Christina jump. Instantly, she regretted it.

Danny Cisco gave a smile that was like watching a reptile stretch its lips. "I'll take that."

"No." She raised a hand to stop him.

The look he gave her was a mix of surprise and something else.

It raised hackles along Christina's spine.

Ignoring her protest, Danny walked swiftly to the TV and hit the EJECT button.

This was her house, Christina reminded herself, tightening her grip on the belt of her robe to hide the trembling in her hands. "You didn't tell me," she said, forcing her lips to move, "you were here that night."

Danny held the DVD in his hand. He was very still, watching her with eyes that were rimmed with red, wary. Watching.

On full alert. She thought again of the raccoon they'd found in the attic last fall, how frightened the thing was when they'd first discovered it and tried to coax it toward an open window.

Just before it bared its fangs and hissed, preparing to attack.

"Don't go there," he said softly, running his fingers lightly over the edge of the DVD, never taking his eyes from her face.

"Why?" Christina couldn't help herself. This was the man she had imagined she would give herself to. "What were you doing here, Daniel?" She used the name she had called him at first, before all this started. Daniel Cunningham.

She was not rewarded with any sort of softening.

Instead, his face hardened and set. He shrugged. "There were people here. We were partying, that's all."

"Bullshit." The word left Christina's mouth before she could catch herself. It was a lie, and they both knew it.

Danny shrugged again. His lips curled into a sneer. "It don't make a difference now." He gave a chuckle that had no mirth. "And you know it."

Horror took root deep in her solar plexus, sending icy tendrils shooting out at lightning speed through her body. "You were here," she said, her voice rising in hysteria. "You were here the night Jason died. You came back, didn't you? You were alone with him, weren't you?"

Danny would no longer look her in the eyes. Staring down at the DVD in his hand, he tightened a grip and motioned with his chin toward the master bedroom. "You need to shut the fuck up. And get dressed. We got things to do."

She was dimly aware that his speech had lost its careful cadence. He sounded, now, like pure Long Island, and blue collar at that. "Dan, what did you do?" Her voice rose higher.

He refused to look at her.

In the space of the seconds that passed, Christina suddenly understood why the paparazzi had been parked outside her drive. Why the tabloids had been running stories about her marriage gone sour, quoting unnamed sources that, she knew full well, were her in-laws. Why the plainclothes detectives had met her at the airport and accompanied her to the morgue to identify her husband's body.

So they could watch her reaction.

Because they thought she had arranged this. "You—" She couldn't finish the sentence. A strangling sound bubbled up from the back of her throat.

This got a reaction from Danny Cisco at last. "Don't you fuckin' tell me," he burst, pointing a thick finger her way. "This was your deal, babe, and now it's gonna play out." He paused. "My way!" He jabbed his thumb at his chest, hard.

The movement made Christina jump.

He saw it and raised his eyes to her at last.

What she saw in them made her count the steps to the door. She blinked, hoping he couldn't read her mind.

"We had a deal," he said, his voice ragged.

"What?" Christina's voice came out in a whisper, her eyes round with horror.

"We had a deal," he repeated, his lips squaring off around the words. "I held up my end, and now you hold up yours."

Christina stared. "What are you talking about?" She tried to force her mind to concentrate so she could understand, but she could not.

"Don't give me that," Danny snapped, waving the DVD in the air. "You know what you wanted, and I did it."

Christina froze. A memory came back. Hazy and hot like a summer afternoon, or maybe a dozen summer afternoons. Lying in the chaise lounge with her legs spread, dipping her fingers in her margarita and leaving a trail for Danny to follow with his tongue . . . Protesting, telling Danny she was too weak to come again. Warning him Jason was due home soon.

"Fuck him," Danny had growled. "Does he do this for you?"

"No." Christina giggled and took another sip of her margarita while Danny worked on her. Everything in her world, at that moment, was right.

"Who needs him?"

"Who needs him?" Christina had echoed.

"He should get fuckin' lost," Danny had said into her clit.

"Get lost and stay lost." Christina had giggled.

"There ya go," had come the response.

Christina shook her head now. "That's crazy. I never asked you . . ." Her voice trailed off, unable to finish the sentence.

"Don't gimme that," Danny's tone had dropped into the danger zone. "It's too late now."

Christina stared. She tried to force her brain to work, focus on what Danny was saying. But it had gone on strike, stuck on one basic fact.

Danny Cisco had killed her husband.

Because she, Christina, had asked him to.

"No." Christina shook her head. She stared at the floor. It was the only part of the room that wasn't spinning.

Danny was going on, about the deal they had made, but Christina couldn't concentrate.

She was too busy trying to figure out if he was telling the truth. If Christina Cardiff was honest about her drinking, she couldn't swear to what she might or might not have said. She'd drunk herself into black-outs for years, waking up the morning after a binge to lie there piecing together fragments of the night before. "I never wanted that," she said, her mind numb.

"Bullshit," Danny said.

He was right, of course. Many times, Christina had imagined a life without Jason, starting with that first Valentine's night she'd spent alone and pregnant on the couch waiting for a husband who never came home.

But she would not, could not, have asked someone to kill him. "No," she repeated, her conviction rising.

"Don't fuck with me," Danny warned, his voice low. Menacing.

The room was silent. Even the rain had stopped.

But dark storm clouds still pressed low and menacing over Jonah's Path.

What was happening? Confused, Christina looked at the lover she had once believed would open new doors for her.

There was nothing in his face that was reassuring.

Just two black holes watching her. Ready to pounce.

She thought again of the raccoon in the attic.

"Let's go," Danny said in a voice that was a perfect match for his eyes. "We're getting married."

If she married him, she would implicate herself in Jason's death, which he almost certainly had caused.

She could spend the rest of her life in prison.

Worse, her in-laws would take Tyler away from her, forever.

She couldn't allow any of those things to happen.

She knew this in her bones, with a certainty she had never felt about her marriage or even about her recent attempt to give up drinking.

Christina Banaczjek Cardiff had lived most of her life going where the current took her.

Not when it came to being Tyler's mother. She couldn't risk losing Tyler, no matter what.

"No," she blurted now. "I mean, we can work things out." Her eyes drifted, and she cleared her throat. Stalling while she tried to come up with the right thing to say.

"Work things out?" Danny echoed.

"Danny," she began, twisting the ring on her finger. She backed up just a tiny bit, taking a small step toward the door.

Giving herself away.

"We had a deal," Danny growled, as Christina froze, frightened now.

Their eyes met, and she knew he sensed her fear.

In that instant, Christina felt everything between them shift, like a tide that changed direction, forming a deadly new current.

He sensed it, too, his eyes flickering from Christina to the door and back.

Measuring the distance, the same as she was.

"You'll never make it," he said softly, already on the move.

But she was moving, too. Christina Cardiff saw her only chance and took it. She was five feet closer to the door than he was.

"Bitch!"

She heard the fury in his voice, felt his hand clamp down on her arm. "I held up my end," he hissed.

"No!" Christina slid out of her robe and raced, naked, into the hallway.

"The cops are gonna find you, OD'd. And you know what, nobody will be surprised," he growled, sprinting after her. "And nobody will give a shit."

Fear lent wings to Christina's feet, propelling her forward so she made it to the stairs in what felt like one giant leap.

Danny Cisco was right behind her.

Christina leapt down the staircase, her feet flying over several steps at a time.

He was muttering about her suicide, coming down practically on top of her, so close she could feel little rushes of air as his hands reached out to grab her.

She jumped down the last four stairs, landing on the bare floor with a crack.

Danny landed practically on top of her, so near Christina cried out in fear as she scrambled to gain traction on the boards of the great-room floor.

The main entrance with its wide door was the fastest way out, but it would be a long sprint to the front gate.

And no guarantee the paparazzi would be there.

The patio door was farther away across the kitchen. But if she reached that door, she'd have less distance to the back gate that opened high onto the dunes where, naked or not, Christina prayed there would be people walking the beach at dawn.

Someone to hear her screams and save her.

She took just a fraction of a second, no more, to opt for the back door.

Danny Cisco lunged for her.

She felt his hands on her.

It was all over. Christina screamed.

But it had been a long night, and Danny hadn't slept. He was off his game.

Christina wriggled from his grasp as he made another grab, his fingers pinching at her bare skin.

Her life depended on this. Too frightened even to scream, she sucked in great, ragged breaths and scrambled for the back door, her bare feet making slapping noises on the floorboards.

"Bitch!" Danny hissed. He was close at her back, just centimeters away.

Luck was with her. She had neglected to lock up last night. She flew at the screen, pushing it open just wide enough to pass through.

Rain had blown inside during the night, forming a puddle on the floor.

Barefoot, Christina's feet flew out behind her. But she made it through.

Danny couldn't get traction with his loafers. He fell to his knees with a curse.

Christina gained a couple of feet and a second or two, no more.

"Get back here," Danny yelled, scrambling to his feet again. He made it through the screen door even before it slammed.

His footsteps made a heavy thudding sound as he raced across the patio pavers.

Her life depended on reaching the back gate.

The grass was soaked, the air laden with moisture from the storm.

Rain clouds pressed right down on top of the dunes, making the gray dawn even grayer.

The sky pressed down on top of her like a lead weight.

The ground shook with waves pounding in to shore.

It was not a beach day.

Danny was off the patio and crossing the back lawn now.

Closing the gap between them.

"Don't you," he yelled, not bothering to finish the sentence.

He didn't have to.

Christina knew what would happen if he caught her. She flung herself at the gate, her fingers scrabbling across the wood in search of the quick-release latch, praying she would get it right the first time . . .

And she did.

In the next instant, Christina was through, her bare feet sinking into the heavy, wet sand.

Danny Cisco was barely two seconds behind, his hands slapping heavily when they came in contact with the wet wood of the gate. He pushed it open again before it had a chance to click shut.

She heard heavy breathing and little grunts of frustration as he, too, landed in the heavy sand at the top of the dune. "Help," she screamed, praying the sound would carry through the mist. "Help! Help! Police!" She kept moving. It was an effort. The sand clung to her like quicksand, dragging her down. She pushed until the fronts of her legs felt like they were on fire, slow as molasses like in a nightmare. Still, she pushed on, moving lower down on the dune.

Heading for the beach.

Christina had the advantage here, being barefoot.

Danny swore aloud, stopping to kick off his shoes.

Christina sprinted onward, her lungs pumping harder than they had ever pumped in her life, thumping so hard she thought they would bounce right out of her body. But it was her only chance. She feared that she would lose her small lead once he got traction with his bare feet in the sand.

And she was right.

In the next instant, he pounded up behind her, so close she could feel little clods of wet sand land on the backs of her legs.

Christina screamed in terror and forced herself on, emerging from the dune path onto the flat expanse of open beach. She risked a glance from side to side and saw no one.

The exclusive stretch of coast extending east from the village of East Hampton to Montauk on the south shore of Long Island, for which the Cardiffs had paid a sizeable fortune, had paid off.

The beach was deserted. The shoreline was chewed up, ravaged by the storm. Waves broke in choppy random sequence, laden with seaweed churned from the bottom of the swollen, racing waters. Spray rose perhaps a dozen feet in the air over this roiling, boiling cauldron of brown water and green-tinged foam.

Christina Cardiff did the only thing she could do.

She raced straight for the pounding waves and dove in.

Danny Cisco followed.

The water was cold, brimming with bits of detritus the ocean swallows and spits back up after a storm. Long strands of seaweed and dark grass snaked through the foam. The tide raced in, carrying tree branches, some of them the size of Christina's legs, tossing them around like matchsticks.

The tide pulled at her, knocking her feet out from under her.

The ocean came alive like an image from a nightmare, sucking Christina into an undertow with deadly force.

The current was stronger than anything she had ever experienced.

A thousand sharp stones pelted her feet, scraping her skin raw like knives.

A wave rose in front of her, sudsing toward her like an angry sea monster.

Every instinct Christina possessed told her to fight her way back, away from the oncoming surf and onto dry land.

But the terror of the ocean was nothing compared to the terror that was at her back.

Christina pushed off the rocky bottom and plunged in. She tried to swim forward and up, as she had countless times before. But it was no use. This sea was like nothing she'd ever experienced, pulsing and heaving with deadly force.

There was no way forward. There was no way *up*.

There was only the ferocious force of the Atlantic, pushing her around like a rag doll, dragging her one way, then another, so Christina lost all sense of direction. She flailed desperately as her lungs grew short of breath and began to hurt. Her bare skin scraped heavy, cold sand, with stones tearing at her bare body like a million razor blades.

It must be the bottom.

Christina cartwheeled around until one foot, at least, made contact. She connected, only for a second, and pushed off with all her might, shooting off to what she prayed was the surface.

She shot up, breaking free at last, sucking down air in gulps. Her feet hung, connecting with nothing, empty and free.

She was in water over her head.

She took in great ragged gulps as another wave broke over her head, making her eyes sting.

Her fingers connected with something that was slippery and smooth like rubber.

She knew in an instant—that thing was Danny Cisco.

The look in his eyes was murderous.

He lunged for her in the roiling sea.

Christina kicked him away.

He grabbed her leg and held on.

Christina screamed and tried to kick him off.

Waves came at them from all sides and, impossibly, from behind. Great, swollen towering columns of darkness, pushing and pulling them every which way.

A heavy piece of wood sped past on a current of brown foam. Six inches closer, and it would have knocked her under. Bits of things, a dead fish and, impossibly, a basketball, whirled past.

One of the waves, followed by two more in rapid succession, crashed on top of them.

Christina was pushed down like a plunger, into the cold depths. She landed on the bottom, scraping it once more while her lungs burned, desperate for air.

Countless shells bit into her skin.

The sheer magnitude of the wave made it impossible to get a foothold to push off.

But the angry sea was fickle, tossing her first one way, then another.

For one single instant, the pressure let up. Christina searched desperately for the bottom with her hands and feet.

She connected just long enough once more to push off with a hand and a foot to what she hoped was the surface.

She broke the top once again, sucking in air while she could.

She swung her hands around wildly in a clumsy attempt to tread water.

Danny Cisco, by far the stronger of the two, was already there.

Christina tried to kick away again, but she was no match.

He clamped down on her, pinning her arms at her sides.

The menace of the waves was lost in the danger of his grip.

Christina realized that her death, in the end, would come at the hands of Danny Cisco.

"Please," she begged between breaths. "Please, my

son!" She tried desperately to kick away. But it was no use.

Danny had her in a vise grip.

She caught a glimpse of shore, tiny and far away in the gray dawn. Out of reach here inside the heaving depths of the sea. Christina's heart sank.

Another wave broke over them, tumbling them and spinning them again.

Danny held her tight even underwater.

Christina struggled back to the surface.

He was holding her down, pinning her beneath the waves.

Christina fought and kicked for all she was worth.

The current helped, scrambling them around like twigs.

Christina managed to break the surface once more.

"Help," she screamed. "Help, help, help, help!"

There was no one to hear, only the cold, dark ocean.

Danny laughed at her, and it was this small act of cruelty in the midst of a cold black tide that could kill them both, that was more evil than anything else he had done.

He was staring at her, his face inches away in the raging waters. "I killed your husband for you, scheming bitch," he rasped. "And now you have to die."

"No!" Christina screamed as the waves rose around them. "I never agreed to that!"

"You asked me to kill him. And I did!" Danny tightened his grip on Christina as his rage mounted.

"No, Danny," Christina said between gulps of air.

The current was changing around them.

Danny didn't seem to feel it. "You did," he spat. "And you were going to let me take the rap. Bullshit!" His eyes glinted. "You know what? They'll find you washed up onshore, and you know what they'll say? What a fuckin' shame it was that Christina Cardiff got wasted again after rehab, so fucked up she went into the ocean and killed herself." He lowered his face to hers, yanking her down by the hair until seawater rushed in to fill her mouth.

Christina struggled to spit it out.

Her head slipped lower as he gave it another vicious yank.

She felt her neck snap back, and water filled her nose. Christina knew he would hold her under until she died.

But the ocean, which had been tossing them every which way, suddenly took a ferocious new turn.

Christina felt herself spin as the current revved around them, pulling her free from Danny's grip like she was a rag doll.

She felt herself spinning away from him, speeding away from him on top of the raging water.

Christina had never experienced anything like it.

A look of panic passed over Danny's face at the sheer force of the current, which was propelling them out to sea with the force of a jet engine. He opened his mouth, but the water tore at him, and this was the last look Christina had of Danny's face, mouth open in a round "O," gasping for air.

He lost interest in her then, turning his back to begin pumping toward shore, fighting the current with all the strength he had in his massive shoulders.

Another wave came towered over her and broke, this time not pushing her down.

This wave dragged her out to sea with supernatural speed.

Christina tried to turn, tried to follow Danny inward to shore but felt herself sucked deeper out to sea. She sped along, faster and faster, churning along in the racing waters.

She screamed, but it was no use. And then she realized what was happening, what this was.

Christina Cardiff was caught in a riptide.

Black water raced all around her, forcing her farther and farther from shore.

Into deep water.

Swimming against it, the way Danny Cisco was, would only tire her.

Not that she could try. The raging water made it impossible even to lift her arms against the force of its fury.

The ocean floor had long since disappeared beneath her feet.

Christina felt herself being flung out into open ocean.

The shore, she knew, was impossible to reach.

Even Danny was gone, in the distance now, his arms pumping like matchsticks, getting nowhere on top of the raging sea.

Christina was too frightened even to scream. She remembered from her water safety course long ago there was no escape from a riptide. The only way out was to surrender, go with it, and try to swim sideways out of it.

And so she did.

She lost sight of the shore each time a wave rose up around her, blocking her view of the only guide she had.

Even as she fought the ocean, Christina Cardiff felt herself in mortal danger of drowning with panic.

Instinct took over, and she battled on, too numb in the cold water to do anything else, kicking her way in what she hoped was a line parallel to a distant shore.

She went on this way, feeling her strength ebb with each kick, until at last—impossibly—the tide released her from its death grip.

It was an act of what some would call luck, and others would call grace.

Christina Cardiff's life was spared.

Danny Cisco's, as the passage of several days would reveal, was not.

Christina Cardiff wondered what kink in the workings of her mind had twisted her thinking so much that she had made this place out to be Oz.

Whatever might have been, her mind was unfurling itself now like a pretzel being pulled apart and laid out straight, end to end for all to see.

It hurt, but it was not the same pain that used to make her duck back under the covers as soon as she awoke, hoping only to escape once more into sleep.

She'd woken up three mornings so far, back in rehab. Three wake-ups without wishing she were dead.

That was something.

Maybe Matt Wallace was right about miracles.

"Recovering alcoholics are special. We get a chance to start life over." He had told her this at least ten times on the drive in to JFK, then when it was time for her flight to leave, taking her back to rehab in Minnesota, he had taken her by the shoulders and squeezed hard.

She got a flutter of hope in her chest every time she pictured the look in his blue eyes.

"Remember what I said, Chrissie, we get a chance to do it right this time."

Christina was beginning to believe he might be right.

"I'll go." She downed the last sip of the bitter swill that passed for coffee around here. "It's my turn."

Peter swiveled to face her in his molded-plastic chair. "Okay, Christina." A smile lightened the worry lines on his face. "The floor is yours."

The circle broke into a round of hearty applause.

The dry-cleaning king of the Midwest, the one facing indictment and a possible prison term, hooted and stamped his feet. "Go, Christina!"

Sylphan from Bucks County leapt to her feet, raising her hands to the acoustic-tiled ceiling to start a wave. "You go, girl!"

The boy-band bass player from Studio City followed suit.

Others, some of the same faces mixed with new ones fresh from the detox unit where Christina had spent the last several days, took up the chant. "Christi-nuh! Christi-nuh! Christi-nuh!"

As though, Christina thought, she was about to accept the Nobel Peace Prize. She ducked her head, embarrassed, staring down at the ugly purple-and-green carpet.

Change or die, she reminded herself.

Another not-so-subtle AA slogan.

She cleared her throat and tried to begin. "I am Christina, and I am an alcoholic and a drug addict." Her voice broke. She let her tears fall, accepting the tissue someone pressed into her hand.

"Hi, Christina," came the chorus from around the room.

Just like in the movies. Except it wasn't so goofy when your life depended on it. Christina wept openly now.

"Tell us how you got here," someone called.

"Now, there's a story," Christina said, when she got control of her voice.

There was a smattering of laughter.

"This is my second try at rehab. I wasn't ready to quit drinking the first time. Things just hadn't gotten bad enough, I guess," she said with a rueful smile. "Even though any sane person would have sobered up if they found themselves in the situation I found myself in." She cringed, closing her eyes against the images that were burned forever in her brain just like they were burned onto Danny's DVD.

Christina forced her eyes open. "I was in the wrong place, with the wrong people, doing the wrong things."

The room erupted into knowing laughter.

Peter gave an encouraging nod.

"It was so bad, my son wouldn't stay with me," she said.

A couple of heads bobbed up and down. Some patients, she knew, had lost custody of their children. That was a "yet" for Christina.

AA-speak for the fate that awaited her if she drank again.

"My in-laws wouldn't have anything to do with me." Christina's voice grew stronger. "And then, things got worse."

The room turned silent.

"My life got so bad, you can read about it this week's *People*," she said.

"Been there, done that," called the dry-cleaning king.

And that was the crazy thing about AA, Christina thought. No matter what you confessed to having done while you were drinking, there was someone else who had done it, too.

Almost.

"If not for the paparazzi," she continued, "I wouldn't be here to tell the tale." It was true. Partly.

It turns out the mean little black dog from next door was the one who woke up and heard Christina's screams over the sound of the wind. The dog barked and barked (like it always did) until Biz finally woke up and let him out.

Little Shep had raced, snarling and yapping, straight for the source of screams in the dunes. The dog's cries caught the attention of the lank-haired Brit (who told the police later he harbored a lifelong hatred of Scotties), who was parked in his usual spot in the cul-de-sac at the bottom of Christina's drive.

The paparazzo used his cell phone to call 911, or Christina would have been swept halfway to Iceland.

She glanced at her counselor.

Peter was watching her with that Miles-and-Miles-of-Compassion look that was his stock-in-trade. "We told you the first time," he said, "the elevator's going to keep going down. You can get off anytime."

"I understand now," Christina said quietly. "Hopefully, I've had my last drink. I want to build a new relationship with my son, be the mother he wants me to be." Her voice broke. "I know that if I stay sober, I can put the past behind me."

The woman sitting beside Christina reached over and patted her shoulder while Christina cried.

"It's okay to cry," Peter said. "Who wouldn't be sad right now if they were you?"

There was no arguing with that, so Christina took a

swipe at her nose with the tissue and got down to business. "I have just returned from my husband's memorial service. Make that two memorial services," she said, correcting herself. "I held one, then my in-laws held a second one, which I managed to attend but only as a guest. Nobody wanted me there, and I got drunk after, but I did manage to sit there quietly without making a scene, for the sake of my son."

She choked up again, thinking about Tyler, and needed a few deep breaths to continue. "And that was after I had been fished from the ocean off the coast of East Hampton, something you all probably saw on the news."

An expectant ripple passed through the room.

Christina had to admit her life—even by rehab standards—had spun wildly out of control.

Even this crowd was silenced by what she spoke of next.

"I nearly drowned in a mishap that claimed the life of a man," she hesitated, searching for the right word. How to describe Danny Cisco, the man she had known as Daniel Cunningham?

"A mishap that claimed the life of a man with whom I had been involved," she said at last. "Ironically, that man drowned in a tragic accident just days after my husband also drowned in a tragic accident . . ."

The classic melody rolled over Ben Jackson's back deck. ". . . They found Amos White in fifteen pieces, fifteen miles apart . . ."

Frank McManus closed his eyes in rapture. "Glendale Train."

"New Riders," Ben Jackson said. "Classic. I chose it for you, my friend."

Frank tipped up his Bud in a toast and took a swig. It helped alleviate the throbbing in his shin. He reached down to rub it, but caught himself in time.

The stitches would open if he rubbed the wound too hard.

They sat in companionable silence, enjoying John Dawson's lyrics, which had stood the test of time.

When the song had ended, Frank took another swig. "My old man used to say, let the dead bury the dead."

"That's cold," Ben Jackson said, taking another sip of his Bud. "You know, whatever went down, it was a clean scene both times. The swim trunks are gone. Nothing left but ash."

"ME ruled both deaths an accident."

"Only she knows what went down."

"And she's off to rehab." Frank McManus raised his Bud in another toast.

"Case closed." Ben Jackson clinked bottles with Frank. "Unless the good widow Cardiff gets to thinking things over and tells a new story someday."

"Could happen," Frank remarked.

"When pigs fly, is my guess," his partner responded.

Frank McManus glanced at the grill. "Those burgers ready to flip or what?"

"'Nother minute," Jackson said, sliding a flipper under one to check. "Chill, bro," he said with a grin. He looked through the kitchen window, to where his wife Cirie was removing baked beans from the oven while Biz Brooks tossed a salad.

The two women were chatting up a storm.

"No worries, man, I'm not about to screw up our family audition night."

Frank took another sip from his tall boy to cover his embarrassment. Truth was, he wanted things to work. He hoped it would be the first of many such nights. Frank rubbed his leg again as the Jackson progeny called for him to come down the deck stairs and into the darkening yard to take a look.

They had managed to catch a firefly in a mayonnaise jar to show Miz Biz, as they called her.

"He can't," Ben Jackson called. "His leg hurts. Come up here now and wash up. Dinner's ready."

This drove the children farther away into the darkness.

Jackson piled burgers onto a platter, waving off Frank's offer to assist. "You just sit," he said, chuckling as Frank lowered himself onto a bench with a small groan. "Hey, old man, you need a cane or what?"

Frank McManus responded with a suggestion that would be anatomically impossible for Ben Jackson to achieve. "Freakin' dog," he muttered. "Came right at me with no warning as soon as I walked into her house."

Jackson laughed harder. "What are you gonna do?"

"What can I do?" Frank McManus grumbled, but he started to laugh, too. Fact was, he was happier than he'd been in a long time.

He'd taken Biz Brooks out to lunch, then out to dinner and a movie, then dinner in a fancy restaurant before asking her here tonight to meet the people that mattered as much as his own kids to him.

Each time he came to pick her up, everything was quiet on Jonah's Path. It had been since Christina

Cardiff—according to what he'd read in the tabloids—had packed up a few weeks back and shipped herself back to rehab.

Things were going pretty well until little Shep took it to the next level, sinking his fangs deep into Frank's leg.

"I'm so sorry." Biz swatted the animal off, uttering the famous last words of dog owners everywhere. "He's never done anything like this before."

And she had smiled at Frank in that sweet way she had, making Frank forget the dog had just ruined a new pair of pants from Brooks Brothers, and the tickling on his ankle was blood. "Are his shots up to date?" Frank had asked, eyeing little Shep, who sat, panting and worn-out with effort, in his usual spot under the hydrangeas.

"Oh, yes," Biz had said, grabbing her purse. "Come on, I'll take you right to my doctor."

And Frank McManus had to admit it wasn't a bad deal because he had got to spend another two hours in Biz's company, if you included driving time to and from Southampton General Hospital and the time it took the ER doc to sew up his shin.

"Man, oh man," Ben Jackson said, balancing the burger platter in one hand and his Bud in the other, "I hate dogs."

"Yeah," Frank McManus nodded. "Me, too."

We turn in at the gate.

Jason's car is there.

He was supposed to be in the city, but if his plans had changed, I wouldn't have known about it. We stopped keeping track of each other's comings and goings early that summer long before now.

"Shit." Danny cuts the engine and the headlights.

Jason is most likely asleep in his room on the ocean side of the house. I suspect my husband wouldn't care even if he did see us.

Danny turns to me in the predawn darkness. "You okay to walk inside by yourself?"

"Yeah," I lie. It is not a terribly long distance, but every inch of my lower body burns like it's on fire. Something hot and painful is leaking inside my panties.

The Ecstasy wore off back at Danny's place. My hangover is beginning to settle in, claiming the territory inside my skull. I can't recall much of the last few hours, and that is a good thing. I know that I don't want to.

All I want right now is to get inside and up to the guest room without running into my husband, so I can be sick in private.

"What the fuck is he doing here?" Danny bangs his hand softly on the steering wheel.

I could point out that Jason lives here, but I am too weary for that. I shrug.

"You know"—Danny leans back against his neck rest—"it would be better without him."

It would. I nod. I have had this idea many times.

Danny reaches over to smooth a lock of hair on my forehead, and I am tired, so tired. "It'd be good if it was just us."

I lean back against my neck rest and close my eyes. "Yeah."

The car is silent.

And then Danny whispers, "It'd be good if he was gone, you know, just gone."

I nod wearily.

Danny makes a cutting motion with one hand. "I mean really gone." He keeps rubbing my head, the way my Nana used to do when I was little and afraid to fall asleep. Before life got so complicated.

"Yeah," I say, practically nodding off right then and there. "Then I could do whatever I want." I smile with my eyes closed.

"It could happen," Danny whispers.

And there we sit, on the edge of a vast watery dark wilderness that I can't see for the green glow of the dashboard light.

But I know it's out there.

"Bad things happens all the time," Danny whispers after a while. "You know what I'm saying?"

I nod in the darkness on the edge of the abyss, not sure whether he sees me or even what we're talking about.

Because yes, they do.

NEED SOMETHING
NEW TO READ?

Download it Now!

Visit www.harpercollinsebooks.com
to choose from thousands of titles
you can easily download to your
computer or PDA.

Save 20% off the printed book price.
Ordering is easy and secure.

HarperCollins e-books

Download to your laptop, PDA, or phone for
convenient, immediate, or on-the-go reading. Visit
www.harpercollinsebooks.com or other online
e-book retailers.

Visit www.AuthorTracker.com for exclusive
information on your favorite HarperCollins authors.

Available wherever books are sold or please call 1-800-331-3761 to order.
HRE 0307